# OGG

## Robert Jones

summersdale

First published by Reed Publishing (NZ) Ltd in 2002.

This edition published in 2003 by Summersdale Publishers Ltd.

Summersdale Publishers Ltd
46 West Street
Chichester
West Sussex
PO19 1RP
UK

www.summersdale.com

Printed and bound in Great Britain.

ISBN 1 84024 354 6

*In a world where everything is ridiculous,*
*Nothing can be ridiculed.*
*You cannot unmask a mask.*

G. K. Chesterton

# PART ONE

## ALCEIDES

# – PROLOGUE –

The Isle of Ogg, comprising a mere nine square miles, lies at the southern end of Scotland's Outer Hebrides Island chain. It is not found in most atlases, and more detailed maps record it as a pinpoint without name.

While its irrelevancy is explicable, it being mistakenly assumed to have been uninhabited since the clearances, Ogg's occupation nevertheless dates from the late eighteenth century, reaching a golden era in 1910 when it numbered nineteen souls. Thereafter followed a steadfast decline, until by the end of the twentieth century a mere nine inhabitants – including one simpleton – eked out a spartan existence untouched by the outside world.

Although flat, the island falls naturally into two parts. The western Upper Ogg lies 60 feet above Lower Ogg, the two plains separated by a near-perpendicular escarpment enlivened by yellow lichen and ribbons of vivid pink thrift flowers, which runs almost the breadth of the island. The upper plateau affords protection from the periodic Atlantic gales to the lusher eastern flats and is accessible only at its western end where on a narrow strip the escarpment fades to a gentle slope. With the exception of a tiny natural harbour at its eastern end Ogg's entire perimeter comprises a wave-pounded, rocky cliff-face about which wheel shrieking kittiwakes, gulls, razor-bills and puffins, while below seals wallow among the wave-washed rocks and swirling kelp beds.

The upper plain sustains a thin veneer of boulder-strewn heath and tussock on which graze approximately nine hundred sheep. They receive shelter from a wind-battered forest along the plain's extremities, nestling at the edge of which can be found the Laird of Ogg's early Victorian granite pile. This is occupied by Upper Ogg's

7

only inhabitants, an ageing caretaker and his wife, who in return for a minuscule salary have managed the flock since 1975. A further twelve hundred sheep on Lower Ogg yield a moderate income for the Edinburgh-ensconced laird.

Bordering Lower Ogg's harbour is a rough cobbled road, along which lie twelve bleak granite crofter cottages, the property of the absentee laird, of which only six remain occupied. The road terminates at its northern end at a small stone kirk that faces down the line of cottages like a monitoring schoolmaster. On mornings when the Atlantic wind abates, the village, like all of Lower Ogg, is often shrouded in fog and mist.

Life on Ogg has scarcely changed over its two hundred years of habitation. There is no electricity and little commerce, while in the harbour two resident fishing boats can be found on most days of the year sheltering from the recurrent storms. Their spasmodic catches are sold at Castlebay, thirty miles to the north on the isle of Barra, from where they are transported to mainland consumers. On such journeys the fishermen also fulfil the rare purchasing orders of their fellow Oggonians, and each spring they derive a supplementary income transporting the annual sheep fleece. The remaining crofters, living by the light, maintain their vegetable gardens and chickens and cut peat for heating and cooking.

A spring-sourced stream, lined with iris and primrose, meanders from the island's dividing escarpment across Lower Ogg, culminating in a shallow, brackish bog to the south of the village. Lower Ogg resonates with the song of skylarks during the day, while at night corncrakes and snipe compete in a harsh percussion, unchallenged by any natural predators.

Oggonians rarely speak, but such utterances as they find necessary comprise a grunting Scottish Gaelic and English mix. Their average age is 58, younger Oggonians having long since fled to the mainland. Oggonians bear an appearance of regressive depravity in their stooped, shuffling gait and demented demeanour. Over two centuries they have created no music, literature, poetry, craft, science, art or cuisine.

Also residing in the village, alone in the largest cottage adjacent to the kirk, is the Reverend Finlay McDonald. Dispatched by the Church 38 years ago, the cleric was the first outsider to visit the island since a failed mission by the Scottish education authorities in 1927.

Like most clergymen, the Reverend McDonald is mildly deranged. From his arrival at theology college as a young man he was intuitively attracted to the decadence and decline end of the religiosity spectrum, and by graduation he had advanced to being a fanatical apocalyptic obsessive. His fiery pulpit condemnations of his former Invergarry congregation's alleged sins engendered much complaint to the Church authorities, who unwisely ignored the protests.

They were moved to intervene, however, following the Reverend McDonald's unlawful middle-of-the-night entry into a parishioner's home and his loud bedroom denunciation of the household's teenage daughter, which incident led to an attempted private prosecution under the 1892 Clergy Discipline Act. Thus the Reverend McDonald was exiled to the long-vacant Ogg living, where he now exists on a small stipend, long forgotten by his employers.

A fierce Scottish nationalist, the cleric devotes his days to writing a never-to-be-published history of the McDonald clan, breaking this daily routine each Sunday morning to deliver a wild-eyed, arm-flailing, incomprehensible, Armageddon pulpit oration. This weekly performance provides Ogg's sole entertainment.

Remove the Reverend McDonald's books and writing materials, the crofters' cartons of matches, their candles and rubber boots, Mrs McDougal's wedding present clock of forty years earlier and take away the engines of the fishing boats, and life on Ogg would be much as it was two hundred years ago.

World wars, penicillin, electricity, fascism, radio, lesbian vogueishness, television game shows, jazz, socialism, changing governments, blue jeans, space travel, scandals, sporting triumphs, frozen food, women's liberation, mass tourism, motor vehicles and high-speed dentist drills – all the momentous occurrences of the twentieth century have bypassed Ogg.

The accomplishments of modern civilisation – of taxation, regulation and welfare, compulsory seat belts and grief counsellors, pensions and policemen – remained detached from the ossified Oggonian life by the year 2000. But in that millennium year events were to transpire to abruptly end this default from the outside world.

# – ONE –

'Listen baby, it's a crocka shit. You know it, I know it, so don't bullshit me,' Finstein wheezed down the phone, but before James could protest the funds manager rasped, 'Mark us down for two million, and take note. I won't be calling. Have us out of this crap one hour after it opens,' and he abruptly cut off the call.

James sighed and wondered if he would ever adjust to the charmless staccato Manhattan approach to every transaction, even the purchase of a coffee. He punched in the BUY and then the SELL details, and not for the first time inwardly mourned at his inability to participate. The Initial Public Offering was being deluged, but allocations were confined to major clients. If the past three months were any guide its price would triple in the first hour. Finstein was right though. Fishtail dot com was nonsense. The institutional subscribers would all be profitably out within a month and replaced by sucker mum and dad shareholders. At the pre-float briefing session three weeks earlier James' analyst colleague Hampton had gently broached the matter, earning himself no points with management.

'Our role is organising broker – end of story,' Minelli, the managing director, had snapped. 'We guarantee nothing. Stocks go up, stocks go down, and I'm talking IBM, I'm talking General Motors, I'm talking Coca-Cola here, boy. Fishtail will go up. That's certain with this demand in this market. Volume equals validation. One day it may go down. You win; you lose. The key point is participation ain't compulsory. This is Wall Street, not a nunnery,' and with a parting glare at Hampton he resumed where he had left off before the interruption.

In fact it was mid-town Third Avenue, but the assembled dealers knew what he meant and had held their silence. Later that day James had joined Hampton in a mock Irish bar that was currently fashionable with the younger brokerage set and listened to his associate's unhappy protest.

'I won the York Prize for my doctoral thesis on value assessment,' the bespectacled Hampton complained, his voice rising a pitch against the riotous noise. 'I feel a fraud. Where's the analysis? Where's the responsibility and professionalism? It's all so barbaric and uncivilised. I feel like a Vegas croupier running a roulette table,' he shouted above the din.

'Russian roulette,' James had bellowed in response.

'Exactly. Why can't they see that? And what about you?' Hampton continued accusingly. 'Is this what you majored in, in … what was it again?' he queried.

'Feudal economics actually,' James replied, grinning.

'Right! Right. I'm not faulting it mind you. And is this what you envisaged – this wild west, this gold rush, this circus? Where's the integrity? Last week I even received an anonymous death threat after my negative report on Amazon.'

Hampton paused and looked anxiously about the crowded bar, distaste crossing his pale features as his eyes settled on an attractive young broker swigging directly from her beer bottle while shouting into a mobile phone.

'Well I'll tell you this,' he continued, barely audible against the background racket, 'I'm not staying. I'm looking … something useful … go home at night feeling … socially worthwhile … a sense of …'

'Why not teach?' James teasingly interrupted, and Hampton had looked at him sharply. For therein lay their conundrum – both were prisoners, chained to six-figure incomes.

Nevertheless the conversation had lingered in James' mind and slowly his dissatisfaction grew. He did not share Hampton's sentiments and considered his colleague precious. Despite its periodic craziness the market had its function. James' discontent lay instead in frustration at the absence of any creativity in his daily routine. He wanted to build something, to see the fruits of each day's efforts add to the previous day's, rather than the hollow repetition of his middleman's broking role.

Four months earlier he had rejoiced at the offer of a six-month stint in the firm's New York office. But now he realised that the frenzied pace of American life, compared with the languid London style, was simply hastening an inevitable decision which may have taken him years to reach back home. The prospect of returning soon heartened him.

Even the Jane threat seemed diminished with the passing of those four months. Her email correspondence was now down to weekly communications, the tone less reprimanding, and the letters shorter and more impersonal. There had been no mention for over a month of her dreaded visit, much talked of by her, when the New York proposal had initially arisen. Would it now be safe to return and quietly resume his old life sans Jane, he wondered.

It had certainly been a close shave back in London. Over the previous year her conversation had increasingly turned to house prices and furnishings, and there had been an awful meeting with the ghastly parents. James had felt himself being gradually drawn down into a vortex, helpless to resist in the face of the subtle but relentless pressure and subjugation of every detail of his life. The New York opportunity, represented to Jane as an order rather than an offer, had provided an escape route while he remarshalled his resistance.

In Manhattan the comparative novelty of his fair hair, blue eyes and English accent had proved attractive to the opposite sex. There had been a ready flow of bedmates, without the accompanying threat of meeting parents or house price discussions.

James was interrupted in this contemplation by his telephone ringing.

'Call from Edinburgh,' the operator snapped. There was a click and he heard his twin sister's soft Scottish drawl.

'Is that you, James?'

'Lucinda! This is a surprise. What's up?'

'I'm afraid it's terrible news, James. Father died this morning.'

James sat stunned, listening to the rush of words. 'Here on Sunday … dinner … fine spirits … can't understand … heart attack … doctors say … no suggestion … regular check-ups … Angus only saying yesterday … live for ever …'

James interrupted. 'I'm very sorry, Luce. Have you contacted Mother?'

'We've tried. We called Miami. A maid answered. Said she's touring somewhere in Europe. I think she was Spanish. We could hardly make sense of anything she said.'

'It doesn't matter,' James said.

His mother had run off with an American businessman over twenty years earlier. He had seen her once since, when he was ten, and rarely thought of her.

'The funeral will be on Thursday, James. I hope you'll be there. Angus has organised everything,' his sister continued.

'Of course,' James replied.

Today was Monday. He'd book a flight for Wednesday, hopefully direct to Edinburgh. He felt a twinge of guilt, and quickly suppressed his mild elation at the thought of returning home early. He endeavoured to console his distressed sister.

'He was a good man, Lucinda. He had a contented life. We've all got to go some time.' James stopped his clumsy rationalisation. 'Look I'm very, very sorry, Luce. I'll make a flight booking now and call you back. Give Angus my best wishes and keep your chin up.'

He rose from his desk and walked to Minelli's office at the end of the dealer room. By the time he reached it he had already concocted a story to justify returning permanently, and again he felt a guilty elation.

His last twenty years, since the age of seven, had been a life of English boarding schools, university, London and now New York. James had scarcely known his father. As a boy he had been cared for during holidays at home in Edinburgh by Mrs McIntosh, his father's widowed housekeeper. His father had remained a detached, shadowy figure, and news of his death induced little more than a nostalgic sadness. On the other hand he felt a mild sibling bond with Lucinda and a quiet pleasure at seeing her again and also Angus McDowell, her genial stockbroker husband, who had secured James' employment with the brokerage house after he left university.

Mostly he felt a sense that this event was about to mark a watershed in his life, and once in Minelli's office he had difficulty maintaining an appropriate solemnity as he recounted his news.

# – TWO –

An elderly secretary escorted James, his sister and brother-in-law into Mr Knox's dimly lit office. It was a step backwards into a gentler, more refined age. A jumble of time-worn leather wing-back chairs blended with the oak-panelled walls, which were lined with glass-fronted book cabinets and framed yellowing law-court sketches. Mr Knox's rotund Pickwickian appearance and his unfashionable waistcoated tweed suit fitted the yesteryear ambience perfectly. The solicitor introduced the party to a similarly clad elderly gentleman who in appearance could have been his brother. He was.

'I've taken the liberty of inviting Jonathan here,' Mr Knox explained, peering over his spectacles. 'Apart from drafting your father's will in 1985 I had no contact with him. However, Jonathan was his accountant and can answer any questions you may have. But first the will. It's really rather elementary. Aside from two other minor beneficiaries everything is divided equally between you both as his surviving heirs, except that as the only son, you, Mr Campbell, automatically become Laird of Ogg. To balance that, your father left the Edinburgh house to Mrs McDowell. Being laird regrettably doesn't count for much any more.' The solicitor sighed wistfully. 'It merely reflects the fact that the island is freehold and owned in its entirety. I'll now hand over to Jonathan to explain the rest,' he said, looking to his brother.

The accountant handed Lucinda and James some sheets of paper.

'Your father's estate is quite simple,' he said. 'Securities and cash total £480,000, which means £200,000 to each of you after the £80,000 your father left to his housekeeper, Mrs McIntosh. Naturally my brother invited her here today for the reading of the will but she declined. I understand she left for Canada this morning to join her married daughter.

'The house, according to an estate agent acquaintance of mine who kindly inspected it yesterday, will fetch about £350,000. Ogg unfortunately is a little more confused. There's a small income from some cottages which returns about £450 each year. As far as I can ascertain only the Church and two fishermen actually pay anything. Your father chose not to press the matter with the other cottages, and we're not sure who's there any more. The annual wool clip fluctuates but over the past ten years has averaged about £30,000 annually. Your father managed comfortably on that and his portfolio dividends. There was rarely any expenditure; there are no rates and no one would insure the Ogg house. Frankly I can't tell you much more about it. I've never been there. I suggest you as beneficiary, Mr Campbell, should do so, although I'm not sure how one gets there. Of course we're quite happy to carry on handling everything if that is your wish.'

'Thank you,' James replied. 'I'm afraid you will have to give me some time to come to terms with everything.'

'I quite understand,' the accountant responded. 'Just as soon as you've decided, let me know. In the meantime, with your consent, I will carry on as before.'

His brother, looking distinctly uncomfortable, now spoke up.

'There's another matter I'm obliged to recount to you both as beneficiaries. Your father also left a bequest to your mother. I'm somewhat at a loss about it, frankly.'

'Really!' Lucinda said, not hiding her astonishment.

The solicitor reached into his desk drawer, withdrew a battered old book and handed it across the desk to James. 'When your father came in to make his will he gave me that book and instructed it be left to your mother. One must be diplomatic when dealing with such matters and I'm afraid he became rather oblique when I quizzed him so I was left with no option but to do as he bid.'

James examined the book, *A History of Bengal Bee-keeping* by Colonel Harold S. Jamieson. Inside the front cover a printed bookplate bore the inscription 'Durapori Methodist College', and below, written in faded black ink copperplate, 'Awarded to Malika Sharma, Runner-up, Fourth Form Divinity Prize, 1927.'

'The thing is, I'm unsure whether I should write to your mother and advise her or just send it with a covering letter,' the solicitor continued.

'Send it,' James said firmly.

'Oh, your mother has an interest in bee-keeping?' Mr Knox enquired.

'No. Just send it.'

At dinner that night Angus said, 'Funny business that about the bee-keeping book, don't you think? What do you suppose it meant?'

'He was taking the piss,' James said. 'It's the same thing as leaving someone 50p. He probably picked it up browsing in a second-hand bookshop.'

Later Angus expressed his disgust as he once again examined the accountant's assets list.

'I raised it more than once with your father but he was a stubborn old mule. Wouldn't let me help. A terrible waste. Look at this rubbish. Government gilts, bank and insurance company debentures; if I'd handled it from the outset the legacy would be five times larger. Still, we'll cash this stuff up smartly. The tricky question is Ogg and I've been thinking about that. The accountant said it's averaged £30,000 over the past ten years. What he failed to say, and probably didn't notice, was the ominous trend. Look at this,' he jabbed at the paper before him. 'It's a typical agriculture story. Ten years ago Ogg returned £64,000 and the pattern, give or take some year-to-year fluctuation, has been decline ever since. Of course it's difficult to comment accurately, none of us knowing anything about the damned place, but in my view, James, you should cut and run.'

'That's all very well, but how? Who would want it?'

'I've been thinking about that,' Angus responded. 'I spoke to an estate agent friend of mine this afternoon. He says there's a market for these sorts of remote islands with rich Americans of Scots ancestry and nouveau riche wide boys. The same apparently goes for Highland estates. He said they buy them, spend a fortune doing up the house – central heating, antique furnishings, the works – jolly up the grounds a bit, then after a few years they lose interest and rarely go near them again. It's your obvious escape route. He gave me the name of a London firm that specialises in this sort of thing, so if you agree I suggest we appoint them. You'll be up for a few quid for helicopter hire for them to inspect the island. You might even want to go with them,' he shuddered as he said this, adding, 'Rather you than me.'

'Angus is right, James,' Lucinda said. 'We went to the Hebrides one Christmas for a holiday. It was awful. Bleak, cold, windy, grim people. After two days we cut it short and came home. I can't imagine Ogg will be any different. It's funny to think we were both born there.'

'Silly idea of course, going in winter,' Angus admitted.

James thought quickly. 'OK,' he said. 'I'll leave it to you to instruct your London people. I'll go back there and organise a flat and we'll see what happens. If I can't sell the island I suppose I'll have to visit the damned place and have a look at this sheep operation. Not a happy thought,' he concluded, grimacing.

'One small silver lining is your early return,' Lucinda said pointedly. 'I'm sure Jane must be pleased.'

'She doesn't know I'm back.'

'Really, James, that's dreadful. I didn't like to raise it when she wasn't here for the funeral. I'm sure she'd have wished to be, after all she met Father on your Edinburgh trip last year. I can't think why you didn't tell her.'

When James said nothing Lucinda continued, her tone scolding, 'You're not a young man any more, James. Attractive girls like Jane can't be expected to wait about at your whim. I was most impressed when I met her.'

'Bloody good legs,' Angus contributed.

'Oh really,' Lucinda flounced. 'You're so infantile. I don't suppose you noticed the equally good mind.' She rose to make coffee, pausing at the door. 'You're the same as you've always been, James. You just float along, accepting whatever comes your way, doing whatever you're told, never initiating anything. One day you will wake up a lonely old man with nothing accomplished, only by then it will be too late …'

'For heaven's sake, Lucinda,' Angus interrupted. 'Leave him alone.'

'Sorry about that, old man,' he said after Lucinda had departed. 'She's a bit upset about your father.'

Still it was true, James thought. At school the masters had criticised him for his passivity, he had been shifted from an inside back position to wing in the university rugby team following a humiliating flow of abuse from the coach for his lack of initiative, and there had been some little 'talks' in the office over his failure to be sufficiently assertive in selling stocks. The transfer to the New York office had been prompted by the hope that this would put some fire in his belly, as Symington, the London office manager, had put it. Yet he knew it was quite foreign to his nature to be pushy. He consoled himself with the thought that perhaps it would be different if he was doing something he could enthuse about.

James thought back to his visit with Jane a year earlier when he had accompanied her to the Edinburgh Festival in her capacity as an Arts Council Grants Officer. Almost immediately she and Lucinda had connected and the visit had evolved into a subtle sort of feminine conspiracy, with the two women constantly talking in undertones, interspersed with accusing glances in James' direction.

The trip had been a disaster. It had begun with a mixed media painting exhibition by the supposed man-of-the-moment, a weedy, unshaven scruff with a permanently anguished demeanour. Jane had been greeted gushingly by the gallery proprietress, and had then waxed squealing enthusiasm at the hodge-podge canvases with their nonsensical *Euphrates Dialogue* and *Dachau Spectre* titles. Reading the artist's notes, James had discovered that the mixed media included crushed dog faeces and he had interrupted the artist's tortured, face-contorting explanation of one of the canvases – 'At one level, as it were, one strives to ...' with, 'So your paintings are basically crap.' This observation had led to protests from the artist and a distraught shrieking duet from Jane and the gallery proprietress, followed by a one-day Jane sulk and even more intense whispering sessions with Lucinda.

Then there had been the play blow-up. Unctuously ushered to front seats in a party comprising the fat, mincing playwright and a supercilious university drama professor, James' initial astonishment soon grew to anger as the performance dragged on.

The curtain had risen on a half-lit, almost bare stage, on which a naked man, his back to the audience, sat intensely studying a glass of water placed on a table before him. For two minutes nothing happened, then the man slowly turned his head to the audience, loudly exclaimed 'No', then equally slowly turned back and resumed his study of the glass. A tremor of excitement had vibrated through the theatre. Bewildered, James had turned to Jane. She was leaning forward, her eyes sparkling with intensity. Conscious of James looking at her, she had turned and whispered, 'Isn't it exhilarating? Are you enjoying it?'

Enraged, James had replied, in a voice clearly audible to his neighbours, 'It's bloody garbage. I'm out of here,' and to angry hissings of 'philistine' and 'barbarian' he had risen noisily and, taking care to tread on the playwright's feet, returned to the hotel. The resulting all-night weeping session from Jane had been followed by two days of non-speaking and further whispering sessions with Lucinda.

The confidence James had felt in New York on the Jane issue now began to evaporate as he contemplated his return to London.

# – THREE –

Having resolved to sell Ogg, James became increasingly glum as the months passed without any interest arising. Following his father's funeral he had returned to his London office and the disenchantment, spawned in New York, gnawed at him daily. He endeavoured to compensate outside of work, resuming playing squash and golf, and taking up then abandoning flying lessons, but overriding everything was a sense of marking time.

Worst of all, the Jane problem was back in full swing. Not content with rebuking James, Lucinda had written to Jane apologising for the failure to advise her of their father's death and funeral. The standard tearful recriminations had been played out then abruptly ceased, and the usual petulance, nagging at his lack of ambition, and required attendance at frequently absurd artistic displays had been resumed. James sensed the net drawing in again and his despair grew.

The estate agents' early enthusiasm had been replaced by a recriminatory tone. 'You must understand, Mr Campbell,' the broker virtually scolded him when he had last called to check on progress, 'Ogg essentially comes into a white elephant property category. Somewhere, some time, there may be a buyer, but frankly, finding that person is like the proverbial needle in the haystack. You must simply wait and hope. Remember we've listed it on the Internet, we've advertised in *Fortune* and other appropriate media, including some American Scottish publications. Now we must be patient.'

James needed no reminder about the advertising. It had cost him £8,000, which when added to the £6,500 he had paid for airfares to Glasgow, a helicopter across to the island and the valuation report, simply compounded his despair. The report had been discouraging, painting a grim picture of Ogg. Its concluding paragraph remained fixed in his mind:

'The island is visually and climatically unappealing. The improvements are primitive and of no meaningful value, lacking all contemporary facilities including electricity and plumbing. There is no transportation to the mainland or telephone connection. Considered as an agricultural unit Ogg has a current value of circa £250,000, arguably discountable because of its geographic remoteness. Conversely, the fact that it is a freehold, wholly owned island invites the possibility of an intangible value premium which we are unable to quantify. The sparse evidence of similar transactions in the Western Hebrides, the Orkney and Shetland Islands and the west coast of Ireland suggest a premium ranging from £250,000 to £1 million, but there is no detectable pattern or formula to these figures.'

Finally, seven months after the funeral, the impasse was broken when James received a telephone call from the estate agent.

'We have an enquiry from a London company,' he said. 'I'm afraid it's not exactly what you're looking for, nevertheless I believe we should pursue it. Their requirement precisely matches Ogg, but the problem is they're not purchasers. They need to check it out, and if it suits they've indicated they would require a five-year lease with a 25-year option.'

'What on earth do they want it for?' James asked.

'To be honest I can't tell you. Naturally I enquired but they became very mysterious so I don't even know what they do. The company name is unhelpful: "Alceides Plc". Sounds a bit foreign to me. But they seem substantial. Occupy an entire building in Dover Street. I looked up the title and they own it. No mortgage registered against it either so any lease they enter into should be meaningful.'

'But that's no good to me,' James protested. 'I want to sell Ogg, not rent it.'

'Look, it's a question of negotiation. It's the five-year initial term then 25-year option that's the stumbling block. I indicated a yearly rental of £100,000 with prescribed annual increments of £5,000 and they seemed relaxed about that. If we can persuade them to take a straight 25-year lease on those terms then I assure you – assuming of course they're as substantial as they seem – we will have no difficulty selling the island for a figure in the million plus range. The insurance companies will snap it up.'

'So where do we go from here?' James asked.

'Well that's the funny thing, and the reason I'm calling. Normally we would conduct the negotiations. But they're adamant they will only deal with the owner. I've made an appointment for you on Thursday morning – 11.30 in their offices. If that's satisfactory I'll confirm it with them. But remember – you must obtain a long-term lease if you want a sale. Five years and a 25-year option simply delays things five years while we wait to see if they exercise the option. It's the income stream tied to the asset we can sell, not the asset.'

James wrote down the company's name and address. 'Alceides' – it seemed familiar.

At university he had endured one year of classics, and the word rang a faint bell in his mind. He rose and entered the office research library, where a never-opened set of *Encyclopaedia Britannica* resided. It was unhelpful. There was Alcestis and Alcibiades and Alcidamas – all Ancient Greek figures – but no Alceides. He decided to leave early on Thursday morning and investigate in Hatchards' classics section since the bookshop was only two minutes' stroll from the mystery company's office.

James resolved to do all within his power to conclude a deal. A million quid, maybe more according to the agent, plus his existing cash and he could quit the City. It wasn't a fortune and he didn't know what he'd do, but he'd worry about that when and if it arose. First things first. Any information about who he was dealing with could only help the negotiations.

He was interrupted in his musings by another call from the agent.

'Sorry to bother you again, Mr Campbell. I forgot to mention something. I told these Alceides people they could inspect the island. I trust that's satisfactory. They're sending two of their chaps up to Scotland tomorrow and have booked a helicopter. Their expense of course. It's a very good sign. Shows they're serious and saves time. No point negotiating a deal only to have them subsequently decide the property doesn't suit. On the other hand, if they do talk turkey with you on Thursday then you're dealing from a strong deck. There's not exactly a lot of choice in this matter. Ogg seems to fit their requirements perfectly, and you've got the only one, so you can afford to be fairly hard-nosed in your dealings.'

What a mad world, James marvelled. Yesterday he possessed a white elephant, worthless because of its uniqueness. Today he possessed a gem, valuable because of its uniqueness. He picked up the printer's proofs of the prospectus he was vetting and laughed out loud as he resumed reading.

# – FOUR –

Here's a good start, James thought, picking up a large pictorial book, *The Magic World of Greek Mythology* in Hatchards' classics section. He studied the index. Eureka, there it was, 'Alceides: Page 187'. Funny it wasn't in *Britannica*, he reflected as he turned to the page and read the entry. Alceides, according to some mythologists, was the real name of Hercules, the hero who travelled the world and overcame evil. It was a small esoteric point, which explained its absence from the encyclopaedia, and there was no further reference to it. He skimmed over the pages of the familiar Hercules guff; serpents attempting to strangle him at eight months, the baby Hercules killing them, murdering his music teacher, slaughtering a lion, impregnating all fifty daughters given him by the king … James' interest faded and he snapped the book shut and looked at his watch. There was almost an hour before his appointment with Mr Upton, the managing director of Alceides, time enough for a coffee, and he left the bookshop and strolled along to the adjacent Ritz Hotel.

The name was certainly a puzzle. If the proprietors wanted a classical Greek name, and with company names such pretension was common enough, James pondered as he sipped his coffee, then why not Heracles or even the more common Latin Hercules; why such an oblique name implying mystique and, if one wanted to stretch a point, subterfuge? Probably he was reading too much into it, he concluded, and he turned his mind to the forthcoming meeting.

Ten minutes later he stood across the street and looked up at the narrow frontage of the Alceides building. It was plainly very old, but otherwise standard Mayfair architectural blandness and anonymity. Eight levels of Georgian-style framed windows, the ground floor set back from the pavement with the usual gold-topped, spiked black railing, black double doors and a small, highly polished brass nameplate to the side of the entrance-way.

James crossed the street and tried the door. It was locked. Then he noticed a buzzer and pushed it. A woman's voice responded from a speaker above him. James gave his name and details, there was a brief pause, a whirling noise followed and he was instructed to come in.

James entered a small lobby where a doe-eyed Eurasian girl greeted him. He followed her through to another equally small chamber, then into a tiny lift which barely accommodated the two of them. On the third floor they emerged to a luxurious chandeliered foyer. They crossed the richly carpeted floor to two double-panelled doors. The young woman pushed them open and they entered a large, opulent office, its walls lined with paintings. 'Bloody hell,' James spluttered, 'Geoffrey bloody Upton.'

'Well, I'll be damned,' the young man facing him said as they shook hands. 'I had no idea it was you. Sit down James, sit down,' and he adjusted an armchair slightly and instructed the secretary to bring in coffee.

James had not seen Geoff Upton for over six years. They had been acquaintances at university and played in the squash team and second rugby fifteen together, but there had always been a touch of mystery and detachment about Geoff. His dark eyes and hair and unrestrained manner hinted at the Levantine, and his possession of a Morgan sports car and constant squiring of the most glamorous university girls had engendered an apartness from the more mundane students. Then, without explanation, he had disappeared. All was now explained as excitedly the two exchanged reminiscences.

'The old man had a heart attack,' Geoff said. 'No surprise, as after my parents divorced he took up with a 28-year-old Peruvian girl. Anyway, the heart attack shook him up so he decided to pack it in and shift to Ibiza and I took over the shop, which is why I buggered off so abruptly. I had my head down for the first couple of years plus I was belting about all over the place; still am, in fact, but at least now I've got a grip on things so Dad pretty much leaves me to it. And what about you?' he queried.

James recounted the events of his past six years, not hiding his disgruntlement with City life.

'Tell you what,' Geoff said. 'How are you placed today, time-wise?'

James thought quickly. He had a great deal of work to do, some of it urgent. 'I'm free,' he replied.

'Good show. There's a smart little French place round the corner with a private room. This calls for a decent all-day lunch.'

In the restaurant they continued reminiscing but eventually turned to the business in hand.

'I gather you want Ogg,' James said.

'Yes. But only on a lease basis,' Geoff replied firmly.

By now they were on to their second bottle of wine. Niceties were abandoned.

'Why, for God's sake? What is it you do?'

'Well, it's a bit tricky to explain. Basically we're in the tourism business.' Geoff hesitated, choosing his words carefully. 'We're in a particular niche market; highly specialised. Ogg suits a specific requirement.'

James stared at him. 'You're taking the piss,' he said accusingly. 'Tourists to Ogg? Why? Who would go there? How would they get there? Why would they want to? Have you seen it?'

'Actually, I've got a thirty-minute video film of it. Our surveyors did it on Tuesday. It looks bloody horrible but basically it matches an exercise we're planning. The thing is we can never be sure, which is why we will only commit to five years. If it works then of course we would take on a long lease. We'd want to, in fact, to protect our interest.'

James explained his predicament.

'What you should realise,' Geoff said when he had finished, 'if this doesn't work for us you would not just enjoy five years' income, you'd come out ahead in a whole lot of other ways as well. For a start the big house would be fully refurbished to a luxurious standard – plumbing, wiring, a generator, heating, outbuildings, landscaping – the works. So too with the occupied crofters' cottages. We'll need their co-operation so we'll bang a generator in the village, the cottages will be wired, we'll fit heaters, stoves, television sets and put in plumbing and a sewage system. It will all cost them nothing. The crofters' incomes will rise dramatically as we'll need them to extend their vegetable gardens to supply us, plus eggs and stuff, and possibly we can offer some of them employment. We'll take the fishing boats' produce, which I gather isn't much but will be sufficient for our purposes and they'll have regular transportation jobs for our supplies.

'Also, we'll be building under the cliff on Lower Ogg, a fairly well-appointed, twelve-guestroom lodge with all the trappings – a large sitting room, dining room, kitchen, various facilities and of course, a generator and sewage system. If at the end of five years we don't want to continue you can take the lot free. We can write that into the lease as it will be no good to us. In total we're budgeting to spend nearly £5 million. Seems to me that's a terrific deal for you. You should jump at it,' Geoff concluded.

James stared at his friend. 'I don't believe it,' he said. 'I don't want to talk against my own book but this is ridiculous. From what little I know about it no one would want to holiday on Ogg. It just doesn't make sense.'

'As I said before, we're a niche marketer. We've identified a market and Ogg fits the bill. I'm sorry but I can't reveal any more details about it. We could carry out the same exercise in the Highlands given a large enough estate, and there's one and the possibility of another available right now. But our first choice is an island, particularly a remote one as hostile to boaties as Ogg is. An island cuts out ramblers, who the bloody stupid government has legislated are free to violate private property. We don't want that,' Geoff concluded adamantly.

The two became thoughtful until eventually James broke the lull.

'Look. It's a generous offer and I appreciate it. The dilemma I face is that I want cash. As I said, I want out of the City. A sale will give me capital and freedom and options. I can't bear the thought of another five years.'

'You could retire on the income,' Geoff suggested. 'If you want it's no problem to us to run it through a tax haven.'

'But I don't want to retire. I want to do something, not just have an income. What I don't understand is, if you're going to spend that sort of money, why not buy Ogg?'

'If it was over to me maybe I would,' Geoff replied. 'Even though my father never bothers me any more about everyday detail he still monitors what he calls fundamental principles. One of those is never to own the ground under our operations. It's not a flexibility or financial issue; rather it's about security. We prefer our resorts to involve a landowner with a vested interest in our success as it ensures secrecy. That would be threatened if we owned the show.'

Noting James' stare, he added, 'Look, it's all quite legal, I can assure you of that. But privacy, or more particularly secrecy, is critical. On reflection my father is right about that, actually,' he concluded.

Again the two fell silent. This time Geoff broke the impasse.

'Give me a day. I'll call you tomorrow after I've telephoned my father. Given what you've said about your frustration with the City, I have an idea which may interest you as well as resolve the matter, but I'll need to talk to him first.'

'What do you have in mind?' James asked, perplexed.

'Actually, it's rather an exciting thought,' Geoff replied. 'But I must talk to my father first so let's leave it until tomorrow.'

The two men shook hands and left the restaurant. As James walked home to Bayswater he felt for the first time in six months that mysterious though it all was, his life was about to take a turn for the better.

# – FIVE –

As promised Geoff telephoned the following day, and the two arranged to meet again on Sunday afternoon in the Alceides offices. On arrival James was surprised to be greeted by the same secretary. 'So, you're the last English slave-owner,' he joked once in Geoff's office.

A flash of alarm crossed Geoff's face. 'Oh. I see what you mean,' he said, his face visibly lightening when he realised James was referring to the girl. 'Actually, we don't adhere to normal conventions in this organisation. I sometimes forget the way the rest of the world operates.'

The secretary brought in afternoon tea and the two settled into armchairs.

'I've spoken to my father,' Geoff began. 'If you're interested in the proposition I'm going to put to you, he'll come over to London tomorrow to meet you.'

'Fire away.'

'Well, first I must warn you that it will all sound a bit mysterious,' Geoff said edgily. 'I can't tell you too many details about us at this stage, but if you accept our offer then of course I will and it will become clear – the need for secrecy that is,' he added hurriedly.

'You've got me on tenterhooks,' James laughed. 'Are you sure you want to tell me? I mean are you up to something a bit …' he hesitated, 'a bit naughty – not quite legal, on the edge as it were?'

'No, no. I told you last week. It's nothing like that. It's just that secrecy is absolutely essential to our business. Look, settle back and I'll explain.'

James shuffled a little in his seat and looked at Geoff expectantly.

'My father owned a fairly substantial travel agency with offices across Britain. About ten years back he woke to the fact that it was getting harder and harder. Deregulation-induced competition was killing profitability despite massively increasing volume. Dad's a highly analytical type and he quickly realised that this dichotomy wasn't peculiar to his company or indeed to the travel business. He's got a theory about it, so if you pursue our offer no doubt he'll explain it to you. In a nutshell he analysed everything that was happening, sold the business to a rival company and eventually set up an entirely new operation. That's Alceides, which basically is still in tourism but targets a particular specialist market. The key point is, we create monopolies which means no competition and therefore high profits. Not many businesses have that these days,' Geoff concluded smugly.

'So, are you going to tell me?' James asked. 'What's your specialist market?'

'The market we cater to is the super-rich.' Geoff lowered his voice for emphasis. 'Over the last ten years there's evolved a hell of a lot of freshly minted newly rich. You know that, given what you've been doing. You may not believe it but there are now over 25,000 individuals with a net worth in excess of $200 million in America alone. It's a new market and we're the only ones catering specifically to it. We've studied it and found certain common denominators which we target with our home-grown creations; because they're off-beat and deliver what the clientele want we have a monopoly. Keeping our activities secret is essential to prevent others horning in and copying them.'

James nodded. Geoff was right. During his five years in brokerage since 1994 he had watched hundreds of investors make major fortunes. The sharemarkets had risen rapidly and relentlessly, contrary to all historic patterns and the numerous Cassandras' warnings.

Geoff continued. 'Now at this stage I can't tell you about our existing operations, only what we're planning for Ogg. Basically, we won't change the deal we've already offered you; that is, a five-year lease at £100,000 rental and a 25-year option. That's not negotiable. Also, I overlooked mentioning this last week but we need the sheep flock. It's not worth much but we'll buy it from you. What we can do, and are here to discuss, is not only pay you the rental but also offer you a quarter equity share in the exercise we're planning. To be frank, your cut will make the £100,000 rental seem peanuts.'

'Hang on,' James interrupted. 'You said you will be spending five million. I can't afford a quarter of that.'

'Forget it. We'll provide the capital. But if it goes as planned it will be repaid in a year, so the outlay is fairly academic.'

James sat up sharply. 'That's a rather extraordinary rate of return. What happens if it doesn't fire?'

Geoff shrugged. 'If the exercise doesn't work then you'll receive five years' income and, as I said last week, you can have the improvements. You won't be up for any of the capital expenditure. Anyway, it will work. We're absolutely certain of that.'

'So where's the catch?' James asked suspiciously, then started as he heard the sound of laughter from the ceiling. When Geoff didn't react he assumed he had imagined it.

'There's no catch,' Geoff said. 'You said you're bored with the City, want to do something hands-on and creative and be your own boss. Well, here's your opportunity. The exercise we're planning needs a manager. That will be you.'

'You mean I have to live on Ogg?'

'Yes. But believe me, when you understand, it won't be as bad as it sounds – in fact it will be quite exciting. There will be weekly helicopter flights in and out so you can come down to London as often as you like. I'd welcome that, as we like regular contact with our managers. I'd certainly come up frequently. There'll be lots of laughs and, as I'll explain, lots of company. There'll be a number of necessarily pretty girls on the Ogg staff and you'll be the only chap. You'll have a field day. You'll also live in great luxury and make a hell of a lot of money, if Brasch – he's our researcher – if he's right. And he always, always is,' Geoff said, emphasising every word slowly.

'Well it all sounds very mysterious,' James said. 'So what's the plan?'

'Actually, there are two plans,' Geoff said. 'Brasch has identified two new markets that are applicable to Ogg. The main one deals with very rich middle-aged Japanese. They'll stay in Lower Ogg in the specially built guesthouse. The other market pertains to rich Americans of Scottish ancestry. There are twenty million people with Scots ancestry abroad, mainly in North America. We're not absolutely sure about that leg of the proposal but if it doesn't work we'll close it and carry on with the Japanese one alone and probably expand it. The Americans will stay in the big house, which will be known as Ogg Castle because with the addition of a few features we're planning it will look like a small castle. We'll need you there to manage both operations. Not directly, mind you,' he added hastily. 'There'll be a pretty Japanese girl managing the guesthouse. Pretty girls are essential when dealing with the Japanese, and she must be Japanese as they're more comfortable dealing with one of their own. Also there'll be a laird managing the castle. You'll just oversee both. There'll be quite a lot of staff in both exercises.'

James gazed at Geoff and the thought crossed his mind that it was an elaborate leg-pull. 'Why would Japanese want to go there, for God's sake?'

Geoff stared at him searchingly for a moment as if weighing whether to go further. Finally he spoke. 'Sheep,' he announced sharply.

'Sheep! Sheep are everywhere. Why go to Ogg to look at sheep?'

'Killer-sheep. Rare, only to be found on Ogg, bloody dangerous killer-sheep. Killer-sheep with a sharp two-foot-long horn in the centre of their heads which can gore a man to death inside a minute. The Japs will go there to shoot them.'

James stared at Geoff in disbelief. 'But they're not bloody killer-sheep. Sheep will run a mile if you so much as look at them.'

'It's not what they are,' Geoff said wearily. 'It's how they're perceived. Our Japanese language brochures will explain it all. The Japanese men will hide in a comfortably equipped, barricaded trench all day, wearing military camouflage uniforms and armed to the teeth. They like that sort of nonsense. We'll be fencing off a large area around the guesthouse so no one, and in particular no sheep, or ordinary sheep that is, can wander in. It will be planted with a thick forest along the fenceline. The Japs will arrive on Ogg by helicopter. While the men are shooting the sheep their wives will be taken on a tour of the village – we'll be creating a bit of Oggonian history there in our Romanian factory – a statue of Ogg's original warrior king who we've named Mugan, the historic gold sword used for ancient ceremonial beheadings on display in the kirk, lots of that sort of thing. Japanese women need all that rubbish when they travel so they can be photographed standing in front of them.'

'You're taking the mickey!'

'Just listen first,' Geoff said resignedly. 'You'll understand better when I'm finished. The Japanese men will be all lined up in the trench. About every hour or so a sheep will charge out in front of them. The sheep will have a horn wired on, only you won't see the wires which will be hidden in its fleece. The Japs will be spread along the trench so whoever's in line will blaze away. Mostly they'll miss because scarcity value is important in this sort of exercise. There'll be a dozen Japanese men there with their wives at any one time, so competition and ego will keep them at it until they've potted one. We're programming an average five-day stay.'

'Why will they mostly miss?' James interrupted, now caught up in the story.

'Because they'll be firing blanks, although naturally they won't know that. There may be a full-time job for a villager but if no one's suitable we'll bring in someone. He'll be the sheep-master. He will be hidden away from the shooters and attach the horn and wire up the sheep before sending it out to face the music. Each trench position will be facing trees. It will be too dangerous for the Japs to venture from the trench for fear of being gored to death so they won't know that behind the trees are some fenced corridors to control the whole exercise.'

'This is bloody absurd.'

'Please let me finish before you pass judgement,' Geoff said impatiently. 'Periodically the sheep-master will send a wired-up sheep off down the corridor. It will have an electrical charger secreted in its fleece and the sheep-master will control it by a remote. He'll also control the hidden gates so all the shooters get a fair go. Off the sheep will trot, kick-started by an electrical shock so it will come charging out at high speed at the entrenched Jap whose turn it is. It will be quite exciting and from the Japanese's point of view fairly frightening. The shooter will blaze away, the gun-shot noise will panic the sheep, it'll turn and rocket back into the holding pen.'

'This is all unbelievable,' James spluttered. 'You're definitely taking the piss.'

'We know what we're doing, James, believe me. What you must remember is that sheep are totally foreign to Japanese. The only sheep you will find in Japan are in zoos. They know nothing about them, they don't eat sheep-meat, and will accept unquestioningly the proposition of a killer variety. The market is there and we know how to reach it. Also, we've researched sheep behaviour and they perform exactly as I said once they're wired up and given the required shocks.'

'But won't the Japs get fed up always missing?' James asked, puzzled.

'That's where finesse comes in, which is why we probably can't use a villager as sheep-master – our preliminary report suggests they're all retarded. The sheep-master needs to carefully monitor each shooter to make sure all get a few dry runs before eventually potting one. Making it difficult builds up the excitement and of course the sense of achievement when they do succeed. We'll actually build the sheep-master a hidden office alongside the sheep pen. He'll have a desk to keep his records on and a television monitor so he can watch the shooters through hidden cameras – they could change places and mess things up allocation-wise.'

'So after a few days you'll replace the blanks with real bullets?' James enquired.

'Good Lord, no. Too dangerous and quite unnecessary. Also rather messy if they only wound the animal. No; when it's time for a successful shot – and we'll only be allocating each hunter one a week – the sheep-master will simply press the super-charge button on his remote once the shooter starts blazing away. As I've said, we've done a trial run and it works. Quite a sensational death apparently. The high-powered electrical shock sends the sheep airborne which is a bonus spectacle-wise. I don't understand this appetite to kill animals but it's certainly there with most males it seems, and the more dramatic the death, the happier they are. That's one of the reasons we'll have a market. Most dangerous animals are now protected and that's left a huge vacuum which we intend to satisfy by creating our own species.'

'But what happens when the Jap sees the dead sheep and there's no bullet-hole?'

'They won't. Far too dangerous to leave the safety of the trench – there could be another killer-sheep lurking about. The dead sheep will be collected by armed guards at night, or that's what the shooters will be told. Oggonian killer-sheep retreat each night to the upper end of the island you see. They only come out in the daytime. All that will have been explained to the Japs and they won't be allowed to take any life-threatening risks. The Japanese are rule-abiding and like being ordered about so they'll buy the story unquestioningly. Anyway, they won't want to take risks. The Japanese are a highly successful race and consequently they value their lives. People with a cavalier

34

disregard for personal safety invariably have mediocre existences so they don't hesitate to place their lives on the line with risky activities because their lives don't amount to much anyway.'

'So they will have no memento of their achievement?' James asked, now caught up in the scheme.

'We've covered that,' Geoff replied. 'Theoretically, the sheep's head will be off to a taxidermist and will be freighted off after a month to Japan. That's what we'll be telling them. Naturally we'll have a warehouse of already made up heads with screwed in horns made from cattle bones. Our Romanian factory will handle that. We can do them there for £10 each and sell them to the successful shooter, nicely mounted with an engraved brass plaque for £400. We can also sell them the sheepskin as a rug and we'll import those already made up from New Zealand. Brasch is uncertain about that potential so it will be something for you to trial in the Oggonian souvenir shop we'll be building.'

'Romanian factory,' James puzzled, 'You mentioned that before.'

'Look, if you want to come aboard I'll explain all of that; in fact you can come with me and see it for yourself. It's an important part of our overall business. I'm calling in there on the way to our African operations next week. Actually, if you do come aboard I'll want you to come along to get the hang of things.'

'What! African killer-sheep?'

'No. Please take this seriously. They're two quite specialist operations. Quite different services. The common denominator with all of them is the customer. In each case they're very rich.'

'Honestly, Geoff. It all sounds …' James searched for the right description. 'It's extraordinary. I can see it when I think about it. But it's so bloody ridiculous.'

'That's its strength. That's why we're so successful. We create markets others never imagine, and if they did, they wouldn't have the gall to do. Credibility is simply never an issue. Perception is reality. I'm sorry I can't go into greater detail at this juncture but if you do come in and you see our other operations, you won't find it all so silly.'

'What about the other bit, the laird in the castle stuff. I can't play a laird role. I'd feel a goose.'

'We don't want you to. We'll be using an actor. But again, I'll go into all that if you come in as overseeing manager. At this stage I want you to take a look at our projection figures.' Geoff rose, walked to his desk, picked up two manila files and handed one to James.

'These are in US dollars and are based on our expected turnover after an initial six months. We're absolutely confident of maintaining a year-round full-house through our Japanese marketing agents, who also handle our Kenyan operation. In fact we expect a waiting list.

'For now I just want you to study the income and expenditure details. The Japs will be paying $1,500 a night, all found, per couple. We expect to have an annual gross of over $6 million a year from the killer-sheep operation and about $4 million off the castle, although that's a quite different market providing a different service. Wages, food, electricity, salaries etc. will eat up about $800,000 each year. Basically, Ogg should pay back its capital expenditure inside a year, maybe longer as we'll take our time getting it right at the start. After that your quarter will yield over a million pounds a year. Furthermore it'll be tax-free. Because we deal in foreign earnings everything goes through tax havens. We'll set you up on that score.'

James studied the sheet, his mind awhirl. He turned the pages. Food, electricity, salaries, helicopter flights, projected shop sales, Japanese agency fees – there were pages and pages of costed details. He looked up.

'It's all so insane, so crazy,' he muttered.

Geoff stared at him solemnly. 'As I said before, we know what we're doing. The market is there. We're already set up through our agency network to exploit it. If you come in you will first see our other operations and then have a better comprehension of everything. To be honest, Ogg will be the least off-beat of any of our divisions. Fairly conventional in fact.'

Again James studied the papers before him. The figures became blurred. His mind was racing and confused. Somehow the very madness of Geoff's proposal gave it allure.

'Why Japanese?' he asked after a pause. 'Why not Americans or Brazilians for that matter?'

'Horses for courses. No American would buy the killer-sheep proposition. They're too independent and questioning in their outlook. The Japanese will accept it unhesitatingly so long as it's presented right. Conversely, no Japanese would buy our royal tours. It's contrary to their collectivist egalitarian culture. Super-rich Americans lap them up.'

'Royal tours?' James asked, puzzled.

'I've jumped the gun. Please forget I mentioned it.'

'Christ. The plot thickens with every revelation,' James laughed. 'It's all so hard to believe. Are you seriously telling me you're making money from this sort of lark?'

Geoff looked hurt. 'Believe me, Ogg will probably be our most orthodox venture. You'll understand it all in the course of time. As for making money, we have an investment division that just deals with our profits. Currently our operations average over $25 million tax-free profit each year. We usually make half as much again from the investment division. I'm quite sure Ogg will make its contribution and you'll get your whack.

'You'll have lots of fun as well. You said you were bored. I can assure you, running Ogg will be far from boring. Your availability and ownership of Ogg, the fact that I know you and our need for an overseeing manager is a wonderful coincidence of events, more so given that as owner you'll have a vested interest in Ogg's success. It's all such a perfect match. Now, if you want to be in it then say so. Hand in your resignation tomorrow and I'll call my father. He'll come to London and we can get under way. The following week I'll take you with me to Bucharest, then we'll nick down to Africa. We'll be away a week or so then once back home you can help plan Ogg. There's lots for you to learn. So how about it? Are you in?'

James thought quickly. He recalled the constant charges of lack of initiative which had been the hallmark of his past. Then again, Jane would be outraged if he left sharebroking. 'I'm a starter,' he said.

Geoff stood up and extended his hand. The two men shook hands solemnly.

'Welcome aboard, mate. I promise you this – it will be a fabulous ride.'

He turned, walked across the office and opened a cabinet door to reveal a bar, and produced a bottle of Bollinger from a fridge. 'Here's the first step,' he said, beaming. 'A toast to our success.'

# – SIX –

For the third time in the space of a week, James sank into an armchair in Geoff's office. Its familiarity relaxed him and he looked expectantly at Geoff's father, eager to hear the background discourse Mr Upton had, the previous evening, undertaken to deliver.

Yesterday morning he had given his notice to Symington, the manager of his firm's London office, and braced himself for a debate. Instead Symington had smugly congratulated him, making it clear he was glad to see him go and implying that his resignation had simply pre-empted a sacking. Quickly coming to terms with that James had suggested he leave immediately rather than serve out a month, a proposal Symington had promptly accepted.

'Always best to pull stumps straight away,' the manager had said unctuously and then, as James reached the door, he added, 'I say Campbell. What are you planning to do?'

'I've received a very good offer,' James replied obliquely.

'Really!' Symington said, smirking and not hiding his disbelief. 'Not commerce, I trust. No disrespect but have you considered schoolteaching?'

'Actually, I stand to make a great deal of money,' James floundered, and angry at Symington's manner he left without further ado. On the street he was filled with a sense of exhilaration and he had walked to the West End, smiling at everyone whose eye he caught, elated by his new-found freedom and optimism.

That night he had dined with Geoff and his father. Initially James thought Mr Upton overly affected, but he soon concluded he was misreading what was in fact merely an old-fashioned, if slightly mannered patrician courtesy. Everything about him, from his exquisitely cut suit, his quiet but confident urbanity and his broad knowledge of the many subjects they had covered, suggested a man in total command of his world. Only his olive-tanned face hinted at bloodlines that were not entirely English.

During dinner he had quietly questioned James about his views on the sharemarkets and listened carefully to his responses, only interrupting to inject periodic spurs to keep him talking.

Realising he was being evaluated, James had become rattled and instead of responding naturally had attempted answers he hoped would impress. But just as the examination began to falter Mr Upton rescued it when he enquired whether James had wondered about the company name. Abandoning the careful strategy of the previous half hour, James revealed the research he had conducted in Hatchards.

Mr Upton had smiled approvingly. 'You're a rare animal. Sadly, few people possess any sense of curiosity. But tell me. What conclusion did you reach?'

James had again begun clumsily. 'At first I thought the name implied subterfuge. But then it occurred to me that if one was seeking that, one would hardly provide clues. That would be self-defeating. So I concluded in a vague sort of way that it was chosen – I don't know off-hand how to put it better – to imply the brains behind the display, or the true heart of something – not so much a disguise as the unobvious reality. I'm afraid I'm making a bit of a mess of this,' he spluttered.

Mr Upton rescued him. 'You have the essence of it. We needed a holding company name and as I have a mild interest in the classics, which nowadays is viewed as rather eccentric, Heracles' spectacular life seemed to fit the bill for our diverse activities. Given that our clientele deal with our various entities by their trade names, Alceides seemed appropriate for the anonymous ownership vehicle. It goes without saying that the imagery of Heracles' immortality holds much appeal in these uncertain times.'

'If I recall rightly,' James said hesitatingly, 'Hercules was rewarded with immortality for choosing virtue over pleasure.'

There was an awkward silence. Eventually Mr Upton asked coolly, 'You prefer the Latin?'

'Heracles,' James corrected himself blushing. 'I did a classics year with Geoff at university,' he quickly added when it was apparent Mr Upton did not wish to explore Heracles' immortality choice, or at least the reason behind it. Immediately he regretted speaking. Far better if Mr Upton had continued to assume his comments stemmed from general knowledge. As it transpired, however, his remarks impressed Mr Upton.

'Was that your decision?' he enquired. On receiving James' affirmation he added, 'A rare animal indeed. Geoffrey only did it because I insisted.'

After that the evening had passed splendidly. Mr Upton congratulated James on his boldness in joining Alceides, making it clear he had gained his approval, then there had followed some small talk about Ogg which Mr Upton soon terminated. 'Tonight's not the appropriate time to delve into all of that.'

They had parted, agreeing to meet in Geoff's office the following morning for an all-day crash course which, Mr Upton had warned, would involve a great deal of talking.

To James' relief Mr Upton arrived the next morning dressed in a well-cut jacket, with matching shirt and tie and a Pringle V-neck pullover. James had pondered over his own dress. All things considered a suit seemed excessive for the occasion. On the other hand casual tie-lessness was not quite right, and eventually he had chosen exactly as had Mr Upton.

Coffee was served and they settled down to business.

'As I warned you last night, I'm going to do a lot of talking,' Mr Upton began. 'But I want you to interrupt as often as you like with questions. First, as a foundation I want to explain the nature of contemporary commerce. That's something few people understand, which fact gives us a head start. Then I want to explain the tourism industry, not as it is generally understood but as it actually is. I rather suspect,' he added airily, 'that Alceides is the only participant who truly understands it. Finally I shall explain the behavioural factors of the super-rich which is the market we cater to.

'I shall leave it to Geoffrey to teach you the specifics of our actual operations. I gather you will accompany him next week to our Romanian factory and to Africa. After that you will have a very good understanding of everything and be in a position to contribute to the planning of Ogg. Of course, before you come in here we will need to draw up a contract outlining our respective roles and obligations. But first things first. Let's deal with the education process. Are you happy with that?'

'I can't wait,' James enthused. 'I'm damned if I know what you're going to say but honestly, I've never been so excited.'

'Good,' Mr Upton said. 'Now, lesson number one, the most important lesson of all, the secret of success, the golden rule. Are you ready?'

James laughed. 'Hit me!'

'Never, never be afraid to ask. Never be afraid to interrupt someone, and that includes me today and Geoffrey next week and every other situation you will encounter – if you don't understand something, speak up and say so.'

Noting James' slight disappointment Mr Upton continued. 'You think that's simple, don't you? Stating the obvious. Not so. If there's one thing that differentiates highly successful people from the masses, it's not brains or flair or luck or taking risks or any of the virtues usually ascribed to explain their achievement – more than any other attribute, successful people, who are a tiny minority, share a common characteristic and that is piping up and saying "I don't understand". It makes no sense to me but most people cannot bring themselves to say that. Instead they learn how to bluff. The general level of ignorance is primarily attributable to that behavioural peculiarity.' His voice rose. 'Ask. Be curious. Develop an enquiring mind. Ask why, ask where, ask how.'

'I'll ask,' James said weakly.

'Good. We'll move on. I'll start with contemporary commerce. The unique characteristic of the current scene compared with the last seventy years is unfettered competition. As a result everyone is working harder than they were five years ago and even harder still than ten years ago, just to stay afloat. This has led to a rather interesting consequence which is delivering sizeable rewards to the few who recognise it or are inadvertently practising the remedy.

'Commercial life was easy under the old regime of designated monopolies, tariff barriers, closed shops and the like. Because it was relaxed, people had time to think. Today they don't. They're far too busy trying to keep their head above water. Relaxed thinking time has gone. It wasn't like that before. Today is the age of the overworked specialist working hard rather than smart. There are very few people with any overview. An overview allows perspective and judgement. In particular, given an enquiring mind, it leads to creativity. That's why we read so often today of overnight fortunes being made by some bright young penniless fellow with a new idea. It never used to be like that. Rather, doing conventional things better than others made one successful. Well, that's not how it works any more and it all comes down to thinking time. The unemployed so-called geek staring at a computer in his bedroom has thinking time that is denied everyone else. Logic says that to make exceptional money, lots, above the herd, then obviously you can't behave like the herd. Do you see my point?'

James nodded thoughtfully. It was all so clear. As a broker his days had been frenetic with non-stop action. Every telephone call was quickly followed by another one. He had routinely trotted out the back office analysts' comments on every share he had been questioned about. There had been no big picture in his responses, no thoughtful consideration, certainly no discussion. And why? Exactly as Mr Upton said: there had been no time.

'You're absolutely right,' he said. 'What's interesting is that it's so obvious – that is now you've pointed it out. Why, if it's obvious, don't people see it?'

Mr Upton laughed. 'I've already told you. They simply don't have the time any more to be contemplative and therefore analytical. As a result they confuse additional productivity with increased profitability and are bewildered when the one doesn't follow the other. So they step up productivity even more, thereby compounding their problem. The answer lies in less work chasing their tails and more thinking time. It's really as elementary as that. Why do you think there's been such an explosion in business seminars and books in recent years? All these purported gurus offer is thinking, which those buying their nonsense intuitively know is absent from their lives.'

'Well, with respect, sir, I gather from Geoff that this organisation's employees work unusually long hours,' James said.

Again Mr Upton laughed. 'That's only on face value. We actually employ full-time thinkers, but I won't go into that now. That's why we want you to be overseeing manager at Ogg. You will have no specific duties but instead will be required to constantly evaluate the existing operation, putting out fires of course – they always arise in any management situation – and thinking up improvements. Other organisations would load you up with menial management work. Anyway, I'm sure you've got the picture. Now I want to move on and talk about tourism. Do you know anything about it?'

'Not really. My field over the past two years has been high-tech stuff and new company floats in that area. We had specialist tourism industry analysts,' James added as he realised yet again the truth of Mr Upton's comments about specialisation and its drawbacks.

'Tourism is an extreme case of modern commerce's futility,' Mr Upton said, 'at least in its conventional form. As you will discover, we've overcome its structural shortcomings as an industry.'

'Structural shortcomings?' James queried, mindful of his mentor's instructions to ask.

'As I said: unabashed, cut-throat price competition,' Mr Upton replied. 'Once participants become caught up with that, profit as a goal goes out the window and is replaced by market-share chasing. But why are they in business in the first place?' He answered his own question. 'To make a profit. The problem is that today's companies are so big and their management so subdivided and specialised that their corporate *raison d'être* – which is profit – becomes forgotten. Market share, being biggest, that sort of silliness becomes the goal. They ignore the obvious, such as that it's far better to make ten pounds with a fifth of the market than five with half of it. Anyway, it's academic because no one in the basic tourism businesses – airlines, hotels and the like – are making any money any more.'

James again spoke up. 'With respect, Mr Upton, airlines make money.'

Mr Upton laughed wryly. 'Are you sure of that?'

James looked puzzled. 'Well, British Air returns profits,' he responded.

'Remember this,' Mr Upton replied. 'Commercial aviation is a modern industry. Until about 1980 it was dominated by state-owned national flag carriers. After that by listed companies. Consequently it's easy to assess the true picture as it's all in the public domain. And what does that reveal? The entire history of commercial aviation is a net loss. That's a matter of record.'

'But how do they carry on? Why are they not all broke?'

'They do go broke, regularly. On average, every two months over the past twenty years a commercial airline has folded somewhere in the world. Everyone treats it as aberrational, attributable to bad luck or poor management. Because of a lack of perspective, that is thinking time, no one sees the situation clearly, that is the inevitability of their eventual demise. As quickly as they collapse new ones begin and foolish investors, bankers and the like put up the capital. Before it finally folded, Pan Am was the world's biggest airline. It made a loss for every one of its last 25 years and was succeeded by TWA which had a similar fate. Any industry characterised by constant amalgamations and euphemistically described "corporate restructurings", is fundamentally flawed. Such activity is merely flailing about, driven out of desperation, only no one recognises it for what it really is. On the contrary, such machinations are generally wrongly viewed as progress by financial commentators, rather than the reality which is survival. Beware of commercial growth which is not organic, and in particular beware of growth which is acquisitive which invariably means debt financed. It always ends in tears. It all comes back to unregulated competition. Good for the consumer; terrible for the operator. If an airline gets on to a good thing, say with a new route, it's no secret. Instantly it's swamped with competitors and suddenly it's no longer a good thing. Basically, airlines are programmed to eventually fail. It's true of most tourism activities. They all lack a monopoly factor which is their major flaw.'

'Hotels?' James broached.

'Even worse. Not a lot of public entities actually own hotels which in itself tells you something. Those that exist are all financial horror stories requiring constant capital injections, just like airlines. Public company boards of so-called independent directors are particularly susceptible to the "next year will be better" mythology fed to them from their executives. And in respect of periodic profit flushes the same situation applies as with airlines. If suddenly Hong Kong or Seattle becomes a good thing for hotels, instantly everyone's there building bigger and brighter ones. Overnight a good thing turns into a very bad thing.'

'But surely their owners must realise all of this if it's true,' James protested.

'Talk to hotel owners and you will find they live on eternal optimism. Always they'll explain about next year, how the new marketing plan, the new chain alliance, the new wing, the new refurbishing plan will make it come right. But with hotels, next year never comes. In an unfettered competitive environment, hotels, like airlines, are programmed to lose money and over any sensible period of assessment, say ten years, they all do.'

'Well, how do they survive then? It doesn't make sense.'

'New foolishly optimistic owners, new injections of capital; a constant shuffling and rearrangement of their financial structures, all driven by eternal optimism.'

'But surely if what you say is true everyone would be awake to it. There would be no new investors,' James argued.

'There are three answers to that,' Mr Upton said. 'First, all tourism activities – airlines, hotels, travel agencies; even the trivial ones, guiding, jetboat operators or whatever – are highly addictive. The players become captivated by what they're doing. But as I have said, when assessed over any reasonable period of time they literally never make money. Actually, I suspect their owners don't care that much. They become satisfied with mere survival so long as they can carry on. And of course, once involved, they're locked in by their financial predicament, compensated only by their addiction.'

'And the other reasons?' James queried, fascinated by these revelations.

'The second answer is that some major players – the big names, Sheraton and the like – are in fact awake to the realities. Consequently they no longer own hotels. Basically they're a franchise operation, renting their name, offering a pooled marketing service and clipping the actual hotel owners' tickets for a piece of their turn-over, only they are not hoteliers as everyone assumes but instead hotel provisioners. They all started out as hotel owners, but eventually they woke up. But I'm not sure the actual hotel owners would swap places with them even if they understood what was happening. They love owning their hotels too much. As I said, it's a highly addictive pursuit, and for some affluent individuals an ego-gratifying hobby.'

'Finally, even if it's a dead duck activity, investors will always be forthcoming for all sorts of reasons, not the least being gullibility. As a sharebroker you know there are just as many profitable opportunities for the astute investor in markets heading south as going the right way. Ordinary punters suffer but smart investors still profit so long as there's a definite trend to exploit.'

James nodded, recalling the series of sure-to-fail Internet floats his old firm had profited from listing during his New York posting.

'So, with a new float in a bad proposition, the underwriters who make it possible still make money simply because they know there'll be mugs to take them out. There always are,' Mr Upton added conclusively.

'But surely the hotel owners must eventually cotton on,' James persisted.

'Never. The owners either die or go broke and a new sucker climbs on board to take the beating. But there's a bit more to it than that, such as the never-to-be-underestimated "human factor" in explaining seemingly wilfully irrational behaviour. If you actually look at the sort of people who own these hotels, they have some common factors. Often they are chaps who have worked very hard doing something rather mundane like engineering or manufacturing. They've made their pile, and when they are about sixty, they suddenly ask themselves, is this it? They want some glamour in their lives and lose all their financial judgement in seeking it because their motivation is basically emotional. They envisage themselves in a sparkling chandeliered hotel lobby; greeting celebrities, politicians and the like when they arrive. The cruel reality is that the owners spend most of their time in backroom financial crisis meetings.

'You can always tell when a hotel is in one of its periodic crisis phases when suddenly all of its staff appear to be mentally deficient. There's a reason for that, which is that they actually are. Under pressure the proprietor has cut wages to the bone and can only attract humanity's dregs. As with most things, cost-cutting forced on a business simply compounds its problems, and never more so than in a service industry that resorts to employing morons. The owners struggle on, periodically changing managers, becoming caught up in the fool's gold from each new manager about new wings, refurbishing, redesign, rebranding and new marketing strategies, and always, always believing that once these things are done, all will be well. They never are. Relief only comes with the owner's death.'

'So glamour hotels have an allure for suckers,' James suggested.

'Oh, it's not just hotels. It's true of lots of commercial activities. Showbiz is the worst by far, especially in America where inexplicably actors are accorded enormous celebrity status. Broadway would collapse overnight if it wasn't for wealthy elderly business dullards and rich widows seeking a last hurrah of some glamour in their lives by financing show business. The actors play along, attending their little parties and being displayed, knowing the so-called investors will bear no end of financial punishment to the celebrities' benefit in return. It's perfectly normal human behaviour. More discerning people behave in exactly the same way, only with politicians or literary or arts celebrities. Arguably it's a fair trade-off because the investors are in their twilight years and, as the saying rightly goes, they can't take it with them. So maybe, viewed that way, they're not suckers at all because they're getting what they want, even if they have to buy it. Prostitution, remember, is a willing exchange by both participants.'

'But what about resort hotels? Glamorous complexes on tropical beaches, that sort of operation. Surely they're an exception?'

'Actually, their plight is worse,' Mr Upton murmured. 'Every tropical hotel complex dealing in cheap low-profit package tours for the low-income sector was once a top glamour hotel, perhaps a decade earlier. As soon as they enjoyed a glimmer of success better, brighter hotels were instantly built further along the beach and usurped their fleeting place in the sun. And the new players are ultimately doomed to the same fate when a younger, stronger lion looms on the scene as invariably it does. But aside from that inevitable decline in fortune, don't be deceived by the apparent success of resort hotels, that is in their early days. Tropical hotels mean Third World labour. Third World labour is the most expensive of all. The individual employee wages are minuscule but a Swiss hotel employee does a job which takes ten in Jamaica or the Seychelles and in those places they still bungle it. Tropical Third World countries are huge consumers of capital through incompetence, graft and all the other negative characteristics of such places. But they continue to suck in optimistic western entrepreneurs, drawn by their apparent cheapness. It's an illusion, and it doesn't just apply to hotels: everyone, manufacturers, banks, insurers, it doesn't matter what activity, gets badly burned by such Third World adventurism. But, caught up by the market-share foolishness they keep coming,' he laughed.

'I still don't understand,' James said. 'If basically hotels are consistently losing money, then surely they'd eventually be forced to close down.'

'You've provided the answer yourself. They don't lose money consistently. Every few years they make a bit, and then it is either a cyclical thing which passes, or new competition pours in. But it's those aberrational profitable years that the owners delude themselves are the norm which keeps them going, just like agriculture and retailing and paper manufacturing and lots of other similar ill-fated activities. In come fresh investors and partners to fund a new wing or a refurbishment or a rebranding programme which never works but takes years to execute. Anyway, even if over a ten-year period it's a net loss, it's still usually better to carry on. Invariably these ventures are heavily geared to banks, so if they can pay 80 per cent of the interest liability by staying in business, that's better than closing and having no income for the interest bill. That's the way they see it anyway, and the banks have no choice but to keep carrying them as they too are locked in. That, incidentally, is the key difference between airlines and hotels. An airline is simply a marketing exercise. It owns virtually no physical assets as its aircraft are usually leased and easily disposed of when it goes broke. By contrast, a hotel is an expensive fixed asset. Consequently hotels as such don't go broke; their owners do, but no matter how poor the performance the actual hotel always carries on, as even at a loss it's still the best option for its creditors. Periodically its fire sale injects a new capital sum, clearing its owner's past accumulated debts and the process begins all over again.'

'Why on earth do banks fund hotels if all this is true?' James demanded.

'Bank stupidity could preoccupy me for several days,' Mr Upton laughed. 'But there are lots of reasons. First, they're in the business of lending money, and like everything else banking is overly competitive. That leads to risky decisions and market-share chasing, as I explained. Banks are just businesses and they behave in these same fundamental ways like all businesses. There's a widespread delusion that banks are a superior echelon in the commercial world. Nothing could be further from the truth.

'Second, as is common with modern commerce, they have a constant turnover of executives so bad experiences are always attributed to past management. But most of all, it's because of what I said earlier. That is, the lack of thinking time and therefore analysis. It's a funny old world we live in, James,' he concluded wistfully.

A silence descended while James mulled over what had been said. Mr Upton gazed out the window. Finally he turned. 'Look, we'll go and have some lunch and this afternoon I'll tell you about the winners in tourism or, perhaps more accurately, entertainment which is what tourism has now become. There are not many but they all share a common denominator which is what we here in Alceides practise. Do you like Japanese?' he asked abruptly.

'I've never really met any,' James replied. 'I suppose that will soon be remedied on Ogg. Why, is there something I should be alert to?'

'No, no, no. I mean Japanese food. You won't have any difficulty with the people. They're the politest and most co-operative on earth. But do you like their food?'

'I don't really mind. It's not my favourite. I probably go to a Japanese restaurant about once a year.'

'Good,' Mr Upton exclaimed. 'Can't stand it myself; no substance to it, but it's supposedly the healthiest food going so I have to eat it regularly. There's quite a good place ten minutes from here. The stroll will do us good. Come on; vamos.'

# – SEVEN –

On arrival at the Fujiyama Mr Upton was greeted effusively, with much bowing. Once inside the private room he said, 'No need for menus. They know my requirements. Given what lies ahead it would be sensible if you ate Japanese food a couple of times a week while Ogg is being prepared. You won't need to once you're there as we'll have a Japanese manager, but it's important to have an understanding of what's required on the food front. It's something Japanese people are particularly fussy about. In every other respect you will find them co-operative and tolerant.'

'As I said, I've had almost no contact with Japanese,' James commented. 'I really know very little about them. My old firm had an office in Tokyo and there was talk of my having a stint out there but it never eventuated.'

'You will find them very easy to deal with,' Mr Upton repeated. 'Apart from their natural politeness the best thing about them is their absolutely patterned and predictable behaviour. To keep them happy everything must be programmed and controlled. They won't be interested in any roaming-in-the-gloaming, free-spirit Scottish adventures. With Japanese women the trick is to provide numerous objects for them to be photographed in front of, and also quality things for them to buy. They must be absurdly expensive. That seems to bring them special pleasure.'

'And the men?' James quizzed.

'Japanese men travelling in a group are also very predictable. They like to do things with a macho characteristic as long as they are safe and highly organised so Ogg's killer-sheep and bracing climate fit the bill nicely there. You will find that with every group of Japanese men one among them automatically adopts the role of group clown.

Always he's the fattest and shortest. The others laugh dutifully and while it can be a bit noisy, it's basically harmless. Have you ever been involved in a major court case?' Mr Upton asked abruptly.

'No,' James replied, puzzled at where this was leading.

'Pity,' Mr Upton mused. 'You would know what I mean if you had. In the course of every litigation at some point the judge will attempt a joke. To the best of my knowledge not once has the joke ever really been funny. Despite that, competition ensues among the barristers to see who can laugh the longest and loudest. It's a bit like that with Japanese males travelling together and responding to the self-appointed group clown. But remember we will be dealing with the upper-income echelon. These are not the sort of people who wear baseball hats indoors at the dining table; indeed, I'm pleased to say they're not the types to wear baseball hats at all, unlike lower and middle-income Japanese tourists. There is an understandable tendency to typecast races based on the more publicised elements. I would not be at all surprised should the average Japanese assume we English are all beer-swilling soccer hooligans. Conversely, you should not assume all Japanese are karaoke-bawling buffoons. Ogg's Japanese clients will not be intellectuals, but as highly successful business types they will display a degree of refinement. You will soon pick up their ways if you pay attention.'

James agreed to do so. 'I've put my hand up on a fairly scantily outlined proposition,' he said. 'Geoff talked about research and things but I haven't heard any of it in detail yet.'

'Don't worry. It's all in hand. When you return from your little education tour you will see the full plans. Hopefully you will have some thoughts of your own to contribute.'

'Geoff mentioned your ideas man Brasch as ...'

He was interrupted as a scowl crossed Mr Upton's face. 'What did he say about Brasch?' he demanded abruptly.

'Well, nothing really,' James said hurriedly. 'Just that Brasch is some sort of researcher. We didn't pursue it. There was so much to talk about.'

Mr Upton relaxed. He thought for a few seconds and then, addressing the wall, said, 'Perhaps you will meet Brasch on your return from Africa. It may be useful.' He paused again, then added, 'Then again it may not be; we'll see.'

A further silence followed then Mr Upton said, 'I take it Geoffrey has warned you that what you will encounter – our enterprises that is – are somewhat unconventional. That's rather true of Brasch as well.'

'Yes,' James said. 'He's certainly reinforced that point. But having outlined the Ogg scheme, I must say, the impressive numbers aside, it's a highly entertaining concept. There was never very much amusing with what I've been doing since I left university.'

Mr Upton smiled. 'Humour is the bride of intelligence. Desirably there should be laughter in everything, but humour only emerges where there is imagination and, in turn, imagination feeds off thinking and knowledge. It all comes back to what I said this morning about no one having thinking time any more. I'm convinced that's why life in the developed world has become rather sober in recent years.'

The waiter entered with eight bowls of various food items and a bottle of chardonnay. Mr Upton set about busily with his chopsticks. A minute passed before he spoke again.

'You know, James, I wouldn't want you to think we're taking advantage of people. It's absolutely not so. Alceides is a very wealthy enterprise that is reliant on its repeat business. Our success rests on happy customers. We deliver the Elysian fields to them, even if …' he stopped and searched for the right words, 'even if there's an element of, what shall I say …' again he hesitated '… let us say an element of illusion in what we offer. What else did Geoffrey mention?' he asked sharply.

'I hope I'm not talking out of school but something he alluded to while endeavouring to explain Alceides, while not really explaining it, was royal tours,' James replied. 'When I reacted he dropped it quickly so I didn't press him.'

'Yes,' Mr Upton said drily. 'Well, as you're going to Madagascar you will see that little exercise. Great fun; very profitable, happy customers; what more could you ask?' he said expansively, extending his arms. 'But we'll take it slowly, bit by bit. Still, that service is different from our others, that is, in the illusion sense. You may be inclined to snigger when you see it but you should be aware that our clients are fully cognisant of everything. The exquisite pleasure they derive and we organise for them, is utterly dependent on their participation in the illusion, as you will see. There's nothing withheld there. But in the final analysis it doesn't matter. What does is that we give value and that's not in debate. Our high repeat business proves that.'

'Needless to say I'm in a state of suspense,' James said excitedly. 'I've been titillated with so many titbits to whet the appetite. I can't wait till next week. But you referred to Madagascar. Geoff didn't mention Madagascar, just your operation in Kenya. I must say that sounds exciting. One never hears anything about it.'

'Exciting!' Mr Upton queried somewhat loftily. 'Perhaps; but it's certainly interesting. As I have said, an introduction bit by bit is best. Just remember to ask plenty of questions. In the meantime, eat up and we'll return to the office for a brief course on tourism. After that you will be ready to go.'

'Actually, talking about going. What about travel arrangements? Should I make some bookings or what?' James enquired hesitatingly, wondering, as he had done since the travelling to Romania and Africa had been first mooted, who would pick up the bill.

Mr Upton stopped eating and raised his eyebrows, 'Has Geoffrey not mentioned that? Well, I am surprised. You will certainly not be flying in commercial airlines. We have our own jet, three in fact; need them for the business. We're a mini-airline ourselves,' he laughed. 'Now come on, we're out of here, there's work to be done,' and they rose and returned to the office.

# – EIGHT –

'I don't wish to be a bore and hog the conversation,' Mr Upton said as James resumed occupation of his now familiar armchair. 'Please remember about speaking up. Let's make this a two-way exchange, or for that matter, three,' he added as Geoff entered the room. 'Stay with us and contribute,' he instructed his son. 'One voice doing all the talking doesn't aid the quick-course educational process.'

James felt simultaneously relaxed and exuberant. Most of all he felt lucky. Inside a week his world had turned on its head thanks to Ogg. Normal life, so mundane, was about to change dramatically for him. He was joining those at the peak of the human pyramid, those who somehow possessed the key to extracting from the everyday meat of existence the juices of affluence, excitement and stimulation. He was filled with a sense of gratitude to Geoff and his father.

'Let us begin,' Mr Upton said. 'The first thing to recognise is that mass tourism, now the world's biggest industry, is a modern phenomenon. People take it for granted and think it has always been like this. Not so. They confuse mass tourism with organised travel, which began with Thomas Cook but was never more than the prerogative of a small minority. Mass tourism began in the mid-1970s with the advent of the jumbo jet. Prior to that even visiting North America and Western Europe was an adventure. Going to Paris was an exciting experience for our middle classes, and as for the working classes, well, they stopped at the coast; Blackpool and Brighton and Butlins holiday camps were their limits. That's not so any more. With the middle classes, as I speak there are bearded quantity surveyors, spinster librarians and dull accountants crossing the Gobi Desert on camels, scuba-diving on once remote Indian Ocean islands, trout fishing in Siberia, climbing Andean mountain peaks, rafting down wild rivers in the Himalayas, and all carefully organised for them, in such ease and comfort that they might just as well be sitting in armchairs at home watching television documentaries about these activities. Yet not too long ago any one of those pursuits would be considered bold adventuring, as indeed they were. As for the lower orders, thirty years ago it was an adventure for lumpen Midlands factory workers to follow their football team to a game in Birmingham. Today they think nothing of following it to Oslo or Mexico City. Once pleasant locations like Ibiza where I reside have been utterly degraded by our barbarous classes. I'm afraid that in elevating workers' material standards we have been unable to similarly elevate their values, which brings me to my point. Foreign travel is now devoid of any exotic appeal because everyone is doing it.'

'Vulgarity is now ubiquitous. Yet a mere forty years ago, anyone doing any one of the things now being experienced by thousands of suburban types would return home and write a best-seller about it.'

'The interesting thing about that,' Geoff intervened, 'is that despite the lack of novelty in contemporary travel, travel-book publishing is booming. Only today it's more guide books than adventure stuff.'

'That's because travel is no longer adventurous,' Mr Upton responded. 'Applying book-writing as a measure of how it has all changed, go back a century and even travellers to Paris and Rome were considered adventurers and wrote about their journeys. Mark Twain's accounts of visiting those cities were best-sellers. Then came the 1920s, an affluent period, particularly in America, which spurred a lot of what was then perceived as exotic voyaging. Travellers to India, to Central America or Africa returned home to write about it. You can still find their output in second-hand bookshops.'

'Surely the changes are a good thing,' James argued. 'Doesn't it simply reflect higher living standards?'

'Of course,' Mr Upton replied. 'But because travel to foreign parts is no longer an adventure, travel promoters are having to create excitement by contriving canoeing trips down the Amazon and balloon voyages across Italy for the middle-class market.'

'Europe has become a vast Noddyland theme park in pursuit of the tourist dollar. Museums and art galleries have been subjected to a debasing Disneyland degradation to lure the masses who only visit such places when abroad because after two days they've run out of things to do. Normally they'd never go near museums; and they certainly don't when they are back at home.'

'Former glamour spots like the south of France are full of overweight Germans, half-naked Scandinavians, backpackers, and even worse, red-faced English yobbos. The skies are dense with jumbo jets transporting millions of Europeans, North Americans and Japanese all over the globe. Modern marketing persuasively evokes new horizons that are portrayed through the rose-tinted perspective of nostalgia, be it a gondola ride in Venice or mounting a camel at the Sphinx, but despite the self-delusion of a photographic record, the overwhelming impression left on the contemporary tourist is as a victim of crass commercialism. For the middle classes a holiday is no longer a holiday unless it's abroad. They demand a foreign ambience, but after an initial flush of excitement, they are soon bored by the increasing uniformity of the experience. They visit whatever attractions are on offer, but how many medieval cathedrals can one inspect without it descending to tedium? Natural wonders are even worse; after all, once you've stared at Victoria Falls or a herd of giraffes in a game reserve for ten minutes, their spectator appeal is exhausted.'

'Yes. I see your point,' James said. 'But the fact is people still do it; travel that is. So what are you suggesting as a solution?'

'All this has created a need for contrivance to fill the tourists' time; that is man-made attractions such as theme-parks and specialist museums,' Mr Upton explained. 'There are now over a hundred Holocaust museums in North America alone, all built in recent years. The Jews were first off the mark in this new victimhood industry but we can expect to see it develop rapidly in the future. The potential's enormous, and not just in Ireland or Armenia or America or Africa. There's scarcely a country which doesn't contain a minority faction with some purported grievance about the past that's open for specialist museum exploitation. There is already an apartheid museum in South Africa and there'll be gulag camps run as resorts in Siberia, and think of the potential for homosexual museums. Widen your perspective and consider the enormous range of human activities and you will see the yet untapped potential for specialist museum development.'

'Like what?' James asked.

'Football and fashion, printing and postage stamps, politics and photography, medicine, surgery, prostitution, pornography, the Olympics, space research, agriculture, machinery; the possibilities are endless for commemorative museums catering to tourists, whereas once such entertainment was the domain of now unfashionable zoos, music halls and circuses. The problem with all of these ventures, however, is that they have no monopoly; once they prove profitable, competitors will emerge, as we're witnessing now with the Holocaust boom. The phenomenal growth in tourism currently maintains the balance in favour of the supplier, but make no mistake, oversupply is inevitable which is why Alceides stays clear of such ventures. These exhibitions fill a void in the tourists' day but if they were really interested in these topics they'd buy a book about them, and they don't. I'm afraid that with the specialist museum industry, oversupply is inevitable and as a consequence unprofitability looms on the horizon. However, it's some time away still as the millions travelling continue to swell in number.'

'Is it all really that bad?' James asked.

'Do you think I'm overstating it?' Mr Upton replied, raising his eyebrows. 'Sadly, I'm not. Take Paris, still the world's top travel destination. Thirty years ago one could stroll up to the Louvre or the Eiffel Tower and enter without delay at the height of summer. Now, on a bitterly cold February day there are lengthy queues and a two-hour waiting time. Thirty years ago going to China was a huge adventure, yet this very day probably several thousand tourists wandered up and down the Great Wall, largely bored out of their minds. And rightly so, because the wall is interesting only in its implications, not in any visual sense. Everyone first knocks off the obvious Paris-type places, then seeks other notches on their travel belts. Next it's Bolivia and Borneo, and as a result the tourist hordes are thick on the ground in these places as well.'

'It's just another ramification of globalisation,' Geoff said.

'It's the most successful aspect of globalisation,' his father retorted. 'Remember, there are still sizeable last-ditch factions fighting a rearguard action against globalisation on political or economic grounds. But the same shallow fools see no contradiction in holidaying overseas. There are negatives in globalisation, but the factors and forces in its favour are relentless and will prevail. Unfortunately the price we pay, which we are already seeing with travel, is a uniformity evolving in politics, attitudes, values, tax, fashion, pop music, fads, food or anything you care to name. You'll find brain-dead youths wearing baseball hats back to front in Lima, Lagos, Los Angeles,

Lahore, you name it, just as you do here in London. Mass travel is inadvertently paving the way to world government as the ultimate outcome of globalisation. Very soon we'll all be provincial.'

'Do you think so?' James said tentatively. 'It strikes me nationalism is alive and well.'

'There are many different emotions blanketed under the term nationalism,' Mr Upton countered. 'The important thing is to recognise their differences. For example, there's a practical reason for supporting one's cricket or football team, simply because if you don't align yourself with one side the spectacle becomes pointless. And there's nothing nationalistic about taking an interest or deriving pleasure from one's country's history. As with nostalgia, reflection on past times is enjoyable and interesting.

'On the other hand, there's the national-identity promoting crowd who are always narrow, small thinkers, lacking any perspective. Invariably you will find they comprise public broadcasters, subsidy-seeking failed authors, theatrical types and other so-called artists whose offerings are rejected in the marketplace. They're charlatans of course and nothing less than well-organised parasites. They know when to strike, and that's with new incoming governments who, swollen with pride at their triumph, naively extrapolate their own flash-in-the-pan success to the dawning of a new age and a national renaissance. During the euphoria of their honeymoon period they are particularly vulnerable to this self-serving blarney. Seasoned governments correctly treat arts' subsidies advocates with contempt. However, we're getting away from the subject which is the homogenisation of the travel experience.'

'If foreign travel loses its novelty then maybe it will no longer be exotic in any meaningful sense and people will stop doing it,' James suggested.

'I'm convinced that's right,' Mr Upton said. 'But we're at least thirty years away from a major backlash. Tourism is still primarily the rich gazing voyeuristically at the poor. Only the rich these days, at least in a global context, include shop assistants and plumbers, so long as they come from a developed nation. But there are huge new markets evolving which are still largely unable to afford travel, such as China and India, which together account for about 40 per cent of the world's population. And of course each new generation may want to see for themselves. Nevertheless, at some stage that understandable desire will diminish as its pointlessness becomes obvious. And despite all its shortcomings contemporary mass tourism does have the redeeming feature of providing large-scale employment for the totally talentless. Nothing else apart from pop music offers that. But the reality is that dumbing down to a universal global culture, which mass tourism is inducing – that is a one-size-fits-all approach – will ironically be the factor which kills the industry as it will destroy the whole point of it. Commentators talk of tourism being the main growth industry of the twenty-first century, but they're quite wrong. The desire to travel implies a curiosity about the world, whereas with most contemporary tourists curiosity plays no part in their motivation. With increasing leisure time, ever-lowering travel costs and the public's total absence of imagination, their true motivation is the pursuit of entertainment.'

'Entertainment?' James queried.

'Entertainment will be the new century's major growth industry,' Mr Upton said adamantly. 'Look at America. Entertainment in the form of film and television output is now its major export industry. Twenty years ago it was armaments.'

'An encouraging change, surely,' James smiled.

'An improvement, yes,' Mr Upton agreed. 'But not without its dangers. The combination of money, leisure time and vacuity has considerable potential to be malevolently exploited. Let me give you a benign example. Two years ago I flew to New Zealand to watch our cricket team in the final test. It was preceded by a one-day game where I witnessed a most extraordinary sight. As spectators entered the ground they were given small cardboard placards with the symbol "4" on one side and "6" on the other. If someone hit a four, they all held up the "four" sign.'

James laughed. 'An exaggeration surely, sir.'

'Sadly no. I swear it was true.'

'But why?'

'That's my point. Because they'd been told to; because they're utterly mindless. Furthermore, the same thing is now spreading to other countries, including ours. In itself it doesn't matter, but the implications are frightening in showing there's no limit to what the masses will unquestioningly do if they're simply told to. We as a commercial enterprise need to understand this sort of behaviour.

Anyway, while it's interesting to speculate about the future, let's concern ourselves with the here and now.'

'I still find the cricket placard business hard to believe,' James said. 'I'd love to see it.'

'I rather wish I hadn't,' Mr Upton said. 'It does tend to destroy any optimism one has about the human condition.'

Geoff, meanwhile, had opened a bottle of wine and he now filled them glasses. 'The salient issue,' he said, 'is how this affects Alceides' customers; that is the approximately 25,000 individuals, mostly in America but also in Japan, with a net worth of several hundred million.'

'Correct,' his father responded. 'Let's look at them and generalise. These are highly successful people. Mainly they're over fifty, and conscious that time is of the essence. They are industrious, imaginative and hungry to squeeze as much out of life as they can. It's that outlook which made them rich in the first place. They're not content with routine ordinariness – golf, an annual holiday abroad, skiing in Austria this year, a Mauritius beach next year, a new car every two years and all the features of the middle-class lifestyle. Yet at the same time they're trapped.'

'I'd have thought having heaps of money gave them immunity,' James said.

'Only on face value,' Mr Upton replied. 'Before the jumbo and mass tourism the rich relied on foreign travel for their pleasures. Thirty years ago countries were still radically different from one another and therefore worth visiting. The rich could afford to travel in style and go to more exotic places once they had the Taj Mahal, Anne Hathaway's cottage and the Prado under their belts. And they did, first-class all the way and regularly. Now, all that's over. Think back twenty years. The term jetsetter was applied to the glamorous celebrity set because of their international travel. You never hear it now, because travel is commonplace. Tens of thousands of people cross borders every day just to go to work.'

'Remember when if you said you were going abroad there was a cliched response,' Geoff said. 'People would say, "Can I carry your bags?" You never hear that any more either.'

'Exactly,' Mr Upton said. 'Without wishing to sound cynical, the fact is that one of the great pleasures of wealth lies less in its material rewards and a great deal more in one's relativity to everyone else; that is, you have things others don't have, which not long ago was the case with foreign travel. Today, everyone's travelling and for the rich travel has become a hollow experience. The marching feet of the masses are everywhere; the only places that are immune are those that are temporarily out of bounds because of civil war or political or religious upheavals. For that reason they can be interesting, even if dangerous and uncomfortable, but they don't appeal to our clients. The rich have every reason to value their lives, and in particular they want maximum comfort and they don't care what it costs. But with the tourist hordes everywhere that can be hard to find. Even the first-class airline lounges, once the privilege of a small minority, are now crowded with vacuous business bores bawling inanities into mobile phones, with badly behaved children, and middle-aged bearded mediocrities in pressed blue jeans, white socks and most pathetic of all – money-belts round their waists.' Mr Upton shuddered and fell silent contemplating these horrors.

'Which is where we come in,' Geoff said, breaking the contemplative lull which had descended on the room. 'Our customers want to avoid contamination with ordinary folk.'

'That sounds a bit snobbish,' James suggested gently.

'Precisely,' Mr Upton snapped. 'That's exactly what it's about. The whole point of great wealth is the options it provides, not the least being a high degree of privacy. Let us continue generalising about the behaviour of the new breed of self-made super-rich. First, once they've cracked it they build a massive mansion, then they acquire a luxury apartment in Los Angeles, London or wherever they're financially based. The next step, the getting away from it all now travel is out, is typically the super-yacht or the 50,000-acre ranch in Montana or the Argentinean pampas. A ranch keeps them interested as a radically different hobby, but only for so long. Very soon they slide into a routine of, say, three visits a year; all good fun, riding horses, fishing in streams, discussing cattle prices with their ranch manager and what-not, but still predictable once they're used to it. The same goes for the luxury yacht. They soon discover what fool's gold that is, and end up paying for a crew and never going near it.'

'I don't know about that,' James said. 'I wouldn't say no to owning a luxury yacht if I could afford it.'

'That's because you don't know,' Mr Upton replied. 'Basically, luxury yachts are simply floating apartments, with the drawback of being surrounded by water; a terrible tedium which is why they invariably end up anchored and unused. Luxury yachts are totally devoid of pleasure, which their owners soon realise once they're past the showing-off stage of hosting friends and celebrities. It's just another predictable behavioural pattern arising from suddenly acquired great wealth. So too with another standard response to their new situation – the art phase – buying expensive paintings, sculptures and antiques, attending then ultimately sponsoring operas and that sort of nonsense. It's sustainable for a time through its novelty but inevitably it all palls with repetition. It's contrary to the mentality of the self-made super-rich to be mere dilettantes. Frankly, in many respects their behaviour, although different from that of the suburban middle-classes, is just as predicable.'

'So there's no point getting rich if one's fate is the same as before,' James proposed mischievously.

'Not so,' Mr Upton argued. 'The nub of their problem is that they have too many choices. Ordinary people accept limitations through necessity. But the super-rich have everything potentially at their fingertips, which leads to frustration. It all boils down to expectations. Ordinary folk expect little; the super-rich everything. People who expect little are easily satisfied. The reverse applies to the super-wealthy. They crave every possible experience and they want it efficiently and in maximum comfort. Most people erroneously assume that the super-rich achieved their wealth through greed. But it is not greed for money which got them there, but greed for life. Their greatest fear is boredom, which ordinary folk accept as part of life. We help solve that problem for them. Over the next few weeks you will see that, and then you will understand better how Ogg will fit into the scheme of things.'

'And your clients are solely American and Japanese?' James asked. 'I didn't think there were that many super-rich Japanese. I thought all their top businessmen lived modestly and paid horrendous rates of tax.'

Mr Upton chuckled. 'Plainly you don't view the Japanese as members of the human race if you believe that.' Then, noticing James' puzzlement, he added, 'Let me give you just one statistic. Japan is the second-biggest merchant ship-owning nation in the world but, of all the major merchant fleet nations, it's by far the highest user of foreign registration; you know, Liberia, Panama and the like. The sole reason for that is tax avoidance. I can assure you, rich Japanese have exactly the same attitude to paying taxes as everyone else.'

'Well, I'm certainly learning,' James laughed.

'No, you're partly right when you refer to them living modestly. That is a cultural factor. The Japanese consider ostentation, which large homes epitomise, to be vulgar. That is why their super-rich are so vulnerable to overpriced baubles such as $50-million Van Goghs or foolish investments such as Hawaiian hotels, which can be categorised as commercial activity rather than the reality of personal indulgence. Once acquired they're easily tucked away out of sight.'

'Earlier you mentioned the absence of a monopoly factor,' James said. 'You haven't explained but I assume your ventures must have that?'

'I gave you a rough outline of Ogg,' Geoff replied. 'It's the only place in the world with killer-sheep, *ipso facto* a natural monopoly.'

'But others could copy it,' James suggested.

'Which is why we place so much emphasis on secrecy,' Geoff responded. 'And as I said, the best protection is ensuring the landowner has a vested interest, which again, is why you're here.'

'Only monopolies make money in tourism,' Mr Upton said. 'As you will learn, Alceides has created its own highly profitable monopolies but with the unique factor of targeting a specialist market, namely the super-wealthy.'

'But foreign travel is bound up in natural wonders which are essentially monopolies,' James argued.

'True. But invariably you will find they are state-owned,' Mr Upton responded. 'We are discussing commercial monopolies, and the best, whether large or small are created. An outstanding example of a large one is Disneyland, while a small one is *The Mousetrap* play here in London. Study the newspaper theatre pages and you will see it's the only West End play which doesn't name the actors. That's because it alone can use low-paid nobodies because as an artistic performance it's a meritless pot-boiler and everyone knows it. But each night tourists pay good money to attend. It's a wonderful created-monopoly, with the single selling point of being the longest-running play in history. For first-time tourists in London, attending rates with going to the Tower or visiting Madame Tussaud's which, incidentally, is another money-spinning created-monopoly and the biggest single tourist attraction in Britain. Go down this evening to *The Mousetrap* and you can see for yourself. The audience queuing are entirely tourists. It's been going for half a century now and it will carry on as long as tourists keep coming to London. The only mistake the producers made was not realising what was happening early enough and placing a series of large, leatherbound visitors' books in the foyer. You can envisage Doreen from Australia on her first trip, checking out Mum and Dad's signatures from quarter of a century earlier. That would have provided a nice pilgrimage-type touch. Still, it is an aptly named exercise – that is as a trap for middle-class mice.'

'But what's to stop someone else barging in and staging the play when the copyright runs out?' James asked.

'Wouldn't work,' Mr Upton replied. 'As I said, its single selling point is being the longest-running play ever. Only the current producers possess that key factor, so long, of course, as they stay open.'

'Yes, I see what you mean,' James said. 'What are some other created-monopolies?'

'The biggest created tourist facility is Las Vegas. It's a truly appalling place centred around gambling and vacuous entertainment targeting the brain-dead and bored. There's no shortage of customers; gambling is simply a tax on dullards. Vegas has created a monopoly by the sheer scale of its vulgarity, and consequently it's America's fastest-growing city. There are many smaller exercises in the same vein such as the Elvis Presley shrine, Gracelands; arts festivals and the Empire State building; the Taj Mahal, and the Oberammergau Passion Play which is another man-made *Mousetrap*-like monopoly. Its monopoly factor lies in the fact that it has been going nearly four hundred years, which is the only reason it pulls an audience. They suffer dreadfully watching it but they endure it because it's another notch on their travel-experience belts. The most recent fad for pulling tourists is the creation of annual Mardi Gras parades, now a huge money-spinner for their host cities despite their repetition and predictability. There's New Orleans, Rio, the homosexual Mardi Gras in Sydney and a similar parade in New York, with more sprouting every year.'

'It's amazing,' James said. 'I never really thought of these things in that light.'

'You may not believe it,' Mr Upton continued, 'but despite its initial difficulties Europe's single biggest tourist attraction is now EuroDisney. Then there's the Hemingway Bar in Havana. The truth is, Hemingway scarcely went near it, but the myth is now well entrenched and reinforces itself with every passing year. So the punters keep coming and are walloped with exorbitant drinks prices. A nice little earner,' Mr Upton said dreamily.

'Anyway, I've talked enough. You now have a complete background and will better understand why we do what we do when you see it. More particularly, you will see the three critical ingredients which underlie our success. The first is identifying and catering to a sizeable new market no one else has recognised; that is, the super-rich. The second is in creating monopolies which means being a price-setter rather than a competition-oppressed price-taker, and finally, we ensure a very high degree of customer satisfaction resulting in demand for our services constantly exceeding our ability to provide it.'

Geoff opened another bottle of wine and topped up the three glasses.

'What we deliver is basically entertainment,' he explained. 'Our clientele don't want to look at things any more. They've seen it all. They want a radically different, stimulating experience. Radically different from their everyday lives and from conventional foreign travel. That's what you will see in our African operations.'

'Talking of which, when exactly are you going?' Mr Upton asked.

'I told the pilots Tuesday,' Geoff responded. 'But if it suits you,' he said, addressing James, 'I wouldn't mind shooting over to Romania this Friday? We could have an amusing weekend in Bucharest and get stuck in first thing Monday morning.'

'That sounds great,' James replied, and turned the conversation to the clothing he should bring.

'Lightweight tropical,' Mr Upton said dismissively. 'But there's still one other very important matter to be dealt with.'

James looked at him quizzically at the same time noting Geoff's slight embarrassment.

'As you will see in the next fortnight, everything Alceides does is immensely profitable and perfectly legal,' Mr Upton said rather formally. 'However, and notwithstanding the very good work we do in bringing considerable pleasure to our clientele, publicity about our operations would destroy them. Accordingly, we require you to sign a confidentiality agreement. It accepts a liability of £50 million should you reveal anything about Alceides.'

'But I don't have £50 million,' James spluttered.

'No, I don't imagine you do,' Mr Upton said drily. 'That, I hope, will be a further incentive to maintain confidentiality. It is not a lot to ask in the circumstances.'

'But you could still wipe me out,' James protested.

'Surely the issue should be academic,' Mr Upton suggested gently. 'I'm afraid your protest sounds rather like that of newspapers with their cries for special immunity from the laws of libel. They rather hypocritically present these demands as being in the public interest whereas the truth of the matter is that newspapers have nothing to fear from the existing defamation laws. All they need do is not libel people. So too with you and our requirement for secrecy. We could waste a great deal of each other's time making absolutely sure of you before we embark on the next step. But time is a commodity I place great value on and I prefer to substitute its expenditure with judgement and trust. The confidentiality agreement is no insurance policy, merely an incentive.'

James thought quickly. Confidentiality agreements had been commonplace in his past employment. Mr Upton was right. If Geoff and his father were willing to trust him then the ball was in his court to honour that trust, and accordingly he had nothing to fear.

'That sounds fair enough to me,' he said. 'I'm happy to sign.'

# – NINE –

At eight on Friday morning an impressively long limousine arrived outside James' apartment. The chauffeur took his bags and he sank into the luxuriously padded seat opposite Geoff. As they glided down the motorway to Gatwick airport Geoff poured coffee from a console. They swept past the terminal towards large gates which were promptly opened by an airport worker who deferentially tipped his cap as they passed through then pulled up alongside a powder blue BA800 jet. 'Alceides' colours,' Geoff explained as they climbed aboard and were greeted by a waiting official who stamped their passports and departed.

The cabin was spaciously configured with eight armchair seats. A startlingly attractive hostess, who Geoff introduced as Miriam, handed them breakfast menus.

'She's Paraguayan,' Geoff explained after she had retired to the galley. 'All our stewardesses are pretty and all Latins. It adds an exotic flavour for our clientele and helps set the right mood.' He picked up a wall-mounted telephone alongside his seat. 'Let her rip, Martin,' he said, and a minute later they were rocketing down the tarmac.

James gazed out the window at the placid countryside of southern England far below. Somehow its detached remoteness seemed appropriate to his new-found sense of elevation above the ordinary.

'You won't see much,' Geoff said. 'We'll be climbing to 45,000 feet. We have to fly at that altitude to stay clear of the commercial flight paths. Best to settle back and relax,' he added, pointing to a neat pile of the morning's newspapers.

Geoff took *The Telegraph* from the pile, but with his mind awhirl he was unable to focus. He put aside the newspaper when Miriam emerged and unfolded a table between the two men, then laid a linen tablecloth and set out silver cutlery. Soon they were preoccupied with breakfast. Half an hour later, now on his second coffee, James finally began to relax.

'I've been thinking about Ogg,' he said. 'I have a few ideas …'

'Don't start,' Geoff interrupted. 'You're wasting your time doing so at this juncture. Wait until this trip is over. By then you will understand the fundamental concept, and once we're back in London there will be a full Ogg briefing. After that, any suggestions will be welcome, but for now it's pointless. Sit back and enjoy yourself.'

Suddenly James recalled something he had been meaning to raise. 'When I was having lunch with your father on Tuesday, he seemed to think we were going to Madagascar.'

'Of course we are,' Geoff said. 'I thought I told you.'

'No, you just said Africa and mentioned Kenya.'

'I see. Well I'm sorry to confuse you. Look, the Kenyan operation is a permanent fixture, you know, buildings and things. But we have another quite different exercise we do in half a dozen African countries. Next week it's in Madagascar so we're going there for that.'

'And you won't tell me about it now?'

'If I told you about everything you will see in Romania, Kenya and Madagascar you'd be massively confused. Deal with it bit by bit. Think of it as a striptease, getting better with each layer coming off. And best of all, as you'll be involved, you get to take the stripper home in the form of the Ogg venture.'

Two hours later the plane began its descent into Bucharest airport. They landed and taxied over to a hangar away from the main buildings. The engines stopped, the pilot and co-pilot emerged from the cockpit and were introduced to James. The pilot opened the door, pulled a lever and the stairs unfolded to the tarmac.

A swarthy official came on board and greeted Geoff and the pilots warmly. He was introduced to James. 'Nicolai is the Romanian Immigration and Customs head banana,' Geoff explained, adding, 'He's been very helpful to us over the years.'

'And you have been very kind to me,' Nicolai smirked.

At that moment Miriam emerged, and after exchanging greetings with Nicolai she handed him a box. 'Your wife's birthday present,' she said.

'Ah, so kind, so kind,' Nicolai oozed, and he set about stamping the travellers' passports.

A burly middle-aged man encased in a black leather jacket now appeared in the doorway and James was introduced to Serban, the head of Alceides' Romanian operations. James, Geoff and Serban descended on to the tarmac and climbed into a waiting Mercedes. Soon they were sweeping through the countryside towards Bucharest.

'The crew will follow later,' Geoff said. 'They tidy up the plane and see it locked away safely. You'd be surprised how much detailed work falls on them when we arrive anywhere.'

They arrived at the Bucuresti, the city's top hotel. Again Geoff was greeted with genial familiarity, and the two men were shown to adjacent suites.

'Unpack and I'll knock on your door in fifteen minutes. We'll take a stroll around the city,' Geoff instructed.

For an hour they explored Bucharest, then they enjoyed a lingering lunch of moussaka and Black Sea wines in an outdoor café. The following morning they obtained a rental car and drove north to Transylvania, where they spent the weekend sightseeing and complaining about the tourist hordes before returning to the capital. By Sunday evening James felt ebullient at the transformation of his life. Pleasure now seemed effortless; everything was possible. He began to view the world with a new perspective.

Over dinner Geoff said, 'It's time to start explaining things. Serban will pick us up tomorrow morning after breakfast. Our factory is about an hour's drive. We bought it for virtually nothing in the early nineties.'

'How does a factory fit into everything?' James enquired. 'I can't imagine what you can make in Romania for a tourist operation. Furniture would not be economic given the freight costs, I simply can't think ...'

'Don't speculate,' Geoff interrupted. 'Let me explain instead and tomorrow you can see for yourself. The first point is the factory's secrecy, which is critical to our operation. That's why it's located sixty miles to the east of Bucharest, near the Black Sea. You will understand the importance of this secrecy soon. As you will see we employ highly skilled craftsmen and artists. In the old communist days they all worked there making statues, sculpting busts and painting portraits of Lenin and Ceausescu; that sort of rubbish. After the fall in 1989 these fellows found themselves pariahs in the new Romania – understandably, as they would have been seen as the ultimate Ceausescu lackeys – so it suits them to remain working at fundamentally the same activities in the countryside, out of sight. And it certainly suits us. Their skills are what we require.'

'But what on earth do they make?' James pressed, puzzled.

'Whatever we require; flags, bunting, crowns, uniforms, statues, electronic golfballs, antique African art. Antiques and ancient artefacts are standard lines. They're very flexible and can turn their hands to anything we require. Tomorrow, for example, we should be able to see their work on the statue of Ogg's first warrior king saviour, designed by Brasch. I gather it's progressing nicely.'

'Flags, bunting, uniforms …' James said, bewildered. 'I don't understand …'

But he was interrupted by Geoff. 'It will all become clear over the next week. In quiet periods they do a nice line in 500-year-old Russian icons. The auction houses snap them up. It's really the only naughty element in our entire operation but as we sell them to a middleman who knows their history our noses are clean. With luck we may see some being made tomorrow. It's rather amusing actually.'

'But this is preposterous,' James exclaimed. 'You can't make antiques.'

'Rubbish,' Geoff said sharply. 'Every genuine antique African carved figure or ancient Celtic adze or whatever antiquity you care to name was manufactured at some point in time. Our output looks identical, so fundamentally it's the same thing. We have a simple rule. If the customer is happy, then we're happy.'

'Oh, come on, Geoff,' James protested. 'You're conning everyone. You're pretending stuff is hundreds of years old when it's not.'

'Ah, but that's the point. We're pretending nothing, and anyway our stuff is centuries old. Take the icons. Eastern Europe's saturated with dilapidated, centuries-old wooden cottages. We've used up three so far, for antiquity production. They've sat there crumbling and we got 'em for a song. Radiocarbon dating tests prove they're hundreds of years old, or the main material anyway. So it's illusory! But if the punters never know, why the hell does it matter? They buy our icons from expert dealers or auction houses, twenty years pass and by then they're family heirlooms, to be handed down to future generations.'

'They'd be a damn sight less happy if they tried to sell them,' James said scathingly.

'Like hell. Our icons fool the best experts. Anyway, people don't buy them intending to sell. They get an intangible return from their ownership in the form of visual pleasure which hoarding gold, or for that matter money, doesn't provide. And I've no doubt they're a more reliable security than money or gold which, if you think about it, are both based on bluff in terms of their value.'

'What do you mean bluff?' James demanded.

'The intrinsic worth of a lump of metal, which is all gold is, or a piece of paper, which is all money or a bank statement is, is basically nil,' Geoff argued. 'Their worth rests on the assumption that their represented value will be retained. History has not always been very supportive of that. Our icons are a far better bet over the long term. Quite frankly, as far as I'm concerned they're not just objects of pleasure but, more important, they're preservers of wealth. Our icons are now in fifteen different museums, mainly in America. The Metropolitan Museum of Art in New York has three and there's one in pride of place in Oxford University's Russian Department. Yeltsin presented one to Hillary Clinton when the President made his first visit to Moscow. Celebrities own them, in fact, we've sold them, indirectly of course, to George Soros, Madonna, the King of Norway, Barbra Streisand – heaps of big names. Jeffrey Archer has five. As I said, it's only a fill-in activity for our factory. We're very conscious of not flooding the market. Anyway, let's not quarrel over semantics. Wait until you see the operation before you rush to judgement, but remember – Alceides may be a bit offbeat but we are responsible.

'There's a difference between illusion and simple fraud and we walk that fine line. For example, we put a stop to it when Serban wanted to create a Fabergé division.'

Discomforted by these revelations, James went to bed in a troubled state, his earlier exhilaration somewhat tempered. He lay awake thinking for a few hours before eventually concluding he was committed to the trip. It was too early to make a conclusive judgement, and he duly fell asleep.

The following morning they set out across the Romanian countryside in a station wagon, eventually turning off the highway at a small village. Arriving at a gate which Serban unlocked they proceeded down a narrow, pot-holed road through a pine forest for about a mile. Finally they emerged into a clearing in which lay a large, high-walled factory.

Serban led the way inside. The front part of the factory had a wooden floor and received natural light from numerous skylights and large windows set eight feet above ground level. At the far end, which was concrete-floored, lay a large kiln with a chimney protruding through the roof, and thereafter the building was divided into a number of sections. In the centre two sculptors were busy moulding an eight-foot-high figure of a rampant and menacing warrior holding an indistinguishable object in one hand and waving a sword triumphantly overhead in the other.

'Ah, Mugan, the great Oggonian hero,' Geoff said, gesturing towards it. 'But we're in luck. Over here first,' and he drew James across to the near corner of the factory where two men and a woman sat huddled at a work-bench. 'They're doing an icon run,' he enthused as they approached the group.

In the corner lay a stack of weather-beaten timber planks. Geoff picked one up. 'Look at this. It was once part of an old country cottage. Probably over four hundred years old. The peasants can't believe their luck when we turn up and buy them. We cut them into icon shapes and Vera here is a dab hand at painting religious scenes. The two chaps are gold and silversmiths and do the overlay metalwork.'

Vera looked up, smiling at the mention of her name and the visitors bent over and studied her efforts. She had almost completed a Messiah figure surrounded by fawning angels.

'Before the metalwork goes on, each painting is covered in four layers of clear lacquer and after each layer the icon is heated in the kiln,' Geoff explained. 'This process ages it nicely, producing fine hairline cracks. Very authentic as you will see.'

'But the metalwork would be shiny new,' James protested.

Geoff laughed. 'Quite right. But wait until you see the ageing process for that. It's bloody funny but it does the trick.' He turned to Serban. 'Any icons ready for metal ageing?'

Serban spoke to the workers then said, 'Is good news. Three are waiting.'

He shouted to the two men working on the sculpture, who immediately abandoned their efforts and came over. The two silversmiths rose from their seats and joined them in an excited chattering group. Serban shouted again and four more men emerged from a large room halfway along the factory. They brought with them portable goal nets which they placed at each side of the factory, facing each other forty yards apart. One of the workers then returned to the side room and re-emerged carrying a completed icon.

Geoff passed it to James. 'Nice work isn't it?' he said. 'But as you can see the metalwork jars. It's all too spanking new. Now you're going to see the second phase of the ageing process.'

James studied the icon. It was a triptych crucifixion scene, and already appeared ancient with its honey-coloured, hairline-cracked lacquer surface. Only the obviously new overlaid gold leaf conflicted.

'Early seventeenth-century Stroganov school,' Geoff remarked casually. 'Very popular at the moment in the Californian market.'

Serban drew out his wallet and placed four American ten-dollar notes on the table. A quarrel broke out among the craftsmen which soon descended into a wildly gesticulating uproar.

'What on earth's going on?' James demanded.

'You'll see shortly,' Geoff laughed. 'Right now they're arguing about who is in which team. It happens every time.'

Serban intervened, resolving the issue by tossing a coin, and finally the slightly disgruntled men formed into two teams.

'They both want Igor,' Geoff explained. 'He's the top goal-scorer. He represented Romania's under-21 side in his youth. Played four internationals. He changes sides with Vitali, who's not so good, after each goal.'

Serban placed the icon face down in the middle of the floor, blew a whistle and the soccer match commenced. James watched in amazement as for ten minutes the two teams frenziedly, and with much shouting, set about their contest. After each goal, all scored by Igor, the former soccer international changed sides. Periodically the match descended into near violence, one incident leading to Serban awarding a penalty, to the outraged protests from the offending side.

Finally, to the triumphant shouts of his team-mates, Igor neatly dispatched the icon into the corner of the goal mouth as the goalie dived the other way, thereby taking the left to right playing side out to a 3:2 goal lead. The match was over. The victorious team each took a ten-dollar note off the table while the losers slunk back to their work, muttering about Serban's refereeing.

'Quite an exciting match,' Geoff commented casually. 'Sometimes they can be uneventful. What we've just witnessed is five hundred years of wear and tear achieved in ten minutes. We've got it down to a fine art. Trial and error shows a five-goal soccer match does the trick perfectly. Even if one side runs up a three nil lead we make them complete the extra two goals to finish the job. When we first started we tried everything imaginable to achieve a plausible ageing effect and ran through over thirty icons but never quite got it right. Then one day Serban came back from a trip to Bucharest and found the chaps playing soccer using one of the icons as a football. Naturally he ripped hell out of them but when he examined it he found it had just the right tone. I gather most great scientific discoveries stem from such misadventures, but it certainly works. Have a look.' He took the icon from Serban and handed it to James.

The icon bore scuff marks on both sides, the metalwork had lost its glow, and small indentations could be detected. A slight cracking was now apparent on the back. Even to James' critical eye it appeared an object of veneration.

'It's not finished yet,' Geoff said. 'Again, if you will excuse the pun, you will think I'm taking the piss with the next step but believe me, experience has proven its virtues.'

'What for God's sake?' James muttered, breaking the astonished silence in which he had watched the previous ten minutes' proceedings.

'The icon goes into the men's urinal for a week. That's why we only do one soccer match at a time. Over the next week the chaps will pee on it every time they use the toilet. It really does add a special frisson but don't ask me why. Again, we discovered it by chance. All I know is it works. After that it will be hosed down, then given a month's weathering outside under a shallow layer of soil, two days in a fish smoker to deliver five centuries of incense and candle-smoke effect and Bob's your uncle; it's ready for the auction house. This one should fetch three to four thousand pounds from our Paris middleman. He's a highly respected icon expert. He'll double that at auction in London or New York. Actually, most of our stuff ends up in America. They're very keen on them there, although we also have a regular buyer in Argentina; a San Telmo antique dealer in Buenos Aires who takes one a month. The Argentinians are big on this sort of stuff. Anyway, enough of that; come and have a look at the statue,' and he led the bewildered James across the factory floor to where the statue was being moulded out of a thick latex material.

'When it's completed we'll cast it in bronze then apply a weathering process to age it a few hundred years,' Geoff explained.

'Hardly soccer match material,' James mocked.

'Actually, ageing bronze is easy. It's all done with chemicals. But we do apply the soccer match principle to achieve the right effect. Before the chemicals are applied the chaps give it half an hour's pounding with croquet mallets then we blast away at it with a shotgun. The lead shot pellets provide random pock marks which fade nicely after the chemical treatment and the overall effect is of mature age.'

James studied the figure and was startled to observe that the object in the warrior's left hand was a decapitated human head, its face contorted in a grimace of agony.

'And precisely what is this supposed to represent?' he asked coolly.

'I told you,' Geoff replied cheerfully. 'It's Ogg's warrior king, Mugan. Brasch has decided to place him in the fifth century as the island's defender who beat off a Viking invasion. The whole history will be explained in our Japanese brochures. The Japs love this sort of thing, especially this,' he added, jabbing at the head.

'It's all so bloody ridiculous,' James muttered.

'Bet you're not saying that in a couple of weeks after you've seen our other operations. Mugan's essential. As I've told you, we need lots of objects for the Japanese wives to be photographed in front of, to pre-occupy them while their husbands are blasting away at the killer-sheep. Of course, once the flower gardens and lawns are developed the problem will diminish. I'm told a decent garden will preoccupy a Japanese woman for days. We'll bang in a fountain as another background object for photographs. Brasch has come up with loads of ideas to absorb the Japanese wives. On our return if you're up to it you can try your hand at writing imaginative texts for the brochures explaining all the objects of historic significance that we'll be creating. Our Tokyo office will then translate them into Japanese and print the brochures.'

Before James could protest further Serban emerged from a storeroom waving a foot-long miniature flag which he handed to Geoff.

'Not bad,' Geoff said. 'The client should be happy. Mind you, he can hardly complain this time, after all, it's basically his design. You've done twenty thousand?' he asked.

'All packed ready to go,' Serban replied. 'I'll tell the men to put the cartons in the station wagon with the electronic golf balls.'

Geoff handed the flag to James. 'Quite nice, isn't it?' he said.

James studied it. The flag had an upper-half gold background with a blue bottom half. Centre-piece was a coat of arms supported on each side by rampant lions, above which lay a silver crown set between two crossed swords. The coat of arms was divided into four quarters, one displaying a wheat sheaf, another an anvil, the third a galleon and the last a bullock's head.

'National flag of Hamastan,' Geoff explained.

'Never heard of it,' James retorted. 'There's no such place.'

'There is now. You will be part of Hamastanian celebrations in Madagascar. Mark my words, you will enjoy it enormously. I'll explain it all before we arrive there. Are the coins ready?' Geoff asked Serban.

Serban barked something to two workers, who entered the storeroom then returned struggling under the weight of a wooden crate. They placed it on the floor and lifted the lid. Geoff took a handful of silver coins and passed one to James.

One side bore a bold relief of the Hamastan cost of arms, and round its perimeter the words 'Ten Hamastanis'.

James turned it over. The reverse side displayed a man's crowned head under which was '1999'. Round its edge was etched 'King Andrew the Third', then 'Kingdom of Hamastan'. The king's face was familiar. 'This is the spitting image of Andrew Clifford, the New York financier,' James exclaimed.

'I should hope so,' Geoff said. 'He's our client. Why, do you know him?'

'Good Lord, no. He was way out of my league.'

'Well, you're going to meet him in Madagascar, only then he won't be Andrew Clifford. He'll be the King of Hamastan and you will be obliged to bow and address him as Your Majesty. The footmen on the royal coach will be tossing these coins to the crowds. We've got a five Hamastani version as well. Experience shows the people tend to horde the higher denominations. Our coinage from previous presidential and monarchial visits are now the predominant currency in quite a number of our territories.'

'But this is preposterous,' James spluttered. 'If that's happening then you're debasing their currency.'

'Don't be so naive,' Geoff snapped. 'We're doing God's work on that front. Take Madagascar, for example, where there's bugger all currency circulating to debase. Our coinage loosens things up a bit and helps facilitate economic activity. Anyway, don't worry about all that now. You'll see it soon enough.' He dropped the coins back in the crate and on Serban's instructions the two men, staggering under the weight, carried it to the station wagon.

'This is all bloody amazing,' James cried. 'I mean, I can see the humour but, bloody hell, it's hard to believe. And what's all this about electronic golf balls?'

'You'll see that in Kenya. Actually, Kenya is our most profitable operation, and I'll tell you why. Basically, it gets back to what I've constantly reiterated, namely, the happiness of our customers. We have it on expert medical advice that our Kenya operation adds ten years to our clients' lives, simply because of the joy we bring them. Just be patient.'

Meanwhile another two workers were unfolding a sixty-foot banner for inspection. Against a white background it bore in bold scarlet lettering the message 'Welcome to their Royal Majesties, King Andrew and Queen Maureen of Hamastan'.

'Beautiful,' Geoff exclaimed. 'Fold it up and shove it in the car. What about the presentation medals. Ready, are they?'

'A very nice job,' Serban said and on his instruction one of the workers produced five red velvet boxes. James opened each of them in turn. All contained medals, with gold and blue striped ribbons attached to a top metal bar clip. The first displayed the Hamastan coat of arms, another a relief of Clifford's crowned head, the third a crown between crossed swords, the fourth was a simple cross and the last a silver version of the Hamastan coat of arms, the others all being gilded in gold.

'We need these for the King to award to officials,' Geoff explained. 'But don't ask any more about this now. I'll explain it before we arrive in Madagascar. All I will say is it's my favourite of all our operations. Enormous fun, believe me. But enough for now. There's lots more we do here and you will see it all in due course, specially the stuff we'll be making for Ogg. Anyway, it's time we buggered off.' He looked at his watch. 'If we step on it we can be off by one o'clock and reach Nairobi by eight then have a decent night's sleep before heading north.'

# – TEN –

As his warrior forefathers had for a thousand years before him, Juma, chief of the Kanju Valley tribe, reached the boulder-strewn crest of the hill and stood silhouetted against the skyline, haughtily erect as he gazed upon his tribal lands stretching below him into the distance.

At 32 Juma was the youngest Kanju chief for two centuries. His magnificent six-and-a-half-foot muscular black body, clad only in a long white kanzu tied at his waist and adorned with the traditional Kanju chieftain's lions-tooth necklace, glistened in the midday sun. In his right hand he held a spear, ready to dispatch any python which might emerge from among the hilltop boulders where they resided.

Far below, glinting in the bright sunlight, the Kanju River wended its way like a silver ribbon down the valley, its red earth banks hidden by clusters of trees and bushes, among which the lilliputian figures of goats could be seen.

Juma watched with satisfaction as six giraffes emerged from the trees, snatching and tearing at the lush leaves of the higher branches. He cast his eye across the verdant valley floor shimmering in the midday heat, on which his tribe's cattle, sharing the plain with a large herd of zebra, grazed undisturbed.

Immediately below, nestled into the foothills, lay a circle of thatch-roofed huts from which twists of smoke rose from cooking fires before fading into oblivion. Only the faint methodical thump of drumbeats gave further testimony to habitation in the morning somnolence. Separating the village from the plain lay fields of maize, beyond which was a stockade wall of sharply pointed sticks, set into the earth and angled outwards to deter any unwelcome visits by lions or elephants.

Abruptly the serenity was shattered by the menacing roar of a lion which resonated across the valley, sending the terrified zebra herd stampeding across the plain. The cattle stiffened and broke into chaotic confusion before setting off in a panic-stricken lumbering black mass after the zebras. Juma tightened his grip on his spear, alarm crossing his features. Scarcely had the lion's roar died away when it was succeeded by the distinctive chimes of Big Ben.

Juma reached into his kanzu and pulled out a mobile telephone. 'Weally, Cecil,' he complained. 'That's quite pwepostewous. I specifically told you to begin quietly. Now you've upset the cattle. I do wish you'd pay attention. Do it again, only for God's sake turn the wolume down,' and he clicked the mobile off and waited.

Again the lion's roar broke the silence, this time at a lower level. Juma spoke again into his mobile. 'Much better. I think that's about wight, so fix the setting at that level,' and he began his descent to the valley below. Halfway down Big Ben's chimes again rang out. Juma clicked on the phone and sat down on a boulder.

'Geoffwey, old man,' he exclaimed after listening to his caller. 'Now don't tell me you're not coming,' and then, 'What, you're alweady at Naiwobi. Well I never. I wasn't expecting you until Fwiday. Why didn't you say you were awiving early?'

He listened for a brief period then said, 'Look, if you've awanged a helicopter you should be here in about two hours. I'm out at the village testing the lion's woar. We've got a performance tomowwow night so you're in luck. The new choweogwapher has done a splendid job. Wery ewotic; you will love it. Also, a super new bunch of girls in fwom Santo Domingo. I've had thwee alweady. Anyway, let's not talk about it now. I'll be back in time for your awival. But I must say, I'm ever so pleased you've come. I'm a bit wowwied about the Dow Jones. I wather think we thould we-weigh towards bonds.'

There was a pause as he listened for a half-minute.

'Yes, of course,' he said. 'I can pwobably shoot over to London at the end of the month. See you shortly, old man,' and he tucked his mobile back into his kanzu and completed his descent to the village. On arrival he climbed into his jeep and, to the sound of Haydn's 94th Symphony, sped across the plain back to the lodge at the end of the valley.

# – ELEVEN –

The helicopter swept low across the plain and James, seated alongside the pilot, studied the vibrant landscape passing 500 feet below him with increasing delight.

Within minutes of leaving Nairobi airport they had reached the Mt Kenya National Park where they had flown over three zebra herds and fifteen zebra-patterned safari vehicles laden with camera-clutching tourists. Geoff pointed out a cluster of lions which remained unperturbed by the helicopter, only one briefly lifting its head in acknowledgement of their intrusion before yawning and returning to its former slumber.

'Tourist crap,' Geoff muttered scathingly. 'They don't even have elephants. We'll soon be into more interesting terrain.' And so it proved as they flashed across forests, rivers and valleys periodically interspersed with villages and small towns. Once they disturbed a herd of elephants which lumbered off into the forest at their approach. Geoff pointed out a group of giraffes on the forest edge. 'If we go too close they could panic and break their necks,' he said. 'Helicopters are no way to see African wildlife.'

James had woken that morning feeling refreshed in Nairobi's most luxurious hotel, where yet again Geoff had been greeted with friendly familiarity. Still troubled by the Romanian experience and Geoff's oblique responses to his questions on the flight, when he reached his room James had telephoned Jane in London.

Any hope of solace from that quarter was quickly dispelled as she had immediately resumed the condemnation that had been her reaction when he had told her he had left the City. She had expressed no interest in the fact that he was in Kenya and afterwards he had slept peacefully, content with the awareness that if doubtful as to what he had let himself in for, he was at least certain about the merits of abandoning his past life.

In the morning they had swum in the hotel pool, then sat at the poolside dining alcove eating breakfast. Toasting in the canopy-shaded tropical warmth, Geoff said as they lingered over coffee, 'Shortly you will see our most profitable operation. We've got a two-hour helicopter journey north towards the Ethiopian border. Our little enterprise is on the edge of the Marsabit National Park but it's over 100 kilometres from the usual tourist routes, not that it matters. We've got a small army of employees patrolling our borders to keep intruders out.'

'But why the alarm?' James queried. 'What on earth are you up to that necessitates such secrecy?'

'Actually, it's not like that with the Kanju resort,' Geoff said. 'Madagascar, yes. When you're there you will appreciate the need for secrecy but with our Kenyan operation it's more an issue of privacy. Our guests are paying $3,000 a day per couple and they certainly get value. They're solely American and Japanese. Not so much the super-wealthy billionaire clients we'll be dealing with in Madagascar but more the $50 to $100 million range. Nevertheless, the last thing they want to see lowering the tone is some scruffy little bearded Birmingham schoolteacher on a motorbike. It's a quality thing.'

'But why would they want to come? The bearded schoolteachers that is,' James pressed.

'Look, it's like my father told you. Africa, and everywhere else for that matter, is now totally infested with mass tourism. Most of them tread a programmed route but about two per cent romanticise that they're Livingstone and naively delude themselves that they're adventurers. But as soon as they suss out the reality they try and, as they put it, get off the beaten track. It's a mistake actually because the so-called beaten track neatly lays out for them whatever's worth seeing and getting away from it is just tedium and hardship. So they're soon drawn to any sign of civilisation, which seems like an oasis in the desert to them. Well, our clientele are not paying $3,000 a day to put up with these dreary types marring the scene.

'Then there's the wildlife filming set. They're everywhere. There seems to be an insatiable market for African wildlife documentaries of big animals pouncing on smaller ones and tearing them apart. We certainly don't want that lot hanging about and we give them the boot in no uncertain terms when they loom up, as they regularly do, hoping to horn in on our dining room and swimming pool.'

'My God. With the build-up I've had over the last week I can't wait to finally see something,' James said. 'Mind you, I'm still a bit shattered by Romania.'

'You'll be a lot happier after you've seen our Kanju resort. You won't need any persuasion from me to see how much good we're doing. It's Brasch's greatest achievement.'

'There's another thing,' James said. 'I can't wait to meet this Brasch character I hear so much about.'

Geoff stiffened slightly. 'Well, we'll see. Brasch rather likes his privacy. Maybe you will meet him, then again maybe you won't,' he added mysteriously.

'So why would people pay $3,000 a day to look at animals and stuff when they can do the same thing elsewhere for a fraction of the price?' James continued, detecting Geoff's sensitivity at the mention of Brasch.

'That's not what they're there for. Sure we give them the standard African experience, you know, wild animals, traditional native dancing, village visiting and all the usual guff, and we neatly encapsulate it without wasting their time. On that front they're perfectly happy, indeed a damn sight happier than the conventional tourist because we lay it on pretty thick. But the main reason they come – that is all the men and about half the wives – is to play golf. We provide a few supplementary excitements as well, as you will see.'

James stared at Geoff, astonished. After a pause he said, 'Golf! Why pay $3,000 a day to play bloody golf? They can do that anywhere.'

Geoff laughed. 'If I was to tell you we accommodate 240 guests, always have a full house and have a six-month waiting list, and that the reason they come is to play golf, I don't suppose you'd believe me, would you?' he quizzed.

'No, I wouldn't.'

'Well, that's our position. The average age of our guests is around sixty. We keep a South African doctor on the premises, who's firmly convinced we're adding about ten years to our guests' lives, simply because of the happiness we bring them. You'll see.'

'But it doesn't make sense!' James insisted.

'Our guests are golfers. Their average handicap is probably about 15. We have a first-rate 18-hole course with a 72 course rating. During any one-week stay – which is the maximum we allow each couple per year – they play seven games and shoot four between 63 and 67, one between 67 and par, and on arrival, first up, one game over par, although never by more than four strokes. It's all carefully programmed and you will understand by tonight, but I'll say this. Our Kanju resort is probably the happiest pocket of humanity in the world. The excitement each night in the dining rooms and lounges is palpable. Believe me, we give value. I'll say no more now so don't ask how we engineer the golf scores. You'll learn that when we're there. There's a surprise waiting for you as well. Now let's pack up and get out to the airport.'

After an hour in the helicopter the landscape changed to desert which seemed endless. James became eager to arrive and was heartened when Geoff tapped him on the shoulder and, pointing to a range of hills in the distance, said, 'That's where we're going. The Kanju Valley is on the other side.'

They reached the range and the helicopter gained height and rose over the hills. As they climbed, the vegetation thinned until eventually it became replaced by giant boulders and smooth rock surfaces. The helicopter skimmed across the top and suddenly before him James saw a green valley divided by a river stretching into the distance. Immediately below lay a lush golf course, its fairways seemingly carved through a dense forest, and on every fairway and green could be seen numerous golf-carts. Spaced round its perimeter were over a hundred expansive bungalows, each enclosed by a high hedge and with its own bright blue swimming pool, colourful parasols, recliners and tables. A tar-sealed road linked the bungalows with the main buildings, while surrounding the entire complex a water-filled moat sparkled in the midday sun. A cluster of buildings lay at one end, in front of which lay a small lake surrounded by numerous figures and nearby, clearly visible from above, a helicopter pad. The helicopter descended and gently cushioned on to the ground. The pilot turned off the engine and as the propeller slowed to a stop a large black figure loomed up and opened the door.

'Welcome to …' he began then he stopped and stared in amazement. 'Well, I'll be damned,' he exclaimed, his face breaking into a grin.

James stared in disbelief. 'Monster, you old bastard,' he cried, and he climbed out and shook Juma's hand vigorously.

'Told you I had a surprise,' Geoff said, grinning as he dismounted.

# – TWELVE –

Juma led the way through the resort's elegant reception areas as waiters scurried with Third World obsequiousness to prepare their terrace table. The three men settled into comfortable padded wicker chairs overlooking the golf course and lake.

The terrace was crowded with groups of late middle-aged and elderly Japanese and American guests, all in a high state of excitement. Snatches of conversation could be overheard as they enthusiastically vied to recount their stories, most describing how sensationally the speaker had played golf that morning, interspersed with tales of fishing triumphs. All seemed to be talking, none listening.

'I swear to God it was over 300 yards …' '60-foot putt, curved to the left then straight as an arrow …' '68 yesterday, 67 this morning …' 'played it for over two hours …' 'Tiger Woods better watch out …' 'still can't believe it …' 'Juma says climate and altitude …' 'strongest fish in 40 years I've …' 'definitely going to enter this year's Florida senior competitions …' 'two holes-in-one since I arrived …' 'I know trout and I tell you …'

The celebratory mood of the balcony's occupants was evident in the multitude of champagne buckets.

James was delighted to see his former university friend Juma again. The giant African, with his faintly ridiculous speech impediment, had been a popular figure. Nicknamed the Masai Monster, which had soon become shortened to just Monster, he had played lock in the university rugby team and caused consternation among opposing sides in the lineouts. But Juma was three years ahead of James, and had completed his studies then disappeared. James had not thought of him since.

He was interrupted in these musings by the arrival of a stunningly beautiful, light-brown-skinned waitress bearing a champagne bucket and three glasses. James stared at her with open admiration and the girl acknowledged his attention with a flirtatious smile.

'My God, she's a stunner,' James gasped after she had gone.

'All our girls are,' Juma retorted. 'Have a look awound.'

James studied the crowded balcony. Monster was right. All the waitresses were extraordinarily beautiful, their copper-skins complementing their dark smouldering eyes.

'I honestly had no idea,' he spluttered. 'I thought African girls were … ah …'

'Pitch black, fwizzy hair, big bums, thick lips?' Juma suggested, raising his eyebrows and grinning.

'Well,' James muttered, 'I wouldn't quite go …'

'That's alwight,' Juma laughed. 'They are; ugly as sin the lot of them, and black as the ace of spades.'

Geoff leaned forward and lowered his voice. 'All these girls are mulattas from the Dominican Republic,' he whispered. 'Of course the guests don't know that. Pretty girls cheer people up. Also, being coloured they leave a favourable impression of Africa, which is specially important with the Japanese who have a derisory view of blacks. Basically they view blacks as part of the African fauna at the dangerous end of the spectrum along with lions and crocodiles. Consequently they tend to stay clear of Africa, which in the case of this resort could be a problem given it's targeting affluent golfers. But once they catch a glimpse of these girls their attitude changes. They really are an important factor in developing a more positive Japanese impression of Africa. We give them an hour's English polishing each morning so they get by. They come for the high wages we pay, and as the guests mostly prefer to eat from the buffet the girls mainly have to deal with drinks orders and they manage that OK. They're strictly forbidden to speak Spanish in front of the guests so the clients never doubt they're African. This is a particularly good crop. I can't wait to see them dancing tonight.'

'The local girls are hopeless for twibal dancing,' Juma said. 'Too ugly and too modest and they won't perform like these ones. You wouldn't want to watch them even if they would. Now tell me, James. What are you doing here?'

Geoff explained about Ogg and James' learning trip to Romania, Kenya and Madagascar. Mention of Madagascar brought an excited response from Juma. 'I say. Woyal or pwesidential?' he demanded.

'Royal; the full palaver, cast of thousands,' Geoff replied.

'Oh super,' Juma exclaimed. 'I'll come along for the wide. Pwesidentials don't excite me any more. Don't forget, Geoffwey, you pwomised I could be Lord High Executioner again on the next woyal tour.'

A frown crossed Geoff's face. 'Well, be bloody careful this time, Monster. Frightening the natives is one thing; causing heart attacks is another. I'm told half the poor buggers still haven't returned to that village where you scared the wits out of them and sent them fleeing into the hills.

'Anyway, let's not talk about that now. I haven't explained the royal tour business to James yet. I'm saving it as a surprise.'

'You'll love it. It's tewiffic,' Juma enthused.

'We haven't got much time,' Geoff continued. 'I'll take James on a tour of Kanju after lunch and we'll attend the traditional dancing tonight. I'm not missing that. I'll show him the golf exercise today and the fishing tomorrow. Then we'll head back to Nairobi first thing on Thursday morning and we can be in Madagascar by early evening. The client arrives on Sunday, which leaves us Friday and Saturday to check Hodge has everything shipshape. First thing Monday morning we'll all zip down to Fianarosa to commence the royal visit. Now let's have lunch and we'll get under way after that.'

'I'll leave you chaps to it,' Juma said. 'I've heaps to do if I'm going to be away a week so I'll see you at dinner before the dancing.'

# – THIRTEEN –

'I ran across Monster walking down Piccadilly six years ago,' Geoff explained over lunch. 'Let's face it, he's hard to miss. We shot off for a drink and he told me his story. Amazing really; it's very similar to yours with Ogg.'

'Oh, how's that?' James asked, puzzled by the suggestion.

'It transpired his father had died and he found himself Chief of the Kanju Valley tribe. About ten thousand people all told. Kenya is a typical African shambles; full of semi-autonomous entities like Kanju, and the lines are not very clear in terms of actual authority. Still, as Monster said, no one in Nairobi gave a damn about them. They're all Kikuyu in control there, and have no interest in helping the other remote tribal factions such as Monster's. Incidentally, he's not actually Masai. At university he was given that nickname and learned to ride with it. As he said to me once, it could have been worse; the Zulu Zombie or Bantu Beast or suchlike.'

'The comparisons with my situation are certainly there,' James agreed. 'Tell me more.'

'Apparently things were fairly grim in this valley,' Geoff continued. 'Few health or education facilities and everything much as it had been for centuries. So Monster took off to London to see the Commonwealth Secretariat for advice on development funds. That's when I encountered him, just after he'd seen them, and he was pretty disconsolate. Claimed they were all ex-political hacks from around the Commonwealth, swanning about doing nothing and all brain-dead, with no idea how to help. Well, one thing led to another. We only had Romania and the Head of State tours divisions under way at that stage, but we had Brasch on board and he'd already come up with the golf idea so we were looking for a suitable location.

Consequently everything fitted into place nicely. It cost us fourteen million dollars to build all of this but we had it back inside a year. Monster's tribe cops a quarter of the profits and we've created over two hundred jobs for the Kanjus who are now probably the richest tribe per capita in all of Africa. They work on the golf courses, in the kitchen and laundry, in the office as you will see, and in the vegetable gardens, that sort of thing, but basically out of sight of the clientele. The only Africans the guests see are in fact all Latin American mulattas from the Dominican Republic. We usually have about seventy Latinas, waitressing and housekeeping. This operation now makes over twenty million US dollars each year and it's rising. We generate our own electricity from a series of turbines in the river, and we provide bogus sets of accounts showing modest returns so Nairobi receives about fifty thousand in taxes each year and that keeps them happy without attracting too much attention. Pay more and they'd be here in a flash and destroy the operation through interference.'

'So what happens to the Kanju money?' James asked.

'Mostly offshore investments handled by our investment division. Monster has eight schools up and running already, plus some health clinics, all funded from the investment income. Every Kanju kid now goes to secondary school and if they've got it up top, on to university. All the Kanjus live twenty miles down the other end of the valley. Our clients think they're in darkest Africa and have no idea of the reality. Mind you, they also think they're in golfers' heaven, as you're about to see. Monster's worked his butt off and has achieved all of this from not much more than five years' earnings from his whack. Spending the money isn't a problem, believe me. Monster's planning to build quality housing, reservoirs, sewage systems, the lot, but his main problem is trying to do all of that and run the resort. He's doing his best training Kanju managers in the office but it takes time. Money's certainly no object.'

'But I still don't understand. I mean the golf course looks very nice but why come all this way and pay $3,000 a day?'

'Come on and I'll show you.' James rose and followed Geoff down a wide staircase to the main dining room. As in the balcony restaurant the diners were all exuberantly describing their just completed rounds and again James heard snatches of excited conversation boasting of astonishing golfing triumphs.

They strolled through the dining room into a large timber-panelled entrance foyer, built and decorated in colonial style. On the walls were crossed African spears and ornate shields, a stretched zebra skin, some colonial-era black and white photographs, some mounted animal heads, and two giant stuffed trout. James stopped before the trout. 'My God, Geoff, these are huge. What's the story?'

'Brown trout from the lake in front of the lodge. Probably the biggest in the world. I'll explain that to you tomorrow.'

Outside the entrance they walked across a paved courtyard to a small forest of trees, through a gate marked Private, and down a path until eventually they arrived at a low concrete, windowless building. Geoff pushed a buzzer, spoke into an intercom and they entered a foyer at the end of which was an office marked 'Manager'. Inside they found Juma studying a computer screen. 'Control room keys, mate,' Geoff said.

'Bwace yourself, James,' Juma laughed as he opened a drawer, took out a set of keys and tossed them to Geoff.

They passed through a side door into a large air-conditioned office where a dozen young Kanju men and women were seated before computer screens. 'Accounting and management,' Geoff said. The two crossed the room, Geoff unlocked a door and they walked down a narrow corridor where, at its end, Geoff unlocked another door.

'Here's why they pay $3,000 a day for golf,' he said smirking. He stood aside, holding the door open. James was almost blinded by the bright light which greeted him in the windowless room. Eighteen young Kanju men and women sat monitoring a mass of flickering television screens built into the walls. The room resembled the NASA space control centre James had sometimes seen on television. Before each operator were three screens set in a line down the wall, and at the top, a large number for each set of screens from one to eighteen was displayed.

The operators occasionally pushed buttons, and sometimes they murmured quietly into their headset microphones. Each had a desk-top computer flickering before them. The pictures on the screens showed groups of golfers, many of them dancing on the spot triumphantly, and even on the small screens James could detect their jubilation.

'OK. You've been in suspense long enough,' Geoff laughed. 'Every golfer on the course is monitored by an operator. Watch a few to get the picture.'

They stood behind the operator of hole 15. 'This is a par 5,' Geoff remarked. 'Watch carefully.'

Four elderly Americans were about to hit off. The first stepped forward, teed up his ball, the standard club waggling took place, then he drove the ball about 160 yards down the left side of the fairway.

'What's he to score this hole?' Geoff asked the operator.

The young woman looked at her computer then replied 'Birdie,' and she pressed a button on the control deck before her.

'Look at the middle screen,' Geoff instructed.

The ball had passed over a ten-foot-high hill that stretched across the fairway about seventy yards from the driving tee and was no longer visible to the player. The middle screen revealed a remote-controlled toy vehicle rocketing across the fairway. It reached the ball, stopped, scooped it into a net arrangement then set off another sixty yards up the fairway, dropped the ball near the centre then scooted back to its original position in the trees.

'Bloody hell,' James muttered.

The second player now teed up and hit his ball a similar distance.

'What's he down for?' Geoff asked.

'Par,' the woman replied, studying the screen and the ball was left where it landed.

The third stepped up to the tee. The operator spoke into her microphone. 'Eagle,' she murmured.

The player drove his ball just clear of the hill, landing about 130 yards up the fairway. The remote controlled vehicle emerged, picked up the ball and ran 80 yards up the fairway before dropping it and returning to the trees.

The final golfer now stepped up and drove his ball to the right side of the fairway. The girl muttered, 'He bogey this hole,' and spoke into her microphone. From the trees the vehicle reappeared, netted the ball and repositioned it behind a tree, necessitating a wasted shot to chip back onto the fairway.

'This is bloody ludicrous,' James muttered.

'Come over here,' Geoff said, ignoring his comment, and the two moved down the room to hole number eight where four Japanese players were shown on the bottom screen approaching the large green. All had balls scattered about, ranging from sixty to twenty feet from the pin.

The furthermost player lined up his putt. 'What's he due for?' Geoff asked.

'He sink this shot,' the operator smiled with a flash of white teeth and she pressed a button on the controls before her.

Carefully the elderly Japanese player lined up the ball then, after a lengthy study, struck it. It ran about fifteen feet then abruptly veered sharply to the left and continued in a straight line the remaining distance. It dropped in the hole and in a most un-Japanese manner the elderly gentleman danced joyfully about the green, waving his putter over his head.

'Tiger Woods would be delighted with that,' Geoff laughed.

The next player lined up his putt. The operator studied the computer screen then said, 'He three putt this hole,' and pushed another button. The player addressed the ball then hit it, it seemed to James, watching dumbstruck, far too hard.

The ball riveted towards the hole then suddenly veered to the right and halted six feet short of it. 'He miss the next shot also,' the operator grinned.

'God help me, Geoff, what's going on?' James demanded.

'All quite simple, old man. Every player is monitored by a network of hidden cameras. We mix it up; the odd duffed shot and lots of sensational ones. We keep 'em interested and over their week's stay we maintain an improving trend but, and this is the big thing, make sure that on their second day they have the round of their lives, usually about two under par. After that it's all carefully programmed so on the last day they go home with a personal record round. They can't wait to get back again because when they return home they can't repeat it. They put it all down to altitude, fresh air and that sort of stuff. But they're very, very happy. We're making a fortune on champagne sales.'

'But how? I mean I can see what you're up to on the fairways, but how do you control the greens?'

'We've a chap hiding in the trees operating the remote toy vehicle on every fairway. He has a walkie-talkie and the operator in here gives him instructions. But the putting is controlled directly from this room. Under every green is a network of electrical wiring. Brasch thought it up. We can make a ball run or stop or go in any direction we want. On every round a player sinks at least ten extraordinary putts, has one three putt and all the rest two. It's all very carefully monitored and each night we calculate the player's next day score. Oh I forgot. The balls are made in the Romanian factory. They have a small computer chip inside them which responds to the electrical instruction.'

'This is bloody ridiculous. I just don't know what to say,' James spluttered.

'Enjoy their joy,' Geoff suggested, grinning.

'But hang on. What if they misdirect their drive and hit into the trees?'

'If it's out of the player's sight, depending on what he's down for on that hole, the remote vehicle worker will find it and relocate it on the fairway. When the player reaches it he thinks he's been lucky and has hit a tree and bounced out. From this control room we can monitor and control every shot.'

'What if he duffs a shot?' James queried weakly.

'We can't do anything about that,' Geoff conceded. 'Strangely enough, however, after a couple of days, duffing becomes quite rare. They all become so confident they actually start playing exceptionally well. You know the story. Golf's a head game. Inside a day we straighten their heads out. Still, if they do bungle a shot and it's out of our control then the operator adjusts the computer program and if they're down for say a par on the next hole then it's changed to a birdie. It's not hard to monitor and our people are now fairly adept at it. Come on, you've seen enough. We'll have a swim and then I'll tell you about the ancillary operations here. We're developing new ones all the time,' and they left the control room and returned to Juma, Geoff carefully locking both doors after him.

# – FOURTEEN –

'I've had a thought,' James exclaimed triumphantly. 'All golfers carry balls in their bags and they don't have electronic chips in them.'

'Needless to say we've covered that,' Geoff replied smugly. 'That's why I told you they have a great second round. On their first day they have lots of disasters and lose all their balls.'

'But what if they don't? What if they're playing well?' James persisted.

'That's simple, old man. On six of the holes we have a narrow bottleneck in the fairway where the trees encroach, about a normal drive's length from the tee-off and we make sure they lose their balls by having our chaps hiding in the trees steal them. Even if they've brought seven or eight with them they'll still buy new balls anticipating a repeat of the same thing, but of course it doesn't happen once they're using our electronic ones and we're deciding their performance. It's another nice earner as we nick over 20,000 new or near new balls each year. We ship them down to Nairobi and sell them to the local golf club pro who on-sells them in South Africa. Mind you, our golfers' first days are still happy ones as we make up for the lost balls' penalty shots with a few extra birdies. We like them to shoot about four over on their first day. Unless they've been here before, most have never done that, so they're still pretty excited and bang on about what might have been without the penalties. Also, losing all their balls has the redeeming virtue of assuring them it's a tough course which adds special lustre to their subsequent performances. Don't worry; we've covered everything.'

'So it seems,' James conceded, still bewildered by all he had seen. The two men were lying in hammocks beside the pool attached to their bungalow, drinking Kenyan beer. 'Another thing,' he continued.

'These bungalows spaced around the course with their own enclosed swimming pools. Seems an expensive arrangement. What's the thinking there?'

'It's another Brasch innovation. Remember our clientele are all around sixty. Half the women don't play golf so we need to keep them happy. At that age they're sensitive about their appearance. Being in the tropics they'd like to swim, but they hate exposing themselves to the public gaze of a common pool. The men couldn't give a damn but the women certainly care. The private pool concept is expensive but it works; the non-golfing ladies happily spend their days often lying naked in complete privacy and feeling twenty again. Believe me, that's every older woman's idea of heaven. Each bungalow has two motorised golf-carts so the guests are mobile and can roll up to the dining rooms and other facilities effortlessly, or out on to the first hole when it's their turn to play. They're each allocated a starting time and we squeeze the lot through each day, specially as they play so well we manage a foursome round in about three and a half hours. The first days take longer, since they waste time looking for their lost balls.'

'So the non-playing wives just lie about for a week, apart from meals, and they're quite happy?' James queried.

'Not entirely. We keep them stimulated with a safari trip and a village tour, and a traditional native dancing performance. Some of them even have a go at trout fishing. The village tour is totally bogus but it's what they want. Bare-breasted girls clutching babies is what people expect although in reality nudity is unheard of in these parts. We have five tours each week, which gets everyone through, and we use twelve of the Latin girls and a couple of the young schoolteachers Monster brought in from Nairobi for the new schools. They're both half-European so they're sufficiently slender and light coloured not to offend the Japanese sensitivities. Anyway, we disguise all the girls' faces with veils of coloured beads Brasch copied from a book on Peruvian crafts and which we make in Romania. We tell the tourists the veils are a Kanju tribal tradition to cover their faces for modesty reasons, and that ensures they can't be recognised as resort staff. Actually, we do quite well selling the veils in the tribal antiquities and crafts shop. The women guests lap them up, although I'm buggered if I know what they do with them. Then again, that's the story of tourism; buying stuff which seems a good idea at the time but is puzzling once you're back home.'

'But why the schoolteachers if you have plenty of Latinas?' James asked.

'They're necessary to bring in the half-dozen babies we borrow from the Kanju mothers at the other end of the valley. We pay the mums a dollar a head for the baby rental and the teachers drive up in a small van specially fitted with six cribs which we hide out of sight.'

'What about blokes?' James enquired. 'Surely the village is incomplete without them.'

'Quite right,' Geoff responded. 'We stick two of the younger golf course workers in the maize fields where they can be seen by the tourists, singing and beavering away with hoes. Only pretending of course. You can't get African men to work in gardens. To them that's women's work. The singing is all recordings. The whole place is wired up. We tell the tourists most of the men are away hunting.'

'This is bloody ridiculous,' James exclaimed.

'Also there's a witch doctor, Clarence Wonja,' Geoff continued, ignoring James' comment. 'He's actually the secondary school principal and has a doctorate in seventeenth-century English literature. For $5 a time he turns up wearing leopard skins, face paint, an elaborate feather headdress and a bone through his nose. It's a plastic clip-on affair Brasch copied from a *National Geographic* story about New Guinea savages. Still, it's the sort of thing tourists expect and react to positively as an African experience.'

'Oh yes,' James, said with a mixture of suspicion and curiosity. 'And what does he do?'

'Clarence sits cross-legged at the entrance to one of the huts, chanting incantations and boiling a pot of muddy water with frogs bobbing about in it. They're plastic of course, as are the human skulls he has around him. More of our Romanian products. The overall result is very satisfactory. Mind you, I rather think Clarence would do it for nothing, he enjoys it so much. He fancies himself as a thespian and has developed quite a successful Shakespearean repertory at the school. He also chucks in a bit of fortune-telling. You know how seriously women respond to that, specially from authentic witch doctors.'

'This is bloody ridiculous,' James muttered yet again.

'No it's not. It's exactly what the wives want,' Geoff responded smugly. 'Every day, across Africa, in Haiti and a few other places, tourists are being carted to primitive villages to watch bloody witch-doctors perform. The net result is tedium as the buggers potter about chanting in monotones. Clarence delivers Act 3 of *The Importance of Being Earnest* – in Kanju of course. Prancing about playing male and female roles, different incantations and the like all results in a very satisfactory animated witch-doctor spectacle. The whole exercise only lasts about an hour after school's finished each day but it provides a diversion for the non-golfing wives and it's all they require in terms of close contact with Africans. They take photos, have their fortune told, gush over the babies, watch a couple of the girls basket-weaving and inspect the huts which, unlike any others in Africa, are light and spacious, then they bugger off, perfectly content, back to their swimming pools. Everything's pristine, which leaves a first-rate impression of Africa, so we're doing a damn good job on that front, specially when you compare our village with the real thing. The Japanese in particular would be shocked if we took them to actual African villages. All that squalor and toothless old crones; very unpleasant compared with ours, I can tell you. We have ornate pots our village women mess about with pretending to cook things in plus wooden carvings and that sort of crap lying about to add to the authenticity. All out of Romania. There are lots of photographic items for the Japanese guests such as a totem pole with historic tribal events carved on it. Brasch designed that of course.

'Off the main foyer we've got a massage room and beauty clinic, and a shop selling our Romanian-made African antiquities and crafts; you know, statues and masks and spears and stuff. Then there's the Kanju primitif art, which goes down a treat with this sort of clientele. They're the types who actually display tourist stuff on their walls. You remember Vera, the icon painter in Romania. She knocks them out. It's actually her main activity. Icons are simply a sideline. Plus there's a bookshop selling magazines and pot-boilers, and a Kanju traditional silver craft shop. That's a big earner.'

'I didn't know there was silver in Kenya,' James exclaimed.

'There's not but the visitors accept it and why shouldn't they? They're not the types to know about that sort of thing. It all comes from our Romanian silversmiths. We do awfully well out of it. Come to think of it, that's another thing the punters see on the village tour.

'One of the golf-course lads sits cross-legged before a large stone tapping away with primitive tools at bits of silver pretending to make the stuff. It's a curious thing but American women are very partial to traditional tribal silverware; you know, necklaces, bracelets and suchlike. At their age, unlike the Japanese, they're much less into photographic mementoes.'

'What I don't understand,' James said, not hiding his puzzlement, 'is why you don't use the genuine article – you know, real spears and crafts and things. After all, you talk about job creation here. Surely that would be a good way to build employment?'

'Out of the question, old man,' Geoff said blithely. 'First, the real McCoy is quite dreary, specially when compared with our Romanian designs. But the main reason is that Juma doesn't want his people doing that sort of thing. He wants them educated and becoming accountants and resort managers and teachers. Far better to knock up decent looking antiquities in Romania and a happier outcome in terms of client satisfaction.'

'But surely the tourists read guidebooks and know what to expect. And what about wildlife? Don't they want that?' James persisted.

'These aren't the billionaire, well-informed, super-rich class. These people are only different because they've got themselves miles above the herd financially, so money's no object, but otherwise they're basically suburban and not exactly sophisticates or intellectuals. They lap up whatever's offered, and the more over the top it is, the happier they are. They believe it all. They're here for a good time, not an anthropology excursion. That's wet bearded schoolteacher territory; you know, taking notes about everything and trying to squeeze the last drop out of it by asking bloody stupid questions and generally being a pest.'

'Wildlife?' James repeated.

'It's all here. The valley has plenty of zebras and giraffes and a herd of elephants. There's the occasional cheetah strolling about and swags of monkeys in the trees on the golf course we shipped in from the Congo as there weren't any here. We've got a dozen tired old lions we bought from a bankrupt South African circus which we feed on zebras the lads shoot. They'd starve otherwise. I hesitate to call them a pride. Most of them seem a bit arthritic and can barely walk a dozen yards. Initially we set up a loudspeaker sound system with recordings of lions roaring in the middle of the night to add to the darkest Africa ambience but we had to drop it. It terrified the hell out of our real lions and they all fled to the hills. Only hunger ultimately saw them drift back again.'

'Doesn't seem much point having them,' James commented.

'On the contrary; it looks bloody good having them lying about toasting in the sun. At night-time we drop the zebra meat just on the other side of the moat so they loll about there. The tourists are convinced they're eyeing them up as a potential meal so it adds hugely to the sense of adventure. But they feel safe because of the moat. Also we've lots of brightly coloured parrots in the trees on the golf course. We imported them from Australia to enhance the African flavour as the indigenous bird life is all rather humdrum. Very unsatisfactory in the African context. We brought in a few ostriches from South Africa once but they terrified our lions so we had to get rid of them. Pity really, as the more variety the better, but we have to be careful. Take rhinos for instance. They'd bugger up the fairways and greens if they barged on to the golf course as the moat is quite shallow and wouldn't stop them coming. You'll have noticed we have a mob of swans on the moat to colour things up a bit.'

'Are the giant trout in the moat?' James asked.

'No. But that's not a bad idea. I'll mention it to Monster. Trying to liven up the moat caused us a spot of consternation recently. The only Brasch idea that's ever bounced.'

'What happened?' James asked, now captivated by the sheer scale of the illusion.

'We had a huge, absolutely authentic-looking artificial crocodile made in Japan. The Japs are very good at this sort of thing. It's controlled by a remote. Monster gave it a trial run six months ago and had it come out of the moat snapping at an elderly couple going for a stroll. The chap promptly dropped dead with a heart attack.'

'Jesus, Geoff, that's a bit rich,' James muttered.

'Well obviously it wasn't part of the plan,' Geoff said defensively. 'Anyway, the widow shot back to New York with the coffin and the next thing her bloody lawyers banged a writ on our New York office for $20 million damages. We applied to have it struck out as vexatious and produced a zoology professor who pointed out, quite correctly I might add, that there are no crocodiles in this part of Kenya. The widow kicked up a hell of a fuss in court, screaming "I know what I saw" and that sort of carry-on – you know what bloody women can be like; totally unreasonable – and the judge ended up fining her for contempt and struck the case out. Still, it was a near thing. The crocodile's all packed up and we'll take it back to England with us on the jet. Bound to be a use for it one day.'

'I must admit the moat does look a bit crocodilish,' James ventured. 'It's a pity you can't think of some use for it. What about hippos?'

'Don't be silly. We'd all be killed. Hippos are bloody dangerous.'

'Really! I thought they just wallowed about in the water.'

'Like bloody hell. Hippos are bad-tempered buggers. They fight one another all the time and don't stop until one's dead. Everyone thinks of lions and crocodiles as Africa's dangerous animals but it's hippos which kill the most Africans every year, literally hundreds in fact; much more than crocs, although they take their share. Juma shot all the hippos in the river and keeps doing so when more drift in. But remember, our punters are mainly here for the golf. The rest is mere flim-flam to provide Africany experiences and keep the non-golfing wives content. We organise a couple of safaris each week; the standard tripe, you know, great white hunters wearing pith helmets and jodhpurs and holding rifles, and everyone in zebra-patterned jeeps.

'The three great white hunters are all ex-South Africans. One's our golf-course manager and the other two are accountants from the office. Mind you, we have to be careful. The lions flee terror-stricken if the punters get too close which is not exactly the imagery we want. They'll get their dangerous lion adventure tonight, so Monster tells me. It's all extremely well-planned. Monster has really done a first-rate job and it will be an excellent education for you vis-à-vis Ogg.'

'So it would seem. Tell me about it.'

'The resort accommodates 240 people. If anyone comes alone they pay double. We bring them all in one lot; they stay exactly a week, then they fly out again and a new lot arrive. That way, being all together, makes it easy to programme everything, specially events like tonight, so they have the complete experience without suspecting any contrivance through repetition. We charge $26,000 per couple for the week, and that includes first-class flights from the States and Japan, the golf, food, the trout-fishing, village tours, traditional dancing; the lot. All they pay extra for apart from their antiquities purchases, which they're all into, are golf balls and their champagne – which consumption, I might add, is substantial after they've knocked up their sensational rounds.'

'$26,000 a week sounds a hell of a lot to me,' James said.

'Actually, it may be too little,' Geoff said smugly. 'You must remember the Kanju clients are rich but not super-rich. Probably mostly in the $50 to $100 million bracket, so the actual cost is insignificant to them. The important thing is their attitude to money, which is where Americans complement the Japanese guests so well. Ordinary middle-class Americans are ultra cost-conscious and hate paying for anything unless it's a bargain or discounted. But our American $50 to $100 million wealth bracket behave in exactly the opposite way. They take pride in boasting how much things cost; the more expensive something is, the happier they feel. Their lives are incredibly money-orientated and they equate value with cost. Talk to them about anything – their homes, cars, boats, health, kids' education or whatever – and invariably they will brag about their high cost.'

'So what about the Japanese?' James asked.

'They're precisely the same in their equation of value and cost, which is something you should be alert to with Ogg. Everything must be the perceived best, which is why they're so susceptible to brands. Offer a Japanese woman two identical handbags, but one at twice the price of the other because it has a brand name, and she will take the expensive one every time. The men are just the same. They'd rather pay twice as much for a brand-name whisky than one without the deemed right label, so as I say, unlike the normal approach, our danger with this market is not pricing ourselves out through being too expensive but instead for being too cheap.'

'Our New York manager used to say something similar about the Japanese,' James said thoughtfully. 'He claimed they were the world's worst investors as they were trophy hunters and could be sold old name American businesses for ridiculous prices.'

'He's right,' Geoff agreed. 'Look at them paying an outrageous amount back in the mid-eighties for the tired old Rockefeller Center and ending up selling it back years later to the Americans at a fraction of the price. There are hundreds of Japanese investment stories like that. Dad says they're the ultimate suckers in the art market, for the same reason. If you've got a dud Van Gogh, and God knows, some of his output was awful, then sell it to the Japs. They'll pay top dollar just for the signature. So you can see our dilemma here. We're probably going to have to lift our tariff 50 per cent just to satisfy our clientele's egos.'

'I'm sure you won't be too upset about that,' James teased. 'Anyway, what's the story on the dancing?' he asked, not disguising his enthusiasm.

'Four nights a week sixty selected guests gather after dinner and are driven in buses ten miles down the valley to our mock native village. Those whose turn it is for each night's traditional dance are informed that morning via the broadsheet delivered to them advising their golf teeing-off time. At the village they see darkest Africa's traditional native dances, rarely observed by outsiders. Naturally they're nothing of the sort. Traditional native dances would send them to sleep. Our Sicilian catering manager, Johnny Persico, is a former Soho night-club choreographer and he puts them through their paces so it's really spicy stuff. We give it a different theme each year; you know, harvest gathering, love stories, hunting, the usual ethnic-dancing guff, but always culminating in a fairly ribald affair which is what the guests really want. Monster says the latest performance is something else and really worth seeing. Tonight's the premiere. I'm quite looking forward to it, as I'm damn sure are the guests who've been here before and know what to expect. But it's always bloody funny watching the reaction from the new chums the first time they see one of our cultural performances.'

'And they never suss they're being had?' James asked, plainly perplexed.

'Don't be silly. They're not being had. They're here to be stimulated and we deliver. These people are highly successful car dealers and building contractors and insurance brokers, that sort of thing, but despite their wealth they are essentially superficial. They believe what they're told. These are the sort of people who go to *The Mousetrap* if they're in London. So long as we say it's traditional ethnic then we can hit 'em with the most outrageous erotica which they rationalise it's OK to watch because it's culture. Don't forget how old these buggers are. They belong to a generation that grew up looking at bare-breasted black women in *National Geographic* magazines; it's the earliest memories which stick, so that's the main thing Africa means to them and what they hope to see.'

'And the dancers are the Latin waitresses?' James asked eagerly.

'Yep. Ten of them shoot off in a bus while everyone's finishing dinner. They actually love doing it. Remember where they come from. These girls are imbued in a culture of sexual sauciness so it's a relief for them to unwind. You'd never get the local girls to carry on like that. They'd collapse in a state of shock if they saw these performances. Not that we'd want them anyway. Far too ugly. Also, four of the youngest golf-course workers join them as village warriors and Clarence prances about doing his witch doctor thing. I've had a crack myself and it was great fun. Only the nuisance of painting myself black all over then having to wash it all off again stops me participating tonight.

'They go to the village and light oil fires in clay pots to provide flickering light and create the right atmosphere. Then they strip naked, oil their bodies to add to the erotica, and don tiny grass skirts which cover nothing. That's another Brasch innovation. We import them from Hawaii and cut them down to bum length. In the half light the guests don't recognise any faces, not that they're looking at faces. It's what people expect when they come to Africa – naked darkies behaving erotically – whereas as I said, the irony is the Africans in these parts are incredibly modest, specially the Kanju, and are usually covered from head to toe. Most would be horrified to even expose an ankle. But we get away with it because it's what the punters hope to see and, like I said, they feel OK about watching because it's culture. It's no different back home. Staging a play with name actors, obscene language, nudity and other salacious behaviour which would put you behind bars in different circumstances is acceptable because being a play, it's deemed to be culture. Serious theatre groups are always doing it. They know it packs in the punters.'

'Well, if you say so,' James conceded. 'But given the numbers you're putting through I'm still surprised you haven't been exposed.'

'Don't be. Remember we target our markets carefully. For example, even though they can afford it none of the Kanju guests would ever be a candidate for the sort of exercise you will see in Madagascar, and conversely, none of the Madagascan clients would ever come to Kanju. Kanju's clientele are middle-class people with middle-class values but with the unusual feature of being extremely wealthy.'

'Surely to God at least once someone's questioned the authenticity,' James ventured.

'Never. The affluent middle classes never question anything. They're the ultimate conservatives so all they ever seek is to preserve society as they find it. They're all self-made and find no fault with the prevailing order which has served them so well. Anyway, the middle classes are totally devoid of imagination and believe implicitly, as an article of faith, in established authority. They accept everything's genuine because we, as the relevant authorities, tell them it is. Our super-rich billionaire category clientele are a different breed altogether and would smell a rat within an hour of arrival – not that you'd ever get them near a resort. You'll see what I mean next week in Madagascar.'

'And with Kanju you only target Japanese and Americans?' James queried. 'Why not rich Germans and other Europeans?'

'I told you. We think everything out clearly. Japanese and Americans are a natural mix. The Yanks make more noise but still share the same peculiarity of excessive politeness. With the Japs it's custom and with the Americans it's fear.'

'Fear; what do you mean fear?'

'American courtesy has its roots in a fear of offending and its consequences. The Germans, Italians, Spanish and the like are just too boisterous. And the English; all that relentless piss-taking is bewildering to Americans. Allow Europeans here and there would be an abrasive undertone between the nationalities which would spoil everything. That's just not so when you mix the Japanese and Americans. They complement each other nicely. Also, the Europeans would never pay our tariffs. They're not susceptible to brand bullshit, probably because they create most of them and know what flannel they are. To them, paying lots is a sign of gullibility, not prestige. It's because we think these things out that we have so much return business. There's no such thing as an unhappy Alceides customer.'

Later that night during dinner Juma stood on a chair in the dining room and rang a bell. The excited buzz of triumphant golfing and fishing anecdotes tapered away and finally ceased. 'Ladies and gentlemen,' Juma said. 'Would the guests attending the culturwal performance tonight please make their way to the buses. But first a caution. What you will see is a twaditional Kanju courting dance in which the village virgins discuss their hopes for husbands and then dance out their expectations. They tire fwom their exertions and fall asleep, and while they're sleeping they're visited by the wawwior spiwit who inspects them for their suitability. Because the Kanju are a wawwior wace there's twaditionally a shortage of men so the village virgins must compete thwough their dancing to attwact a husband. It's a very ancient twaditional dance which is still widely pwactised.

103

Please be wespectful as it is most unusual for outsiders to be allowed to witness such an event. The villagers will not permit camewas so please, no flashes.'

'Can't afford the risk of someone knowing seeing photographs,' Geoff whispered to James. 'Could blow us out of the water otherwise. You know the bullshit subjects cluttering universities these days – degrees in frisbee throwing and ballroom dancing. One of this lot could have some hare-brained offspring doing African studies or some such tripe and recognise it all as a load of cock so we take no chances.'

They rose and, escorted by great white hunters bearing rifles, joined the guests on one of the buses which set off over the moat's drawbridge and drove into the darkness across the plain.

'Adds to the romance,' Geoff whispered. 'Too stagey if we held it here. The drawbridge is good too. Makes 'em feel that once they're over it, they're out in savage African heartland exposed to danger.'

The clatter of American voices began to irritate James as the reliving of the day's golf and fishing triumphs was kept up at full volume. Eventually the bus pulled up beside the village palisade. The guests were led theatrically in single file under armed guard into the central compound which was lit by flickering fires. Four rows of deckchairs were arranged at one end. The golfing and fishing anecdotes ceased abruptly when a penetrating drumbeat began from among the huts.

Suddenly ten Latina girls, their glistening golden bodies naked except for their flimsy grass skirts, ran daintily into the clearing. There was a few minutes of mock chattering and girlish tittering as they knelt in a group purporting to discuss their marital hopes then they rose and began a wild limb-flailing, high-kicking prancing while all the time singing loudly. They leapt, squatted, fell to all fours and generally adopted outrageously erotic postures, visible only in flashes of firelight while the methodical drumbeating continued in the background.

The audience sat dumbstruck. James looked across to his neighbour, an elderly gentleman and plainly a first-timer to Kanju. His spectacles had fallen down his nose and his mouth dropped open as he stared awestruck at the girls.

'I'm in love,' James muttered.

'We'll gather up a couple of them afterwards,' Geoff whispered. 'How's your Spanish?'

'To hell with talking. Still, I must say their singing's not bad.'

'It's a recording. The Bucharest City Opera made it for us for $1,000. The girls are just miming but they seem to have mastered it and in the half-light it's perfect.'

Gradually the drums and singing faded and one by one the girls collapsed to the ground, their limbs spread enticingly while purporting to be asleep and in the process, providing flickering fire-light glimpses of African culture far in excess of the audience's wildest hopes.

Clarence now emerged holding a carved feather-clustered spear and wearing a leopard-skin loin-cloth, his body daubed with white painted stripes. Chanting loudly he pranced among the girls, pausing before each to point his spear at them, before eventually disappearing back into the huts.

Next four well-oiled golf-course workers wearing only short grass skirts leapt into the ring, the drumbeating resumed even louder and the girls slowly rose from their slumber, exaggeratedly rubbing their eyes and began wildly cavorting among the male dancers, by their erotic posturing, plainly competing for the men's favour.

'Christ,' James muttered. 'Am I seeing what I'm seeing?'

'Don't be alarmed,' Geoff reassured him. 'They're foot-long latex dildoes attached to a string round their waists. We make them in the Romanian factory. It fulfils the lady guests' fantasies about Africans. The husbands never notice; they're too busy watching the girls. When I had a go I tied mine on too loose and it slipped down six inches and two Japanese ladies fainted. Bloody embarrassing, I can tell you.'

Just as the traditional dance seemed to be reaching a crescendo it was brought to an abrupt halt by a terrifying lion's roar which penetrated the night and echoed off the hills.

'Bloody hell! Monster's got it far too loud,' Geoff muttered.

As rehearsed, the dancers fled shrieking into the huts. Some of the ladies began to sob noisily and Juma leapt to his feet and shouted, 'Don't be fwightened, ladies and gentlemen. Stay in your seats while we close off the bawicade,' and he shouted at the armed guards who, rifles cocked, ran outside the compound. Almost immediately another lion's roar, this time closer, rang out heightening the consternation among the guests.

'Jesus Christ, we're done for,' a panicky American male voice bawled. Two elderly ladies dropped to their knees and, hands clasped, began loudly praying. Four of the Japanese men set about industriously building a fort with the deck chairs behind which their wives cowered, whimpering piteously.

Half a minute later a volley of gunshots echoed off the hills and shortly afterwards the riflemen returned and spoke to Juma.

'OK. Ladies and gentlemen. We hope we've scared the lion away but it may be wounded so it could be very, very dangewous. For evewyone's safety, please do exactly as instwucted. Ladies first please. The guards will escort you on to the buses,' and, trembling with fright, the ladies ran huddled together to the bus alongside the guards and fell into their seats, emotionally drained. Soon they were joined by their menfolk, all affecting a nonchalant air but unable to hide their relief once safely aboard. Minutes later the buses were bouncing across the plain back to the resort, golf and giant trout forgotten as the ladies chattered excitedly about their adventure. Most of the men, James observed, remained silent, plainly deeply moved by the cultural performance.

'We have to think up new angles every year,' Geoff whispered. 'This year we're dishing up onc lion fright each week. But Monster's definitely got it too loud. We don't want any unnecessary heart attacks, other than with holes in one. We've had two of those so far; still, it's not a bad way to go. I know it's only a recording and I knew it was coming but Christ, it even frightened me.'

'So it's all part of the African adventure,' James said drily.

'Don't mock it. You watch this lot boasting to the other guests later. Anyway, forget about that. I'll get some drinks over to our bungalow. The girls will be back in fifteen minutes once the coast is clear so I'll try and pull a couple over, preferably still oiled,' Geoff added, laughing.

# – FIFTEEN –

The following morning James woke feeling slightly hung over. He lay for a few minutes contemplating the previous evening's events, until the door opened and Geoff entered wearing swimming trunks and sipping a glass of orange juice.

'The girls have trotted off to work. Breakfast is here so get up, shower and shave then have a swim and I'll tell you about today's programme while we eat.'

James rose and ten minutes later felt recharged as he languidly stroked through a dozen laps of the pool. He climbed out and joined Geoff under a parasoled table on which stood a pitcher of orange juice, a bowl of fruit salad and, on a heating apparatus, metal canisters containing toast, bacon, sausages, eggs and coffee.

'I want to head off by midday,' Geoff said. 'It's quite a few hours down to Madagascar and I don't trust those flight control buggers in Antananarivo with night arrivals. One of them sends us the occasional note handwritten in capital letters, which is a sure sign of lunacy. But I want you to see the trout-fishing exercise first.'

'Ah yes. That I do want an explanation for,' James said, spearing a sausage. 'I knew Kenya had trout in the tablelands but I thought they were fairly small.'

'They are. It's ours that aren't. Right at the beginning when the resort was being constructed we shipped in a thousand hatchery fingerlings, built holding ponds and then began a fattening programme with zebra meat. We've got over two thousand there now and I'd say their average weight is about twelve pounds. Some are real giants, as they should be given we feed 'em non-stop.'

'So you put them in the lake for the guests to catch?' James enquired.

'Not quite, old man, although there are actually two swimming about which broke the lines when they were being played. We chuck in a zebra flank for them each week. These fish would never take a fly. They've been gorging themselves on zebra meat all their lives so they wouldn't make the effort. After breakfast I'll show you how it works rather than tell you, but for now, all you need to know is why.'

'What do you mean, why?' James asked.

'After the golfers have their daily round they have nothing to do for half the day. Unlike their wives and because of the types they are, most are not into lying round swimming pools or reading. If they don't know how to cast a fly rod then we teach them so usually there's about fifty chaps and a handful of wives standing round the lake edge casting streamer flies and retrieving them. Every day we allow three or four of them to hook into one, or that's what they think anyway, and they play them for a couple of hours each before the fish escapes.'

'What do you mean they escape? You can't organise that.'

'Oh yes we can. Shortly I'll show you how it works,' Geoff replied smugly. 'The guests get bloody excited carrying on about the one that got away. Actually I reckon it's a toss-up as to which gives them the biggest thrill; playing a huge trout for two hours or hitting a sub-par round. It's just another example of what an outstanding job we do in terms of customer joy. And among each week's batch of guests four actually land giant trout, which is a hell of a thrill for the successful anglers. It keeps three of Monster's people employed mounting them, along with tanning the zebra skins we sell in the shop. We sent them down to Johannesburg to learn taxidermy, which has been another useful diversification skill for Monster's tribe. It's a nice little supplementary earner for the resort too as we slug them $3,000 for each mounted fish. That's another $600,000 in the pot annually.'

'But I don't understand,' James muttered. 'Are you telling me this is another monitoring scheme like the golf? I can't see how that's possible.'

'Then down your coffee and I'll show you.'

The two strolled through the garden to the road, jumped into the golf buggy and set off towards the resort headquarters. On arrival they walked across to the lake around which fifty anglers were casting.

'Christ, one of them's into one,' James said excitedly, and he ran round the lake edge towards a small group of tourists who were shouting encouragement to a perspiring elderly Japanese man who was desperately trying to control his bucking rod.

The trout charged across the lake at high speed, the reel reaching a high screaming pitch as the line raced out. Suddenly the trout stopped, its huge tail fin flickering as it broke the surface, and gradually the angler played it back towards him. He brought it to the lake edge, winding carefully and steadily, his rod bent under the strain. But abruptly the fish was off again, racing towards a different part of the lake, the reel screaming and the rod bucking and jerking as the Japanese angler frantically hung on.

Geoff ambled up slowly and addressed the group of spectators.

'How long has he had it on?' he asked.

An elderly American responded. 'Ah been watching this for over an hour. Ah tell you, man, this baby is sure one big fish.'

'It's enormous,' James cried excitedly. 'I saw its tail.'

'Come on,' Geoff whispered to James. 'He's got another forty minutes to go. Follow me and we'll see what's going to happen.'

Reluctantly James left the group and the two walked round to the far side of the lake, Geoff occasionally congratulating anglers on their casting, and once stopping and coaching an elderly lady who was clearly a novice and was bringing her back-cast too far behind her.

At the end of the lake lay a thick, fence-enclosed forest with a large sign reading 'Resort Guests. This forest contains highly dangerous animals. Do not enter under any circumstances.'

'Over here mate,' Geoff said, and he clambered up the fence and dropped down to the other side.

James followed. 'What about the dangerous animals?' he asked nervously.

'That's just to keep the guests out,' Geoff grinned. They entered the forest where a path led to a small wooden building which they entered through a door marked 'No admission'.

Inside, a young African in swimming trunks was sitting in an armchair sipping coffee and reading a book. He looked up. 'Hello Geoff. I didn't know you were here.'

'Arrived yesterday. How's the extramural study going?'

'Not bad,' the young man replied. 'I passed the mid-year exams. The Aristotle stuff was plain sailing but this Schopenhauer is giving me some bother,' he said, waving the book.

'Talk to Monster. He'll explain it.'

'Yes, he's terrific. But I don't like troubling him. He's so busy all the time.'

Geoff introduced the African to James. 'This is Jomo. He's one of Monster's managerial trainees. Second-year philosophy student but having two months off to help out with the resort. We're here to show James the operation,' he explained. 'I see you have someone hooked up. Is he going to land it?'

'No. This is day three for the current intake. We had a fourteen-pounder caught yesterday so the next one's due tomorrow. Four per intake don't forget.'

'I heard about your disgrace,' Geoff said.

Jomo looked at the floor, plainly embarrassed. 'I thought I had broken through understanding Schopenhauer,' he mumbled. 'I became so engrossed I forgot.'

'A bad show, Jomo. Some of these guests are fairly frail. Letting the poor bugger play one for five hours could damn near have killed him. I'm surprised Juma didn't put you in the torture chamber as punishment.'

'Well, what the hell are they playing?' James demanded.

Geoff and Jomo laughed conspiratorially.

'Get undressed,' Geoff said.

'What do you mean, get undressed?'

'Strip off. The water's fairly warm. Jomo will show you. You're not going to believe it unless you see for yourself.'

Somewhat hesitatingly, James undressed.

Jomo put down his book, walked to the centre of the room and lifted a manhole. The two men descended a ladder into a ten-foot-high water-pipe filled with waist-deep water. They splashed down the tunnel for about twenty yards until they came to a ledge on which lay some scuba gear.

'Can you scuba?' Jomo asked. On receiving James' assent he said, 'Put the gear on then follow me and make sure you don't surface. We're going into the lake.'

James pulled on the flippers, strapped the tank on his back and tested the oxygen flow. He pulled on the goggles and then, following Jomo who had also donned scuba gear, ducked under the water and they swam along the pipe. After about ten yards they reached the lake, the bottom falling away to a depth of about fifteen feet. To James' surprise the lake-bed had a concrete surface.

Jomo dived to the bottom and, leading the way, swam about thirty yards towards the centre of the lake, then stopped and pointed. James saw a steel rail set on small blocks about three inches off the bottom which disappeared towards the centre of the lake.

They set out again, staying close to the bottom and following the rail track. After another fifty yards Jomo stopped again and pointed to two tracks which were connected to the original one but headed off in different directions. Jomo sat down and signalled to James to wait.

A minute elapsed then suddenly Jomo grabbed James' arm and pointed. Racing along the track towards them was a two-foot-long bullet-shaped object with a wire loop on its top. Caught round it was a large streamer wet fly attached to a fishing line that stretched away into the distance. At the rear of the vehicle a three-foot steel rod extended upwards, and fixed to its end was a plastic imitation of a huge tail fin.

As the vehicle neared them and reached the conjunction with the other tracks, it paused then slowly set off again in a different direction. As it passed Jomo reached out, grabbed the line and pulled the fly free, then turned to James and signalled their return.

They swam back to the tunnel and soon emerged near the ledge. Jomo stood up, removed his face mask and tank and then his flippers and placed them on the ledge. James followed suit. 'This is bloody ridiculous,' he gasped, conscious that this had been the tenor of his response to everything he had encountered over the past two weeks.

They splashed down the tunnel, climbed the ladder and Geoff, grinning broadly, handed both men towels.

'Got away I'm afraid,' Jomo said, laughing. 'I saved the fly.'

'Do you have the picture, old man?' Geoff chortled.

For the first time James checked his 'Bloody ridiculous' impulse. 'Explain,' he said sharply.

'Well, it's all quite simple. Brasch invented it. Five times a day Jomo dons the scuba gear and hooks someone up to the vehicle. It runs on an electric engine he controls in here. He lets the angler play it for a couple of hours then unhooks it by throwing this lever.' Geoff pointed to a lever set in the wall. 'That activates a trip wire which whips the fly off the loop. Still, the angler has had one hell of a battle. Also, he gets to see the fish occasionally when the vehicle runs up over humps in the track which are set at the right height for the tail fin to emerge.

111

The vehicle can only travel away from the lake edge towards the centre. Once at the centre it changes direction and its motor cuts off automatically. That allows the angler to play it back again to the edge which activates it to set off on another run. We usually have someone hooked up from dawn to dusk so it has spectator value for the other guests as well.'

'But what about the fish you said do get caught?' James demanded.

'Four times a week Jomo drives down to the holding tanks and puts a giant trout in a wire cage inside an aquarium filled with water. He brings it back, puts it under the water, takes out the cage and swims into the lake with it. When the vehicle comes by hooked up to an angler he grabs the fly at the junction where it stops, opens the cage door and quickly hooks the trout through the mouth, then lets it go. Usually it takes another hour or more to land. The successful anglers are absolutely exhausted. As I said, four get caught each week. Scarcity plus the others getting away after two-hour battles simply adds to the excitement when one's landed. The punters are very, very happy.'

'It's bloody ridiculous,' James muttered. 'What I don't understand is why you don't simply drop a foot or so of soil on the lake bottom, put in some plants – and fill the lake with trout and let the anglers genuinely try and catch them. It seems to me you enjoy making monkeys out of your clients.'

Geoff looked hurt. 'Far from it,' he said caustically. 'You certainly don't understand. Unlike any other tourist organisation anywhere, as my father explained to you, we alone make big money. And that success rests on one solid foundation, namely overwhelming customer satisfaction.'

'What's wrong with my idea then?' James persisted.

'I was hoping you might put your finger on the one flaw with Kanju,' Geoff replied. 'In the event you've failed.'

'Tell me.'

'The only drawback with the golf operation is that all the guests play sensationally. It's partly compensated for by the fact that with golf one is essentially playing against oneself, but it's still a weakness. Takes some of the shine off a great performance when everyone else turns one in. The same goes with the fishing. If we set it up so every angler landed a big fish each day it would lose its lustre. Brasch anticipated the golf problem and invented the giant trout scenario to compensate. The absolutely critical factor with the trout is the scarcity value.

'But remember, the reason these fish are so huge is that we stuff them with zebra meat in holding tanks. If we put them in the lake they'd be normal size. And if we simply put them in the lake from our holding tanks they'd never take a fly. They're not used to it, and they're too big and bulky to go after them.'

'Bloody hell,' James muttered. 'You really have thought of everything.' He thought for a while, then said, 'The problem I have is the underlying dishonesty. Everything I've seen, including Romania, is basically fraudulent and I can't imagine what lies ahead in Madagascar. This resort is lovely. Why not run it honestly without all the bullshit?'

Geoff looked at him, sighed and shook his head slowly. 'You still haven't woken up, have you? If we did that it would die in six months. You said it yourself; why come all this way just to play golf? Look at the benefits to Juma and his people. That alone is a justification. But most of all think about it from the clientele's viewpoint. It's a wonderful thing at 65 years of age, when every day seems a downhill ride, to suddenly start burning up the golf course and shoot rounds twelve or fifteen strokes better than you ever managed in your heyday.

'It's a wonderful thing at 65 years of age to play for three hours, catch and mount a 17-pound trout after a lifetime of taking two pounders in prissy American and Japanese catch-and-release rivers. And just maybe most of all, it's a wonderful thing at 65 years of age to feel the juices stirring again after watching one of our cultural performances. And I'll tell you something about that. As you know, the bungalows have two bedrooms, each with a king-size bed. Ninety per cent of our guests use both bedrooms for the first night or two after their arrival. But after two days here their spirits are so elevated that suddenly – perhaps for the first time in years – they're sharing the one bed and I don't think it's for discussion purposes. If nothing else, that confirms what a fantastic job we're doing. Saves on our laundry costs too,' he added breezily. 'You say it's all based on deception but so what! It's the outcome that matters and we deliver the ultimate dream to our clients – that is, a rebirth, a second innings, another chance. I was serious when I said we add years to their lives. We do that by bringing achievement and happiness they had long thought belonged in their past. Look at our champagne sales. They're phenomenal, only the clients are buying it to toast themselves, not the birth of a bloody grandchild. Get real, James. We're doing a fabulous job.'

There was a lengthy pause and finally James spoke. 'How can I quarrel with any of that?' he said thoughtfully. 'I suppose it's all such a shock it takes time to come to terms with.'

'Glad you can see it now,' Geoff said triumphantly. 'Come on. It's time we packed and got out of here.' They rose and farewelled Jomo who was climbing back down the ladder to hook up another angler, and headed back to their bungalow.

# – SIXTEEN –

For the first thirty minutes of the helicopter journey south from Kanju James, oblivious to the passing terrain, silently mulled over all he had seen. In the rear Juma and Geoff discussed the resort accounts, the murmur of their voices only faintly audible above the *tisk, tisk, tisk* of the whirling helicopter blade. Eventually James turned and addressed Geoff.

'I've been thinking. If the demand is such that you can only allocate everyone an annual visit, why not build more golf resorts, say closer to America or even in America?'

'You ain't been thinking deep enough, chum,' Geoff replied, looking up from his papers. 'You're ignoring the critical points I've emphasised over the past week – secrecy and privacy, and also the right landowner with a vested interest in ensuring those things. Consider our investment. It's not exactly peanuts. We couldn't pull this deal in a developed country and maintain secrecy for more than a month before one of the staff ran to the news media. We'd be history, and not only with that resort it would probably blow Kanju out of the water too. Everyone would wake up to what's happening there.'

'Quite wight,' Juma piped up. 'Absolutely essential to box carefully before embarking on another. That's why we're looking at an additional back-up golf course and twout lake in the Kanju Valley.'

'But there are lots of Third World places where you could apply the supplementary local exotica like Kanju,' James insisted.

'Actually, there are bugger all that are suitable,' Geoff countered. 'Don't think we haven't explored the idea. The problem is all Third World countries are so damned corrupt; their top brass would be on to us in a flash trying to get a piece of the action once they saw the number of tourists the resort's pulling. Believe me, it would end in tears.

'Kanju is perfect. The climate's right, with little rainfall unlike most tropical places; the location is remote and well away from busybody authorities; there's the African angle to add some exotica and most of all, Monster is the big boss in the valley. We know him, he's highly competent; Kanju has all the ingredients. But aside from that, if say we had another four similar exercises they would lose all meaning if the golfers achieved sensational results wherever they went, after all, those medium-rich types are workaholics and they're not going to be continuously on vacation. That's why we're looking at duplicating Kanju with an adjacent golf course and a similar guest capacity. The market's certainly there. But they have to be separate entities. Huge resorts are OK for the masses but they lack the sense of specialness our clients want.'

At Nairobi Geoff carefully supervised the loading of the artificial crocodile into the hold of the Alceides jet. 'Bloody expensive animal,' he grumbled. 'Cost us the best part of a hundred thousand dollars. Sooner or later we'll find a use for it.'

Two Immigration officials came on board, stamped their passports, and then they were off, heading east to the Indian Ocean and down to Madagascar.

Miriam served lunch and afterwards, nestling his wine glass, Geoff leant back in his seat and said, 'Well, old man, next comes the real fun operation in our enterprises. I'll explain it now. You will want to be involved and can choose a role for yourself.'

'I'm Lord High Executioner,' Juma insisted anxiously. 'He's not having that wole.'

'So what's it all about?' James asked, bracing himself for a fresh absurdity.

'Well, the background goes back ten years, after Dad sold the travel business. He came out with a sizeable dollop of money so for a year he was simply an investor. Ultimately that took him to America as Wall Street looked ready to run. Being a big player he met the top financial people there. You've heard of Oscar Goldsmith?'

'What – the billionaire takeover fellow?'

'Yes, him. Dad and Goldsmith met, hit it off and became good friends. One day Goldsmith mentioned the frustrations of modern travel; you know, the things Dad explained in London. What

116

ultimately emerged was that Goldsmith was bored, and when pressed he made a remark about regretting his choice of career, which naturally surprised Dad. He claimed that having heaps of money was all very well up to a point but if he could have his time over again, he'd go into politics because if he was capable of becoming one of America's richest men, then he would have had a fair chance of getting to be President had he tried, or so he argued. Of course Dad was astonished but when he delved further he found out what Goldsmith was really on about. On face value he had everything, but he was still dissatisfied.'

'So money can't buy you everything after all,' James suggested lightly.

'Of course it can't and that's the frustrating thing for the super-rich because that's what they expect. In Goldsmith's case it was more the grass being greener etc. It transpired he was deeply envious of the presidential role, solely, and I emphasise this, solely, because of the mass public accolades Presidents cop; you know, visiting China and fifty thousand schoolchildren waving flags as the motor procession passes, that sort of crap. Mostly he envied the Queen, the ceremonial riding in horse-drawn gilded carriages to open Parliament and all that palaver. But he realised that while he could never have been a hereditary monarch, being President was open to everyone, only for him it was too late now. In a nutshell, there was only one thing he'd never experienced in an otherwise full life and that was mass adulation.'

'Bloody childish,' James muttered.

'Well, be that as it may,' Geoff continued blithely, 'the fact is the super-rich crave every experience and, unlike any other time in history, nowadays great wealth is not automatically accompanied by fame. And even when it is, it's a temporal fame which becomes dulled with familiarity and is never accompanied by mass adulation or glory; indeed, usually the contrary applies when it's simply wealth-based. Then the most passionate of all human emotions arises, namely envy. The super-rich are usually super-bright so they know how important it is to keep their heads down when so many bastards are keen to lop them off. Invariably grubby journalists will spy on them, hoping to profit from producing a book revealing all. And if they can't find anything questionable, being well practised in the art they simply make it up and resort to personal attacks and innuendo. So after that conversation Dad thought about it and came up with an idea. I suspect by then he was a bit bored himself, so the next time he saw Goldsmith he told him he could deliver him the Presidential State Visit experience. That first exercise was simply a lark for the fun of it, but it was such a success Dad discreetly offered it to two other billionaires and they too snapped it up. Dad thought he had drawn a line under his old life, only to realise that, lo and behold, he'd created a brand new industry. That led to Brasch and in turn to the Romanian factory, then Monster's resort plus our Indian and African Head of State Tour divisions, and now Ogg. The key point, however, was Dad's realisation of the emergence of an entirely new market no one was catering to, namely the super-rich. More particularly he realised, thanks to Goldsmith, that while outwardly the super-rich appeared to have everything, the one thing they hadn't been able to purchase – but desperately craved – was mass adulation. Brasch has a lot more proposals on the drawing board to tap this market once Ogg is established.'

'But what did he do? What happened with Goldsmith?' James demanded.

'As I said, initially it started as a lark. Dad shot off to India and found lots of very sizeable regions with quite large towns which were actually quite remote and, in a sense, ignorant and uncivilised. Even the top brass, the mayor and police chief and so on, were all uneducated and living simple peasant lives out of touch with the rest of the world. So, through a translator Dad told them he was the Polish Ambassador and that they were about to receive a visit from the Polish President. Even though most of them had never heard of Poland they were absolutely thrilled. Nothing like that had ever happened to them before. A public holiday was called on the day of the visit. Dad had elephants brought in, he organised a run of ten thousand Polish flags for the locals to wave, shipped in an open limousine – which those cart and bullock towns had never seen – hired five hundred spear-carrying men at $2 a day each and issued them with colourful uniforms he had knocked up in China for a song, plus a few more bits of trim such as a brass band he brought up from Delhi. In due course Goldsmith flew to Delhi, then up to the selected town in a helicopter and away they went. It was a one-day job but it ran perfectly. Goldsmith, dressed in a white, bemedalled admiral's uniform and a gold-braided cap, rolled slowly into town in the back of the limo waving a white gloved hand, preceded by one of the elephants, the band and half the spear-carrying soldiers, with the rest of them and the remaining elephant bringing up the rear. The entire population was on the streets cheering wildly and waving the Polish flags. There was a civic reception, Goldsmith gave a speech which naturally no one understood, presented some medals, knighted the mayor and that was that. Dad realised he was on to something big and the next thing he was back in business. Now our Head of State Tours are taking place somewhere in Africa or the subcontinent every three weeks.'

'I've been on six,' Juma said. 'Wouldn't miss one at all if I had the time.'

'This is absolute madness,' James muttered. 'Surely to God someone's sussed it?'

'We've never even had a close shave,' Geoff said. 'Mind you, we're fairly careful. As I said, we stick to a few sure-thing territories like rural India, Madagascar, and certain African locations. Over the last four years we've averaged fifteen Royal or Presidential Visits a year.'

'Royals! For God's sake, what are those?' James spluttered.

'Visits by monarchs of course. That's what you'll see next week in Madagascar. Usually whether it's a Royal or a Presidential depends if they bring their wives. The women nearly always insist on a Royal. They become quite bombastic as queens and can't get enough of it. We've also done three Papal Tours and five Dalai Lama Visits, although we've now scrubbed both of those. The Papals were too boring, just waving to mobs of sullen Bolivian Indians from a Popemobile. Also, too many tourists in the Andes now so the risk of exposure is high. We could get away with a Royal there as the tourists would assume it was just another of those interminable Catholic processions they go in for but the problem is the Andean Indians. A terribly dour lot. We wouldn't get the crowd fervour the Africans and Indians deliver, which is fundamental to the whole exercise. The same goes with the Dalai Lama Visits. They were OK for half a day, just sitting on a throne and issuing the odd platitude to oodles of grovelling Indians, but the clients weren't seeking deference. They already had that in their lives. They wanted mass cheering and adulation, not servility, which is why we've pulled the plug on Dalai Lama Tours. Now our Royal and Presidential Visits total three days as we've added lots of refinements Brasch has thought up. The grand parade through the streets is probably the highlight but Brasch continues to embellish them with new ideas.'

'And me,' Juma intruded. 'I thought up the Lord High Executioner and the court jesters.'

'But what about the organisation of all of this and the cost; God knows, it must be horrendous?' James exclaimed.

'We have a permanent State Visits management team of sixteen people including accounting and management staff,' Geoff replied calmly. 'Eight in India and eight in Madagascar which is the headquarters for the African division. They've got it down pat. As for the cost, remember the places we pull these exercises. Everything's dirt cheap. Next week, for example, we have a four-hundred-man uniformed army costing $2 a head per day. That's only $4,000 for five days. As I said, the actual tours are three days but there are always dress rehearsals and we pay the soldiers for that. In these locations $2 a day is big money so our temporary soldiers take it seriously for fear of losing the job. Mind you, they don't know the monarchs and presidents aren't real. The medals and coinage and uniforms and flags and stuff all come out of the Romanian factory. Total disbursements are usually only about $20,000 as we've now built up quite an inventory of uniforms and other paraphernalia. We also offer a number of costly extras if they want them which they always do. Over and above disbursements we charge a flat fee of $500,000 for a Presidential Visit and $600,000 for a Royal Tour and the extras are on top of that. There's a lot more preparation required with the Royals; gilded carriages, eighteenth-century uniformed footmen, court jesters, ladies in waiting, ornate crowns …'

'Lord High Executioners,' Juma added.

'Lord High Executioners,' Geoff recited. 'Heaps and heaps of frills with a Royal unlike say a Papal Tour when the only special requirement was our Popemobile.'

'They pay $600,000 for this Ruritanian delusion? You're pulling my leg,' James muttered incredulously.

'Why not?' Geoff responded coolly. 'Look at Goldsmith. He's worth about eight billion. His daily investment income alone would be at least two million. He forfeits a few hours' income for three days of wonderful exhilaration. The cost is meaningless to him and anyway, it's tax deductible. He's done three Royal Visits, a Papal Tour and two Presidentials so far. Frankly, we can't keep up with the demand given the limited number of suitable territories, although we're working on some new locations. It's a very successful operation yielding annual profits of over six million dollars.'

'What do you mean tax deductible?' James protested. 'How can it possibly be tax deductible?'

'Simple, old man. We don't formally sell them a Royal Visit; we sell them a purported full consultancy analysis of some element of their commercial activity. They receive a set of four cloth-bound, hardcover 200-page reports. Brasch writes them for each client. It usually takes him about half an hour for each one. He only has to knock out a ten-page preamble tailored to each client; the rest is all standard consultancy guff – statistical data, charts, lots of nonsensical jargon. We have a storeroom filled with them already made up, but the finished article certainly looks the job and would pass any auditing test.'

'But surely the auditors want to see the reports?' James argued.

'Don't be absurd. At $600,000 a time it's understandable their contents are highly confidential. All the auditors need to satisfy themselves is that payment has been made to a consultancy company – that's us of course – and that the work's been done. The contents are none of their business. Not even the tax authorities have the right to see them.'

'So the billionaires deduct your fee but the Kanju medium-rich clientele can't,' James remarked, after a pause adding facetiously, 'The same old story; one rule for the rich, another for the poor.'

'Actually, the Kanju clientele do even better,' Geoff responded cheerfully. 'We don't formally sell them a golf holiday. Kanju is presented as a permanent investment study centre. So ostensibly they come to attend an investment seminar, and deduct the lot. For tax record purposes we give them a complete set of speech notes to take back, which we change each year. Brasch knocks them out.'

'I don't see how that's doing better,' James said a little grumpily.

'They do better,' Geoff explained, 'because our investment office also provides them with a sharemarket tip. As a broker you know that at any given time there's always a handful of stocks which are undervalued and due for a correction. We tip the clients into them and most, being in such a positive mood because of their golfing triumphs, buy in big so it becomes a self-fulfilling process, the price correction that is. Most turn a profit on their annual visit. We'd offer the same to our Head of State Tour billionaire clientele too but they'd consider it impertinent if we gave them financial advice. The Kanju-type clients are innately deferential to purported experts and much more receptive.'

'Geoffwey's wight,' Juma said. 'The clients always tell me how well they did fwom the pwevious year's advice.'

'I just can't believe it,' James spluttered. 'It's, it's …' he searched for words, reluctant to say it again. But he did. 'It's bloody ridiculous,' he mumbled.

'No it's not,' Geoff said calmly. 'It's classic market economics in action. We offer a service and our customers enthusiastically buy it. We do a very good job so the Head of State Tour clients consider it great value. We give them a six-hour video recording of the tour's highlights, which they really appreciate. Two of our staff are adept cameramen, so much so that I very much doubt you'll notice their presence. Everyone's happy. That's the only test.'

'But what about the poor bloody mugs who believe this nonsense? The Madagascans and Indians and Bolivians waving the flags and being conned?'

'Far from being mugs, in many respects they're the biggest winners of all. First, it costs them nothing. Second, it brings huge excitement into their relentlessly dreary lives, lots of colourful pageantry and noise. Africans in particular like noise. And think about those poor buggers in the Andes; the peasants whose lives are saturated in destructive Catholic mumbo-jumbo. Seeing the Pope would normally be beyond their wildest dreams although, as I said, we're no longer doing Papal Tours. Third, it honours their otherwise uncelebrated civic leaders, that's the presentation medals and in India the knighthoods our monarchs dish out, and finally, and perhaps most important for them, it increases their virtually non-existent wealth through our tossing coins into the crowd. Usually we dish out about five hundred coins per visit, or the footmen do that is.'

'That's always a highlight,' Juma observed.

'It's preposterous,' James said indignantly. 'It's a totally bogus currency.'

'Not where we go, old boy. If anything it's the local money that's bogus in any meaningful value sense, not that the locals ever see much of it. Anyway, how can it be bogus if it works? Our coinage has absolute credibility which is all that counts. It's the predominant currency now in some of our stamping grounds and has brightened up their economies considerably, believe me. The big thing of course is that it has the client's head on it, otherwise we'd toss out the local currency – not that we could, as in the Third World where corruption and incompetence have destroyed their economies it's always paper money, but it doesn't matter anyway as ours works much better.'

'That's absurd,' James retorted. 'I don't believe it.'

'Really,' Geoff said coolly. 'Well consider this if you want to know how bloody hopeless African governments are with money. In Malawi, Government securities currently sell on the secondary market at 70 per cent yields, which simply says they're worthless. The same in Zimbabwe. The biggest building in Zimbabwe is the Reserve Bank. It's even worse in Malawi. Their bloody Central Bank has two buildings, one in the capital Lilongwe and the other in Blantyre, and they're both the biggest in town. It's vintage Third World; all show and no substance. Make no mistake, our little distributions do a damn fine job.'

'Then there's the schools and health clinics,' Juma added.

'Good point,' Geoff said. 'On every tour we suggest the visiting monarch or President donates a new school or health clinic and establishes a capital fund to keep it going. We've never had a refusal. It gives our billionaire clients a kick and the cost is neither here nor there to them. We organise it all. Off the top I'd say there are at least sixty schools or medical clinics operating in our territories, all with suitable plaques commemorating their donation from the King of Hamastan or the Emperor of Mythenia as the case may be. We actually employ people in both our Delhi and Madagascan offices just administering the ones already set up from past tours. We could probably pay for the schools and clinics with our own currency and make a turn on that when we charge the client but we'd ultimately end up devaluing our coinage. By any measure we're running a relatively responsible monetary policy which any western central banker would applaud and everyone's a winner.'

'And the jobs,' Juma prompted.

'Yes. Don't overlook that,' Geoff continued. 'It would be interesting to do an economic analysis of Alceides' positive economic effects in job creation. Our London offices have thirty employees, Romania about sixty, Monster has over two hundred and fifty, the tours division another twenty full-time and during a tour as many as six hundred part-timers. And none of that takes into account the flow-on economic benefits from the impetus of our currency. Believe me, we're making an outstanding contribution on the employment and economic stimulation fronts. We're a damn sight more beneficial than a lot of the aid agencies in these places.'

'And next week it's Andrew Clifford, the New York financier? I can't believe it. He seems such a cold-blooded, hard-headed type.'

'This is his seventh State Visit. Mind you, I think his wife pushes him a bit. He ran through the gambit in the first couple of years. Began with a Royal in Mali, six months later he did a Presidential Visit to India, then a Papal Tour of the Andes and after that he was the Dalai Lama, again in India. That went very well. He then had a Royal in northern Pakistan, by which time his wife was hooked. She loves being a queen so that was the end of religious and presidential tours for him. Last year they had a very successful Royal in Mauritania and were given a state banquet by the President. Their third main street was renamed King Andrew Avenue to commemorate the visit. They were even special guests of honour at a beheading.'

'That's disgraceful,' James exploded.

'Not at all. Mauritania is a Sharia law Muslim country. That's what they do there,' Geoff replied in a matter-of-fact voice.

'It's all so utterly hedonistic,' James muttered.

'Don't be silly,' Geoff said. 'You're forgetting who our clientele are. They're mostly self-made men. It's not in their nature to be spectators like everyone else. Think about it. How many tens of thousands of tourists wandered fascinated through preserved royal palaces somewhere in the world today? Our clients are behaving in the same way, only they taste the experience rather than just ogle at it.'

'But it's a charade,' James protested.

'Rubbish. It's nothing of the sort. It's totally real. Where we go the viewing public believe they're seeing a real live monarch and act accordingly. That's the important thing. And as for our clients, they know all monarchs are actually ordinary people who circumstances have elevated. Look at Princess Di. A dim kindergarten teacher fate plucked from obscurity. Everyone loves the idea of royalty and if they don't have it then they create it. Think about Eva Peron, or Jackie Kennedy, or Nelson Mandela. In the absence of a royal family they were effectively substituted. There's no such thing as royal blood, just chance rearing its head. In every respect our monarchs are as real as the Queen of England while they're on the job. They wouldn't fork out so much money if they thought otherwise.'

'James could be a coach footman,' Juma intervened. 'He could toss coins to the cwowd.'

'Too public for a first go. He might cock it up,' Geoff said adamantly. 'Perhaps he could be the Admiral. That's not too demanding. The Admiral's outfit in the Antananarivo warehouse is about his size. All he has to do is to model himself on the Duke of Edinburgh; you know, lurk about behind with his hands clasped behind his back. Normally the Alceides jet pilots fill the Field Marshal and Admiral roles but as we're here we certainly won't pass up the opportunity.'

'Can't I just watch?' James said weakly.

Juma and Geoff stared at him, flabbergasted.

'Are you mad?' Geoff barked. 'Why watch when you can participate? It's tremendous; every bugger cheering and waving flags. You'd kick yourself afterwards. Anyway,' he added conclusively, 'it will be good practice for Ogg. From time to time you may need to take on a role there.'

'James could be the Bishop,' Juma suggested.

'I'm not being a bloody Bishop,' James shouted.

'No he can't,' Geoff said. 'Hodgie has commandeered that role. He's our African region State Visits manager,' he explained. 'Hodgie won't give it up for anyone. He gets a real charge out of blessing cripples and babies and so on. Once he took confession from the President of Mali during a tour there. He'd kick up merry hell if he had to be a general or an admiral. Mind you, I can't say I'm entirely happy about it. In my view it's an unsuitable role from a management overseeing point of view and particularly in Hodgie's case. He's an Australian you see, so he can be quite uncouth. He was a judge in Malawi but he got kicked out after he impregnated two of his female court staff; and then there was the incident where he sentenced the wrong fellow to death and they shot the poor bugger. Turned out he was a court official and Hodgie mixed him up with the accused. Mind you, in fairness Hodgie was drunk at the time. Nevertheless, I thought it most unbecoming of him on the last Royal Tour in Madagascar when he leapt off his carriage and started beating some of the soldiers for not marching straight. And then he became tangled in his robes and fell over, and all the time shouting profanities. The Madagascans are Catholics. It's not the sort of thing they expect from a bishop.

125

Also, it left a poor impression with the client watching his Bishop rolling on the ground brawling with his army. And then there was the incident where he had it off with the pretty young nun. I thought that was abusing his ecclesiastical authority.'

'Perk of office,' Juma said cheerfully. 'The people expect it.'

'That may be so,' Geoff grumbled. 'But this time he's on notice. Any more undignified behaviour and I'm relegating him to Field Marshal. It's a much more suitable role for keeping an eye on things. Someone else can be the Bishop.'

'James could be a lady-in-waiting,' Juma proposed mischievously.

'I'll be the Admiral,' James said sharply.

'That's the spirit, mate,' Geoff laughed, and he called to Miriam for another bottle of wine.

# – SEVENTEEN –

Just on dusk the jet reached Madagascar's capital, Antananarivo. It skimmed over the hills studded with colonial mansions beyond which, sprawling across the island's central plain, lay the city's extensive slums.

Geoff drew James' attention to a spectacular complex of grandiose white buildings set among a protective park of high trees. 'President's palace,' he said scornfully. 'Typical disgraceful Third World corruption. This is one of the two or three poorest countries in the world. Tana, which is what the locals call the capital, is mainly slums. They'll blow you away, but the street life is something else.'

A few minutes later they landed at the airport, thirty miles to the south of the city and taxied past the arrival buildings to a hangar at the end of the runway.

'As you will see, no silly passport nonsense here,' Geoff remarked casually. '$5,000 a year to the chief immigration official and we come and go as we please. The same with all our tour locations, so there's no evidence our clients have ever been there.'

'You bloody hypocrite,' James erupted. 'You've been railing away about Third World corruption yet here you are encouraging it.'

'With cause, old man. There's corruption and corruption. Paying officials to do what they're supposed to do is OK if it facilitates efficiency. But paying them to do what they're not supposed to do – that's the immoral category.'

'But that's precisely what you're doing here,' James protested.

'Not so; that's if you think about it properly. In today's world of mass travel, passports are like diplomats; totally redundant and anachronistic. The only function both serve is to provide employment for screaming no-hopers. Passports purport to stop those they don't want from coming in but of course they fail at that. All they achieve is to make it irksome for the unwanted, and in the process stuff everyone else up. Our little gratuity promotes efficiency and convenience.'

'You've got a rationalisation for everything,' James grumbled.

'Your problem, James, is that you haven't come to terms with the modern world,' Geoff said impatiently. 'You still believe governments are useful and enhance life. Well, they do in part but in many respects their impact is largely negative. It's a multitude of vested interests, not logic, which keeps governments going at their current level of activity.'

'That's hugely overstating it,' James retorted.

'No ith not,' Juma intruded. 'Kanju would never have got off the gwound if the government had any say. I live in dwead of their awival on the scene.'

As the engines died Martin emerged from the flight deck, opened the door and lowered the steps. Immediately a dishevelled, pot-bellied, middle-aged man wearing sloppy, unpressed khaki trousers and a loose scarlet T-shirt burst into the cabin.

'Good evening, Your Gwace,' Juma greeted him.

'Oh fuck, not you again. More bloody trouble. I've enough bloody problems with this tour,' the newcomer complained angrily as he sank into a seat opposite Geoff and took a whisky from Miriam.

'This is John Hodge, our African State Tours director,' Geoff said. 'Meet James. He's coming on board.' Then he added sharply, 'What problems?'

'Problems, problems, I'm awash in fucking problems. First my ladies-in-bloody-waiting have buggered off with two Frenchmen to Mauritius for a week's debauchery, one of my court bloody jester dwarfs had his throat slit last night, those Madagascan airline arseholes have lost the Zambian brass bloody band's instruments and I'm fifty fucking foot-soldiers short because of rice harvesting.'

'So everything's under control then,' Geoff said lightly.

'Yeah, yeah. You can mock. It's not easy dealing with African savages.'

'Be weasonable,' Juma taunted. 'Wemember, we're not long out of the twees.'

Hodge glared at Juma as the four men disembarked and climbed into two waiting Mercedes, James travelling with Geoff. The forty-minute journey to the city's only modern hotel, the Hilton, left James wide-eyed. He gazed awestruck at the turbulent scenes of numerous vendors, tumble-down dwellings and makeshift shop-fronts. Bedraggled children played in the dirt among the multitude of hawkers and scrawny chickens scratching among the dust and rubble. Colourfully dressed women, erect as mannequins, threaded their way through the turmoil with laden baskets balanced on their heads. The car weaved a path among bullock-drawn carts loaded with firewood and ramshackle buses belching smoke and dangling passengers off their sides as, gears slipping and grinding, they lurched in fits and starts along the potholed road.

'This is fantastic,' James cried. 'I feel like I'm on the set of *Porgy and Bess*.'

'Great place,' Geoff said. 'Curiously enough it's still largely a secret and one of the few countries that are still unpolluted by mass tourism. You certainly won't see many Europeans in Tana apart from some business types, although God knows what they buy or sell. No one has any money here. At the airport you'll find the occasional bearded bird-watching dullard and his fat wife in tramping boots and shorts. They've been sold a line about the island's unique fauna – they disappear into the forests to watch silly bloody lemurs leaping about and that sort of rubbish so they're not a problem. It won't last of course,' he added ruefully. 'The State Tour business has only about another five years left and then the game will be up. We're simply making hay while it's still a goer.'

'I've been wondering about that,' James said, puzzled. 'Surely no matter how remote the place, when your Head of State has his street parade, there must be a risk of the odd European backpacker or tourist being there?'

'Quite right,' Geoff replied. 'But we have it covered. That's why we like to have all our administration staff in the parade, so among other things they can study the crowds. Everyone watches out for European faces and if they spot one they pull out their mobile phone and advise Jacques. He's Hodgie's odd-job man. Being French he's specially valuable as 95 per cent of the few visitors here are French. He sidles up to the European, engages in conversation, and naturally the subject of what the hell's going on arises. Jacques expresses surprise at the visitor's ignorance and tells them it's an "important traditional cultural event". That always does the trick. As I told you in Kenya, mention the word "culture" and you can get away with damn near anything. With a few exceptions the word "research" works nicely too.'

'Research? What do you mean research?' James asked, puzzled.

'Try it when we're home,' Geoff suggested. 'Do something outrageous. Don a white coat then tip a bucket of water over someone's child who's playing in a front garden. When the mother hangs out the window and asks what the hell you're playing at, wave a notebook and pen and bark "research" and I guarantee she'll apologise for troubling you. Probably bring the rest of her kids out for a drenching. It always works.'

'I'll take your word for it,' James laughed. He thought for a while. 'What about missionaries?' he asked. 'Aren't there lots of those in these sorts of places?'

'Have you ever met one?' Geoff asked. 'When it comes to gullibility they're in the vanguard. The same goes with the clergy, or at least the nuns. It's not just an Irish tradition to put dim daughters into nunneries. The European priests were potentially a worry, but over here they're mostly elderly and out of touch and anyway, once they spot our bishop in the procession they intuitively become obsequious. It's the principal reason we have a bishop in the entourage, otherwise his role is just to add a hierarchical element to the royal court. But basically we apply a simple test for the suitability of an African location. We confine tours to places where the locals only possess used clothing provided by western charities. As you'll see next week, nothing anyone's wearing actually fits them in the towns we're going to. On the other hand, in Tana there are quite a few people wearing clothes they actually bought new, so Tana's out as a tour location. It's a failsafe test. The only real problem we have is accommodation. It can be fairly wonky at times and not exactly what billionaires are accustomed to.'

At that moment the car stopped as a bullock cart lurched into its path. A smiling teenage girl thrust a tray of roasted corn cobs at James. 'My God, some of these girls are striking,' he enthused. 'But they've unusual features. I've never seen faces like these.'

'Fascinating history,' Geoff explained. 'Up to fifteen hundred years ago Madagascar was uninhabited. Then a great mob arrived from Sumatra.'

'What? Sumatra in Indonesia?'

'Correct. They sailed across the Indian Ocean; no one knows why. A few centuries later Africans arrived, and then over the past five hundred years there have been Portuguese, Dutch and our lot here, mainly pirates and other rogues. England's produced more than her share of scoundrels in the past. Then in the last century, up until independence in 1960, Madagascar was a French colony. Needless to say, throughout all of these invasions nature took its course and you're seeing the result, which, as you rightly observe, is very satisfactory. Appearances aside, they're also super people.'

'Why don't you use these girls at Kanju?' James suggested. 'They look great and it's a lot closer than Latin America.'

'We thought about that but it wouldn't work. Out of the question. They're too African to be suitable for Africa. They lack the all-important sassiness factor which our Kanju clientele react positively to. Latin girls begin swaying their hips from the moment they learn to walk. They're different here; more restrained. Look at their history. The Malagasy inherited from their Sumatran antecedents rice as their staple diet, an industrious culture and wood-carving skills. Wait till you see the royal carriages we had made here. They're nothing more than a bullock cart chassis and wooden wheels with a plywood body and 1950s Citroën car leather seats. They're painted gold and look fantastic. Total cost about $300. We've got a dozen in warehouses in all our Royal Tour locations. The Africans' contribution to the make-up here was to add animism and dark skins and the French lightened the colouring and contributed finer features. They gave them Catholicism as well which they've mixed in with their existing African spiritualism. The Malagasy are perfect material in a receptive sense for our royal tours but they'd be hopeless at Kanju. Too reserved. Still, as I said, it's a grand place as evidenced by the fact that Hodgie has chosen it for his headquarters. He could have picked anywhere, not even necessarily in Africa.'

Eventually they arrived at the Hilton where they were joined by Juma and Hodge at the reception desk. 'Take a look behind you,' Geoff suggested.

James turned and gazed at the lounge area. A dozen attractive girls were sitting elegantly in armchairs sipping on pretend drinks. 'My word they're knock-outs,' he gasped and quickly turned back, embarrassed as the girls smiled, acknowledging his attention.

'Hodgie knows most of them,' Geoff said. 'The hotel allows in a

131

few good-looking ones for the guests. We usually hire a batch if we have a tour with just a monarch or president and their wives don't come along. If the clients are on their own we offer a village virgin deflowering service. Our clients really lap that up. Some of these girls have been village virgins on half a dozen or more past tours.'

'They don't look too village virginy to me. Surely the client realises?'

'Never,' Geoff replied. 'Mind you, the girls are bloody good at it. They know the ropes: no make-up naturally, a simple wrap-around robe and lots of colourful beads to look the part; terrified cowering and lots of squealing and groaning and the following morning, quietly sobbing in a corner. We pay them well but I gather they hugely enjoy the role in the context of their usual situation. The important thing is the client. We charge them extra disbursements of $5,000 per virgin so it's a nice little money-spinner. Clifford deflowered six, or so he thought, on his first tour before his damned wife came on board and became addicted to being a queen. It's the same story with all of the wives. Hodgie had a go at convincing them that it's an important local tradition for visiting Heads of State to deflower village virgins and to refuse to do so is considered a great cultural insult and a gross breach of etiquette. But the wives are always totally unco-operative. It's typical of western insensitivity when dealing with the Third World.'

'Perhaps you could sell the wives on the research angle,' James teased.

Geoff laughed. 'Yeah, well, maybe deflowering could be an exception to the research rule.'

Finally, the receptionist handed over three keys. 'Everyone unpack then meet down here in fifteen minutes for a pre-dinner drink so we can map out the next few days,' Geoff instructed.

When they reconvened and after drinks had been served Geoff spoke, adopting a brisk, business-like tone James had not previously encountered. 'Right; I've been thinking about everything so here's the drill. Tomorrow I'll personally take over dealing with the airline. We've three days to locate the band's instruments so we'll assume success.'

'Bloody no-hopers,' Hodge muttered.

'We'll sort out two girls from the crop in here to be ladies-in-waiting,' Geoff continued. 'Preferably two who speak some English.

It's an important role and the Queen will become shitty if they're not in place. Tomorrow they can go to the warehouse for ball gown fittings and at the same time James can try on his admiral's outfit. There's plenty of time for any adjustments to be made. The outfits must be a good fit as it doesn't look right if the senior military personnel aren't up to scratch. Then James and Monster can spend the day training the girls. You know what's required, Monster; remaining constantly just behind Her Majesty, carrying her train when she moves and proper curtsying. Make sure they get that right. There's nothing worse than a clumsy curtsy so I want them up to speed. We won't worry about the murdered court jester; one's enough, and Their Majesties won't notice any difference between 350 and 400 soldiers. We'll space 'em out a bit.

'Before dinner Monster and James can select the ladies-in-waiting. They'll all want to be in it, but best to choose two who have been village virgins on previous tours as they know the score. Offer them $200 each seeing as it's an emergency. Go to it now as I want to have a chat with Hodgie about the rest of the planning.'

Juma and James rose and, wine glasses in hand, enthusiastically began moving round the lounge chatting up the girls. After they were out of earshot Geoff resumed.

'I don't know why you make such a song and dance about everything,' he scolded. 'Of course things go wrong. It's your job to handle such contingencies.'

'Yeah, you're right. I always get a bit edgy in the days just before each tour,' Hodge muttered. 'It's not bloody easy dealing with these black bastards. Clifford's OK though and not too demanding. He never complains, but his wife gives us hell if everything's not up to scratch.'

'Well relax. Now, let's go over everything. How's the dress rehearsal gone?'

'The same as bloody usual. Getting the stupid buggers to march in step is a nightmare. I kicked the shit out of them yesterday; laid out three and sacked another five. All the officers are bloody useless.'

'Well that raises another issue,' Geoff said firmly. 'I'm going to have to defrock you and relegate you to Field Marshal. It's much more appropriate for keeping an eye on things. You left a very bad impression brawling with the troops on the last tour. It was quite disgraceful behaviour from a bishop.'

133

'Jesus Christ, Geoff; you can't do that,' Hodge cried, a note of panic in his voice. 'I'm a bloody natural for the spiritual role. Why can't Juma take charge of the troops?'

'Because he's Lord High Executioner, that's why.'

'But that's perfect,' Hodge exclaimed triumphantly. 'Remember the last Royal here? The soldiers were bloody terrified of him and his axe. He'll have their respect once he threatens the bastards with a beheading.'

Geoff thought for a while then spoke.

'OK. I'll give you one last chance. No brawling, and watch the bad language; in fact, cut it out altogether. It ill behoves a bishop to be constantly uttering profanities. And lay off the young nuns. It's a poor show having your way with them and exploiting your clerical office. You can have one of the ladies-in-waiting. Now tell me. How's everything else going?'

Visibly relieved, Hodge lit a cigar and began a recital. 'The zoo elephant and four camels will go down to the encampment just outside Fianarosa on Saturday. The zoo's supplying their riders and the elephant's hay. We've done the uniform fittings for the riders. The bloody camels can eat grass.'

'How much?'

'I cut a deal for the whole shebang for $500 to the chief zookeeper. Remember this is our first run with animals here, and where we're going the locals have never seen an elephant or camel. The bastards could flee.'

'We'll take that risk. And the rest?'

'The bloody gorilla's fine, the royal carriages and thrones are in the Fiana warehouse and Jacques and the rest of the team are going down on Saturday to check everything. The tent city and mobile kitchens go tomorrow with the flags, coins, medals and bunting, and all the troops will be in place for a final dress rehearsal on Sunday. The horse floats for the cavalry go down on Saturday with the riders. That's a new one and should add to the quality of the procession. We've made them ceremonial flagstaffs with the Hamastan flag. Should look bloody good. I hired half a dozen horses and riders from the equestrian school here. Only cost $600.'

'Statues?'

'All in place under wraps.'

'OK. Run through the programme,' Geoff demanded.

'Their Majesties arrive at 1 p.m. on Sunday. The limo will pick them up and take them to the hotel where their outfits will be waiting for fitting with the seamstress, and we'll go over the procedures.'

'Managed a motorcycle escort?'

'Yeah. Cost $100 to the police captain. Six in front and four behind with sirens. The fee's a bit steep but it includes the return journey to the airport on Monday morning.'

'What are Their Majesties wearing?'

'The Queen wants to stay permanently in bloody ball gowns so we have four for this tour. Different ones for each day plus the evening banquet. The King's chosen the replica nineteenth-century Montenegro monarch's outfit from the uniform catalogue for daywear, and in the evening he's switching to the regalia King George the Fifth wore at his coronation. Personally, I think it's over the bloody top but his wife insisted. She's calling all the shots. All of you in full dress jet down to Fiana, leaving about ten on Monday morning. Their bloody Majesties will follow with me in the other jet ten minutes later and you'll greet them on arrival. We've organised jeeps down there as we need the limo for the clients here in Tana. Still, the Fiana airstrip's not far from the encampment.'

'On arrival there'll be the usual flag-raising and anthem ceremonies, then the King will inspect the troops on parade and decorate the Battalion Commander. A bloody good kick in the arse would be more appropriate if you ask me,' Hodge grumbled. 'The bastard's useless.'

'Never mind all of that,' Geoff snapped. 'Get on with it.'

'About 11.30 the parade into town will start. The mayor's declared a two-day public holiday so the entire population will be on the streets. I'm expecting about 65,000. Jacques will be dishing the flags out early that morning. I made the bloody mayor patch up all the potholes in the main drag; otherwise, I told him, the Royal Visit was off. They've spent the entire year's budget on it, so as you can see they're taking it bloody seriously.'

'Good show,' Geoff said. 'What's the order of the parade?'

'The bloody gorilla's going first, then the court jester, the elephant and the camels. After that come one hundred infantry plus drummers, then the cavalry, another hundred soldiers and drummers followed by the brass band, and in the middle the royal carriage with four footmen. It's a nice build-up before Their Majesties loom up, so the flag-waving should be fairly frenzied for them.

'Behind Their Majesties is the ladies-in-bloody-waiting carriage, and then in an open jeep come you and James as Field Marshal and Admiral. Juma told me in the car you're taking those roles. I'm glad you're here. It leaves more staff for other roles. Juma can bloody well walk, and he'll be followed by 150 soldiers.'

'How far does the parade travel?' Geoff asked. 'Remember, that's why I'm here, as it's our pioneer tour in this part of the island.'

'About two miles. We all end up just after midday at the town hall for the formal greeting ceremony, and the band will play the Madagascan and Hamastan national anthems. The mayor's staging a civic banquet then after that the mayor, a Turkish shopkeeper, the Indian hotel owner and a Mother Superior from the convent cop medals from His Majesty. Clifford wanted to knight a few bastards but I knocked that on the head. He doesn't seem to understand it's meaningless here. He likes bloody knighting and did a swag of them on his Royal Visit to India.'

'Then what?'

'While the banquet's going on inside, the troops will have half an hour off for lunch. The band will play a concert outside. It will be the first one those buggers down there have ever heard so it should keep the town square jammed.

'After the banquet Their Majesties emerge with the mayor, dish out the medals and unveil the statue of His Majesty, then we wrap up with the execution and bugger off to the Indian's hotel. It's rough but it's the only tolerable place in town and the food's good. We've taken over the entire joint free of charge, including meals and liquor and the reciprocal royal banquet in return for the Indian copping the medal. The little bastard was so bloody thrilled I was going to insist he chuck in one of his daughters for the night until I saw them. They're all fat with moustaches. It's a bloody disgrace.'

'Well just remember – lay off the young nuns,' Geoff commanded. 'Why's the Turk on the awards list?'

'No one's got any money down there,' Hodge grumbled. 'The best I could get from him is to feed the troops for four days in return for the Hamastan Medal of Honour. Can't say I'm pleased about it. It devalues our awards if we dish 'em out too cheaply.'

'What's the hotel Indian receiving?' Geoff asked anxiously. 'Not the Medal of Honour I hope.'

'Christ, no,' Hodge exclaimed, visibly shocked. 'He's getting the Hamastan Service Medal, second class.'

'Yes,' Geoff mused. 'It's good we have graduated honours but you still mustn't let them go too cheap to these commercial types, specially wogs. Make 'em pay plenty. They're not like the Mother Superior, who I don't doubt has well and truly earned hers. Anyway, what's next?'

'At eight that night there's the reciprocal Royal Banquet for the civic leaders. I'll need you and James present in full dress uniform as I've had trouble scraping up suitable local worthies. They're a bloody motley lot down there. To keep the crowds at bay I've delegated a hundred soldiers outside the hotel, and Juma can prance about and scare the shit out of them as well. Can't trust the bloody soldiers not to stuff up.'

'Entertainment at the Royal Banquet?' Geoff quizzed.

'The court bloody jester performs with the gorilla. That'll be enough. They like that sort of crap.'

'The video cameraman organised?' Geoff asked.

'Yeah. He's one bugger I can rely on. We get no complaints on that score.'

'Tuesday?' Geoff demanded.

'Another full procession through town to chuck out the coins then everyone down to Ambarosita where we repeat the whole performance; the parade, civic lunch and medals. That afternoon the bloody local school's putting on a gymnastics and choral performance for Their Majesties, then we wrap the day up with the public hanging. We'll all take the night off and motor back to Fiana to stay in the hotel. There's nothing suitable in Ambarosita. The troops and cavalry will set up their tents just out of town, so on the final day we drive back early and join up with the troops and the rest of the mob. There's another bloody parade to dish out the coins, then the Queen opens the new medical clinic Clifford's paying for, after which His Majesty unveils the Queen's statue and that's it. Their Majesties piss off back to Fiana and fly home.'

'Hang on a minute,' Geoff exclaimed. 'What about floggings? I thought Clifford's wife was big on those.'

The Australian sighed, 'I can't squeeze them in. I warned Clifford they'd have to go, so no doubt he'll cop it from his wife. It's a bloody nuisance too. We're going to have to pay the flogees $5 each as I

137

promised them $25. Sets a bad example giving them something for nothing.'

'What's the problem?' Geoff demanded. 'You've got plenty of time. You know how much the Queens enjoy floggings.'

'That's the bloody problem,' the Australian replied. 'We haven't got plenty of time. Clifford rang last week to say he now had to fly back to Washington leaving Fiana no later than 3 p.m. Apparently he's Chairman of a Presidential Commission promoting family bloody values. He says he has a Senate Committee reporting session set down for the following day. Clifford claims it wasn't due until Friday, then suddenly he was notified of a two-day earlier starting date. Still, they should be happy with the executions.'

'OK,' Geoff said. 'Pity about the floggings but it sounds like everything else is in hand. I want you to carefully monitor the new features carefully. There's no point wasting money on elephants and cavalry if there's no good effect. When's the next tour?'

'I've got Lucas, the billionaire Californian software whiz, in three weeks' time on a Presidential. We're going south. That's as much as I can put through Madagascar this year. After that there's a month's lull then we're off to Mauritania for a Royal with Bramington and his wife; you know, the Texas oil heirs. They did a Royal last year in India. The bastard's demanding a 21-gun salute so I'm going to have to organise a bloody cannon. Christ knows where I'll find one in Mauritania.'

'Extras?'

'Not bad,' Hodge replied. 'Lucas has bought one obelisk, a beheading, two public floggings and nine village virgin deflowerings. He wants three each night so I'll have to rally up nine different tarts. Still, it's another $275,000 in the kitty. Bramington's bloody wife won't let him do deflowerings. Claims it's immoral but she's real keen on the executions so we've sold them two beheadings, a hanging and a statue which is another $400,000 to help keep the cat fed. I offered them floggings but they didn't bite so I'm throwing one in free to whet their appetite for future tours.'

'New territory; how's that going?'

'It's bloody difficult,' Hodge grumbled. 'I shot over and had a look at Botswana a couple of weeks back but there's too many bloody tourists. Central Africa's out. Bloody aid workers are falling over themselves everywhere after the civil war. I'll take a look at Burkina

Faso after the Mauritania tour but I'm not optimistic. Don't forget we're breaking in new territory in July with a Presidential to Gambia. I'm bloody confident about that one, and I think Guinea-Bissau could be a starter. I'll have a look next month. How are you going on that front?'

'There's still a few nooks and crannies here and there,' Geoff replied. 'We've located three small Caribbean island states which look promising. Problem is we'd be pushing it to get more than two tours a year out of them. And then there's the racket factor; incessant drumbeating and bawling passing itself off as music. That rubbish is all very well for the cheap tourist market but it will drive our clients mad so we're not absolutely certain about those spots. We think the Caribbean coastal strip of Honduras could be a goer. There's a big enough town called Ceiba and a couple of nearby smaller ones. And there's still Bangladesh waiting to break in which should be a winner. But that brings to mind something I want to raise with you. Brasch has come up with a new idea. He reckons there's about five countries in West Africa which are all dictatorships and all broke, where we could buy the President's co-operation for $100,000 a tour. I want you to check that out, starting with Liberia. We won't need to stay away from the capital where the embassies and western commercial types are because if we've got the actual President participating then we control everything.'

'Jesus, I don't know about that,' Hodge said thoughtfully. 'Nothing happens in those places. They're hardship postings for embassy personnel so they tend to be dumping grounds for wet buggers who take everything seriously. I met lots of them at functions when I was in the judging game in Malawi. Tedious little statistics-quoting pricks with thin ostrichy necks and spectacles and unbelievably ugly wives, always prattling a lot of crap about African culture. Have a full street parade turn-out and those bastards will be writing reports back home about it. They've got nothing else to do.'

'Brasch has thought of that,' Geoff said. 'He claims no one ever reads embassy reports sent from dead-beat countries, but even if they did our Royal Tours wouldn't be out of line with the usual nonsense which constantly goes on in them, so no one in Washington or London or Paris would take any notice. Nowhere else counts. Anyway, it's certainly worth looking at. Brasch believes we could lift our fees if we've got the actual President hosting the tour. He's suggested a lot of new twists that could be added – you know; State dinners, receiving lines, ceremonial signing of peace treaties, free trade agreements, exchanging of decorations, signing joint space research projects and whaling ban agreements – the sort of rubbish Heads of State like doing.'

'Yeah, maybe it's not a bad idea,' Hodge said as he pondered the concept. 'It would certainly make things a bloody sight easier dealing at that level. On reflection, Brasch is probably right. The host Presidents would be rapt to have showy tours from visiting Heads of State. They'd see it as enhancing their prestige with the locals. But hang on; it might be the end of executions. We wouldn't want to give those away. I'm averaging fifteen a year; that's a million and a half dollars extra in the pot.'

'Brasch has thought of that too,' Geoff replied. 'All we need to do is leave the capital for one day – visit the hinterland inspecting crops or leper colonies or whatever they've got on offer. The executions could be that day's highlight, nicely out of sight.'

'Yeah,' the Australian mused. 'I think Brasch may be on to something. With actual Presidential co-operation we could step up productivity. At $100,000 a visit the bloody Presidents would want as many as possible. We could do one a month, which we can't get away with anywhere else. That would be serious money in the President's pocket. It would be bloody helpful to the local economy too as the Presidents might stop siphoning off the meagre State funds and World Bank grants. With that incentive they'd declare three-day public holidays with each tour and order the locals on to the streets for cheering purposes. But what about statues? We don't want to lose those. These places would become cluttered with them if we had a monthly tour.'

'Brasch has covered that too,' Geoff replied. 'Claims those sort of Mickey-Mouse capitals always have large avenues leading up to a grandiose presidential palace. It would add to their grandeur if they're lined with statues, and their leaders are always keen on anything which does that. I don't see it as a problem. Look into it as soon as possible.'

'How's Brasch going anyway?' Hodge enquired.

'OK. We're keeping him around 440 at the moment.'

'Well, shit; you surprise me,' the Australian responded. 'I thought you said he performed best nearer the 500 mark.'

'He does, but we can't risk losing him.'

'I ran across a Bulgarian here a couple of weeks ago,' Hodge said, changing the subject. 'He flogs second-hand bulldozers to Third World countries. Told me he'd been in Mongolia, and from how he described it, I reckon it'd be worth a bloody look.'

'No, no,' Geoff replied. 'Too cold. Places like that, you'd get the locals out for the procession but there's no fervour. People in cold places are always dour. Remember, that was the problem with the Papal Visits in the Andes. It's the fervour and frenzy the clients want. You must have coloured people. Nothing worse than a passive parade no matter how many are on the street. Our clients want adulation and hysteria.'

At that moment Juma and James loomed up with two happy girls in tow who greeted Hodge warmly. 'Good picks,' he said. 'They've been bloody virgins several times before so they know the score,' and he rose and led the party into the dining room for dinner.

# – EIGHTEEN –

A wave of panic hit James when he woke on Monday morning and contemplated the day ahead, despite Geoff's reassurances the previous evening after he had confessed to his trepidation.

'Everyone has butterflies the first time,' Geoff had assured him. 'Don't worry about it. I promise you'll be into the swing of things after the first half hour, specially once the cheering starts. Remember your role is fairly passive. Just stay a few paces behind Their Majesties, nice and erect and hand on sword. I'll be alongside you all the time so pick up your cues from me. Believe me, you're going to love it. Look at Monster. He's awfully busy at Kanju but he never passes up the opportunity of participating in a Royal.'

James thought back to the past three days in Antananarivo. It had been a non-stop riot. On Friday he and Juma had begun the day with Nicole and Simone, the chosen ladies-in-waiting, at the Alceides warehouse. He had tried on the dashing white admiral's uniform, with its epaulettes and gold-braided cap, and following some waistband tightening by the seamstress, admired himself in the full-length mirror. His delight had been compounded when Juma handed him his ceremonial sword, which slotted into a loop on the right side of his uniform.

'The cowect position is to have your wight hand loosely over the hilt at all times,' Juma instructed.

James took up the posture in front of the mirror to acclamation from the girls and his chest swelled. He considered his long blond hair. It matched the white uniform but it wasn't quite right. Not sufficiently military, he concluded, and resolved to have it cut short at the Hilton's hairdressing salon.

Then followed the girls' fittings. Excitedly they had pulled the

142

gowns from the racks until, after half an hour had elapsed and they were still undecided, Juma intervened and chose for them. Quickly they stripped to their knickers and pulled on the gowns. The seamstress noted some adjustments then the girls undressed and donned their street clothes and with a great deal of laughter, they practised their curtsying for an hour under the men's instruction.

Shortly after midday the four of them had left the warehouse and hailed a battered old taxi. They had driven back past the Hilton, round the polluted central city lake, then spluttered up the hill to the town centre's main avenue where they pulled up outside a faded colonial-era hotel. Inside they climbed a sweeping stairway before emerging on to a balcony restaurant that overlooked the city market. James had gazed fascinated at the teeming street-scene below and the array of brightly coloured cheap imported plastic goods. However, he'd quickly retreated horror-struck when confronted by hordes of ragged beggars with imploring outstretched hands after he had dropped a Malagasy 5,000-franc note to the first woebegone ragamuffin who had appeared.

By late afternoon all four were tipsy and in high spirits. They tumbled down the stairs, fended off the beggars, found a taxi and drove back to the warehouse. The girls' gowns were tried on again and fitted perfectly. Once more they had hailed a dilapidated taxi and James sat in the front with Nicole on his lap while Juma lay spread-eagled over the rear seat holding Simone sprawled across him.

Back at the hotel they had found Geoff in a benevolent mood. After some hours of shouting and threats, he reported, the band's instruments had been located in Zanzibar and were already on their way via Dar Es Salaam to be delivered to the warehouse on Saturday.

The girls had stayed the night, then on Saturday morning escorted James and Juma around the city. Followed for the first ten minutes by a jerky-limbed, drooling madman, the foursome had wandered wide-eyed through the teeming Antananarivo shanty-town. Overwhelmed with shock, it was only after an hour had passed that James became accustomed to the squalor and could relax. The narrow, crumbling cobblestone alleys with their open fetid drains were lined with rough adobe brick hovels, their ramshackle upper portions comprising rotting unpainted timber planks, scraps of tin and sometimes even sacking, roofed over by rusted corrugated-iron sheeting. Vendors squatted before a single battered shoe, a pair of tarnished spoons, an ancient teapot and other such items, inconceivably of any value. Underfoot numerous children, dogs and chickens formed a lively synthesis as they wallowed in the dirt. Laden bullock-drawn carts patiently plodded through the disarray.

Blind beggars played harmonicas and accordions, knife-sharpeners wended their way through the congestion with their bell-tinkling, whetstone contraptions, bloodshot eyes peered out from dingy bars, open-air butchers presented slabs of blackened and fly-strewn meat, trestle tables displayed rows of tiny silver fish and scribes sat patiently on three-legged stools awaiting commissions to write letters or complete government forms. Faded and peeling plaster-walled churches occupied many street corners, bundles of cruelly leg-bound ducks lay resignedly on their sides in the dust; it was like a vast open-air junkyard and only the multitude of squatting fruit vendors and bread salesmen, with their freshly baked long french loaves, seemed to offer saleable items. A cacophony of noises – peddlers' urgings, laughter, shouting, dogs barking, hens squawking, children's cries and blaring radios – made conversation difficult.

Eventually they retreated to a more amenable part of the city. The girls led the way to a Madagascan restaurant where for three hours they dined and drank local wines until all were mildly tipsy.

The bill when finally presented totalled 110,000 Madagascan francs which equated to $22. Juma attempted to pay with US dollars, a gesture that was received with suspicious hostility, so James tendered three 50,000 Madagascan franc notes. He received a saucer of change comprising three banknotes and a single coin. He picked up the coin and studied it. 'Bloody hell. Look at this, Monster,' he exclaimed. 'It's one of ours, isn't it?'

On one side the coin bore a relief of a crowned male head and the inscription 'King Ronald the First – Kingdom of Melani'. James recognised Ron Brierley, the Australian financier. The reverse side displayed a rampant lion with the date 1998 and round its edge the words 'Five Melanis'.

Juma inspected the coin. 'I was on this Woyal,' he said excitedly. 'We were down in the south. That was when Hodge disgwaced himself with the nun.'

'Hang on,' James said. 'Let's see what value they're placing on it,' and he picked up the Malagasy banknotes. There were one 5,000 and two 10,000 franc notes.

'Well, I'll be damned,' he exclaimed. 'Geoff's right. They're valuing it at 15,000 Malagasy francs. That's three US dollars. It's bloody amazing.' He pocketed the coin, leaving the banknotes as a tip, and the party returned to the hotel.

On Sunday morning Geoff bailed James up while he was sunbathing with Nicole beside the hotel swimming pool. 'The clients arrive today. I know you'll find it awkward but I want to meet in the foyer at four and take you both with Simone to their suite for introductions.'

'What's awkward about that?' James had asked.

'Because you're to bow slightly and if you have cause to speak address Clifford as Your Majesty. The girls will only be introduced to the Queen. They mustn't speak. I want Nicole in a respectable dress if she possesses such a thing. Also, a hat. Women always look demure and innocent in hats. We'll be telling the clients they're trainee nuns borrowed from a convent. They curtsy then back off studying the ground. After that I'll whisk you all away.'

'I'll feel a bloody idiot, Geoff,' James complained.

'I know. It's not easy at first. But I promise you will quickly get used to it and it will actually make your job this week easier. Don't forget, the Cliffords are forking out a million dollars for this excursion. They're entitled to expect what they're paying for.'

'I thought royal visits were $600,000,' James queried.

'They are. That's the flat rate. As you will see, the Cliffords have bought some extras. I'm keeping those as a surprise for you.'

In the event the client meeting had passed quickly. As instructed, James had bowed, shaken hands with the King then stepped back two paces. Geoff had then brought forward Nicole who, head subdued, had curtsied to Clifford's wife, and Simone had followed. The Queen glanced at both haughtily, sniffed and looked away. No word was exchanged, and Geoff quickly ushered them from the room.

Now was D-day. James rose, showered and shaved then went downstairs for breakfast where he found Geoff and Juma. 'I want you in full dress uniform down here precisely at nine,' Geoff said. 'The limo will be outside so we want to be away quickly, attracting as little attention as possible. Make sure you call the service desk to have your bag in the car by quarter to nine. It doesn't look right to see an admiral carrying a suitcase. When we reach Fianarosa the pilots will take our bags to the hotel as we'll be swinging into action right away.

In public you and I will address each other as Field Marshal and Admiral, and you will address Hodgie as Your Grace. As I said yesterday, you'll find it easy after a time.'

At 8.40 James called the service desk and a few minutes later there was a tap on his door. When he opened it the bellboy's eyes widened and he quickly stepped backwards and bowed deeply. James pointed to his bag and the bellboy entered the room, cringing. He took the bag and, head bent, retreated from the room then scurried away.

At two minutes to nine, his white-gloved hand resting on the hilt of his sword, James strolled down the corridor to the lifts and was mildly disappointed to find it empty. When he emerged on the ground floor two guests who were waiting for the lift quickly stepped aside, adopting a respectful deference. Conscious of all eyes on him James strode across the foyer, the bell captain snapped to attention and four doormen made a fuss of opening the doors and stood, heads bowed, as he sailed past.

At the foot of the steps stood the waiting limo, flying the Hamastan standard from its bonnet. James felt an absurd tinge of nationalistic pride. Two of the doormen rushed to open the rear door. Inside the limo Juma sat in the front passenger seat while Geoff was in the rear in his Field Marshal's uniform, a swagger stick on his lap. A minute later they were on their way.

'Tell you what,' James said, 'I look a damn sight more impressive than you.' Then he started. 'Bloody hell,' he exclaimed. 'Do I get any of those?' For in a neat row on Geoff's chest lay a row of medals.

'Not yet, old man,' Geoff laughed. 'I don't want you pulling rank. On this trip I'm the Commander-in-Chief.' He showed James his medals, which were all from previous tours he had participated in. On one James recognised the head of one of his former New York office's major clients, Albert Castillo, the Californian banana tycoon. The inscription read 'Albert V – Emperor of Mythenia'.

Forty minutes later they reached the airport, passed through some high gates and crossed the tarmac to where both Alceides jets waited with their steps extended. The limousine pulled up, the chauffeur leapt out and stood at attention holding James' door open before skipping round the back to the two doors on the other side. James climbed the steps slowly, adopting what he considered to be an appropriate solemnity as befitting his station.

He entered the cabin then shrieked and fell backwards against Geoff for inside, facing the doorway, sat an enormous gorilla.

'For Christ's sake, James,' Geoff muttered as he pushed him back inside. This time James noticed that the gorilla was reading a book and had a cup of coffee beside him.

'Meet James,' Geoff said. 'This is Claude, one of Hodgie's assistants. He's the gorilla on each trip. Vital role in Madagascar. Even more frightening than Juma to the locals. We mostly use him for crowd control.'

The gorilla rose and extended a huge paw which James shook nervously. 'How do you do?' the gorilla greeted him in a French accent as Miriam appeared with a coffee pot and mugs.

James collapsed into a seat, took his coffee from Miriam, and shortly afterwards they were off. Ten minutes later the landscape changed and James marvelled at the spectacular beauty below. Rolling, parched brown hills encrusted with massive boulders and rock faces extended into the distance. Rivers, sparkling in the morning sun, wound their way down the valleys which were dotted with clusters of double-storey tile-roof houses surrounded by lush rice paddies.

'Great countryside,' Geoff said. 'Terrific climate too. We should seriously consider another golf course here. It's only a few hours from Johannesburg. It's a question of locating a suitable owner.'

'Pissing in the wind,' Juma said adamantly. 'It's all in small parcels.'

'That can't be right,' Geoff retorted. 'There are tea and coffee plantations and in recent years they've started wineries. Super grape country and the wines are not too bad. I'll get Hodgie on to it.'

'Wains non-stop four months of the year,' Juma countered then he rose and retreated to the bathroom with his bag. A few minutes later he emerged. 'How's this, chaps?' he enquired.

Juma was stripped to the waist. He wore a black mask over his eyes, black leggings and calf-high black boots. In his right hand he held a six-foot-long axe.

'Jesus Christ,' James started. 'What next?'

'Lord High Executioner,' Juma proclaimed. 'Scares the cwap out of the locals.'

'Yes,' Geoff said. 'But this time we don't want any of that. Just scare the crap out of the army. I'm sick to death of Hodgie moaning about them.'

Miriam returned and topped up their coffee mugs. 'What about Miriam?' James asked. 'Does she play a role?'

Miriam giggled. 'She's bloody useless,' Geoff replied. 'She did a lady-in-waiting once in an emergency and made a right old cock-up of it. No dignity whatsoever. Waving to the crowds, laughing and carrying on. The Queen cut up very nasty. Now she just watches the parade.'

A few minutes later they scudded across Fianarosa's airstrip, braking violently before shuddering to a halt. 'Like everywhere they're trying to create a tourist trade,' Geoff explained. 'This airstrip is hardly used. There's a national park nearby and it was built in anticipation of tourists. The runway's about fifty yards too short for us. We can land and take off but it's always a rough affair. Now we wait for Their Majesties.'

The party descended from the jet and on the ground found five jeeps, all flying the Hamastan flag from their bonnets. The drivers snapped to attention and saluted.

'Piss off you two,' Geoff said and the Lord High Executioner and the gorilla climbed into one of the jeeps and departed. A few minutes later the jeep returned.

Twenty minutes passed then suddenly the other Alceides jet whistled across the sky, wheeled around and began its descent. It screeched across the tarmac, tyres smoking as the pilots braked hard, then at the end of the runway it turned and taxied slowly back to the waiting party.

'This is it,' Geoff said. 'Just don't forget. Follow my cue and lay it on in truckloads.'

The jet pulled up and the engines gradually slowed then stopped. The door opened and the King appeared at the top of the steps and stood for a few seconds, surveying the scene. He wore a lurid medal and braid be-decked uniform divided by a scarlet sash across his chest and his right hand rested loosely over an emerald-encrusted sword at his side.

A fanfare of trumpets hailed his arrival. James turned and saw two black trumpeters, their eyes and cheeks bulging, dressed in Regency-era style with white lace at their necks and wrists, while below their instruments hung banners emblazoned with the Hamastan coat of arms.

'Come on,' Geoff hissed. James faltered then caught up with him and the two marched rigidly to the jet's steps, taking up positions opposite each other at the bottom.

Regally the King descended. Geoff snapped into a fixed salute and James followed suit. The Queen, in an Elizabeth the First replica gown and wearing a jewel-studded coronet, now emerged. From the corner of his eye James observed Nicole and Simone, dressed in their ball gowns and tiaras, descend solemnly behind her. As the Queen stepped on to the tarmac the two ladies-in-waiting dipped and gathered up the corners of her trailing robe.

'Stay,' Geoff hissed, for now came Hodge in full bishop's regalia, a mitre on his head and holding a gold shepherd's crook in one hand and a large Bible in the other. He winked at James as he passed. 'That's the fucking caper, mate,' His Grace muttered encouragingly.

The party moved towards the jeeps. Four black footmen, like the trumpeters dressed in Regency-era knee-breeches, buckled shoes and high-horned wigs, emerged and held open the vehicles' doors.

Their Majesties climbed slowly into the first jeep, the ladies-in-waiting into the second, Geoff and James entered the third, and the Bishop and two footmen the fourth. The remaining two footmen and the trumpeters piled into the last one and the procession of jeeps, each with a white-gloved and uniformed driver, proceeded slowly out of the airport.

The convoy headed south and a minute later spun off the road on to a firm grassy plain. They rounded a foothill and there to one side lay a 200-strong tent city, while spread across the plain waiting in formation was the Hamastanian army.

'Jesus,' James muttered. 'That's bloody impressive, Geoff.'

'Told you we do it well,' Geoff said smugly as they climbed out of the jeep. Before them waited the ornately decorated elephant and the camels, all with uniformed riders, and behind them stood the twelve mounted cavalry riders, ten carrying lances, while two others held erect standards bearing the Hamastanian coat of arms. Spread across the field in formation were three hundred uniformed soldiers all holding rifles across their chests. They wore blue vests, scarlet Napoleonic-era hats with ostrich feather plumage, white leggings and black calf-length boots.

Another fifty soldiers bearing drums on their fronts waited to one side. On the other side of the parade ground the eighteen-man Zambian brass band, now reconnected with their instruments and dressed in bright scarlet uniforms, stood stiffly in formation. In front of them were the gorilla, the Lord High Executioner and the remaining court jester dwarf, wearing a blue satin tunic, red tights and a tassled fez.

As the convoy halted the footmen leapt from the rear jeep and rushed forward to open the doors. Their Majesties, followed by the ladies-in-waiting, descended and took up positions before a high flagpole in front of the parade.

'Quick, James,' Geoff hissed and the two fell in slightly behind the royal couple and stood at attention. The Bishop moved alongside the ladies-in-waiting.

A Battalion Commander now marched forward from the ranks, wheeled and in a stentorian bellow roared, 'Men of the Royal Hamastanian Foreign Legion Reserve. Three cheers for Their Majesties, King Andrew the Third and Queen Maureen of Hamastan. Hip, hip ...'

'Hooray!' bellowed the army.

'Hip, hip ...'

'Hooray!'

'Hip, hip ...'

'Hooray!'

Instantly the Zambian band broke into 'Men of Harlech'.

'Hamastanian national anthem,' Geoff whispered as the royal entourage and the army stood erect in the warm morning sun while a soldier slowly raised the Hamastan flag.

When the band finished Geoff hissed, 'Follow me and do as I do,' and he set off on a rigid, jerky march, his swagger stick under his arm. His hand on his sword, James fell in behind. They proceeded ten paces then stopped. 'Turn,' Geoff commanded, and they wheeled round. From the front of the standing army the Battalion Commander, sword pointing skywards in front of his chest, goose-stepped forward and halted before them.

'Salute,' Geoff instructed, and the Commander, Admiral and Field Marshal saluted one another.

'In a straight line turn,' Geoff ordered and the three spun round, marched towards the King and saluted him again.

The King casually returned the salute then stepped forward and the battalion inspection began. The party proceeded slowly down the front ranks, the Commander, his sword erect against his chest, beside the King with Geoff and James following behind. James was thoroughly enjoying himself. At the end of the line they turned, then they inspected the next seven rows. When all were done they returned to their original position.

The band now broke into 'White Christmas' while the troops remained at attention.

'Bastards,' Geoff muttered. 'Bloody limited repertoire.'

When the band finished a liveried white-gloved footman, holding before him a velvet-lined tray on which lay the Hamastan Order of Merit, the crossed swords medal, marched towards the King.

The King took the medal, the footman retreated backwards, and now the Commander goose-stepped forward, saluted and stood at attention. The King pinned the medal on his tunic and uttered a few congratulatory remarks. The Commander snapped another salute, rigidly retreated three paces backwards, saluted again, wheeled about and bawled, 'Battalion. From the front, quick march,' and the parade was under way.

'We're about three minutes from the city,' Geoff whispered. 'We ride in the jeep two behind the royal carriage. The ladies-in-waiting are in front of us.'

An open carriage ornately painted in gold and drawn by four white horses with scarlet-feathered plumage on their heads emerged from behind the tents and pulled up in front of Their Majesties. A footman held open the door as first the King and then the Queen entered the carriage. The footman placed a crown on the King's head then joined the other three footmen in their positions, one on each corner of the coach.

A smaller version of the same gilt carriage, drawn by a pair of horses, now pulled up behind the royal carriage. One of the jeep drivers stepped forward and held the doors open as the ladies-in-waiting climbed in.

The gorilla, elephant, court jester, camels, fifteen drummers and the mounted lancers, their Hamastanian banners erect, set off first, with a hundred soldiers marching behind them. The band struck up 'Swanee River' as it joined the procession behind the first wave of soldiers. Then came the royal carriage followed by the ladies-in-waiting, and James and Geoff clambered into their jeep and joined the parade behind them.

James looked behind, just in time to observe the Bishop boxing his driver's ears with his Bible as he climbed into his jeep. He said nothing.

# – NINETEEN –

'So; how do you like it?' Geoff enquired casually as the procession joined the road.

'It's bloody marvellous,' James cried excitedly. 'Now I understand completely.'

'As you can see, the King and Queen are old hands and know the ropes, but you ain't seen nothing yet. By tonight you'll appreciate why Monster and I always take part in the Royals when we can spare the time. We lay it on a bit but I think Hodgie has it about right for this market and location. It's a fine line, the divide between impressive grandeur and circus frivolity.'

At that moment the band launched into 'The Flower of Scotland' as the first faint sounds of the cheering crowds ahead wafted into earshot. The procession rounded a corner then crossed a bridge and they found themselves on the outskirts of the city. Ahead could be seen thousands of people lining the streets and very soon they were among them.

The band now began 'The Skye Boat Song'. Suddenly they were awash in a sea of waving Hamastanian flags, joyous black faces and flashing white teeth, twenty deep on each side of the street. Hamastanian gold and blue bunting stretched across the road between the buildings into the distance. The sky was filled with flowers thrown from the packed balconies. James noticed a bevy of nuns drop to their knees and cross themselves as the royal carriage passed.

'Discreet waving's in order,' Geoff roared above the cheering. James raised a white-gloved hand and affecting an appropriate solemnity, somewhat pompously acknowledged the crowds.

Stretched across the street between the city's two tallest buildings, each of three levels, extended the welcoming banner James had last seen in the Romanian factory. From every window cheering, Hamastanian flag-waving figures distracted from the buildings' ramshackle façades.

Children were held above their parents' heads to see the royal couple while bedraggled small boys ran excitedly alongside the procession. An elderly man caught James' eye, genuflected and respectfully removed his hat. James acknowledged him with a casually dismissive wave. Many of the older ladies were still dabbing their eyes as James' jeep reached them, overcome with emotion at having seen the royal couple.

The dissonant noise and excitement was now at such a level that the band could barely be heard but James detected the faint strains of 'Danny Boy' above the roar of the crowd, the cries of 'Vive Le Roi' and the methodical thumping from the drummers spread along the procession. He turned and looked behind him, just in time to witness the Bishop's massive enrobed posterior jerk skywards as Hodge lunged over the back of his jeep and cracked two out-of-step soldiers' heads with his Bishop's staff. As before, James held his silence.

Geoff leant across. 'You can see why the gorilla has to march at the front,' he bellowed. 'The locals are terrified of it, otherwise we'd come to a complete halt. Claude clears a path for the procession.'

'Is it always like this?' James shouted back.

'Always,' Geoff bawled, grinning.

Emboldened, James blew a kiss at a pretty girl who clasped both hands to her heart and swooned against her female companion. The thought crossed his mind that only three weeks earlier he had been stuck at a desk in London, engaged in a daily tedium of polite telephone earnestness, and now events had transpired so that he was riding in a jeep in a scruffy run-down city in the heart of Madagascar, dressed as an admiral of a non-existent nation, being cheered by tens of thousands of people. The surrealistic absurdity of it all, and the thought of Jane's outrage if she had known, delighted him and he began to laugh until his body shook and tears ran down his face.

The roofs of the buildings were crowded with waving cheering figures and as James, still rocking with barely controllable mirth, scanned the scene, he started and grabbed Geoff's arm. 'Christ, it's an assassin,' he roared as he directed Geoff's attention to a rooftop figure pointing a barrel at the royal coach.

'Relax,' Geoff bawled back. 'It's only Jacques,' whereupon the

Frenchman fired and the sky was filled with confetti which floated down over the royal carriages.

They approached a large jacaranda tree dotted with several dozen ragged boys among its branches. James observed one, overzealously waving, tumble from the foliage on to the heads of the crowd below. Faint snatches of 'The Toreadors' Song' from *Carmen* could now be heard over the roar of the crowd as the band worked through its repertoire. They passed a special roped-off section where invalids in wheelchairs and cripples on crutches waited and again James turned in time to observe the Bishop rise and solemnly bless them, as tears of gratitude ran down the faces of the inflicted.

For almost an hour they bathed in the mass adulation then suddenly the procession turned into a square at the far end of which lay the incongruous neoclassical town hall. Its main entrance was flanked by twin Corinthian columns while from its rooftop drooped Madagascan and Hamastanian flags.

The first wave of soldiers had already formed up on each side of the square to hold back the crowds, aided by the gorilla who pranced along their ranks, the people, with a caterwaul of shrieks, falling back in a flurry of collapsing bodies as it passed. A crescendo of church bells rang out and continued peeling as the royal carriage rumbled across the cobblestoned paving.

At the top of the town hall steps waited the mayor and other local dignitaries. The royal carriage pulled up and the liveried footmen descended. As two held open the carriage door for Their Majesties the others worked their way along the vehicles, first opening the ladies-in-waiting's door, then Geoff and James' and finally the Bishop's. The party took up their positions, with the Battalion Commander and four officers behind the royal couple, as the mayor, a shrivelled, elderly black in a shabby purple crimplene suit at least two sizes too large, flappingly descended the steps. He was followed by his gargantuan wife who was wearing a pink 1950s-vintage ball gown. At the bottom of the steps the mayor bowed deeply to Their Majesties then introduced the mayoress who, despite her enormous bulk, managed to semi-curtsy in an elephantine implosion. Then the official party solemnly ascended the steps to the town hall landing where gold thrones beneath a large gold-tasselled awning awaited them. Their Majesties were duly enthroned, the King now holding a

154

gold sceptre in his right hand, and Geoff, James, the ladies-in-waiting, the Hamastanian army officers and the Bishop fell in behind them.

James looked out at the scene before him. The elephant, the camels, the cavalry, the Zambian band and the dwarf – who to the delight of the crowd was performing a series of backward flips – had now formed at the foot of the steps, exactly as on the parade ground an hour earlier. The remaining soldiers were still marching into the square, now jammed with over 20,000 cheering citizens.

James observed Juma, his axe poised menacingly, pacing up and down one side of the wall of soldiers and striking fear into the citizenry, as was the gorilla, working the other side.

The mayor now stepped forward to a microphone and as the crowd fell silent he began a welcoming speech.

'How's your French?' Geoff whispered.

'Non-existent. What's he saying?'

'Pity you can't understand, and Clifford for that matter. He'd love it. Lots of Lion of Hamastan, smiter of foes and sire of multitudes blather. Let's hope he doesn't babble on too long though.'

Unfortunately he did. After what seemed an interminable time the mayor finally finished and the band struck up the Hamastanian national anthem, 'Men of Harlech', followed by the Madagascan anthem. When it concluded the crowd, now restless after their fifteen minutes of restraint, broke into tumultuous cheering, and as a flock of white doves were released and fluttered skyward the official party rose and entered the town hall. Inside, the crumbling plastered walls and pervading gloom were relieved only by the gold and blue crêpe-paper bunting hanging across the hall to add a festive atmosphere, just as, James recalled, he and Lucinda had created every Christmas back home in Edinburgh as children.

The King and Queen sat at the centre of the elevated front table, facing the already seated VIP guests. To the Queen's side sat the ladies-in-waiting, then the mayor's wife and Jacques. Adjacent the King sat the mayor, then Geoff, James and the Bishop. Before them, officers of the Hamastanian army filled two tables while the remaining eight were occupied by conspicuously ill-dressed local dignitaries, most of whom would be justifiably arrested on suspicion by any discerning policeman back home. A dozen nuns and the convent Mother Superior claimed one long table in the centre of the hall. On each table, mounted on plastic pedestals, stood miniature Hamastanian flags from the Romanian factory.

The welcoming banquet was conducted in an awkward silence, disturbed only by regular thumps from all except the royal and Mother Superior's tables as the guests crushed the scarlet ants that darted among the dishes. The diners' conversations rarely rose above a respectful murmur as, largely unaided by the cutlery, they concentrated on the food. Throughout, the band could be heard from outside as it ran through its programme beginning with 'White Christmas'.

The banquet began with a fried locust entrée, which was followed by platters of curried goat meat and steamed rice and an ominous looking bowl of swill containing dark chunks of meat which Geoff later explained was cat, a Madagascan favourite. At the head table only the mayor and mayoress ate. Copious quantities of wine were present, and after half an hour James observed that many of the guests were becoming drunk.

'The local wines are bloody good,' Geoff muttered, and so it proved. Uncomfortable with the stiffness of the proceedings, James drank five glasses and soon became light-headed.

'What's next?' he whispered.

'A surprise, mate. The best is yet to come.'

When the banquet was finished the King and Queen, who throughout the proceedings had not uttered a word to their neighbours, rose at a signal from Jacques, and all present stood in respectful silence as they retired to a private room. Without the intimidating presence of royalty, excited conversation broke out as the guests relaxed and, aided by the wine, celebrated their prestigious status as chosen ones in the presence of the great.

'Comfort stop,' Geoff explained. 'We resume in fifteen minutes,' and they joined the milling throng in the dank town hall toilets before resuming their places.

In due course the royal couple returned, silence again fell then, escorted by the mayor, the official party resumed their places on the town hall landing where they were greeted by a stupendous roar from the patiently waiting masses. Once Their Majesties were enthroned the diners filed out to seats placed during the banquet at the foot of the town hall steps, while the two Alceides jets screamed low across the square in a royal fly-past.

James' excessive wine consumption on his empty stomach suddenly made him wobbly, and he stumbled and gripped the back of the King's throne. Geoff turned and spoke to the Hamastan Battalion Commander who beckoned to four of his officers. They retreated back into the town hall then returned with five seats from the banquet tables and placed them behind the royal couple. James, Geoff, the Bishop and the ladies-in-waiting sat down and James began to feel more comfortable.

Jacques now emerged from the town hall having changed into a Grenadier Guard's uniform. He stepped up to the microphone and addressed the crowd in French. A roar of approval followed his concluding remarks. Jacques gestured to the four liveried footmen and the first stepped forward bearing a tray on which lay a medal.

The King now rose and, following some words from Jacques, the mayor, resembling an animated scarecrow, marched forward and stood, head bowed before His Majesty. The King pinned the medal on him, uttered a few congratulatory remarks and the crowd broke into applause. This exercise was repeated with a different footman on each occasion.

Next came the Indian hotel proprietor. He wore an ill-fitting, unpressed, chocolate-coloured suit with bell-bottom trousers, open sandals exposing yellow woollen socks, and an orange-and-green-striped tie. After shuffling forward curled almost double in deference, he collapsed in a grovelling heap before His Majesty and kissed his feet. Jacques pulled him upright while the King did the honours and again the crowd applauded. Overcome by the occasion, the bemedalled Indian retreated obsequiously backwards, bowing and genuflecting, with tears running down his cheeks until he was eventually escorted by Jacques to a seat where he sat hunched, fingering his silver medal and wiping his eyes with his sleeve. Then came the Mother Superior. On this occasion the Bishop joined the King as the Mother Superior, her elbow held lightly by Jacques, was escorted forward. She knelt, head bowed before His Majesty, then assisted by Jacques, rose and kissed the Bishop's ringed fingers. Again the King did the honours to public acclamation. Finally came the Turk, whose appearance befitted that of a serial killer, and the awards ceremony was over.

'On your feet, chum,' Geoff instructed and the escort retinue fell in behind Their Majesties who, accompanied by the mayor, descended the steps. They crossed at a regal pace to the side of the square while the soldiers, assisted by the capering gorilla and the Lord High Executioner waving his axe, restrained the surging crowd. The official party halted before a large shroud-enclosed object and, unassisted by amplification, the mayor bellowed out a short address. When he had finished, Jacques handed the King a tasselled rope-end. He gave the rope a sharp tug, then Jacques completed the removal of the cover to an approving roar from the spectators.

Before them on a six-foot-high stone plinth stood a life-sized statue of the King. A polished brass plaque recorded the occasion. The King was portrayed in a jaw-jutting posture, wearing a morning coat and leaning forward from the waist, his right arm extended and pointing futuristically into the distance while in his left hand he held a book. Something about it jarred. The likeness of Clifford's crowned head was faultless but it seemed to James the statue's body language didn't ring true.

'That's one of our $100,000 extras,' Geoff whispered. 'It's a nice little earner but we're going to have to tidy it up in future. Tell you about it later.'

Once more the party climbed the town hall steps. James looked at his watch. It was 4.30 p.m. The excitement and events of the day, which had begun back in the Hilton ten hours earlier, combined with the tropical heat and the five glasses of wine, now made him sleepy.

'What now?' he muttered to Geoff.

'Here comes the crescendo,' Geoff whispered mysteriously. 'Believe me, this one will knock your head off. It's another hundred grand in the till. Then we're back to the hotel for a few hours' rest before the reciprocal banquet.'

The mayor now stepped up to the microphone. He seemed enraged, and gesticulated wildly as he spoke to angry supportive muttering from the crowd. He finished his address with what seemed to be an appeal, and the huge audience responded, 'oui, oui, oui' as fists were raised and shaken menacingly.

Now desperately sleepy, James watched in a hazy mental fog, puzzled as to what was occurring. He turned to Geoff for an explanation, only to find him leaning across whispering in the Bishop's ear.

Then he noticed the massed soldiers at the end of the square part and a dozen others emerge pulling a large wooden enclosed platform on which stood Juma, holding his axe in both hands, his arms extended above his head. The crowd hushed as the apparatus rattled across the cobblestones to the foot of the town hall steps, stopping before the Bishop who had now descended and was waiting at the bottom with his Bible clasped between his hands.

From among the standing army two soldiers emerged, dragging between them a sobbing young black man, like Juma also stripped to the waist but with his wrists tied behind him. The soldiers pulled him roughly up the steps at the rear of the platform and held him between them until he collapsed to his knees and looked up imploringly at Their Majesties.

James gazed dumbstruck at the scene as the Bishop climbed the steps and, kneeling beside the young man, opened his Bible and began reading aloud. Still the young man begged Their Majesties for mercy, his pleading and sobbing intensifying as the Bishop completed his reading, flamboyantly snapped his Bible closed, then rose and stood dispassionately alongside.

Juma now stepped forward. Facing the official party he grabbed the black's woolly head, jerking it upright, seemingly as an offering to Their Majesties.

'Watch the Queen,' Geoff hissed. Bewildered, James turned to Her Majesty.

Her entire body was convulsing, her lips quivering and her eyes bulging insanely. Slowly she extended her right arm, her fist clenched and her thumb extended sideways. She stared mad-eyed at the desperately pleading, kneeling black for what seemed an age and then, as the huge crowd waited in an eerie expectant silence, a crazed grin slowly formed on her face and she rolled her fist, pointing her thumb sharply downwards. An approving roar from the assembly broke the silence and resounded across the square.

The two soldiers quickly tied a band over the prisoner's eyes then roughly pushed him downwards. The crowd fell silent. A drum-roll echoed across the square then Juma stepped forward and raised his axe high over his head, at which point James leapt to this feet and desperately shouted, 'Stop, stop, stop it …'

But it was too late. Juma crashed the axe down in a huge arc; blood sprayed into the air, then he bent down and, grinning maniacally, held up a blood-dripping head to the wildly cheering crowds before placing it on a pole at the corner of the platform just as James fainted, crashing his forehead against the back of the King's throne as he fell.

# – TWENTY –

James woke, opened his eyes then quickly closed them again. The room he was lying in was washed in a twilight dimness but the foreignness of its weird furnishings sent him into a mental retreat. Despite a strange sensation above his right eye he felt a blissful soothing restfulness, and for a minute he lay still, eyes closed, while his consciousness slowly returned.

Again he opened his eyes and he now recognised Nicole, concern etched on her features, sitting beside him. She reached forward and gently mopped his face with a damp cloth as he heard Geoff's voice say, 'He's waking up.'

In the dim light of the curtain-drawn room James saw Geoff, still in his Field Marshal's uniform, sitting in a corner. Beside him sat Juma who now had removed his mask but was otherwise unchanged. Both were drinking red wine. The memory of the execution flooded back and brought James sharply to his senses.

He sat up on the bed. 'That's it for me,' he shouted. 'I can run with the bullshit when it's fun but as far as I'm concerned you're both bastards. I want no part of this. I'm going home to tell the world what you're up to.'

'Settle down, old man,' Geoff said. 'You're jumping to conclusions.'

'Oh no I'm bloody well not!' James bellowed. 'Don't you shits have any morality? I'm shocked at you, Monster. You'd sell your bloody soul for sixpence.'

'Perhaps a glass of wine would help,' Juma said. 'What about the dwugs, Geoff? Does it matter?'

'It was only pethidine. Pour him a glass.'

'Get stuffed the both of you,' James shouted and he rose, then suddenly fell back, weakened by his exertions.

'Is this what's botherwing you, James?' Juma asked, and he reached down into an airline bag at his feet, pulled out the still eye-bandaged Negro head, and tossed it on to James' bed.

James shrieked and leapt from the bed and across the floor, stumbling as he hit the wall. The two men rose to help him. Nicole picked up the head from the bed and James recoiled, collapsing against the wall.

'For Christ's sake, James, it's not real!' Geoff shouted in his face.

James relaxed slightly. 'What do you mean not real?' he quavered.

'It's not real, mate. The head's a latex model. Another of our Romanian products. It's all a charade.'

'Oh shit,' James said, and he slithered to the floor. He looked up at his two colleagues, now laughing noisily. Juma took the head from Nicole and brought it over. James, studied it warily, then tentatively took it. It was latex.

'You bastards,' he complained. 'You might have warned me. I'll have that bloody glass of wine,' and as Juma poured it Geoff helped him back to the bed.

'You gave yourself one hell of a crack when you fell. Went out like a light. Blood everywhere. Hodgie was ready to give you the last rites,' Geoff explained. 'You've got six stitches over your right eye so the doctor gave you a shot of pethidine. You've been asleep for an hour and a half. If you're not up to it you can scrub the Royal Reception tonight.'

Still confused, James endeavoured to collect his thoughts. 'For God's sake, Geoff, what about the blood? I saw it for Christ's sake.' Then, remembering he had just handled the head, 'OK, spill the beans.'

'Quite simple, old man,' Geoff laughed. 'The executed bloke was Ramantsoa. He's one of Hodgie's management staff. Been decapitated fifteen times now across Africa. It's another hundred grand in the kitty.'

'But what about the blood?' James demanded. 'I mean, damn it all, I saw it.'

'It's all an illusion, mate. We tell the mayor the condemned bloke is a convicted child rapist and murderer and he works up the crowd. They certainly want his neck but it becomes the Queen's prerogative. Experience shows the wives couldn't give a damn about the offence. It might just as well be jay-walking. They all love delivering death sentences. We discovered it by chance after the Mauritanian tour when the Cliffords were actually at a genuine beheading. They were terribly keen for a repeat performance, or the Queen was anyway, so we tested the water gently with the other clients and they were all bloody enthusiastic. So here we are, a hundred grand better off per lopping. It's pretty unusual now not to have at least two executions on every tour.'

'Christ, Geoff. It's bloody fraudulent,' James spluttered.

'Not a bit, old man. We do it so well no one's any the wiser so the effect's the same. And anyway,' Geoff added, 'even in the improbable event that the client discovered the truth I don't think too many of them would want it known they purchase executions for thrills. We're on a win to nothing with this one.'

'I still don't understand,' James said. 'I mean, my God, it was absolutely authentic; the blood and everything.'

'Thank you, James,' Juma teased. 'I pwide myself on my cwaftsmanship.'

'It's like all illusions,' Geoff explained. 'People believe they're seeing what they expect to see. When the soldiers pushed Ramantsoa down, almost immediately Juma raised his axe and everyone's eyes were on him. What nobody notices is that Ramantsoa had disappeared behind the parapet and was lying flat on the floor. Juma crashed the axe into a large sponge soaked in goat's blood, thus the spraying, then quickly bent down and held up our friend here,' and at that Geoff picked up the latex head and kissed it on the lips.

'Wait till you see the hanging on Wednesday,' Juma enthused. 'Another illusion but very wealistic.'

'And another hundred grand,' Geoff said.

'It's bloody disgusting,' James muttered.

'Not in terms of client satisfaction,' Geoff said. 'You certainly won't think that when you watch the Queens slavering every time. I get special delight knowing I'm taking them to the cleaners for their obscene tastes.'

'But why on earth do they get pleasure from it?' James persisted. 'It's perverted.'

'I'm not so sure about that, at least not in terms of perversity being inconsistent with general sentiment,' Geoff argued. 'There's not a country in the world where, when asked, the public don't usually poll in favour of capital punishment, even if few actually practise it. It's one thing one can say in the politicians' favour. As for the crowd's

162

enthusiasm, remember public executions were regular events in London up until a hundred and fifty years ago and drew huge audiences, solely for the entertainment. Same thing today every Friday afternoon in Saudi Arabia although with our clients I think different factors apply. It comes back to what I told you about the super-rich wanting to experience everything, even the power of life and death. So we deliver. Mind you, in fairness you must remember all the Head of State Tour clients are Americans and capital punishment is well entrenched there for extreme offenders, which is what the clients think our executed are.'

'It's still disgusting,' James insisted. 'Specially when you remember they're buying the executions.'

'I'll put up with that at a hundred grand a time,' Geoff replied. 'Anyway, are you up to the reciprocal Royal Banquet tonight?'

'Must I come?'

'Nope. We'll get along without you. We'll have to leave now as it starts in fifteen minutes. You'll miss the performance by the gorilla and Court jester which is actually bloody pathetic, but the locals like it. Maybe it's better if you take a spell. Ring for room service if you're hungry. Nicole will need to come to the banquet but she can join you later.' At that the party rose and left James to his very confused thoughts.

But half an hour later loud cheering from outside drew him to the window. He pulled back the drapes and opened the window. The tangy tropical aroma of smoke and perfume wafted into the room. On the road a dense crowd hoping for a glimpse of the royal couple were being restrained by a hundred Hamastanian soldiers while Juma, his axe poised menacingly, was pacing along their ranks. Washed with a twilight orange hue an untidy vista of rusty tin roofs broken by the fronds of palm trees stretched before him while the distant hills sparkled with the camp-fires of thousands of villagers in town for the royal visit. Immediately below in the courtyard a huge mottled pig and a dozen scrawny chickens fossicked in a giant pile of rubbish.

It was all too much for one day. James pulled the drapes closed, undressed and was soon asleep.

# – TWENTY-ONE –

Twice during the night James was woken, first when Nicole returned from the Royal Banquet and slipped into the bed beside him, then half an hour later by a noisy commotion outside his room. There was much yelling. James heard Juma shout, 'Pith off, you wotten barthded,' followed by a loud crash against the wall, a stream of Hodge profanities, a woman shrieking, then the sound of splintering timber as Juma's axe penetrated the wall just above his head, causing Nicole to leap screaming from the bed. Almost immediately came Geoff's angry denunciations, the axe was wrenched free and silence descended again over the darkened room.

The following morning James woke early, feeling refreshed and energetic. He showered, then dressed in his Admiral's uniform but was dismayed to discover his former polished image was now marred by a strip of plaster over his right eye. He was interrupted in these contemplations by a series of horrific blood-curdling screams which seemed to stem from the very soul of their perpetrator. There was a brief lull then the screams began again. James rushed to the window, threw it open and stared aghast at five men violently tussling atop a writhing body below in the yard. Suddenly one of the men raised a long, blood-stained knife high over his head and plunged it into the victim, who emitted an awful spine-chilling shriek signalling imminent death.

'Nicole, Nicole,' James shouted ashen-faced. 'Wake up for God's sake. Someone's being murdered.'

The girl rolled over, muttering sleepily, 'Eet's only a peeg, James,' and resumed her slumber.

Badly rattled, James descended the stairway to the foyer of Le Grand Hotel International only to stop abruptly, startled by the spectacle before him. For a full minute he stood flabbergasted beneath a green wrought-iron archway intertwined with dust-covered pink plastic flowers, taking in the hotel's gloomy lobby. The floor was covered in purple and orange tiles, and at the foot of the stairs were tarnished brass bowls holding potted palms, one, by its brown colouring and limp leaves, plainly dead.

To his left lay the hotel's reception where a Malagasy receptionist was being noisily scolded by one of the proprietor's sari-clad, moustachioed daughters.

Two early Stalinish-style brown vinyl sofas faced the reception counter, one displaying a lengthy tear patched with a strip of black tape. Between them hovered an eight-foot-high stuffed brown bear, acquired many years earlier when still alive as part payment of a travelling circus's debt. These furnishings were complemented by two purple felt armchairs, still in their, now much smeared, plastic delivery wrappings, while before this cluster stood a chipped, pink Formica coffee table on which sat a bowl of plastic flowers and two ashtrays overflowing with cigarette butts.

Doric columns without structural purpose or discernible pattern were scattered about the lobby, while centre-piece in a rock-bordered pool stood a ten-foot-high, silver-painted wooden replica of the Eiffel Tower, its entire length dotted with tiny red and green lights which flashed on and off at three-second intervals. At its base, poised beside a luminous pink plastic mermaid dangling a fishing line, a small turtle stared morosely at the stagnant olive-green water.

On the far wall, glimpsed between the Doric columns, hung the Indian hotelier's art collection. Stunned, James crossed the foyer to examine the works more closely. They comprised five large carpet squares enclosed in elaborate gold frames, displaying garishly coloured, crude portrayals of, respectively, a pouncing tiger, a cigar-smoking Winston Churchill, the Sphinx, a leering Mona Lisa, and a bare-breasted Hawaiian hula girl. Beneath them a sign bore the warning 'LOOKING ONLY. TUTCHING NOT PERMIT'.

At one end of this display, beyond a cluster of protruding electrical wires and a Korean shipping company's calendar bearing a photograph of a container ship, framed certificates testified to the proprietor's diverse achievements. They recorded his membership of the Bombay Theosophical Society; his 1968 graduation from the Leeds Correspondence School in ballroom dancing; his Doctorate of

Philosophy from The International Postal University of Scholarship located in Paterson, New Jersey; his crossing the equator in 1971 on the SS Prince of York bound between Bombay and Capetown, from where he had found his way to Madagascar, and his possession of number 17,271 of a limited edition porcelain plate commemorating the Queen Mother's eightieth birthday. In pride of place an ornate certificate celebrated his inclusion in the International Dictionary of Outstanding Accomplishment, for which entry he had forwarded $450 to a London post office box although only the certificate had turned up.

As he stood transfixed by this eclectic display James became aware of a peculiar animal-like snuffling behind him and he turned to find the Indian, clad in a lurid green suit made of some non-organic material and still wearing his medal from yesterday's award ceremony. The hotelier clasped his hands together under his chin. 'Mr Admiral, sir. I am saying for your happiness no stone will be spared.'

'Thank you,' James replied, nervously edging away.

'You are liking my very fine baintings, sir?'

James re-examined the grotesque carpet squares. Perhaps the Indian was trying to sell them and the temptation crossed his mind, that if the price was low enough, he could hang one in his bedroom when Jane was there. Her apoplectic reaction would be well worth paying for.

'Splendid workmanship,' he responded. 'A local artist, I presume?'

The Indian was visibly shocked. 'Oh, Mr Admiral, most certainly not. I am not being a damn fool, sir. They are gumming from Gairo.' Adopting an even more wheedling tone, the Indian changed the subject. 'Also I am saying, sir, the 'amastan beople are speaging very fine English.'

'Compulsory subject at school,' James muttered and excused himself. Slightly bewildered he entered the dining room through an entrance of hanging multicoloured plastic strips where he found Geoff in angry conversation with Juma.

'The Bishop's in disgwace,' Juma gleefully informed him as a barefooted waiter rushed to pull out a chair.

'And you,' Geoff blurted angrily. 'You're just as bloody bad.'

'What's wrong?' James enquired. He was looking forward to the day ahead and the disharmony cast a pall over his ebullience.

'He twied to steal Simone fwom me last night,' Juma explained. 'That's what all the wacket was.'

At that moment, unshaven and wearing his Bishop's vestments, Hodge arrived smoking a large cigar.

'You can forget about that outfit,' Geoff snapped. 'This time you're definitely defrocked. That was scandalous last night, right under the royal bedroom. I had to tell Their Majesties we were fighting off royalty fans who had invaded the hotel. It was bloody embarrassing and I don't think the Queen believed me. Fortunately I was able to draw their attention to the crowd maintaining an all night vigil outside otherwise we'd be right in the crap. I'm sick and tired of this irresponsible behaviour.'

'Pull up right fucking there, sunshine,' His Grace said coldly. 'You told me loud and bloody clear back in the Hilton; if I laid off the nuns I could have a lady-in-bloody-waiting.'

'Oh shit,' Geoff said and he put his head in his hands. After a time he looked up. 'Anyway,' he said conclusively, 'you can't be a Bishop; you've smashed your bishop's staff. It's your symbol of ecclesiastic authority and you're dead meat without it.'

'Swinging it at me,' Juma intruded.

'Jesus bloody Christ,' His Grace protested. 'What about you swinging your fucking axe at me?'

'Pwovocation and wetaliation.'

'For Christ's sake, shut up both of you,' Geoff shouted.

'It's called a crosier,' James said quietly, temporarily bringing the angry denunciations to a halt as the three stared at him perplexed.

'What is?' Geoff demanded.

'The bishop's staff. Its correct title is a crosier.'

Geoff regarded him suspiciously. 'How do you know?'

James shrugged. 'I don't know. I just do. That's what it's called.'

'Stuff what it's called,' the Bishop said, bored by this diversion. 'Who gives a shit? I've got my bloody Bible. It's a big bastard so it'll do for today. I've telephoned Tana and a replacement staff or whatever you bloody call it will be down tonight.'

'OK,' Geoff said angrily. 'So there's been a misunderstanding. But for God's sake let's have some self-control for the rest of the tour. It's preposterous carrying on like that over a dime-a-dozen slattern.'

'So can I knock off a nun?' His Grace enquired lightly.

'Certainly not,' Geoff snapped. 'There's no function tonight so you can snare one of the locals, only make sure you're in civvies. As a senior churchman it's time you acted more responsibly. Where the hell do you think religion would be back home if bishops wore their vestments every time they picked up tarts?'

Ignoring the reprimand, Hodge brightened. 'I see they've knocked off that bloody pig,' he said. 'Bloody good show too. Pork chops for me tonight. The bastard ate my cap when I was down here making arrangements for the tour. It blew off a window ledge and he scoffed it before my very eyes.'

Geoff rolled his eyes. 'Their Majesties will be grouching to me about all that screaming, mark my words.'

'There's a claim to fame,' James suggested thoughtfully. 'If John eats the pig he will probably be the first person in history who can honestly claim to have eaten his hat, even if indirectly.'

'Food poisoning all wound then,' Juma suggested brightly.

'For God's sake stop it,' Geoff complained. 'I'm sick and tired of all this quarrelling. We're trying to run a Royal Tour, not a war, so let's show some professionalism. Is everything in order for today?'

'When I run things everything's always in bloody order,' His Grace sulked. And so it proved.

It seemed to James the crowds for the procession were even larger than the previous day. Certainly they were more exuberant and he watched incredulously as men and women, pursuing the coins thrown by the royal coach footmen up ahead, thrashed in wild limb-flailing scrambles, creating whirlpools of violence among the sea of black heads. James felt mildly disappointed that he was not permitted to throw any. 'Undignified for senior military personnel,' Geoff had replied stiffly when he had broached the subject at the commencement of the parade.

After an hour the royal retinue, accompanied by two hundred soldiers retained for crowd-control duties, turned into the square and to the peeling of church bells the carriages rattled across the cobbled open space to the town hall steps. The remaining parade continued through the town to the buses and animal floats that were to take them on to Ambarosita.

Once more the royal couple, followed by the official entourage, climbed the town hall steps and resumed their thrones. The mayor gave a farewell speech, interspersed by loud sobbing from the Indian hotelier who, uninvited, was lurking behind the official party, still

168

wearing his medal. For the first time the King rose and approached the microphone. A hush fell over the square.

'Citizens of Fianarosa,' he began, reading from notes and speaking slowly in a strong American accent. 'Her Royal Majesty, Queen Maureen, and I have greatly enjoyed our visit to your magnificent city.'

He paused while Jacques translated.

'Yesterday and today will forever be remembered in the history of our two great nations. Our visit has forged a bond between the peoples of Hamastan and Fianarosa that I have no doubt will be but a first small step in an ever deepening relationship.'

Again Jacques translated and when he had finished the crowd broke into applause. As it died away the Indian hotelier's muffled sobbing rose in hysteria, culminating in a loud elongated sniff which echoed through the loudspeakers and across the square.

'Fucking Indians,' the Bishop muttered, and the Queen stiffened, her back arching in disapproval.

The King concluded, 'Her Majesty and I will treasure always the affection and respect you have demonstrated and the memory of your noble civic leaders whom we have been privileged to anoint with Hamastan's highest honours.'

Again Jacques translated and to the tumultuous roar of the crowd the King returned to his throne, while the now distraught Indian, overcome with emotion, collapsed, weeping and babbling incoherently, to the ground. The Bishop turned and kicked him hard in the groin then smashed his Bible over his head, the Indian's shrieks fortunately being lost amongst the crowd noise.

Now came the formal Hamastan flag-lowering ceremony, conducted by the Battalion Commander, following which the royal party descended the steps and rejoined their carriages and vehicles.

The rest of the day passed largely without incident. Shortly after noon they paraded through Ambarosita to identical mass adulation as in Fiana; there was a similar civic reception and banquet followed by the twin jets fly-past and more medal-awarding. Then in mid-afternoon fifty schoolgirl gymnasts performed, marred only by the Bishop's, 'shit, I could rip into some of them' observation which, Geoff was to later angrily complain, had been heard by Their Majesties.

The school choral performance, conducted by a blushing nun,

regrettably ran for twenty minutes, causing some restlessness in the official party. 'Could have been worse,' Geoff muttered. 'At least it wasn't traditional dancing. We draw a bloody line at that ethnic rubbish.' The mood lightened, however, when Her Majesty, for the first time on the tour playing the dominant role – which she plainly relished – formally opened the new health clinic that Clifford was funding. She was then introduced and curtsied to by the eight nuns into whose care it was entrusted. The clinic lay at the end of a rough dirt road, Their Majesties being conveyed to it in ornate sedan chairs carried by the footmen.

Following the Bishop's blessing of the new facility, the official party, weary after the long day, rejoined their vehicles for the return trip to the Indian's hotel. The royal couple rode in the standard-bearing limo, which had arrived down from Tana, while the animals and troops remained encamped outside Ambarosita to await the final day of the royal visit.

That evening Nicole disappeared with Simone to visit an aunt, and James joined Geoff for dinner. They studied their menus and placed their orders with the waiter, James declining the roast pork special. In the corner of the dining room, seated at the bar, the now derobed Bishop was entertaining two local tarts. Raucous laughter from the trio occasionally drifted across the room.

Geoff looked across at Hodge and sighed. 'I suppose you wonder why we put up with him?'

'He can certainly be a bit rough,' James proffered, unwilling to be too damning as he felt a bemused affection for the Australian. 'Still, he seems a pretty good organiser. How did you find him?'

'The usual. We advertised in every English language newspaper south of the Sahara. Had over a hundred replies but most were hopeless and lots were alcoholics. Africa's full of colonial-era relics who've become used to the indolent lifestyle and climate and can never go home. Their only asset is their white skin and its implied authority but when it comes to actually doing anything they're totally useless. They flounder on, obtaining management jobs, stuffing up, getting the sack, changing countries and repeating the exercise. It's like a bloody great game of musical chairs with them all periodically swapping jobs, but the market for their white-skinned status sustains it. They're all late middle-aged or older so there's probably only another decade left in it by which time, hopefully, there'll be plenty of Jumas to actually run the show.'

'Sounds like you're lucky to have Hodge,' James said, conscious that Geoff was in a talkative mood and eager to grill him about Alceides' operations.

'No doubt about it. Hodgie was a stand-out. He understands that just ordering people to do things is pointless in Africa. You either do it yourself or closely monitor it with a great deal of force. Plus he's intelligent, imaginative and has a hooligan streak which suits the job. He's a very wealthy man now, you realise.'

'Oh, how's that?'

'Because in the past five years with his commissions he's earnt over a million dollars tax-free annually and our investment division has doubled that for him in the sharemarket.'

'So you could lose him,' James prompted as he topped up their wine glasses.

Geoff laughed. 'Never. He's a prisoner of Africa. Hodgie would wither up and die if he returned to the west with all its rules and regulations. He's 52 now and will probably want to pack it in, in a few years' time; about the same time as the growth of tourism everywhere means the game's up for the Head of State Tours. There are heaps of Hodge clones all over the continent. A divorced wife and family back home they haven't seen for years. Hodgie has two adult daughters in Australia. One's a lawyer and another's a doctor. I suspect he likes the thought of their existence but that's about the sum of his relationship with them now. He's not untypical of the sort of ex-pat you find in these places. As I understand it he was a top barrister back in Melbourne; one of those colourful, always sailing on the edge of propriety types law seems to attract. Apparently there was a tremendous blow-up when he abused a judge, and Hodgie was quietly shipped out to Vanuatu as Chief Justice. His wife wouldn't come so after a few months he shacked up with a native girl which caused a bit of a stew. Next thing he ended up in Malawi as a judge but that ended in yet another blow-up.

'He's perfect for Africa because he understands it. The only thing that works here is shouting and physical force, specially as no one speaks English. He'd be hopeless in India. More subtlety's required there. Shouting at Indians simply causes them to collapse into quivering heaps although they do seem responsive to ear-boxing. Our

171

man Rama there is a former army general and knows how to handle things. What he does ...' but Geoff was abruptly interrupted in his discourse by a woman's scream followed by a loud crash, the tinkle of breaking glass and a string of Hodge profanities from the corner bar. One of the Bishop's lady friends had fallen off her bar stool. A minute later Hodge, an arm round each girl's waist, loomed up and paused before them, swaying precariously. His enormous belly hung over his pants, his fly zip at half mast.

'Blesh you, my children,' he slurred before lurching off towards the stairway, the ascent of which was accompanied by a mixture of Hodge curses and gales of female laughter.

Geoff sighed. 'It's not as if I demand piety or that he behave like the Archangel Gabriel,' he complained. 'But being a Bishop, surely some discretion would be reasonable. Whenever I protest he argues that debauchery and ribald behaviour by senior clergy is part of the Catholic tradition.'

'Well he's certainly right on that score,' James said, eager to protect the Australian from his latest indiscretion. 'I must say I'm enormously impressed by his organisational skills, specially knowing he's doing one of these tours somewhere in Africa every six weeks.'

'Oh you're right. There's no doubt he's bloody good at his job. It's just a pity he's so uncouth, more so as he insists on being the Bishop. Mind you, there's plenty of room for improvement. I've just copped a bollocking from the Queen. First she complained about the entertainment at the banquet last night – which I must confess was a bit disappointing. The dwarf was definitely drunk and kept missing his cue with the gorilla. The Queen claimed it was inappropriate for royalty and there should have been a concert pianist or opera singer. That's all very well for her but it's the guests we have to think about. We couldn't guarantee their behaviour if we delivered that.'

'So what exactly do they do?' James enquired.

'What do who do?'

'The dwarf and the gorilla. What do they do to entertain?'

Geoff looked puzzled. 'They don't do anything. They just cavort about.'

'Cavort about!'

'Well, they kick one another in the bum; that sort of carry-on. But that's the problem. The bloody dwarf was so drunk he couldn't even do that. It's not good enough,' Geoff grumbled.

'For God's sake, Geoff. That's hardly entertainment.'

Geoff looked hurt. 'Well normally there are two dwarfs,' he said defensively. 'Anyway, you're rather missing the point. Remember who we're dealing with. When it comes to entertainment these buggers have the sophistication level of a ten-year-old back home.'

'And they don't care that the gorilla's a fake?'

'Good God, man,' Geoff exclaimed. 'They don't know he's a fake. They'd be bewildered by the concept. Acting is never just confined to the players. It requires audience participation and their suspension of reality and substitution of imagination. That's light years beyond this lot's competence. Still, you must remember the gorilla's principal role is crowd control. He's worth a hundred African soldiers on that count and is a damn sight more effective and reliable.'

'Talking of African soldiers,' James pressed on, 'that's another thing which puzzles me. Surely the people realise something's amiss when the King and Queen are white and the Hamastanian army's black and, for that matter, obviously Malagasies?'

'Never. Wouldn't cross their minds. The few whites they ever encounter are always figures of authority, otherwise they probably believe the whole world comprises black people. Besides, their attention is totally focused on the King and Queen. They're so overwhelmed by the presence of greatness and all the pageantry of the parade, the troops are simply a blur in their perception.'

'Doesn't seem much sense having them then,' James commented. 'You could save the cost and trouble and run with a glittering royal court.'

'You're missing the point again,' Geoff frowned. 'We don't have the army to impress the people. We have it for the client. Adds to their sense of importance and power.'

'So why the dwarf?' James continued, keen to push Geoff into further elaboration.

'A symbol of wealth. Bloody important in the Third World. To be able to afford a house dwarf is a clear sign of great affluence which is what these people expect of a monarch. Brasch says that in the seventeenth century every European royal house had a house dwarf, and the practice quickly spread to the aristocracy. Nevertheless, it's a tricky business trying to get the right balance between impressing the clients and impressing the locals and the dwarf issue epitomises it. If the Queens had their way there would be no dwarfs, as they tend to view their capering as frivolous and undignified. But we're the experts and know what impresses the locals, and in that respect the dwarfs are essential. Anyway,' he added somewhat aggressively, 'if you object to the dwarf's cavorting with the gorilla then tell me what the hell he should be doing?'

'Well,' James said hesitantly, 'if he's supposed to be a court jester then I suppose he … well … I don't know … well I suppose he should jest,' he added feebly.

'You mean tell jokes?'

Realising he was trapped, James thought frantically. 'Perhaps he could be a juggler or something like that.'

'Something like that, as you put it, is what the little bastard is supposed to do now with the gorilla. Believe me, that's as far as you can go. We had one once who was a fire-eater.'

'Well, there you go,' James said encouragingly. 'That's the sort of thing I mean. Why have you dropped it?'

'We didn't. It's exactly what I mean if you demand too much of Africans. First time up the little bugger caught on fire and charged about like a fireball screaming at the top of his voice. Most undignified behaviour for a royal and bloody embarrassing. Furthermore, he damn near incinerated the Queen. She was in an elaborate Catherine the Great coronation outfit and would have been history. Hodgie saved the day. Almost took the little bugger's head off with his staff or whatever you call it.'

'Crosier,' James said weakly. 'So the dwarf was OK?'

'Him! No, he was buggered. Once Hodgie laid him out he burnt to a frizzle.'

'Good Lord! That's awful.'

'No, no. It was perfectly all right,' Geoff assured him. 'At the time we had an extensive dwarf stock across Africa. Problem is, Hodgie's almost used them all up. That's why we're always looking for new innovations, like the elephant we hired from the zoo.'

'I thought African elephants were untameable,' James quizzed, happy to change the subject.

'It's not African. It's from Thailand. The zoo uses it for rides so it's fairly used to people and shouldn't cause any problems. But make no mistake; like I said, it's a tricky business trying to get the right balance with everything. Being a Royal Visit and mindful of the audience we put the emphasis on pageantry. Only the footmen and the ladies-in-waiting, and I suppose the dwarf in his role as court jester, and of course the Bishop, provide any element of a royal court. The problem is that the damn Queens study up on royal protocol and ceremonies and expect the entire tour to be like a coronation. But by and large we get it right. We've thought it all out very carefully, or at least Brasch has,' Geoff concluded adamantly.

'Still, you can understand the Queen's point of view,' James said. 'What else did she complain about?'

'She moaned about the confetti yesterday. Argued it was undignified for royalty. She's got a point actually. Normally we have a ticker-tape display, but only on Presidential Tours. The confetti was a new innovation as we constantly look for fresh embellishments. It's definitely a Hodge botch. Then she bitched about Hodgie's bad language, which she apparently overheard. And the King climbed into me about his statue. He's right of course. At a hundred grand a pop he's entitled to better.'

'I must say there was something about it which didn't ring true,' James said as he beckoned to the waiter for another bottle of wine.

'Yes. We've been cutting corners there,' Geoff conceded. 'Serban will have to find extra sculpting staff given the current demand. When we took over the factory we found 31 Lenin statues stored in a room. Apparently Ceausescu had been gradually taking them down all over Romania and substituting statues of himself. We cut off their heads and replace them with our client's, but they're definitely not right, not that it matters now. We've just about used up all our Lenins.'

'That's a bit rich,' James said. 'What about the Romanian factory staff? Don't they view it as sacrilege cutting the Lenins up; after all, from what you told me I presume they made them in the first place?'

'There's an old Chinese proverb, he who carves the Buddha never worships him, which I rather think applies there,' Geoff replied loftily. He paused for a moment, then brightened. 'The trick is to finish the Royal Visits on a high note, and that means pleasing the wives. The Queen should be happy on that score tomorrow. Hodgie says her statue is first-rate plus she's got another execution. Pity there's no time for any floggings though,' he mused. 'The Queens are always very keen on those.'

'Floggings?' James queried.

'Oh don't worry. They're authentic. No charade there. We pay

175

$25 a head to the flogees who each receive six lashes. We charge the client $5000 per flogee. Most buy half a dozen.'

'So how do you rig that then?'

'Rig? What do you mean rig?'

'How do you pull the illusion, like with the executions?'

'For God's sake, James, there's no illusion with floggings. If they weren't real the screams would lack authenticity.'

'That's disgraceful,' James exploded.

Geoff looked at him in puzzlement, a pained expression crossing his face. 'Don't be so bloody precious,' he snapped. 'We're doing wonderful work on the flogging front. Have you any idea what the average income is in these places? $25 is a fortune.'

'Then why not pay them more?' James suggested weakly.

'We'd be only too happy to, but we'd simply mess up the market. The first time we introduced floggings we ended up losing an entire territory in India through incorrect pricing. Paid $100 per flogee and the word got out. Mind you, that was for ten lashes. Nevertheless, when General Rama returned to organise another tour he was besieged by a crowd of over ten thousand, all demanding to be whipped. It's always the biggest problem dealing with the Third World. We tend to unwittingly apply our civilised values and, being too generous, end up creating a cargo-cult mentality which is what happened with the overpaid floggings.'

Uncomfortable with these revelations, James changed the subject. 'Well I must say you really took me in with the execution.'

'Yes, they're certainly well done. Mind you, Brasch is working on some new concepts. At $100,000 a pop he reckons there's a danger of the clients tiring of them after they've had half a dozen, although personally I don't think it's a risk. You've seen the Queen. Her reaction's typical. Executions are plainly a highlight which they look forward to immensely.'

'What's Brasch got in mind?' James enquired warily.

'He's been investigating chucking people to lions. That would certainly go down a treat. We could probably charge $150,000 a head for that.'

'So how would it work?' James asked hesitantly, mentally bracing himself for a fresh atrocity.

'Well naturally the lion end of the exercise would be no problem. We'd starve the buggers for four or five days first. It's the victims we

176

haven't sorted out. Obviously we'd have plenty of real candidates, specially in India, if we paid their families say $10,000, but we steer clear of that. Floggings are as far as we'll go on that score. Pity really but far too risky. If Delhi found out we could be banned from India. Ridiculous when you think about it, given their overpopulation problem.'

'Yes,' James said wryly. 'It does seem a bit shortsighted.'

Not detecting James' sarcasm, Geoff continued. 'At the moment we've got the Japanese manufacturers working on robotic victims made with imitation flesh and blood but they haven't got it right yet. The difficulty lies in creating a robot which cringes and flees, but to do that it needs to be packed with instruments which would be exposed once the lions tear it apart. It's a super idea if we can put it together with proper cowering and screaming and so on. The market's certainly there so I'm keeping my fingers crossed the Japs will work it out. Of course, what would really go down big is burning buggers at the stake, but whichever way we look at it I'm damned if we can work out how to pull it off. Same with impaling. We actually had a request for that from one of our Queens.'

'What are the King and Queen up to tonight?' James asked, eager to both change the subject and keep Geoff talking.

'They're dining in their suite. The footmen are waiting on them. I've posted Juma outside their door to keep the bloody Indian at bay. When I went up for the bitching session I caught the little bastard in the hall. I gave him a clip over the head, banned him from the floor and warned him if there's any more insolence we'll strip him of his medal. He's an extreme case of royalty-worshipping, which is usually only a problem with old ladies. No doubt about it, the medal's gone to his head. Hodgie stuffed up there. Far too free-handed, even if it was our lowest Hamastanian order. The Indian would have provided the hotel and meals free for the honour of having us stay. Now Hodgie's generosity has corrupted him and the greedy bugger will be expecting an award with every tour. Still I must say the food's pretty good here,' Geoff added, brightening. 'The banquet last night was first rate. How's yours?' he asked, gesturing at James' plate. James was enjoying a veal mornay concoction, and he admitted to its quality.

'There's the answer,' Geoff proclaimed triumphantly. 'That's another thing the Queen whined about; the food at the civic banquet yesterday. It was rather dreadful but of course, as I explained, it was out of our hands. We were guests, not the hosts. In future Hodgie can insist the Indian does the civic banquet catering. We'll make him do it free to ensure the mayor agrees. It'll provide some redressing for the medal,' and he called to the waiter for the sweets menu.

Somewhat hesitatingly James said, 'You don't think it's a bit much, swapping the hotel rooms and meals just for a medal?'

Geoff stared at him wide-eyed. 'A bit much,' he spluttered. 'You're damn right it's a bit much. There's not a hotel proprietor back home who wouldn't gladly provide the same for the British Empire medal or whatever the equivalent is to ours. We've been far too munificent.'

'But those medals are real,' James persevered. 'Ours are bogus.'

'Bogus my bum,' Geoff snapped. 'All medals are simply symbolic gestures. Look at the rubbish back home; knighthoods for example. Real knights rode horses and killed people for a living. The average knight today wouldn't know a horse's front end from its rear and would panic if he had to kill a mouse.'

'Be that as it may,' James persisted. 'The fact is Hamastan doesn't exist.'

'So what! Does the British Empire? Well damn it all, twice a year back home British Empire medals are dished out to general acclamation. So long as everyone here thinks our monarchs are the real thing, and everyone does, then our medals are every bit as legitimate in their effect. Anyway, it's only two nights for a handful of rooms.'

'And meals and liquor,' James battled on. 'And it's not a handful of rooms. There's the royal couple's suite, and a room for you and one for me, and then there's the gorilla and the Bishop and Juma and the video man and Jacques and the ladies-in-waiting and the dwarf ...'

'Don't be absurd,' Geoff cut in. 'We certainly don't let the bloody dwarf stay in the hotel. With a Royal in particular, everyone knowing their place is damned important, which is precisely why Hodgie's cocked up giving a medal to the Indian. It downgrades the whole tone of the tour. We're going to have to introduce a lower range of awards to cater for service providers – certificates or something of that nature.'

Realising he was wasting his time, James changed the subject again. 'Are all the Presidentials and Royal Tour clients Americans?' he asked.

'Yep. Only works with them. Interesting isn't it?' Geoff mused. 'We tried some of our super-rich Japanese clients but they weren't interested. Quite puzzled and uncomprehending in fact. They're not natural parvenus like the Americans and probably lack the necessary imagination but I rather think it's more than that. The Japs actually have a Royal Family and believe in it implicitly so I suspect they simply can't buy into our proposition with any conviction. The same goes with Presidentials. The egalitarian sentiment is well entrenched in Japan, so humility rather than personal aggrandisement prevails.

'On the other hand republicanism, democratic values, equality, meritocracy – all those sorts of sentiments are articles of faith installed into Americans from birth, so in a perverse sort of way they're vulnerable to indulging themselves in a concept so extremely at odds with that indoctrination. It adds to the excitement to do something utterly opposed to everything they've been preached at about. The same goes with Hodgie who's a fierce atheist yet insists on being the Bishop. Human nature's a funny thing,' he mused.

'What's with the Bishop's nun obsession?' James asked.

'Oh, it's nothing to do with them being nuns, although I suspect there's an element of property rights with it. He is, after all, a Bishop and things are different on that count in Africa. Personally I think it's the uniform. It's well known that uniforms have sexual allure, and I've noticed Hodgie ogling our air-hostesses when they're on duty yet ignoring them when they're in everyday clothing. You won't see too many uniforms here in Madagascar and with women, none whatsoever, apart from nuns. The annoying thing was that the incident with the nun was totally unnecessary. The Australian financier Brierley was the client on that tour as King of Melani. He'd booked six village virgin deflowerings spread over the three days, so Hodgie could have helped himself from the off-duty ones in that crop.'

Mention of Melani reminded James of the Melani coin he'd received in his change in the restaurant, and excitedly he recounted the incident.

'Yes,' Geoff said thoughtfully, 'there goes another out of that issue. Give it another three or four years and there'll be almost none left. They get lost or hoarded and lots are turned into decorative jewellery for the tribal women. Still, they provide a nice little one-off economic stimulus following each tour, before they disappear from circulation.'

The final day of the Royal Visit in Ambarosita proceeded to plan. It began with the coin-tossing parade at eleven then the official party retired to a local hostelry for lunch and at 1.30 came the unveiling of the Queen's statue in the Ambarosita town square which clearly delighted Her Majesty when it was revealed. It portrayed her wearing a simple full-length gown, her arms welcomingly extended as she gazed serenely down at a cluster of cherubic children kneeling at her feet and looking up at her with adoring expressions.

'We modelled it on those trashy Mary statues Catholics go in for,' Geoff whispered to James. 'Bloody good, isn't it? The Queen's certainly pleased. It's important to finish on a happy note with the wives.'

It was now 2 p.m. and the official party re-formed in the town square to wrap up the royal visit.

First came the execution. It began as James had witnessed on Monday, except this time a different, much larger tumbrel apparatus was pushed into the square, Juma was without his axe, and a gallows with a noose hanging from it was now present on the platform.

Once again the mayor worked the crowd up to a fever pitch, while this time a different young black, his hands tied behind his back, was roughly pushed up on to the platform then to his knees from where he pleaded desperately to Their Majesties, tears rolling down his cheeks.

'That's Radama,' Geoff whispered. 'He's our Tana office accountant. Been hanged five times now across Africa and has it down to a tee.'

As in Fiana the crowd fell silent, waiting on the Queen who, slavering and rocking with obvious pleasure, after a lengthy arm-extended consideration, gave the thumbs down. The crowd roared their approval, the Bishop stepped forward and read a few passages from his Bible, then Juma jerked Radama to his feet, fitted a black bag over his head and placed the noose round his neck. Again the crowd hushed, there was a drum roll, then Juma pulled a lever and Radama dropped out of sight. The rope quivered then became taut and after waiting half a minute Juma stepped forward and pulled Radama back up, his legs kicking violently as he swung by the neck for all to see. Cheering resounded across the square and the Queen clapped her hands delightedly, while the dwarf capered and cartwheeled round the platform as, for two minutes, the shrouded figure kicked out its death throes before eventually its grotesque writhings faded and it hung still.

Juma tied the end of the rope to the platform, then, to the delight of the crowd, their laughter rippling across the square, he engaged the corpse in a finger-wagging mock conversation culminating in him taking its limp hand and shaking it vigorously. Then he set it spinning, whereupon the dwarf ceased his cartwheeling, clambered up the steps and somersaulted at the corpse. Holding on with one arm round its neck, he waved to the cheering crowd as he spun round and round.

James felt faint. 'Explain it all later,' Geoff whispered to him nonchalantly.

Now the King stepped up to the microphone and standing before the slowly revolving corpse with the dwarf still clinging to its neck, he delivered an identical speech to his Fianarosa rendition, substituting only the names of the towns.

There was one remaining ceremony, signalled by a roll of drums.

'Here's a surprise for you, old man,' Geoff whispered. 'Your turn for a medal. March slowly down to the front. When you reach the corpse, wheel about, pause, salute His Majesty and step forward to be decorated.'

James did as bid. Strangely he did not feel foolish. Indeed, as the King took the Hamastan Order of Merit from the footman's tray and pinned it on his breast pocket, then congratulated him on his service to Hamastan, he flushed with pride, as did Nicole, who was smiling proudly at him from her seat behind the Queen.

Without need of guidance James briskly retreated two paces, saluted again, wheeled and marched back to his former position to the accompaniment of generous applause from the multitudes jamming the square.

'Congratulations,' Geoff hissed.

'Thanks,' James whispered, and he realised he was hooked. He had revelled in the crowd's acclamation during the parade but this time the applause was directed solely at him. For the first time he empathised with the Head of State Tour clientele.

The Royal Tour was over. James followed Geoff as side by side with the Battalion Commander they marched forward and saluted the King then shook hands with the mayor. Their Majesties entered the limousine and rode a lap of honour round the square before speeding back to Fiana airport where the Alceides jet waited to return them to Washington via the Bahamas.

In the absence of the royal couple the official party could now relax. James observed the Bishop violently beating off a cowering group of benediction-seeking cripples with his new staff, the crook upending one when it caught his crutches. Behind him the sobbing Indian hotelier sat crestfallen on the town hall steps, one hand fondling his medal while in the other drooped a Hamastanian flag.

They rode back to the hotel and packed their bags. An hour later they found the Indian hotelier waiting to farewell them in the dusty reception area. 'I am telling you, it is a very wonderful honour ...' but he was interrupted by the arrival of the Bishop, plainly in a bad mood. 'Fuck off,' he snarled, and the Indian quickly scuttled out of sight. 'Another bloody dwarf drama,' His Grace complained. 'The little bastard was drunk as a skunk all day and was taunting the elephant. Now I'm completely dwarfless.'

'What happened?' Geoff cried.

'Bloody elephant trod on him. Flat as a pancake. Worse still his outfit's stuffed. Still, it saves us his ten dollars fee.'

'Christ,' Geoff worried. 'Did Their Majesties see it?'

'No. They'd gone. But it's a bloody nuisance. There's a serious dwarf shortage in Africa. I suspect they knock 'em off at birth and I don't blame them either. Never had a troublefree one yet. That's the sixth bastard I've lost.'

'I'll check with the Indian office when I get back to London,' Geoff promised. 'We may be able to ship some of their stock out here.'

James still felt queasy about the hanging and questioned Geoff.

'Same as the beheadings, old man,' Geoff said cheerfully. 'Everyone sees what they expect to see. When Radama disappeared he landed on a mattress beneath the platform, where Jacques was waiting. Jacques quickly grabbed the rope and pulled it taut while Radama slipped the black bag and the noose over the head of our identically dressed robot's neck then Monster yanked it back up. We had the robot made in Japan. It's a pretty simple affair. Works by clockwork, as all it has to do is twitch and kick its legs. Clockwork's perfect as it winds down nicely, just like the real thing. Clever, isn't it?' he concluded gaily.

They farewelled the girls, who tearfully extracted pledges for their return, and an hour later were enjoying dinner in the jet on their way to Nairobi to drop off Juma and then home to England. James' educational tour was over.

# PART TWO

---

# OGG

# – ONE –

Having arrived back in London after midnight, James spent Friday morning in bed contemplating the events of the past fortnight and periodically dozing off. He rose at midday, showered, drank several black coffees, half-heartedly scanned through the pile of newspapers accumulated during his absence and generally pottered aimlessly about. By mid-afternoon, overcome with restlessness, he left the flat and wandered purposelessly down Bayswater Road and into Oxford Street.

London's leaden sky and crowded but orderly streets now seemed deadly dull after the effervescence of Madagascar and James felt discordant among the shoppers and their seemingly trivial pursuits. His sense of alienation increased when two gypsy women, clutching babies and accosting passing pedestrians, approached but abruptly withdrew as he neared. A Bible-waving preacher with a hit-by-lightning creased face stopped in mid-rant and smiled as he passed. These people, outside the norms of society, James suspected, intuitively recognised a kindred spirit.

At six, having eaten nothing all day, he dined in a Soho Chinese restaurant filled with noisy young tourists, cloned penguin-like with their jeans carefully torn at the knee, their inane message-bearing T-shirts and clusters of fashionable brands, plastic shopping bags. His feeling of apartness intensified as he realised he was now emotionally committed to Alceides' cavalier disregard for conventionality.

Despite that, his mood remained confusingly ambivalent. In part James felt euphoric at escaping the predictability of normal existence, tempered by a loneliness at the prospect of abandoning everything of his previous life for he knew that joining Alceides would necessitate an irrevocable and total rejection of his past.

Was the lure of Alceides, he wondered, simply a reversion to childish delights, to circuses and fantasies and a devil-may-care irresponsibility? But he quickly rejected that notion for in the context of his former career, in which there was only one guideline, money, Alceides was a winner and its success lay in its deep comprehension of human nature, precisely as Mr Upton had outlined.

Afterwards he continued wandering, ghost-like and oblivious to the evening crowds, until eventually he found himself opposite St Martin's Theatre, home of *The Mousetrap*. A queue of tourists waiting for the doors to open stretched fifty yards along the road, exactly as Mr Upton had described three weeks earlier. James studied them from across the street as they stood patiently, quietly murmuring to their companions with an air of resignation rather than expectation. They were middle-aged, middle-class suburbanites; paid up members of a social contract of order and respectability, vacuumed in from Melbourne and Montreal, Denver and Durban, their lives pre-programmed to a world of pyjama-wearing, tax-paying, saving for a rainy day, committee-serving, funds-manager fodder fuelling, mundane predictability.

Theirs was an existence which only three weeks earlier was his until fate had intervened to deliver him into the zany world of Alceides. James envisaged the conversation back home months later as photographs were passed among family members.

'Now let me see. Oh yes, that's right. On our last night before leaving for Paris we went to *The Mousetrap*.'

'Ooh, Mum; what was it like?'

'Well your father liked it. I was a little tired after Buckingham Palace and the Tower and we didn't have time for dinner.'

'Can't imagine Dad liking Shakespeare.'

'Oh, Bill. You're so dumb. *The Mousetrap* is Dickens.'

'Well, whatever. They're all the same to me.'

Suddenly the skies opened, and as the rain pounded down, with military-like precision the tourists unfurled their hotel-supplied umbrellas and huddled closer as they continued their dutiful vigil, planned and purchased in a distant land many months before.

James hailed a taxi. Riding home he looked at his watch and felt a pang of nostalgia. It was after 10 p.m. in Kenya. The Latin girls would have completed their traditional African tribal dance and he wondered how they had concluded the performance without the lion scare which, as Geoff had explained, was always a Tuesday night event.

His thoughts turned to Nicole, doubtless now gracing the Hilton lounge, and to Hodge back in Tana, probably rampant in a bar, and Clifford in America, an inconsequential million dollars lighter but enriched by his recent fantasy fulfilment. The Romanian factory would be closed, the craftsmen at home in their cottages watching television game shows after another productive day of statue, coin and icon manufacturing.

Thoughts of the looming weekend dismayed him. Fortunately Jane was not expecting him back until next week, for the prospect of listening to her complaining about his irresponsible abandonment of a respectable career for some pie-in-the-sky unknown – her dominant theme during their last evening before he had left for Romania – seemed intolerable. He had not dared mention his planned shift to Ogg. Alternatively, resuming acquaintance with his former friends seemed hollow; to listen to their sharemarket prattle as they drank themselves into a joyless Saturday night stupor culminating in a melancholy Sunday morning in a strange girl's flat.

Back home, on an impulse he telephoned the Alceides office and was unsurprised when his call was answered by a secretary who responded as if telephoning at eight o'clock on a Friday night was perfectly normal, which in the case of Alceides, he reassured himself, it probably was. Geoff came on the line.

'I'm sorry to bother you at this hour,' James spluttered, 'but I've been thinking. Need we wait until Monday to get under way?'

A burst of laughter greeted this overture. 'Nicely corrupted already I see,' Geoff chuckled. 'Mind you, I shouldn't say that. Obviously you've broken through the slavery mindset of normal employment. Brasch has a theory that slavery is impossible without the tacit consent of the enslaved and that weekends are for workers and wankers.'

'So you're working now?' James asked eagerly.

'Nope. I've just had dinner with Amy. She's my right-hand man …' James heard some background girlish squeals then Geoff, laughing, continued. 'But we've been at it all day. Going over the Ogg building plans actually.'

'Can I come in tomorrow?' James begged.

'Sure. See you about nine. The sooner we get under way the better. Bye, old man.'

James put down the receiver, selected a book from his shelves and contentedly went to bed.

# – TWO –

The following morning at the Alceides building, James pressed the door buzzer, and was greeted more warmly than on his past visits by the Eurasian girl who now introduced herself as Amy. In the lift James enquired what she did at Alceides.

Amy looked puzzled. 'Has Geoff not told you? I live here with him.' Then, observing James' surprise, she added, 'I don't really work for him; more for Brasch actually, organising the various innovations. I've been full-time on Ogg over the past fortnight.'

'So how's it going?' James enquired, surprised by this revelation and the realisation of how little he still knew about Geoff and Alceides.

'We're getting there. No major problems so far,' Amy said. 'But there's lots to do. We're going to be awfully busy.'

They entered Geoff's office. Strewn about the desk and a side table were numerous architects' plans and files. Geoff looked up from behind his desk. 'I'm glad you've come in,' he said. 'We've heaps to do over the next week; lots of decisions to make before we can start construction. As we'll work together there's no point in providing you with an office. First we'll go over the plans, and unless we have any modifications, construction can start immediately. We've reached agreement with a Polish construction company who will ship in eighty tradesmen. They'll prefabricate the lot and helicopter it all in from the mainland.'

'Polish! Why Polish?' James exclaimed. 'Surely it's more sensible to use local firms from the mainland?'

'Come on, James. Haven't you learnt anything over the last fortnight?' Geoff replied, not hiding his annoyance.

'You mean secrecy?'

'Of course. Absolutely vital. The Poles are only a decade out of communism and still bewildered by the west. They'll question nothing. But it doesn't stop there. They'll do the job for half the price and in a fifth the time of any local outfit. We used them to build the Kanju resort.'

'But surely that can't be economic,' James queried.

'It certainly is. You may not believe this but they'll complete the whole project in nine weeks. Using British contractors would take at least eighteen months. Apply enough labour and you'd be surprised how quickly things can be built. The Empire State Building was constructed in only nine months and that was back in 1933. But then the Depression was in full swing and labour was plentiful and bloody cheap. Well it's just like that with the Poles. They'll sleep in tents and work eighty-hour weeks so they can get home as soon as possible. We've offered them a quarter million pounds bonus to complete on target. That's huge money to them. You'd never get British workmen to do that no matter what you gave them. We'd be lucky to get thirty hours a week from them, and they'd demand all sorts of conditions and luxury accommodation and God only knows what else. If we give the Poles the go-ahead next week you'll be living there inside two months. We can shoot up in about three weeks' time and check on progress.'

'What about the architects?' James enquired. 'Are they local? How about secrecy with them?'

'Not a problem,' Geoff said cheerfully. 'Of course they're local. We need them close by for instruction purposes. They hate it of course, but obviously we refuse to tell them where the project is. We gave them a topographical plan and told them exactly what we want. It's only curiosity which makes them want to know where it's all going and what it's about. Amy told them to mind their bloody business when they kept pressing her. Their brief is to draft in line with our instructions.'

Amy giggled. 'They did go on at me terribly while you two were away. They kept saying if they knew where it was they could make suggestions. Can you imagine that?'

'Well, yes I can as a matter of fact,' James replied coolly. 'Surely that's what architects are supposed to do?'

Geoff and Amy stared at James, dumbstruck. Eventually Geoff broke the lull. 'Are you mad?' he demanded. 'Have you ever actually worked with architects? Good grief, man. Forget all the jokes about

190

accountants. With the exception of quantity surveyors, architects are the dreariest of all professionals. Look at the give-away sign. They're the only profession who wear uniforms.'

'Uniforms?' James puzzled. 'What uniforms?'

'Bloody bow ties. They all do, all over the world. It's simply fashion-following which is the sure sign of a dullard. It's no different from tattoos, and who has them? Prison inmates, primitive savages, the armed forces, witless shop girls; anyone who's been reduced to virtually a number or whose life is so humdrum they must contrive an identity to purport individuality. But as they don't actually have any individuality they end up mimicking one another with their tattoos and bow ties or whatever. Ask an architect for ideas, oh dear me,' and he chuckled at the absurdity of the notion. 'When we want ideas and creativity we'll stick to Brasch, thank you very much.'

'Well, to be perfectly frank I find all of that rather cynical,' James said. 'It's ridiculous to blanket dismiss architects like that. Every great building is the inspiration of an architect.'

'I think you're rather missing the point,' Geoff said. 'Look, it's a bit like dining out. Sometimes you know exactly what you feel like eating so you go to a particular restaurant which will deliver that. Other times you simply go to a damn good restaurant and indulge in one of the chef's concoctions. We're not being cynical, we're being practical because we know exactly what we want with the Ogg buildings and we don't want the damn architect messing us about with his concoctions.'

'Well, be that as it may. I still think you're being a bit unreasonable. Isn't the reason for the bow tie because a normal tie will get in the way at the drawing board?'

'Absolute rubbish. Mostly the drawing board is upright so it's not an issue. But even if it's flat, why doesn't every other male white-collar worker have the same problem? I'll tell you; because there isn't a problem. But look, don't think I'm picking on architects. The real supremos when it comes to dull predictability are the CEOs of big companies. Furthermore, they know it, so they always try and compensate in interviews by the inference that at heart and in private they're actually a bit of a lad with a buccaneering spirit. Of course if that was true they wouldn't be where they are. Large companies can't risk having anyone who's not excruciatingly boring at the helm. Too dangerous for shareholders. Like the threat with architects, the buggers might start having inspirations. But CEOs are the same worldwide. They all have wives who could pass as their mothers, and, again like the architects, a universal uniform if I can put it that way.'

'Oh yes. And what's that?' James asked, his curiosity aroused.

'They all have a Harley-Davidson motorbike as their purported weekend recreation. I'll scream if I read another magazine interview with one of these middle-age bores with an accompanying photograph showing him astride a Harley-Davidson wearing a black Lenin cap and trying to look macho. God they're pathetic. As if dressing up can make you a swashbuckling type but they only do it because they know they're so dull.'

As with his earlier meeting a month ago, a faint sound of laughter came from overhead. Startled, James looked up at the ceiling and then to Geoff. When he displayed no reaction James again concluded he had imagined it. He pondered the Harley-Davidson observation and realised how true it was. Geoff's description fitted numerous CEO interviews he had read in business magazines in his sharebroking days.

'So why Harley-Davidsons?' he asked.

'Two things. First the cost, so that's simply boasting. But mainly because the brand became famous as the Hell's Angels' bike of choice. The CEOs like the association as compensation for their dreariness, even though most nuns would have more in common with the Hell's Angels than they ever will. You should hear Brasch on the subject. He's very funny.'

'Well, that's another thing,' James said. 'When will I meet Brasch? I've heard so much about him, I can't wait.'

A frown crossed Geoff's features. He thought for a moment then said quietly, 'Look. Brasch is a bit on the shy side. Probably there's no need to meet him.'

'What are you hiding Geoff?' James demanded. 'Why all this mystery every time Brasch's name is mentioned? Your father told me to ask questions. What's the point of doing so if you don't answer them?'

Again Geoff hesitated. He rose from the desk, walked to a window and stood silently, his back to James as he looked out. After a lengthy pause he turned and said, 'There could be value in discussing things with Brasch. But I must warn you. He's somewhat unconventional. It could be a bit of a shock.'

'You've already told me that in Africa,' James said tersely. 'So what is it about him? Does he have two heads?'

'Let's see how we go today,' Geoff proposed cautiously. 'If by the end of the day issues arise, we could visit Brasch tomorrow. But there's lots to do. First there's the building plans, then we must decide the employment programme and purchase all the furnishings and whatnot. There's a hell of a lot of interviewing to do. Remember, we're taking on a fairly large staff for Ogg.'

'I can't believe we can do all of this so quickly,' James said. 'People are always complaining about building permits and how long they take. I'd have thought you wouldn't even have those in six months.'

Geoff looked at him, amazement again crossing his face. 'Damn it all. Haven't you learnt anything at all in the past couple of weeks? We're not getting bloody building permits. We'd be lucky to be under way in three years, if at all in fact, if we sought permits. Chances are a hundred per cent there'd be cardigan-wearing planning officers or busy-body councillors or bearded conservationists who would all oppose it on totally nonsensical grounds.'

'But we have to have building permits. The law requires it.'

'I really am surprised at you, James. You don't seem to have any cognisance of modern society. The entire governmental process effectively boils down to stopping people doing things. It's even true of undeveloped countries. Do you think Kanju would exist if we had applied for permits? Look at the excellent work we're doing with the Royal and Presidential Tours – all the employment and economic stimulation we create. Imagine if we sought permission in India or Africa or Peru when we did Papal Visits. We'd literally never have any tours under our belts. People are always going on about judicial activism, and rightly so as it's simply a civilised form of political dictatorship. But what always staggers me is how readily the public turn a blind eye to bureaucratic activism which is now completely out of hand and immensely more damaging.'

'I don't suppose it's occurred to you that the public's apparent passivity might reflect their tacit concurrence with well-meaning regulation,' James countered.

'No, you're right, it bloody well hasn't,' Geoff replied sharply. 'What has, however, is that what you call passivity I would call apathy. You're

193

supposed to be an economic historian. Study the last two hundred years and you'll find every economic boom has invariably been sparked by a new innovation or technology or new territory being opened up for development. But the surge only ever lasts about five or six years and why? Because in the early stages the innovation is unregulated and exuberant. Then in come the bureaucrats with their spirit-crushing rules and regulations and taxes and the music stops. When you joined Alceides we didn't just expect your body and mind but your spirit as well. Applying for permits indeed,' and Geoff shook his head in wonderment. 'Dear me, you really do astonish me at times, James. What next I can't imagine. You'll be wanting us to pay tax soon with that line of thinking.'

Again James thought he heard the faint sound of laughter from overhead but as Geoff remained unperturbed he, stung by the rebuke, responded, 'Well that's all very well if you can get away with it, but what if everyone took that line?'

'Get away with it. Get away with it,' Geoff exclaimed, his voice rising. 'Are you completely naive? Getting away with it, as you put it, is hardly the issue. Of course we get away with it. And why? As everyone thinks like you do, the bully-boy bureaucrats take their compliance for granted so they're not programmed to deal with those who don't. They don't believe such thinking exists, they're so convinced they have everyone subdued. Listen, James. We get on with our lives and simply ignore their preposterous regulations. You really will have to rethink things, old man. Alceides is not based on law-breaking; it's based on law-ignoring, which is a quite different proposition.'

'Come on, Geoff,' James retorted indignantly. 'Surely you're not suggesting building regulations – fire and electrical safety standards, health issues and all the rest of it – are wrong or silly?'

'You're missing the point. Of course our buildings largely comply with those standards, not because they're there but because in most cases they're sensible and therefore in our interest. That's not the problem. It's the interference and procrastination which accompanies them that we're not prepared to tolerate, so it's damn the torpedoes and full speed ahead. It's the only way to get anything done in the modern world.'

'But the whole show could be closed down,' James persisted.

'Rubbish! First they'll never know about it. There are over eight hundred islands off the coast of Scotland and less than a fifth of them are inhabited, specially in the Hebrides archipelago where only the main ones have any people. Second, even if they did find out, and they won't, they can't get there. Brasch has come up with an idea to prevent access to the harbour, and the rest of the coast is too rugged to land on. And finally, we've searched the land titles offices and you probably won't believe this but Ogg literally doesn't exist in any legal context. Obviously it's part of Britain by dint of its geographic situation, but in a jurisdiction sense no local authority has any recorded power over it.'

'They could land by helicopter,' James tendered weakly.

'Brasch has even thought of that. That's why part and parcel of your little empire will be two rottweilers. They'll be penned up and under the command of the sheep-master who will have very clear instructions about releasing them should there ever be any unauthorised visitors. Believe me, they would be very short visits indeed. Now, I suggest you stop all this hand-wringing and we get down to work.'

# – THREE –

It was not in James' nature to be pushy but that night in a restaurant with Amy and Geoff and in high spirits after a hugely enjoyable day discussing the Ogg plans and emboldened by wine, he again raised the subject of Brasch. This time he was more forceful.

'I'd like to meet Brasch,' he said adamantly during a lull in the conversation. As the familiar frown crossed Geoff's face he continued, 'Look, I've thrown in my lot with Alceides. Damn it all, I'm part of the team now. Brasch is obviously the pivotal brains-trust so why can't I meet him without all this hedging?' he demanded.

Amy stiffened and cast an anxious glance at Geoff who leant back in his chair, wineglass in hand, contemplating James' demand as if this was the first time the proposition had been raised.

'No reason at all,' he said lightly. 'Actually Brasch likes meeting people. We'll see him tomorrow.'

Bewildered by the volte-face and noting Amy's surprise, James pressed on. 'You mean Brasch will be in tomorrow?' a suggestion which brought giggling from Amy.

'Brasch lives in the building. He occupies half the fourth floor right above my office,' Geoff replied in a matter of fact voice. 'So do I. Amy's and my flat takes up the remaining third floor next to my office, and Dad has one on the sixth for when he's in London. Next time he's here ask to see his Audubon paintings. He has the third-largest private collection in existence. That's if you're interested.'

'So what goes on in the rest of the building?' James asked, unwilling to be distracted from his broader enquiry.

'The ground floor is storage. There's a cart-dock at the rear serving a large coolroom for storing meat and other frozen goods and another dried goods, foodstuffs room. Amy looks after it.'

'What on earth do you need all that for?' James asked, puzzled.

Geoff laughed mysteriously. 'Don't ask. You'll learn the details in the course of time but suffice to say quite a lot of people, all employees of course, live on the premises. Matter of fact, the building's usage is entirely residential apart from my office.'

'You're kidding me. Surely Brasch has an office?'

Amy gave a little hoot of laughter.

'Well, no actually,' Geoff said calmly. 'But don't ask any more. It will be clearer after tomorrow. I suppose you could say Brasch works from home, as it were. A very nice home mind you,' he added hastily. Then obviously eager to change the subject he continued, 'There's a small collection of Hogarth etchings which are worth a look on the fifth-floor lobby. Actually, I don't know if you're interested or not but the Alceides building is a veritable art gallery and I'm not just referring to the things in my office,' he added, referring to the large Francis Bacon and two Freud oils James had admired on the walls. 'There's a Rodin, a couple of Epstein busts of his mistress, two early Picassos, a Gauguin; heaps of things scattered throughout. Dad's a collector but they're also part of our investment strategy. Once the artist is dead and output has ceased, the monopoly factor we place so much emphasis on comes into play. Our art collection, value-wise, has outperformed our global utilities portfolio over the past five years. The stuff is spread all over the building in the staff flats and lobbies.'

But James was not to be distracted. 'Well if Brasch lives in the building why haven't I met him before? Why wasn't he there today instead of us listing all the things we were to ask him about?'

'Brasch doesn't go anywhere. We go to him.'

'So the mountain comes to Mohammed.'

Geoff stared pointedly at James and Amy began to giggle again.

'I did warn you Brasch is a bit unusual,' Geoff said tentatively after a pause.

'Come on, Geoff. What is he? Some kind of freak or what?'

'You could say that actually,' Geoff replied thoughtfully. 'Brasch is big. Very big in fact.'

'So's Monster. So bloody what!'

'He's not big like that. He's just …' Geoff paused. 'He's just rather large; enormous in fact.'

'You mean he's fat.'

197

This time Geoff tittered along with Amy. 'Yes, you could certainly say that.'

'And you've been hiding him all the time just because he's fat. I don't believe it. It's ridiculous. There are plenty of fat people in the world.'

'True, but not too many like Brasch.'

'Well, what the hell is he like then? I mean what's so peculiar?'

'Mmm. Well um, Brasch doesn't have many visitors.'

'But you said he quite likes meeting people. Is he odd in some way?'

'Um, odd, no, no, he's not odd,' Geoff stumbled. 'Quite normal actually, that is apart from his size. Bloody bright mind you. Quite a droll sense of humour in fact. It's just basically been company policy for him not to have much contact with people.'

'Oh come on, Geoff,' James said angrily. 'You can't stop him. What about when he goes out with his family and whatever else he does recreationally.'

'Brasch doesn't go out.'

James stared at him. 'What do you mean he doesn't go out?'

'Brasch hasn't left his flat in, well, let me think, at least four years now.'

'You mean he's a recluse?'

'Well, I suppose you could say that, in a sense that is. Well, not in the normal meaning of a recluse; inadvertent rather. He simply doesn't go out,' Geoff floundered.

'I'm looking forward very much to meeting Brasch tomorrow,' James said firmly. Sensing he had pushed the Brasch issue as far as was desirable, he reverted to Geoff's earlier diversions. 'The Audubons and Picassos; products of Romania are they?' he enquired lightly.

A flash of annoyance crossed Geoff's face then he relaxed and laughed. 'The artwork in this building is insured for over £12 million. I've told you; you mustn't take the icons lark too seriously. In the scale of our overall operations it's a mere frippery.'

'But Brasch is genuine?' James retorted.

'Larger than life,' Geoff laughed. 'Tomorrow you will see for yourself.'

# – FOUR –

On Sunday morning James arrived at the office determined that procrastination on the Brasch front would induce a showdown even though there was no reason to meet him other than curiosity.

'Where's Brasch?' he said abruptly to Geoff.

'I told you. Brasch doesn't leave his flat. We're going to him.'

'Now?'

'Yes. He's expecting us. But don't forget he's very large. It can be quite a shock.'

'This is silly,' James snapped. 'And there's another thing. Doesn't he have a Christian name? What do I call him?'

'Oh no; well, that is he has, but it's always been just Brasch. That's the way he prefers it.'

'Really! How odd. What's his name?'

'You can't call him that. He'll order us out.' Geoff shuffled awkwardly. 'Look for Christ's sake don't let on I told you but it's Egbert. Understandably he was taunted about it as a child so now he insists on just being called Brasch. You'll get used to it.'

'What a strange thing,' James exclaimed. 'If he's that bothered by it, why doesn't he change it by deed poll?'

'I said that to him once,' Geoff said resignedly. 'Heaps of people do after suffering being Damian or Elvis throughout their adolescence. I was no different. My second Christian name is Pericles – my father's input needless to say – and I lived in fear of anyone finding out when I was a kid. Now I don't give a damn. But it made no difference to Brasch when I told him that. He cut up quite nasty and wouldn't discuss it. The Danes have it right. Their Birth Registrars have the power to reject names which might cause their recipients

199

embarrassment in later years. The problem is where do you draw the line? What about the Kevins for example?'

'What about the Kevins?'

'Oh come on, James. Get real. If you were a bank manager would you give credit to someone called Kevin?'

James pondered the Kevin credit poser until eventually Amy broke the silence. 'I like Brasch,' she said. 'He's funny.'

Geoff rose and took a manila file from his desk. 'Here's the list of yesterday's unresolved issues. Let's go,' and the three of them left and crowded into the tiny lift. They arrived at the fourth floor to a bland lobby, at each end of which was a single door. Geoff knocked on the left-hand door then opened it and, followed by Amy, led the way into a large wooden-floored room. The walls were lined with books, and as Amy and Geoff stepped aside James saw, at the end of the room, a massive human colossus.

Enveloped in a blue tent-like kaftan, Brasch sprawled like an enormous whale, semi-reclining in a six-foot-wide wheel-chair contraption. Thick black horn-rimmed glasses contrasted against his pasty white face and lank black hair layered across his great block-like head.

'Come in, come in,' he boomed in a deep voice which resonated round the room. 'So this is James, or would you prefer Admiral? I watched the video of your Madagascan performance yesterday. You need to smarten those salutes up my man,' he laughed.

Following the others, James approached and extended his hand. Brasch acknowledged the gesture dismissively with a brief flicker of his huge paw which was lying along an armrest on which lay a series of buttons. 'A timely arrival. Just in time for morning tea,' he bellowed as he pressed a button with a large, sausage-like finger.

From the rear a tiny middle-aged Asian woman emerged pushing a trolley containing a coffee-pot, milk jug, sugar bowl, three cups and saucers, an enormous mug and a platter with a dozen chocolate eclairs oozing whipped cream.

'That's Hoon,' Geoff said. 'She looks after Brasch. She's Cambodian and doesn't speak English so there's no point introducing you.'

Hoon knelt and set the items on a table alongside Brasch then rose and scurried from the room. Brasch promptly took an eclair and bit it in half. Almost immediately he swallowed it and then finished off the other half. James and Geoff sat in armchairs facing Brasch as Amy poured the coffee. 'Three sugars please,' Brasch instructed, reaching for another eclair. 'Chaps having something to eat?' he enquired. 'Hoon can rustle up some more eclairs.'

'Ah no, I'm fine thanks,' James muttered.

'Excellent,' Brasch whinnied happily, not hiding his relief. He took another eclair and in two bites it was gone. Over the next five minutes he polished off the lot. After the last had disappeared he stared wistfully at the empty plate. 'Funny things, eclairs. Why is it one always feels so peckish after one or two?' he enquired sadly then turned to the business in hand.

The various unresolved issues were raised and James marvelled as Brasch listened while they were recounted then neatly summarised the problem and presented the solution. His clarity of thinking and mental dexterity, and sometimes offbeat solutions, astonished James. Brasch was plainly a genius. No topic seemed beyond his knowledge, no problem beyond his capacity to resolve. He laced his comments with witticisms which at times had his three visitors doubled up with laughter.

Finally they were done. 'Sure you won't stay for lunch,' Brasch enquired. 'Hoon's roasted a suckling pig. Even though I'm absolutely famished I wouldn't want to hog the lot and make a pig of myself, if you'll excuse the puns.'

'No, no,' Geoff said. 'We've an awful lot to do. There are bound to be more problems so we'll come and see you again,' and the three returned to Geoff's office where Amy brought in sandwiches and coffee while they continued discussing Ogg.

At five Geoff rose and opened the drinks cabinet, drawing forth two bottles of red wine. 'Let's pack it in until tomorrow,' he said. It had been a long day with a great deal of detailed discussion and James welcomed the relief of the wine. The first bottle was quickly emptied.

'I must say, Brasch is an extraordinary fellow,' James commented after they had almost finished the second bottle and Geoff was opening a third.

'Yes. He's a genius. Literally in fact,' Geoff boasted. 'Has an IQ of 185. That's better than Einstein.'

'How did you find him?' James enquired.

'Find him! We didn't find him. We searched him out. There are a lot of Brasches out there going to waste.'

'What do you mean you searched him out?'

Geoff topped up James' glass, slopping some wine on the table as he did so. Plainly he was a little tiddly as Amy had scarcely contributed to the demise of the first two bottles and her original glass was still half full. He peered at James, swaying slightly. 'You still haven't got it, have you?' he said accusingly.

'Got what?'

'Nothing in Alceides is an accident. My father imagined Brasch then sought out the seed, planted it and reaped the crop,' he said mysteriously.

'What the hell are you on about?'

Geoff sat down heavily in an armchair. 'I'll tell you,' he said flatly. 'After all you seem to have taken everything else in your stride.'

'Why don't we go out to dinner?' Amy suggested nervously.

Geoff cast her a hood-eyed glance. 'Bugger dinner. We're having a quiet drink first, James and I are. Having a little chat; all part of James' education. He can cope. Handled the Royal Tours and Kanju OK. What's Brasch in the scheme of things? No different.'

Amy cast a scathing look at Geoff then shrugged dismissively, rose and left the office.

'So what's the story then?' James pressed.

'Goes back to what my father told you. All the changes in the world today. Dad was always ahead of the game. Like every other so-called captain of bloody industry he was constantly on the look-out for management talent; trotting up to Oxford and Cambridge and the other universities. Only got cast-offs. The elite were snaffled up by the City. Didn't matter. None of them any good anyway,' he slurred.

'So what happened?'

'Once Alceides began to grow Dad applied some analysis. He needed really bright lateral thinkers. Soon realised, academic achievement aside, in his former travel industry days he had made the mistake of evaluating candidates by the usual criteria, just like everyone else. Targeting presentable and personable types, giving them extra points if they had sporting and other accomplishments under their belts. Dodging the beard wearers and MBAs and other wets. And then it was a waste of time as the so-called desirable ones turned their noses up at the travel business, which is how he had to represent Alceides. Not sufficiently prestigious. Can't blame 'em either.

'Anyway, it occurred to him that what he really needed was creative brain-power. Couldn't give a damn if they were any good at cricket or president of the debating society. Cut a long story short, he sought out fat buggers, not just fat but massively so – obese, monstrous, gigantic – but with the proviso that they were bloody bright. And that's how he found Brasch. No one else wanted him. Everyone despises fat buggers.'

'But surely Alceides could match the City salaries?' James queried.

'Ah! Not the point! Dad was seeking a particular outlook. Basically he wanted brilliant people with a total comprehension of human behaviour, which is where the fat factor came in. Problem with the attractive ones, the people everyone seeks who seem obvious stand-out candidates, is their easy success at everything which distorts their comprehension of life. Because life's a breeze for them they have no understanding of what it's like for normal people so they make poor judgements on others' behalves. It's why bright buggers make poor teachers. They assume everyone has their mental capacity. Same with sport. The best coaches are always those who played the game but weren't great at it. They understand their pupils' difficulties because they had them too. Well, if you think back to your school days there was no greater pariah than the fat kid. No bugger talks to them; they're total outcasts, the ultimate social misfits. So if they're clever two things happen to them. First, they become bloody astute observers of human behaviour for the damn good reason that that's all they ever are socially, that is observers rather than participators.'

'That's rather devious thinking,' James said. 'What's the other point?'

'The second thing is their extreme loyalty to anyone or anything which will accept them. That's why you always find fatties in weirdo movements; you know, communist clubs at university, new age nonsense movements, minor political parties, North Korean Friendship Societies; any outfit desperate for members. Everyone else shuns them. Misfit organisations attract misfit members. As losers bound up in their victimhood, they feel an affinity. Poor old Brasch was no exception – out of loneliness he once joined a yodelling club at university, but don't ever mention I told you that. He'd kill me. It had been started by a bearded Swiss nutter and the only other members were a blind five-foot Welshman and a paraplegic sociology student. So all things considered you can understand why in the case of employment a fatty's loyalty's not just to the company but to the job itself. Their lives are so empty the job's the only thing they have to live for so they deliver in bucketloads.'

'Brasch is a classic example. Hasn't left the premises in four years. He reads, watches television news and current affairs, eats and thinks. His whole world is Alceides. He derives enormous vicarious satisfaction watching the videos of every Royal and Presidential Tour. Every now and again Juma sends him a tape of golfers dropping 60-foot putts and chaps playing a trout for two hours. As I told you, this building is over two centuries old and has well worn, thin wooden floorboards separating each level. I always know when he's watching a video as I can hear him down here booming away laughing. We've checked it out and he can't hear us talking, thank God, it's just he has such a loud laugh.'

James nodded, relieved to learn the laughter he'd heard was not a figment of his imagination.

'Why don't you insulate his floor?' James suggested. 'Bang down some carpet.'

'Can't. With his weight Brasch's motorised wheelchair wouldn't move on it. He needs mobility to access his books. I make no bones about it. We'd be lost without him. He knows absolutely everything. Any problem that arises, take it to Brasch and he works out the answer, often straight away. You saw that today.'

'I certainly did,' James conceded.

'Compare the likes of Brasch with the so-called elite, the golden ones everyone chases,' Geoff continued. 'They change jobs frequently because everyone constantly woos them. For them work's just a necessary evil as they have too big a life outside of it and they don't give a damn about their jobs because they don't have to. They could never come up with Brasch-type ideas. They're too busy enjoying the good life to be bothered even trying, not that they're actually capable of doing so.'

'And your father worked all this out?' James marvelled.

'He did and he's been proven right. Putting aside intelligence it all boils down to a single factor and that is the degree of Brasch's obesity. The only initial concern Dad had was that being social misfits they'd all be left-wingers. But we pay bloody big tax-free salaries so that problem instantly takes care of itself, as it always does with left-wingers once they realise they've escaped their destiny as a £20,000 a year local government employee. I can't imagine what Brasch does with it all but presumably the money accumulating in his bank account makes him happy.'

'He'll die,' James said sharply.

'That of course is the only flaw,' Geoff remarked casually. 'We monitor his weight. He performs best when he's over 440 pounds. We pull him down to four hundred periodically for health reasons.'

'And he co-operates with that?'

'He doesn't know. His bed rests on an industrial weighing machine. When he gets out of hand, approaching 500 pounds, as he has recently, Hoon changes his diet in subtle ways. Those chocolate eclairs this morning, for example. He likes those. Currently we're bringing him down fifty pounds so the chocolate, the pastry and the cream are made with artificial fat-free substances.'

'And he never ever goes out?' James marvelled. 'You'd think curiosity would get the better of him?'

'We don't want him to go out or develop outside interests. Anyway, he can't. He couldn't fit through the door or in the lift and he could never squeeze down the stairs even if he could walk, which in fact he now barely can.'

James stared at Geoff. 'So he's a prisoner?' he said accusingly.

'It's his choice.'

It was then James recalled Geoff's startled reaction when he had joked about slavery on his second visit to Alceides a month ago. 'It's appalling. You're taking advantage of his weakness. He's virtually a slave.'

'If he's a slave then he's a voluntary one,' Geoff said breezily.

'So what if he does die? You'd be stuffed then.'

'We've anticipated that. We have three other trainees – I suppose you could call them mini-Brasches – ensconced in flats on the sixth and seventh floors currently being fattened up. Three are still only around 300 to 340 pounds at the moment, but coming along nicely. One's reached 370 pounds and is beginning to produce. He came up with the Royal Tour hangings idea. Brasch was the same. Once he passed the 400-pound mark he really oozed ideas. We know why too. At 400 pounds it's almost impossible to move. There's nothing to do but read and think, and of course eat. There are two other Cambodian ladies living upstairs who look after them.'

'Why Cambodians?' James asked, sensing yet another offbeat twist looming.

Geoff laughed. 'You'll say it's more devious thinking. Basically security is the main reason. They're all widows from the Pol Pot era; simple village women with no idea where they are. We pay them heaps and none of them can speak English which means they're too terrified to go out. They do a couple of years here, cooking, washing and what have you for our fatties, and go home rich women, at least in the Cambodian context.'

'But if they can't speak English how on earth do they communicate?'

'That's the whole point. We don't want them distracting the tubbies from eating and thinking, and as well there's always the risk of a fatty getting a minder to take a message, or God knows what, to the outside world. Amy's half English and half Thai and although Thai's different from Cambodian, there are enough common words for her to be able to instruct them, such as on food issues. We don't let the fatties have the Internet or telephones so basically they're isolated apart from television and newspapers. We want them to stay informed about the outside world but not in touch, if you know what I mean. It was a bit of a treat for Brasch, us visiting him this morning.'

'It's disgraceful,' James protested. 'It's just like factory farming and, anyway, what if they prove duds? What happens then? Have the other three trainees come up with anything?'

'Different field. Two are attached to our investment division so they've got a bit more learning to go and anyway, they're still in the anorexic 300-pound region so we can't expect spectacular results yet. We're hoping they'll produce some interesting new financial market concepts. Ultimately they'll be part of a six-man complement of obese giants, only they won't be a team in the sense of working together. We'll be bringing in two more for fattening this year. Another thing; you say it's like factory farming. Well so what! This is a commercial venture in a commercial building and the activities we engage in here are eating and thinking. The two are mutually dependent. Why should we be ashamed of that?'

'So you're telling me someone wanders about universities looking for obese people and approaching them with job offers,' James asked, not hiding his astonishment.

'Good heavens no. We're more efficient than that. We've a network of history professors across England in the better universities who turn 'em up for us. They receive a five thousand pound finder's fee,

206

and if the candidate turns out OK we pay another five thousand after a year. We only consider history graduates. They tend to lack any personal ambition so they make ideal employees. Most other tertiary subjects are basically advanced mechanics in any academic sense and their graduates, no matter how bright, are useless for our purposes. We want people with imagination and that requires a broad knowledge and a sense of enquiry which history students seem to have most of all. I've eight new prospects for interviewing once Ogg is put to bed. All blokes of course. Too many emotional problems with fat girls. That's a point you're overlooking when you moralise about our strategy. Fat girls, even when their problem is self-inflicted, don't like being fat girls. The fellows are different. To be able to eat non-stop and think up offbeat schemes is paradise in their eyes. Any latent interest they may have had in sex soon fades away. Their only nocturnal bedroom noises are the rustle of chocolate wrappings.'

'This is just unbelievable,' James muttered. 'Surely given how bright Brasch is he understands what's going on. I'm surprised he doesn't warn the new chaps.'

'None of them know of the others' existence. Obviously that would be disastrous as they'd work out what's going on. Anyway, like I said; Brasch is in glutton's heaven. He eats a normal person's weekly intake almost every day. It's his choice. He could diet and depart but he doesn't want to.'

'What about Brasch's laughing? Can't the fatties above him hear and are their floors the same; you know, paper-thin?'

'Of course,' Geoff said. 'But we covered that. They all think it's my mother. We told them she's a madwoman locked away with a minder so they're used to it now and think nothing of it.'

'It's disgusting,' James protested. 'It's exploitation of personal vulnerability. Totally beyond my ...' He was interrupted as Amy returned waving a fax sheet.

'Super news,' she said. 'Tokyo's found our Ogg manageress,' and she handed the letter to Geoff.

'Aha, listen to this from our Tokyo office,' he exclaimed triumphantly. '"Pleased to advise have secured excellent Ogg manageress. Miyumi Todaka, aged 26, single, pretty, personable, speaks excellent English, former Japanese tennis champion, at peak reached seventh in world rankings, retired recently as fed up with constant travel, popular heroine with Japanese. Available immediately." It's all

207

here. It's tremendous news. The Japanese are almost as bad as the Americans when it comes to celebrity worshipping, specially sporting stars. What a lucky break. She'll really pull the punters.'

'I remember her,' James said slowly, searching his memory and forgetting for the moment his concern about Brasch and the other tubbies. 'I saw her at Wimbledon about three years ago when she made the semis. She's a dainty little thing and the crowd were right behind her when she knocked over the number two seed, a six-foot American giantess.'

'Well, it's certainly a wonderful omen for the future,' Geoff said. 'Let's go and have some dinner and celebrate,' and they rose and left the building.

# – FIVE –

Over the following fortnight James worked twelve-hour days at the Alceides offices, returning home late each evening, frequently to lengthy telephone complaining sessions from Jane.

The deterioration in their relationship grew with every contact marked by acrimony. On their last meeting he had actually walked out on her when she was the guest-speaker launching a novel subsidised by the Arts Council. The evening had erupted into a row when driving to the function, James had interrupted her babble about the book's brilliance with 'If it's that good then I don't see why taxpayers should pay for it' whereupon had followed the standard Jane diatribe about his insensitivity to finer things.

They had arrived at the usual crowded room of garrulous bearded men and plain, desperate-looking thirtyish women. Jane had plunged in full gush into the throng so James secured a glass of wine and drifted over to the host bookseller's table piled high with copies of *My Horse Has Three Legs* and read the opening page. No mention of horses, instead a lengthy and detailed description of autumn leaves falling. He turned to the last page; the leaves were still falling. James had slipped out of the room and returned home. He had not spoken to Jane until this morning when, adopting an untypical conciliatory tone, she had telephoned and asked him to accompany her to an art opening that night. Emboldened he had refused, but following a bout of sobbing he eventually weakened and agreed to pick her up afterwards at 7.30 and take her to dinner.

Meanwhile construction at Ogg had commenced. Amy had purchased numerous furnishings and other requirements which had been sent north to the small warehouse at Oban she had leased as a permanent supplies depot where a local had been employed as a part-time warehouseman.

'Once Ogg's fully operational, he'll be fairly busy,' Geoff pointed out after James had expressed surprise at how much Amy had accomplished while they had been away. Her inventories filled a hard-bound folio and James marvelled as he flicked through and noted the range of esoteric and trivial purchases such as scissors, first-aid kits, scotch tape, printed stationery, cartons of light-bulbs, framed historic Scottish lithographs, oil paintings of Scottish landscapes, gardening tools, toothpaste … the list seemed endless.

'It really wasn't that difficult,' Amy said modestly. 'It's no different from buying for a household except for the volume. But there'll be lots more things needed so just keep faxing any requirements once you're there and I will send them to Oban. The helicopter will bring them in with each new guest intake.'

'Which is why we'll take it slowly at first,' Geoff remarked. 'Just a few guests at a time until things are running smoothly.'

Now that the lease was signed and James was receiving a monthly rental, the management of Ogg's sheep business was transferred from the Edinburgh accountants to Alceides. In the second week, staffing interviews were about to commence when Mr Upton arrived for his monthly visit.

'So, James. How did you find our operations?' he enquired lightly.

'Most impressive, sir. Obviously very innovative and well managed.' Noting Mr Upton's briefly raised eyebrows, James quickly added, 'And of course, highly profitable.'

'Dear me, James,' Mr Upton murmured. 'I rather hoped you would recognise more important attributes than those. Did you not observe the very high degree of customer satisfaction? We pride ourselves on that at Alceides. Profit follows automatically in the wake of customer pleasure with a monopoly so one naturally takes it for granted.'

'Indeed, sir. And of course there's the amusement.'

'Ah, the amusement,' Mr Upton responded soothingly. 'That is perhaps our greatest achievement, at least with our Head of State Tour clients.' He pondered for a while then added, 'Well, some of them at least. I'm afraid many of our monarchs, and particularly their consorts, are susceptible to the Ozymandias virus and sadly derive little humour from our services, satisfied though they otherwise are.'

'Don't knock them. They pay extra for lacking a sense of humour,' Geoff said sharply. 'Only the serious ones who really believe they're monarchs buy executions remember.'

'Quite so,' Mr Upton said dryly. 'Perhaps we should view that additional expenditure as a tax on their sobriety. Now tell me,' he said abruptly changing the subject, 'how is the Ogg planning proceeding?'

For ten minutes, interspersed by periodic questions from Mr Upton, Geoff outlined all that had been accomplished, concluding by reporting that he, Amy and James would be flying north to inspect construction on the island in the near future.

It was then that Mr Upton dropped his bombshell.

'I've been giving the Ogg exercise a great deal of thought,' he said. 'I rather think it is ill-considered, or at least one part; fortunately the lesser of the two proposed activities.'

James, Geoff and Amy gazed at him stunned.

'There is no doubt in my mind that the Japanese killer-sheep exercise will succeed,' Mr Upton continued. 'But I now have serious reservations about Ogg Castle.'

'Good Lord,' Geoff protested. 'We're well down the track on it. The construction work on Ogg Castle is under way. We've shifted the shepherd couple down to one of the empty village cottages, purchased all the furniture and trimmings and we're about to interview thespians for the laird role. It's a hell of a time to change your mind.'

'None of that will be wasted,' Mr Upton elaborated. 'There are other more desirable activities for the refurbished castle. As I said, I have no qualms about the killer-sheep operation. It will suit the Japanese taste very well. But targeting the Scots, or even those of Scottish ancestry, now seems to me extremely unwise. Frankly, it is difficult to imagine a less suitable race to ...', he hesitated, searching for the right words, '... to apply illusions to,' he concluded clumsily.

'But what's the problem? What do you object to?' Geoff demanded.

'It's not for nothing that the Scots are referred to as canny,' Mr Upton explained. 'No other racial stereotype is so favourable.' Warming to his subject he continued, 'I have come to the conclusion that the Scots are the most accomplished race of all. Considering there's only five million of them, their creative and innovative contribution to the world is unmatched.'

211

'Like what?' Geoff enquired suspiciously.

'Television, merchant banking, the jet engine, golf, whisky, tartans, the bagpipes; the list of their innovations is eclectic and lengthy,' Mr Upton responded. 'People think of the Jews and the Germans, the two races which share respect for education as much as the Scots, as the great innovators, but they're not in the same league when one considers their relative numbers. Scots have dominated British politics over the past century, they've produced great thinkers with a pragmatic emphasis, perhaps best epitomised by Adam Smith. And that gets to the nub of the difficulty. For all their disproportionate contribution they are essentially practical people as illustrated by the nature of their innovations. But where are their truly outstanding poets, artists, playwrights and authors? They don't exist, which suggests a certain hard-headed lack of romance in their character. For that reason alone the Scots diaspora is not a suitable target for Alceides operations. Unlike the Irish, their interest in their ancestral roots is intellectual and detached rather than nostalgic. I said they are called canny. There's a less kind interpretation illustrated by their reputation for being careful with their pennies. Hardly our material surely?'

Silence fell. Eventually James spoke up. 'So what are you proposing, sir?'

'I believe you should continue with your planning but concentrate solely on the killer-sheep operation. If it goes as planned then Upper Ogg, with the security of the island's isolation, offers a wonderful opportunity to replicate our Kenyan golf-course operation. It would complement the killer-sheep operation nicely given the Japanese obsession with golf and induce longer stays. The guests would have a four-day killer-sheep experience and then another four days on the golf-course racking up sensational scores. They're an excellent combination, just like the golf and trout fishing in Kanju, and the two together provide justification to the client for the expense of travelling so far.'

'What about Ogg Castle and all the money we've spent on it?' Geoff complained.

'James will still reside in Ogg Castle which can also serve as the clubhouse. As I see it not a lot changes. You will still need chefs and waitresses for the golf-course exercise, and a much larger staff for the course management and the computer control room. The only significant change to your present planning will be the requirement to greatly increase Ogg Castle's accommodation to cope with the much larger guest numbers and the increased staffing. The architects will need to design bigger facilities.'

'Oh come off it, Dad,' Geoff protested. 'What about the climate? Not much fun playing golf in the rain and cold and winter gales.'

'Obviously it will be a links type course and therefore rather bracing, particularly in winter,' Mr Upton replied, unperturbed by the criticism. 'That will not be to the taste of Americans, but I do not believe it will deter the Japanese so we will market Ogg solely to them. Ogg's climate is no more rigorous than Japan's and as well, the Japanese are great traditionalists. Remember, Scotland is the home of golf so to play there sensationally, as of course they will, should deliver a great deal of happiness to the clients especially when compounded by the bracing climate as another hurdle they have overcome. While I question whether you will sell the Japanese kilts, I believe the Ogg shop will do very well with the sale of tweed plus-fours. As I said, the Japanese are traditionalists and will want to act the part.'

'It does make sense,' James said thoughtfully.

'It's not that simple,' Geoff said coldly. 'It will take at least a year to develop the golf course.'

'Really?' Mr Upton questioned, raising his eyebrows. 'It's a links course remember. It's just a matter of shifting the sheep to Lower Ogg, beginning a tree-planting programme alongside the intended fairways, and building the electronic greens. Remember; we've been searching for another Kanju operation for three years now and here it is in our lap only we didn't see it. Ogg is an ideal location for our second golf-course exercise. Frankly, I thought you would be pleased. It will certainly be a great deal more profitable and easier to run than the original proposal.'

'If it's a links course with few trees we won't be able to shift their fairway drives,' James said.

Mr Upton was unmoved. 'I've thought about that. It will not be an issue. In the first few years we will ignore their drives as it's hard to get into fairway trouble on a links course. The firm Upper Ogg ground will add thirty yards to every drive anyway. The clientele will logically all be competent golfers, otherwise they wouldn't go to the trouble of travelling halfway round the world to play. Instead we will have large and challenging greens; sharply sloping, different levels, bumpy, that sort of thing, so all the score adjustment action will initially take place with the electronically controlled putting. We can build some fairly deep sandtraps to provide additional interest.'

'It still limits the options,' James said. 'We'll have less control over their results than at Kanju.'

'I agree,' Mr Upton replied patiently. 'As I said, that's only for the first few years. The important thing is to lay the fairways out running north to south against the prevailing winds and start a forestation programme immediately down the fairway sides. In six or seven years' time the trees will be sufficiently high to act as a windbreak and also provide cover for the fairway workers to shift the balls. In the interim I suggest that on arrival each guest be presented with half a dozen new Ogg balls to ensure they use ours from the outset and any lost should be replaced free of charge. Of course once the trees are grown and it's no longer windswept, the grass will become lusher and it won't be a links course any more. Remember, the Japanese have one stand-out peculiarity and that is their obsession with vegetation, be it a simple daisy or a giant oak, so we must completely transform Ogg from its current barren landscape to a lush forested island. I believe we can accomplish that inside five years by planting thousands of saplings this coming winter. But additionally, we must focus attention on garden development and, of course, ensure we plant hundreds of cherry blossom trees. That is another Japanese oddity. When they travel abroad they like things to be as much like home as possible.'

'New York has already sold the first month's guests,' Geoff persisted. 'We've a party of five McDonald couples arriving from San Francisco a week after we open and a steady flow booked for two months after that. And we're about to interview actors for the laird position.'

'Let them come,' Mr Upton replied airily. 'There's no harm in it while the golf course is being built. But obviously you will have to defer their arrival, as James won't be able to open in the scheduled time. Still, he will now avoid winter, which is a plus surely at the teething stage of the operation.'

'But we don't want to employ a laird for something which is not going to last,' Geoff protested.

'Oh come now. They're actors,' Mr Upton said curtly. 'Actors take in their stride abrupt terminations of their employment. Their lives are steeped in eternal hope and constant failure. Anyway, if the laird is a success he should be retained. It would be an added attraction to be a paying guest at a Scottish laird's private golf course.'

When James arrived the following morning Geoff said, 'I've been thinking about it. I have to admit the old man's right. The golf course idea is rather obvious. It certainly complements the killer-sheep exercise nicely and will be a hell of a lot easier for you management-wise. Plus, the delay allows time to get the sheep operation functioning smoothly. Best of all, it will certainly be more profitable than the original concept.'

'I agree, but in case we've overlooked something, perhaps we should talk to Brasch about it,' James suggested.

'Amy and I did that last night. He sulked and carried on no end as the Scottish laird concept was his idea. I reminded him that the principal exercise was always the killer-sheep operation which was also his creation so he was a bit better about it this morning, specially when I pointed out we will still run the already booked clients through to see how the laird lark goes. He's made me promise just to prove his point, so I've undertaken to let the five McDonald couples from San Francisco visit when we're ready. You wouldn't think a man that intelligent would be so childish. But the more I think about it, the more the golf course makes sense. We'll have to get the architects in smartly. Remember, we were programming for a dozen Japanese killer-sheep couples and only ten American couples in Ogg Castle at any one time. Now it's an entirely different exercise catering for up to two hundred guests. Building the facilities for that is a huge exercise and then there's the staff quarters and large-scale sewage plants and we'll need much bigger generators; it's thrown all our planning on its head.'

'Not really,' James said. 'If it will take at least a year to have the links course ready we've actually got plenty of time for redesigning and construction. We can operate the killer-sheep concept while all of that's happening; iron out the wrinkles and establish a solid staff base. I've never done this sort of thing before so it will allow me time to learn the ropes.'

'Nevertheless, it's still an entirely different concept,' Geoff insisted. 'Basically it's now a golf course like Kanju. We'd lose credibility if we tried to run a hundred killer-sheep shooters at the same time, specially if we allowed each client one sheep each. Good Lord, we'd go through ...' Geoff stopped and did a quick mental calculation, 'we'd go through five thousand a year. That's ridiculous … all those corpses. We must confine the killer-sheep exercise to a peripheral attraction once the golf course is going; you know, in the same category as the Kanju cultural performances.'

'But all the Kanju guests experienced that,' James retorted.

'Market forces old man,' Geoff replied smugly. 'Brasch has been reading up on this killing dangerous animals craving. The few countries which still allow it charge the earth for a successful shot. You can shoot a bear in Georgia but it will cost you $80,000. Same in Mongolia and other wild-west places. We'll hit 'em say $5,000 a sheep for starters as a licence fee, and if the demand exceeds available shooting places we'll lift the price until we find an equilibrium. Anyway, we must refocus our thinking to running a golf course, which is ultimately what Ogg will be about now. As in Kenya, doubtless once they start knocking up sensational scores they'll be back in droves.'

'I've thought about it too,' James said. 'There's one difficulty we need to consider and that's the golf-course employees, specially those in the computer operations room. We can't take the risk of using Brits.'

'Jesus, yes,' Geoff said, clasping his head. 'We're in trouble there. Still, there's plenty of time to work that one out. I'll have the architects come in tomorrow. The Japanese girl is due in from Tokyo this morning. Amy's picking her up at Heathrow. It seemed a good idea to get her here as soon as possible and break her in slowly to the Ogg concept, plus get to know her. If she's any good she'll be helpful with planning as she'll understand the Japanese taste, but we will need to be a bit oblique at first about the electrical wiring aspect of the killer-sheep and the golf-course greens until we've got a feel for her. I hope to God she's OK; still, we'll know soon. We've a busy day today. There are six actor interviews for the laird's role and the first is due in half an hour. You had better have a look at these CVs,' and he handed James four manila files.

# – SIX –

Throughout the morning Geoff and James interviewed the six actor applicants sifted from the 83 responses to their advertisement in *The Stage* for the Laird of Ogg role.

Geoff outlined the job to each aspirant. The news that it would be a permanent position startled the actors, this not having been a feature of their past lives. The successful applicant would be required to execute a managerial function, overseeing the staff, kitchen, gardens and other duties, as well as acting as host to the guests, and would potentially be on call 24 hours each day.

He would dine with the guests each evening and sound off expansively Laird-like at the head of the table with Scots theme anecdotal items while during the day, outside of management duties, he would be responsible for the guests' entertainment, namely the village tour and explaining and showing the relics of the yet to be created Oggonian history. To date only the statue of the twelve-century-old warrior king Mugan and the ancient whisky still, both currently under construction, had been devised as historic background photography objects for the Japanese ladies.

Listening to Geoff recounting the obligations reinforced James' view that Mr Upton was right. It wasn't good enough. For a day and perhaps two evenings of baronial-style dining the guests might be amused, but that was it. The Scottish ancestry market idea was a poor one; the electronic golf course perfect.

After the first applicant had departed James mentioned his reservations. 'I thought exactly the same when I was outlining it,' Geoff admitted, and with the subsequent interviews he expanded the story.

217

As the guests would be solely Japanese, he explained, the laird could adopt a less Bridesheadish and more flamboyant caricature approach without any pedantic concern for authenticity, and could forego the Scots accent which would only confuse. Permanently wearing a kilt and sporran, smoking a pipe and regular bellowing rages would provide sufficient lairdish flavour. A piper would be employed for a weekly ceremonial dinner, and also to provide eccentric middle-of-the-night bursts on the bagpipes from the depths of the forest to provide an appropriate remote Scottish island, pervading insanity ambience. During the day the piper would fill another role such as a chef or greenkeeper.

In the normal course of events, Geoff elaborated, they would simply seek a golf-course resort manager, but the added flavour of the laird would please the Japanese. Thus the requirement for an actor, who would desirably be an older man-of-the-world type who was capable of applying common-sense management principles. The commencing salary would be £100,000, plus luxury accommodation including meals and liquor. Nightly drunkenness would be encouraged as appropriate lairdish behaviour and also to set an example to the Japanese men, thereby promoting the sale of Oggonian whisky. The job would entail being on call seven days a week but the successful applicant would receive two weeks' paid holiday every four months and receive return first-class travel expenses to London.

The six applicants, although ranging in age between 45 and 66, were remarkably similar. All spoke in a refined manner and affected an air of gentlemanly pomposity and self-importance, and all were dressed in well-cut but unfashionable suits, relics of rare moments of fleeting past success. But despite their outward confidence, their fragility was apparent, and none disguised their desperate hunger for the position, particularly when Geoff outlined the salary package.

Only the oldest and final interviewee allowed the veil of contrived detachment to slip and, embarrassingly, he suddenly burst into tears. 'It's a cruel, cruel joke,' he sobbed. 'It's a wonderful job, made in heaven. I know you will consider me too old but if only I could be allowed a chance.' He paused, wiped away a tear and seemingly insensitive to the awkward lull that had arisen, abruptly remarshalled his original composure, rose and, arms extended, flamboyantly and loudly recited:

*'Ah fortune,*
*What God is more cruel to us than thou!*
*How thou delightest,*
*ever to make sport of human life.'*

A faint burst of hysterical laughter erupted from overhead. Brasch was obviously watching a Head of State Tour video.

Geoff and James stared dumbstruck at the actor who, sensing he had blown it and rattled by the unexpected and unseen mocking ceiling audience, seemed to visibly shrink before their eyes. He suddenly looked very old. Abandoning his recitation bravado he muttered, 'Horace, gentlemen; a personal favourite; always with an apt phrase for every situation. Thank you for seeing me,' and defeated, he rose and left the room.

Geoff sighed. 'The poor old bastard. I'm almost tempted to give him a crack at it.'

'No. Definitely not,' James insisted. 'Too temperamental. Given the change in plans it's really a manager we want. The laird bit's a plus but only if the actor's right. Personally, I thought the Shakespearean bloke, Sanderson, was the best.'

'You can never really tell,' Geoff said. 'Dad's got a theory about management. He strongly believes it's not a teachable subject, just common sense, and a manager's performance reflects his personality and attitude and nothing else. Look at Hodgie, or for that matter Juma. They're both outstanding and yet neither are doing things they were trained for. That's why any of those actors could well prove OK.'

'Well if desperation is a consideration you certainly couldn't go past that lot,' James ventured. 'Their craving for the job after you outlined it was palpable. I felt like a torturer dangling a piece of meat just out of reach of a starving caged dog.'

At that moment Mr Upton entered. 'Finished the laird interviews?' he enquired breezily. Then, detecting the sombre mood he added, 'Not a task I would relish, interviewing actors that is.'

'It's hard to tell 'em apart,' Geoff said. 'Probably any one of them would be satisfactory.'

Mr Upton took the CVs file off the desk and flicked through them.

'Yes,' he said slowly as he quickly scanned the applications. 'A fairly typical story for thespians. Basically a litany of frustrated aspirations and personal failure. Listen to this. Bit parts in television and radio dramas, provincial repertories, television advertising, Christmas pantomimes, minor short-run West End roles; very sad, very sad,' he concluded, shaking his head.

'So they're all duds?' James enquired.

'Oh dear me, no,' Mr Upton responded quickly. 'Far from it. Possibly all six are perfect. These CVs would be duplicated by 99 per cent of actors. Duds? Goodness, no; at least not in the context of the theatre. But in a different perspective such as life itself, well yes, arguably they're massive failures but that is the lot of the actor.'

'You mean it's overly competitive, like you explained about modern commerce,' James asked.

'No, that's not what I mean,' Mr Upton replied stiffly. 'Although like everything else acting is certainly over-competitive, with more supply than demand but it goes much deeper than that. Think about what they do. They get one crack at life but do they take it? No, they do not. On the contrary they reject life from the outset in choosing a career pretending to be someone else. Consider it from a psychologist's viewpoint. Would one not conclude that spending one's life pretending to be someone else, making no choices but having a totally prescribed experience, demonstrates a rather large character flaw? Is it unreasonable to conclude that actors are actually afraid of life and are simply opting out of its risks and uncertainties at the price of forfeiting its rewards? The one great puzzle is their curious popularity with the masses, but perhaps that tells one more about the masses' shortcomings than about actors.'

'Well surely if they're weak characters we don't want them as managers,' James suggested.

'Not so fast, James,' Mr Upton responded. 'Actors are undoubtedly weak in character but they are not generally unintelligent. In the right circumstances they can be very useful, and looking at these CVs I suspect all of them fit our bill nicely. None are married and at their age, like many in their profession, they are possibly all restrained homosexuals. That I concede could be a problem with the kilt-wearing requirement. We certainly don't want any unsavoury incidents which kilts might induce. Alternatively, their wives, should they ever have had any, would have long past given up on their perpetual poverty, which is the lot of the actor. That might be a plus as wives could be a problem on Ogg; after all, they're usually a problem in most circumstances. But their greatest attribute is their age combined with their poverty. This job will seem like paradise to an impoverished actor staring at the abyss of imminent old age. I'm sure whoever you select will be first-rate and will do everything in his power to perform to our satisfaction.'

'The question is who!' Geoff said resignedly.

'Let me have a closer look,' Mr Upton replied and for two minutes they sat in silence as he read through the CVs. 'Ah, here's your man,' Mr Upton announced triumphantly. 'Sanderson'.

'He was my pick too,' James said, pleased with the endorsement. 'What is it you specially like?'

'One-man shows. He's done three: Lloyd George, Gladstone and the Yorkshire Ripper. A refreshing change from the usual tired subjects – Mark Twain, Oscar Wilde, Dickens and who have you. Almost certainly he wrote the scripts himself, which reveals some get-up-and-go spirit not usually found in thespians. None of the others have done any one-man shows.'

'So what!' Geoff said. 'What's special about those?'

Mr Upton laughed. 'Well for a start they're even more tortuous for the audience than the usual play. But that's incidental. All actors are pathologically self-centred. For our laird role that will be a plus. Delivering a one-man show is an egotist's dream – for an hour and a half you talk non-stop with all eyes fixed on you, even if the actual audience response is intense loathing which, I might add, one can certainly understand.'

'If that's the case why on earth do audiences attend?' James demanded.

Mr Upton laughed again. 'Theatre audiences comprise middle-class people. The middle classes are programmed to behave conventionally no matter how insufferable those conventions may be. One can only assume they view theatre-going, like church attending, as a self-imposed discipline, albeit an irrational one. In recent years, periodically attending theatrical performances has evolved into a middle-class rite of duty. It's not all bad; the ecstatic high the audience feels when the performance ends almost compensates for the two hours of tedium from watching mildly disturbed inadequates prancing about bellowing on a stage. I imagine that, as with Sunday sermons, most people have mastered the art of mentally turning off during the actual performance.'

'Oh come on, Mr Upton,' James laughed. 'That's a bit rich.'

'What is?'

'Well, all that mildly disturbed inadequates stuff about actors and suggesting the audience is only there because of social pressure.'

'Do you think so?' Mr Upton said, raising his eyebrows. 'Well, let me present a different tangent on the situation. Consider matrimonial columns, now found in all western world newspapers. They are of course a recent innovation copied from the very practical system in India, only with one important difference.

'In India the parents, not the candidates, advertise and the eligible son or daughter is oblivious to these behind-the-scene machinations. The parents check out the responses and then devise surreptitious ways for likely spouse material to meet. They don't actually select the spouse, instead they merely ensure a wide range of suitable partners encounter one another. It's an admirable process, so much so that the west has endeavoured to copy it over the past decade. Even the most respectable newspapers and magazines today carry matrimonial advertisements. But there's one important difference. In the west the lonely hearts actually advertise themselves. Study those advertisements and you will find half a dozen common denominators. For example, the women invariably describe themselves as 'said to be attractive' although by whom we are never told, and frequently as 'young at heart', as clear a message as one could ever receive of their out-of-the-race age, probably, I assume, over 45.

'The men hint at material comfort and a tolerant nature; sensitive to the reality that these are the most sought-after attributes. But note this. The single common denominator nearly all of these desperate advertisers share, both men and women, can be found when they describe their interests. While walking on the beach at sunset and dining out are popular selections, I would venture 80 per cent list going to the theatre. Now let us for the moment allow the highly improbable contingency that they're telling the truth. If so, that purported theatre-going interest alone would explain their sadly pathetic need to resort to advertising for a spouse – namely that they are excruciating dullards.

'Conversely, if they're lying in claiming this interest – which I don't doubt they are – then it simply proves my earlier point insofar as these lonely heart advertisers, by dint of their need to advertise, have plainly slipped out of the grooves of normal middle-class intercourse, know it, and are pasting labels on themselves suggesting otherwise, thus the expressed interest in the theatre.'

Geoff and James gazed astonished at Mr Upton following this diatribe. 'Really, sir,' James spluttered. 'Surely that's rather stretching things.'

'Not at all, not at all,' Mr Upton said airily. 'Personally I subscribe to the Augustinian viewpoint on the subject. Perhaps you are unaware but St Augustine described the theatre as disgraceful, absurd, shameful and false, and suggested thespians would be denied eternal life which from his outlook plainly meant eternal damnation, a prospect I find rather enticing.' As if to terminate further discussion on the matter he reverted to the original subject. 'As I said, Sanderson's the pick of the bunch. Good name too; excellent roots. Doubtless you assume it stems from the Latin.' Geoff and James adopted suitably blank looks having assumed nothing of the sort. 'But I can assure you,' Mr Upton continued, 'as with so many words Latin claims, the specific origin is Greek.' Geoff and James both nodded dutifully. 'The warrior and defender connotations of the Greek origin of the name Sanderson do suggest a certain verve which will be useful on Ogg and indeed our man has already demonstrated that with his appalling one-man shows.'

Silence fell across the room. Sensing disquiet at these observations, Mr Upton continued, 'You must not think I am picking on actors. To varying degrees the same charges could be made of all stage performers and certainly of their audiences. In an age when technology delivers perfect recordings there can be no logic in attending orchestral performances for there is absolutely no spectacle element. Orchestra audiences are sustained by middle-class peer pressure. In their dull minds attending is an obligatory social ritual. So too with opera, which purports to combine music and theatre. But its origins lie in the eighteenth century when there were few entertainments. That is not the case today and the theatrical element of traditional opera is, in the modern context, painfully thin and undeserving of an audience. Furthermore, the spectacle of a middle-aged 250-pound woman thundering about a stage purporting to be a young maiden dying of consumption while being lusted after by rival young men played by plump homosexuals sorely tests the imagination. I'm afraid I have reached an age where my tolerance is boundless but my patience is nil. With the middle classes the reverse is true, which is why they are such exploitable audience fodder for stage performances.'

Just as James began to fear they were in for another lengthy diatribe Mr Upton looked at his watch. 'It's nearly one o'clock. I thought I might stroll along to the Fujiyama. Would you gentlemen care to join me?' But before they could answer the door opened and Amy entered.

'Come in, Miyumi,' she said, holding the door open, and into the room came a pretty Japanese girl. She wore a simple white linen dress and a boater hat with a light blue ribbon which was matched by a blue brooch on her breast and blue shoes. She bowed her head to the three men.

'This is Miyumi,' Amy said. 'I picked her up at Heathrow this morning and took her to her hotel. She's used to constant travel so now she's unpacked and showered she insists she's ready to go. I tried to persuade her to have a day's rest but she said it's unnecessary.'

Amy introduced the three men.

'I watched you at Wimbledon three years ago,' James mumbled.

'Thank you,' the girl replied and gave another little bow. The room fell silent as everyone stared at the visitor.

Mr Upton broke the impasse. 'Well, Miyumi, a very timely arrival. We were just leaving for my favourite Japanese restaurant. Come along and we can hear all about you over lunch.'

Miyumi gave another little dip of her head and the party rose and left for the Fujiyama.

# – SEVEN –

In the restaurant Miyumi sat demurely, her hands clasped in her lap, speaking only when directly addressed. Geoff rather aggressively endeavoured to draw her out. 'So Miyumi, our Tokyo office explained the Ogg resort job to you?'

'Yes,' she virtually whispered, lowering her eyes.

'A regular flow of Japanese guests; supervising the staff, making sure the food's right, laundry up to scratch, wives entertained, everyone happy; all that palaver.'

'Yes.'

There was a pregnant pause, followed by Geoff's doubting suggestion, 'And you think you can do all that OK?'

'Yes.'

An awkward silence descended. James had been captivated by the girl from his first glimpse and leapt to her rescue, determined to save the situation.

'You were fantastic at Wimbledon when you made the semis,' he began. Miyumi smiled at him and his heart leapt. 'I was amazed how you could hold your own against those giantesses and their power shots. I suppose it all lies in excellent timing.'

This time Miyumi, her coal-black eyes twinkling, laughed daintily, exposing perfect white teeth. James was smitten. 'Do you play?' she enquired.

'Not very well,' James stumbled. 'There's a thought,' he said suddenly. 'We should bang in a hard-surface all-weather court on Ogg. We could have racquets on hand and if Miyumi could bear it, the guests would be thrilled to say they'd had a hit with her. Think of the photo opportunities.'

'Too windy,' Geoff retorted dismissively.

'Rubbish,' James snapped with uncharacteristic aggression. 'We could surround the court with hedges and trees and it would add to the general enhancement. But that's if Miyumi wouldn't mind. I suppose it would be a bit tiresome for you,' he added hurriedly.

'I am happy to play with guests.'

'Excellent,' James exuded. 'The more facilities and diversions the better. I'll get it under way as soon as I'm back in the office.'

But Geoff was not done. 'Hope you've plenty of warm clothes, Miyumi. Ogg's not exactly tropical.'

'I told you. Neither is Japan in winter,' Mr Upton said firmly, not hiding his annoyance at Geoff's aggressive tone. 'I'm sure Miyumi is used to cold climates.'

Another tinkle of laughter. 'It is eight years since I experienced winter. With tennis it was always summer. I am looking forward very much to snow and cold; but it is true, I must buy some warm clothes.'

'You don't think you'll get bored stuck in the one place after all those years of travel?' Geoff persevered, not disguising his scepticism at the girl's suitability.

'I am looking forward very much to not travelling. I have been travelling for twelve years.'

This time Amy leapt to the rescue. 'I can take Miyumi shopping tomorrow. She will need lots of woollen pullovers and slacks, and fur-lined boots and warm stockings.'

'Thank you,' Miyumi smiled. Mesmerised, James wished dreadfully he could go with them.

'We're all going up to Ogg in about three weeks' time for an inspection trip,' Geoff said conciliatorily, detecting the opposition to his gruffness. 'You'd better get stuck in smartly on the clothing front.'

After lunch they returned to the office and showed Miyumi the original building plans and a general outline of the proposals, although no one mentioned that the killer-sheep were not quite the real thing or that the golf course would be rigged. Gradually Miyumi came out of her shell and by the end of the day was chatting happily, asking questions and laughing at the jokes. To James' delight, when the wine was opened at 5.30 she did not demur and drank two glasses of chardonnay. James returned the discussion to tennis. 'You did win some tournaments?' he began.

'Yes, I won five. But I did not win any Grand Slams. Now that is behind me. It is not a good life always travelling. I wish very much to not travel for a long time. I think I will like the job on Ogg where I am still and everyone else is moving,' she smiled at James.

'Not a bad description of your role,' Geoff commented to James' relief as his earlier reservations now appeared allayed.

'It is nice on Ogg?' Miyumi enquired.

When no one replied Miyumi looked at them each in turn, puzzled by the silence her question had induced.

'Well, actually,' James fumbled, breaking the impasse, 'none of us have actually in fact been there, or at least not in any meaningful sense. I was born on Ogg but I left when I was four. It will be a first trip for Amy and Geoff.'

'You are making a joke, I think,' Miyumi laughed.

'James inherited the island,' Geoff explained. 'Some of our people have been there and we have a video. But we have a pretty good idea what it's like.'

Miyumi clapped her hands and laughed again. 'So, we are all explorers. Perhaps there will be dangerous animals and we will all be eaten.'

Not if I don't eat you first, James thought and for the first time since the Ogg proposition had been raised two months earlier he felt excited at the thought of living on the island.

Suddenly he remembered he had promised to collect Jane from the Chelsea art opening at 7.30. He looked at his watch. It was 7.25. Reluctantly he left the party and dashed outside for a taxi.

He arrived at the gallery at a quarter to eight. The inevitable art opening stragglers, their voices now shrill, lingered as long as wine remained. Having accompanied Jane to many such functions, James was well familiar with the scene. Art openings were only deemed successful if crowded, and the laggards comprised journalists, house salesmen and other similar social dregs invited as roughage, who neither could nor would purchase a painting. There was an unspoken understanding with the gallery that in return for their filler role they could extract the last drop from the occasion, long after the more glamorous potential buyers had left for fashionable restaurants, frequently with the models and celebrities invited to add sparkle to the proceedings, in tow. Social flotsam though the stragglers were, at times it was a questionable exchange as sometimes there were guest speakers. On one occasion, which was etched in James' memory, an ancient Labour peer had rambled for an excruciating hour and a quarter and only been halted by the gallery owner's desperate action in setting off the fire alarm.

James glanced about the room. All the canvases comprised a large white surface with a single diagonal black stripe in the top left corner. Only a variation in the width of the stripe distinguished one painting from another. There were no red stickers, an observation James took pleasure in noting.

Jane emerged from the throng looking pointedly at her watch, and twenty minutes later they were seated in a restaurant. Immediately she opened her attack with the familiar refrains, but James was uncaring and he picked at his food, oblivious to the mantra of complaints: 'promising career recklessly discarded ... Lucinda bewildered ... Mummy says ... utter disregard ...' The litany of his crimes wafted around the table but he barely heard them and cared not a whit, for he was content to allow Jane her head, leaving his free for thoughts of Miyumi.

And afterwards, as Jane played her strongest card, in bed, it was those thoughts of Miyumi which lifted his performance from the mechanical to the passionate which peculiarity had a subduing effect on Jane so that the following morning over breakfast she was disconcertingly pleasant.

Encouraged by this untypical harmony, and the fact that Jane had not mentioned his disappearance from the book launch, James raised a matter that had been puzzling him. 'That book last week; I looked through it and couldn't find any mention of horses.'

'James, James, James,' this accompanied by slow head-shaking. 'Don't you understand? It's a metaphorical allegory.'

'You mean all that guff about leaves falling?'

'Oh dear me, James. Will you ever understand? It's not just black and white leaves falling. It's the shades and nuances of the descriptive narrative. It's a brilliant work which I have no doubt will win the Parker Prize this year for best new novel.'

Jane's comparatively passive response egged him on.

'No red stickers last night,' he gloated.

Jane carefully put down her coffee cup and stared pointedly at him. Adopting a patronising singsong tone as if talking firmly but sympathetically to a recalcitrant child she said, 'You know, James, if there's one reason I'm important in your life then it is to assist you develop a necessary appreciation of the intangible higher plane of our existence. Art is illusion, and it is illusion which tests the imagination and invites a dialogue with the artistic expression. And that is why I am so very sad that you should engage in this appalling plebeian travel business which is so utterly devoid of any imaginative qualities.'

'Cock and nonsense,' James retorted gaily. 'That's sheer snobbishness. You liked the thought of me being a sharebroker, or merchant banker, as you always chose to introduce me. Anyway, we're not in the travel business; we own and run resorts.'

'I happen to know that Claude Ebbington, the highly respected contemporary art consultant, is going to the gallery today and will probably buy two of those magnificent works you choose to mock,' Jane continued in a supercilious tone. 'And Claude's clients are solely merchant banks. I also know that when it comes to sponsorship our Arts Council research demonstrates that the most supportive patronage comes from the financial industry. I certainly don't recall any support from travel firms, or resorts as you call them,' she sneered.

James thought back to his sharebroking days. At regular intervals in both the London and New York offices, new and always absurd paintings and nonsensical sculptures were placed by the firm's art consultants in the reception areas. The response from his colleagues was always ridicule, borne out by the after-hours practice by some of the brokers of rehanging the pictures upside down, in which position they invariably remained until the consultants' visit.

On the other hand, the Alceides building was a veritable treasure-trove of fine art. James briefly flirted with the idea of taking Jane there, until he remembered that her acceptance of his new life was most certainly not what he was seeking. It would be impossible anyway as most of the artworks were displayed in the fatties' flats. Nevertheless, emboldened by the extreme inaccuracy of her assessment, he said, 'I shall be away a great deal in the coming months.'

'And what precisely does that mean?'

'I won't be around, at least during the week. I'll be back occasionally but I'll be studying resort management on site.'

'I see,' Jane said coldly, and tossing her head haughtily she rose and, leaving the door open, her refined equivalent of slamming it, she left without a further word. Later that morning James advised the letting agent that he would be giving up the flat, something he had held off doing as if reluctant to sever the last lifeline linkage with his past existence.

# – EIGHT –

Later that morning the two architects arrived, both, James noted, wearing bow ties. Geoff outlined the proposed changes.

'Did Amy mention our view that we could possibly do a better job if we knew the site location?' the senior architect, Mr Titmouse, whose bow tie was slightly the larger, timidly broached.

'She did. Quite unnecessary,' Geoff snapped dismissively. 'Now let's get on with it.' The two architects cowered and began dutifully taking notes, as instructed, on the substantial expansion of Ogg Castle.

'Do you have any particular period style in mind?' Mr Titmouse enquired nervously.

'Rambling,' Geoff barked. 'That's the style we want. It must have no discernible form or symmetry. Gild every lily. Plenty of nooks and crannies, turrets and parapets, alcoves and window boxes here but not there, Grecian columns, terraces, balconies, extrudences, bay mullion windows, gables, vaulted ceilings, different ceiling heights in the aisles, fancy architraves, no corridors in a straight line, instead bends and recesses, fireplaces with ornate surrounds, steps up and then down again, a fireplace in every bedroom but no chimney for them. We want the entire castle to have underground central heating. The only functioning fireplaces will be in the lounges and dining rooms. Make sure they're huge. Got the picture?' he asked rubbing his hands gleefully at the satisfactory image of the completed castle.

Mr Titmouse looked distraught at this prescription. 'We could provide a distinctive style,' he ventured tentatively. 'Gothic, teutonic, baroque ...' but he was interrupted by Geoff.

'Yes. Excellent. We want all of them. Mix the lot in.'

'Well,' Mr Titmouse persisted. 'You don't think it may look perhaps

231

…' but his voice faded under Geoff's withering glare and he fluttered his hands, his eyes panic-filled while his lips moved soundlessly.

'We absolutely must have the revised plans and specifications inside a week,' Geoff insisted. 'Work your staff night and day and charge us. Don't forget we'll need a much larger generator and sewage plant so the requirement is basically to redo everything on a tenfold scale, expanding the castle to accommodate one hundred guestrooms plus the ancillary lounges and dining rooms and other flow-on requirements. And bang in a new wing for staff quarters. Eighty bedrooms, dining and recreation rooms. Communal bathrooms will do for the staff. But the main thing to remember is irrationality. Got that, gentlemen? Fix it in your mind. If there's a rational way to design something, such as a straight corridor, then change it. We want bends; lots of them. If there's a natural pattern or sequence such as the bedrooms all in a row, then de-pattern it. Remember the watchword gentlemen – rambling – keep it in your minds and you won't go wrong.' At that he rose, beckoned to Amy, and she escorted the two bewildered architects out.

'Wait,' Geoff shouted as they reached the door. 'Panelling. Panelling. I nearly forgot. We want the entire interior panelled. Rococo panelling actually, just the thing. And come to think of it, gargoyles. Bang in some of those near the entrance.'

With a shudder Mr Titmouse, his shoulders slumped in defeat, nodded and closed the door.

'Don't want to over-egg the soufflé of course,' Geoff said rubbing his hands together contentedly, 'but overall it should look bloody good.'

'I thought the Japanese taste was for austere simplicity,' James said puzzled. 'Isn't that what we're doing with the killer-sheep lodge?'

'Exactly,' Geoff exclaimed. 'And that's why the castle will be a success. The Japs will have no reference standard to judge it by and best of all it will reinforce their sense of being in a foreign land. Remember my father explaining how difficult that is to achieve these days with the universal sameness of travel, specially with accommodation.'

'I still think the castle will look silly being all brand new,' James ventured.

'Rubbish!' Geoff declared. 'If those architects follow their instructions it will have a terrific disorderly ambience which will be very Scots baronial castle in flavour.'

'But it will still be new,' James persisted.

'True; but only for a few weeks. As soon as it's finished we'll fly in the Romanian lads. They'll age the joint two centuries in a matter of days and we'll get ivy and Virginia creeper planted smartly. Apply force-feeding and we'll cover the exterior inside five years which will finish it off nicely. We'll fill the halls and lounges with battered old leather couches and Victorian oak furniture, gloomy oil paintings and lithographs, suits of armour, stags' heads, the Campbell coat of arms in the hall and other trimmings to achieve the appropriate image. Amy's heading north next month to scout out auction rooms and antique shops and buy up big. Once you've placed all that stuff about, no one will doubt Ogg Castle isn't centuries old. Let those National Trust clowns near and they'll want to list it, mark my words.'

'Miyumi might care to comment on the lodge's internal arrangements,' James suggested and was pleased when Geoff readily agreed. They pored over the existing plans and were surprised by the number of variations she proposed.

The dining room seating arrangements were wrong, she observed. When on holiday in a group the Japanese prefer larger table settings than pairs and foursomes. Amy promptly telephoned the furniture manufacturers to change the order. Miyumi made many similar suggestions to cater to the Japanese taste. In mid-afternoon she left with Amy to visit a lighting shop, having been dismissive of the existing proposals as 'not what Japanese people like'.

'Looks like Miyumi's going to work out OK,' Geoff acknowledged grudgingly when they were alone. 'She's a bit more assertive than I first thought. But look here,' he added. 'What about taking her to dinner each night and around and about and working her over. Get her confidence so you can gradually break her into what will actually be happening on Ogg,' a task James willingly accepted.

When the two women returned after 5 p.m., and following the daily ritual of a few glasses of wine, James suggested dinner to Miyumi and the two left together. 'We could stroll along to the Fujiyama?' James suggested.

'But, James. I have been travelling for twelve years. Now I eat western food.' So they continued walking until in the heart of Mayfair they found a dimly lit Italian restaurant. Later James walked the girl

233

to her hotel. Thereafter dining together became a nightly affair, which led on to spending the weekends with James as tour guide escorting Miyumi to museums and art galleries. They took boat rides down the Thames, visited the Natural History Museum and Madame Tussaud's and the other standard London visitor attractions, always in the company of numerous other tourists. All this delighted Miyumi and her happiness softened James' outlook to contemporary tourism after Mr Upton's cynical dissertation two months earlier but he took care not to describe these weekend activities to Geoff for fear of being mocked.

Three weeks after Miyumi's arrival James cancelled his home telephone to avoid calls from Jane and acquired a mobile phone.

Inevitably the two became closer. Soon they were holding hands when walking or in darkened theatres. Finally matters came to a head when Miyumi suggested they remain at home and she cook at James' flat one Saturday evening, which ended with her staying, an event which flabbergasted James when he discovered she was a virgin.

Her innocence did not stop there. Discussion revealed that life as an international tennis star was far from glamorous. In eight years of constant travel Miyumi had used up five passports and been to 63 countries. But, as she explained, she could describe her hotel room and the tennis stadium in each place and nothing more, then she added with a giggle, that in fact she couldn't even do that as the hotels and courts all seemed identical anyway. Socially, her past eight years' existence had been as cloistered as a nun's, which is why she had abruptly stopped, feeling life was slipping by.

But the four months at home had proved disappointing. She had been fêted as a celebrity and paid sizeable appearance fees by department stores and television shows, but it had all seemed rather empty and in many respects simply a continuation of her previous eight years. The appearance fees were meaningless anyway as she was a very wealthy young woman. She had been bordering on depression when fortune had intervened and she had been discreetly approached by Alceides' Japanese office manager with the Ogg offer. Now, here she was in London, in love and happier than at any time in her life.

James was similarly smitten but he did not overlook his task of explaining the true nature of Ogg. He began carefully, first outlining the Head of State Tours while they were sitting in a quiet corner of a restaurant one night and when both were in an expansively happy mood. Initially Miyumi was disbelieving but she still delighted at the concept. Emboldened by her reaction James recounted his own experiences as the Admiral in Madagascar, each episode inducing increasing mirth. Soon they were attracting frowns from the other diners so they left and wandered back to the flat, stopping periodically as Miyumi doubled up with laughter when James told her about the Bishop and the executions and medal ceremonies and the statues and the Queen's pomposity. He carefully omitted any reference to the floggings and dwarf consumption, and most certainly made no mention of the village virgin deflowering service.

'Oh how I would love to see it all,' Miyumi said between bouts of laughter.

'But you can, you can,' James replied excitedly. 'Brasch has tapes of all the tours.'

'Brasch! Who is Brasch?'

'Brasch is the librarian,' James said quickly. Mention of Brasch was a mistake. Intuition told him it was far too early to explain the fatties strategy and given his own discomfort about them he automatically ascribed the same reaction to Miyumi.

And so the following night at his flat, frequently collapsing with laughter, they watched the two-hour tape of James' Madagascan Royal Tour. They were ecstatically happy.

Nevertheless, James waited another week before raising the subject of Kanju. Over dinner one night he explained the exercise and was hugely relieved when Miyumi clapped her hands delightedly as he outlined the golfing and trout fishing manipulation and the guests' happiness. He demurred, however, at describing the cultural performances.

The following morning he visited Brasch, who he found steadfastly demolishing a dozen chocolate eclairs while reading a book on medieval tortures. 'Looking for new services for the Royal Tours,' Brasch explained. 'I think the rack could be a goer,' and for a few minutes they discussed ways and means of contriving a rack torture illusion. 'The great virtue it has over beheadings and hangings,' Brasch explained, 'is its slowness. We could reasonably expect two or three minutes of agonised screaming before the limbs are torn off which should please the Queens. We have to culminate with death to justify the $100,000 fee but if we can engineer all of that it should prove a major attraction compared with the abruptness of beheadings.'

'Why bother?' James asked as they faltered over some of the difficulties of creating a successful rack illusion. 'No one's complaining about the current offerings.'

'Not complaining, James,' Brasch boomed. 'Perhaps not. But to the discerning analyst they're sending signals. I've been studying the last twelve tours' execution purchases and they're running three to one in favour of hangings over beheadings. My theory is the appeal of the kicking corpse. More bangs for bucks. Surely you agree the Queens would prefer three minutes pre-death screaming on the rack over two minutes' twitching legs. That's what I'm here for, James, to constantly examine our services and search for improvements. Alceides prides itself on being progressive.'

'Yes, I'm sure it does,' James said wryly. 'I'll be interested to hear how you do it,' and he moved on to explain the reason for his visit.

'No problem,' Brasch boomed. 'I'll put together a tape of golfing and fishing exploits only.'

'Make sure half the punters are Japanese,' James instructed.

That night he played the video for Miyumi. At the sight of an elderly Japanese golfer lining up a 60-foot putt Miyumi became solemn. The golfer hit the ball and they watched it slowly roll across the green then suddenly change direction, gather momentum and rocket to the hole. At first Miyumi sat expressionless, but as the camera panned to the golfer dancing with joy a slow smile broke across her face. 'Perhaps we should have electronic greens at Ogg,' she suggested.

'I say, that's a great idea,' James exuded. 'I'll discuss it with Geoff tomorrow.'

'Well done, Miyumi,' Geoff said to her the following morning, having been primed by James. 'It's a brilliant idea. It would never have occurred to us,' and Miyumi flushed with pleasure.

That was enough to be going on with, James concluded. It would be at least a month before they would shift to Ogg so he held off explaining the facts about the killer-sheep proposition until Miyumi was thoroughly indoctrinated into the Alceides culture, a process he hastened and shared her delight in by borrowing tapes of other Royal and Presidential Tours. Eventually, as she was spending most nights in James' flat, there seemed little point in continuing with the hotel and Miyumi shifted in with him.

# – NINE –

Invited back, ostensibly for a second interview but in fact to be advised of his appointment as Laird of Ogg, Sanderson arrived wearing the same suit, tie and shoes. Noting a small tear in the actor's shirt cuff that he had observed at their first meeting James could only admire the actor's sangfroid. Despite Mr Upton's scathing and probably accurate condemnation of the bleak life of the stage, there was something to be said for thespian skills.

'We'll lay it on a bit,' Geoff warned prior to the actor's arrival. 'I've made some arrangements to set the tone as to what's expected,' but before he could elaborate Amy was ushering Sanderson in and a few minutes later they were toasting the overwhelmed thespian with champagne.

'Up to a spot of lunch?' Geoff casually enquired, knowing full well the answer. Again James marvelled at Sanderson's carefully calculated hesitation, briefly furrowed brow, examination of his watch, contemplative pause, further check of the time and then, with a plainly contrived reluctance, 'I can probably spare an hour or so,' when if truth be told he could probably spare a decade.

Waiting outside was the limousine James had ridden in on his first day with Alceides. The chauffeur held open the door, doffing his cap to Sanderson as the others stood aside to allow him in first. Geoff uncorked another bottle of champagne and, flutes in hand, they cruised across London, Sanderson affecting a blasé manner as if this were an everyday experience. Their collective unspoken sense of well-being was heightened when it suddenly began to rain and from the opulent comfort of the limousine they watched contented as office workers scurried along the pavements and huddled, bedraggled, under verandahs.

Once while stopped at traffic lights, a rain-drenched middle-aged man made a desperate late attempt to dash across the street just as the lights changed and the limousine began to slowly move off, only to crash against the rear passenger window. James found himself briefly staring into the astonished eyes of his former boss, Symington, and he raised his flute to him as the limo sped away. God was most certainly in his heaven and all was well. Eventually they arrived at a riverside restaurant notorious for its outrageous expense.

The chauffeur again tipped his cap to Sanderson as he emerged to be in turn saluted by the umbrella-wielding, uniformed doorman. Inside the maître d' glided forward, silkily murmuring, 'We're delighted to have you with us today, Mr Upton. Just Mr Sanderson and Mr Campbell in the party I presume,' and he led the way to a corner table already set for three, overlooking the Thames.

Following this obviously pre-arranged greeting James became uneasy. What was Geoff playing at and he noted Sanderson's contrived nonchalance was beginning to crack. The actor was affecting an even plummier voice than earlier and could not resist repeated pop-eyed glances at the former Prime Minister, ageing pop star and famous newspaper tycoon who were among the diners.

James endeavoured to put Sanderson at ease but was constantly sabotaged by Geoff's remarks to the actor such as, 'I don't know about you, old man, but I've never much cared for the merlot they stock here,' and 'Where are you skiing this winter? The reports from Vail look promising,' and most preposterous of all, 'I've found a first-rate chap for Bentley maintenance. I'll send you his card but don't let on to too many of your chums,' a suggestion Sanderson in his confusion reacted to with a simultaneous nodding and head-shaking, resulting in a bewildered circular motion.

The luncheon continued in this awkward vein until following the main course Sanderson, now badly rattled, declined the sweets menu, looked at his watch and said, 'I'm dreadfully sorry, gentlemen. Can you excuse me? I didn't anticipate luncheon and regrettably have an appointment with my stockbroker.'

It was a brave effort, and much relieved James escorted him to the door and instructed the chauffeur to drive Mr Sanderson to his next appointment.

'What the bloody hell was that all about?' he demanded angrily on his return to the table.

'What was what about?' Geoff asked, feigning innocence.

'You know damn well. That was probably the biggest day in years for that poor bugger, maybe even in his life, and you went out of your way to embarrass him.'

'Not at all, old man,' Geoff retorted chummily. 'Believe me, he didn't think I was taking the mickey. He'll have the chauffeur drop him off in St James or somewhere like that then sneak off to the underground and back to some grotty little basement flat. But it will still be the highlight of his life. Nerves got him in the end but I'll guarantee he thinks he's finally made it, simply because I treated him as one of us.'

'Oh horseshit, Geoff. Why spoil it for him with all that nonsense?' James persisted.

'I told you before. Important to set a tone. You're forgetting he's going to Scotland to run a contrivance. I want him thinking we're aristocrats, not bloody wide-boy spivs.' Geoff looked at his watch. 'The day's gone. I know a nice little pub near here. Let's go and quaff an ale or two.'

Ten minutes later they were settled into comfortable armchairs. 'I'm constantly knocked off my beat by your oblique angles on everything,' James declared, quickly adding, 'which is not to say I always agree with them.'

'I've told you,' Geoff said smugly, 'nothing in Alceides is an accident. Everything's carefully thought out, whether it be staffing or marketing or management ...'

'Management,' James interrupted excitedly. 'There's something you haven't explained. If the Alceides building is all eating and thinking, where the hell's everything run from?'

Geoff looked at his watch again. 'I'll show you if you like but steel yourself for a surprise. It's not as you might imagine. Actually our management headquarters aren't far from here. Come on,' and they rose and went outside and hailed a cab.

Geoff gave the taxi-driver the address. 'You sure, guv?' he queried.

'Quite sure, thank you.'

Ten minutes later they were in Hackney. They drove through the seedy streets and eventually pulled up outside a decrepit two-level warehouse. 'Hang about,' Geoff said to the driver. 'We'll only be five minutes then you can take us back to Mayfair.'

They approached a wooden door bearing a sign reading

'Encyclopaedia Sales' and entered a poorly lit dingy entrance foyer at the end of which was a lift.

'Is this some sort of joke?' James demanded.

'Far from it. It's Alceides management headquarters. I warned you it'll be a bit of a surprise; more of our lateral, or as you prefer to call it, devious thinking coming up,' Geoff added mysteriously as he pressed the lift button.

With a disturbing clanking the lift car arrived and the door slowly opened. They entered and it shuddered its way up. 'Hydraulic lift,' Geoff explained. 'Really meant for industrial usage but ideal for our purposes.' Finally, with an unsettling series of jolts, the lift stopped, the doors opened and before them lay the most unpleasant office premises James had ever encountered.

The floor was rough concrete, there was no ceiling under the pitched iron roof and the brick walls were unlined. A dozen old wooden desks, about half with computers, were spaced round the room and before them sat the ugliest women James had ever seen. None acknowledged the visitors.

All were fat; not in the Brasch league but still grossly overweight, and all were spectacularly hideous. James stared aghast in shocked silence, broken only by the hesitant arrival before them of a shabby, balding, slight middle-aged man.

'Hello, Mr Upton,' he said timidly in a thin reedy voice.

'Afternoon, Albert,' Geoff said and he introduced him to James. 'This is Albert Frumpton, the office manager. I'd like you to meet Lord Bellvue, our company chairman,' and Albert limply shook hands with a bewildered James.

'Everything in order, Albert?' Geoff asked and on receiving a squeaky affirmation he added, 'We won't stop. Just taking Lord Bellvue on a tour of our London properties,' and without further ado he escorted James to the lift.

'Bloody hell!' James spluttered. 'What's with the Lord Bellvue bullshit and also, those women; my God, Geoff, I mean to say …'

But he was interrupted by Geoff's 'Bloody frightful aren't they? But say no more. I'll explain it all back in the office,' and they re-entered the taxi and drove in silence to Dover Street. Geoff, a smug self-congratulatory look on his face, was clearly enjoying James' frustration. 'First things first, old man,' he replied to his demands for an explanation, and he turned to the cabinet, opened a bottle of wine and poured two glasses.

'OK, spit it out,' James urged.

'Spit what out?' Geoff teased.

'Those appalling creatures, that awful office, the Lord Bellvue nonsense! What's going on? I can't believe that was Alceides' management headquarters.'

'Really? Well you'd better believe it because it's true. And I'll tell you this. The personnel in that office are arguably the most carefully handpicked of any organisation in London. In every respect they're precisely what we require.'

'What, fat and hideous! Good God, Geoff; it was like a freak show.'

'Exactly. Just what we need. But if you want an explanation then it's necessary to go back to the beginning, which in point of fact is over half a century ago. You remember Professor Parkinson?'

'You mean the comedic economist fellow?'

Geoff looked pained. 'I don't think my father would describe him that way and, frankly, nor would I. In some respects he ranks up with Hayek and Keynes among the twentieth-century economists.'

'Oh cut it out, Geoff. Anyway, what's this got to do with ugly women and me being introduced as Lord bloody Bellvue?'

'Everything. But first Professor Parkinson. The reason we rate him is that along with Keynes and Hayek he treated economics as a behavioural subject and not a branch of accountancy as most economists do. Do you recall reading about the last stages of the war when the Allies targeted the massive Krupps armament factories which literally spread over hundreds of acres and employed tens of thousands of workers? They wiped out the factories in one thousand-plane carpet-bombing blitz and the next morning all the workers turned up only to find everything destroyed. That's where Parkinson came into the picture. He was an academic economist and, acting on a hunch, he obtained permission to go in and study the actual effects after the Allies had captured that territory a couple of months later.'

'What on earth has this to do with employing ugly women?' James complained.

'I'm getting there, so listen. What Parkinson discovered was terribly important and had a huge influence on my father's thinking and in particular the way he's structured Alceides' various divisions and management, all of which led to the harridan employment strategy.'

By now James was caught up in the story. 'Well come on; what was it?' he insisted.

'Parkinson concentrated on the one unaffected component of the Krupps organisation because the bombers deliberately ignored it as irrelevant once the factories were eliminated. That component was the administration. The Krupps office buildings, containing the various managers and designers and raw material orderers and pay clerks and staff officers and accounts clerks and all the other range of white-collar jobs found in any huge organisation, were all housed in offices located miles away from the factories. After the factories were obliterated Parkinson discovered that all the white-collar employees actually continued turning up each day and not a single damn Jack of them found their actual job changed one iota, despite the elimination of their fundamental *raison d'être*. Consider it at its simplest level and you'll understand better. Take say the office cleaners and tea ladies. As long as the rest of the staff turned up, their jobs were unchanged. Conversely, their continuing presence necessitated pay clerks, and so it went, all the way up the food chain. Don't you see the implications?'

'Not in terms of deliberately employing grotesque women half a century later, no I don't.'

Geoff sighed resignedly. 'I haven't quite got there yet. The thing is, after my father read about this he thought through its ramifications. They were lost on the world at the time because the peak growth in State and large organisation bureaucracies didn't really eventuate until the mid-seventies so Parkinson was describing a virus which hadn't then arisen.

'The point is that once organisations reach a certain size, they develop a natural tendency in their management component for self-fulfilling, yet fundamentally non-essential growth to the extent that they ultimately become living, functioning, complete entities in their own right. And once the momentum's under way somehow it becomes impossible to stop.'

'I'm damned if I see what any of this has to do with employing ugly women,' James muttered.

'Well you're about to. Once Dad awoke to the super-rich market's potential, specially the fact that he had it to himself, he realised it was unavoidable that Alceides would build up a bureaucracy. It wasn't the unnecessary salaries and offices that primarily concerned him but the all-important secrecy factor. You understand that now. If Alceides

242

was structured in a conventional way and the staff were all housed in one administrative building, the staff numbers would grow on their own account and we'd be shot out of the water every day with someone, deliberately or even accidentally, letting on to the world what we're up to. And that would be the end of us. So Dad turned his mind on how to overcome the problem.'

'And what's that?' James asked, now curious and beginning vaguely to sense the point.

'Bloody simple actually,' Geoff said, topping up James' glass. 'Compartmentalising.'

'I don't understand.'

'Dad compartmentalised every Alceides operation. They now all run as totally separate entities, mostly knowing nothing about anything else in Alceides. It's exactly the opposite approach of the conventional organisation structure and driven solely by the need for secrecy. Every division is lean and mean but, more importantly, knows nothing about the others or has any overall picture of what goes on. There are exceptions, such as Hodgie who knows about Romania and the fatties and of course the Indian operation. But General Rama isn't aware of the fatties let alone Romania or Kanju because there's no need for him to. Same with the pilots. They know about the Head of State division of necessity but they have no idea why we occasionally go to Romania or Nairobi, and Romania has no idea about anything. They just manufacture what we tell them to; but as to who 'we' are, they really haven't a clue. Anyone could turn up and give them instructions and they'd just do it, so long as the fellow said he was from Head Office, although that's hardly an issue as obviously no one would do so.

'So in a nutshell everything's compartmentalised and almost no one knows even who they work for. Divisions such as our New York and Tokyo offices receive client payments which automatically flow through to our anonymous tax-free Bahamas bank accounts, and our investments are all in tax haven entities and conducted within different sharebroking houses entirely outside the banking systems, and so it goes.

'All this compartmentalising has not only led to a highly efficient organisation but has the all important virtue of maximum security. More particularly, one unit could collapse for some reason and the rest of the operation would just sail along, exactly as with Parkinson's discovery in Germany.'

'So where do the ugly women come in?' James pressed.

'It's as I've always said, nothing's an accident in Alceides. When Dad was analysing all of this he realised that once we attained a certain size we'd need a hell of a lot of humdrum accounting people, mainly dealing with payments and bookkeeping. Mindful of the secrecy factor, Dad applied the fatties' brains trust concept, only in reverse. First we deliberately created unpleasant offices. Anyone prepared to tolerate those fitted our requirement nicely. Basically we sought employees who could never find a job anywhere else. Instead of the usual approach of seeking smart young women we targeted harridans, and the more stupid and slovenly they were, the better. Those appalling creatures you saw today will be there for life, if for no other reason than that no one else would ever employ them, let alone marry them. They're absolutely perfect for our requirement. None of them even know who they work for or what we do, and they're all far too dull to even wonder, let alone ask. Officially their employer is a token company called Paragon Services although we put the Encyclopaedia Sales sign on the door to deter anyone coming in trying to sell advertising space or whatever.'

'Oh lay off it, Geoff,' James objected. 'They must know who they work for. After all, what do they tell their friends?'

'They don't have friends, that's the whole point and part of their appeal. Just like the fatties upstairs, we're the only point of reference in their lives. We're doing them a huge favour, not only in providing employment they would never otherwise obtain, tedious though it is, but also in marginally lifting their spirits. Nothing worse for an awesomely ugly girl than to be surrounded by pretty ones. Going to work makes them feel normal when everyone else is a beast. Funny thing; they all have names like Sharon Frump or Myra Stoke, you know, the sort of darkest working-class sounds which one feels can only properly be pronounced with a heavy head-cold. Lunch time's a highlight. I don't know if you noticed the cake shop on the corner but every day they pile in there and come out with bloody great bags of cream buns and other crap. They waddle back to the office and sit in a row and put in about forty minutes' solid eating. They never speak, literally not a peep, because they've so bloody dim they've got nothing to say. They just sit in a row, munching away and staring blankly straight ahead. Their only outside interest is watching television.'

'Hang on a minute,' James said. 'I remember you telling me once fat girls are no good for Alceides because they're unhappy about being fat.'

'Precisely. But that's in respect of the extreme cleverness requirement. With the menial administration tasks we actually want extreme stupidity. Their dimness ensures they have no curiosity about what they're doing, and their unhappiness provides extra insurance. A World War could break out and that lot would neither know nor care. Look, the quickest way to find out what's happening in any organisation is to sight all its payments, so if we ran a conventional organisation it would be our most vulnerable security point. I tell you, it all works very well.'

James shook his head slowly in wonderment. 'What about the drab boss chap, what was his name?'

'Albert. He's an accountant. Again, carefully chosen. Absolutely perfect for the job. He once did three years inside for grossly indecent behaviour when the law used to be down on that sort of thing. The usual mackintosh brigade public toilet stuff. Today, of course, it's categorised as art and virtually encouraged but the important point is Albert's prison record makes him unemployable anywhere else so he values the job immensely, not that it's difficult. Basically he simply oversees and checks everything; after all, being so dumb the harridans do make lots of mistakes. But again, even he has no idea who he works for or what it's all about and he's such a bloody mouse he'd never dare ask. Amy picks up a box of prepared cheques every fortnight and brings them back here. She checks and signs them then sends them off. That's why I introduced you as Lord Bellvue. I knew you'd want an explanation and probably wouldn't believe it, and that little charade proved Albert had no idea who we are. As with Romania, anyone could walk in and say he's from Head Office and tell him to do things and he would. Still, that's hardly an issue for obviously it would never occur to anyone to do so, specially with the Encyclopaedia Sales notice to frighten the hell out of them. What you saw today was the payments processing and recording for every Alceides operation. One of those monsters is already handling Ogg, dealing with all the expenditure to date.'

James again shook his head in astonishment as he contemplated these revelations, a gesture Geoff responded to with bemusement.

'You know, James,' he said, 'I'll tell you how well we've created a block of self-sustaining entities. The bloody IRA could blow up this building and all inside it to eternity and so long as someone continued signing the cheques and, let's face it, anyone could as banks no longer check signatures, the existing ventures would carry on as if absolutely nothing had happened. None of it goes through here, thank God,' he laughed as again he topped up James' glass but further discussion of the ugly women strategy was abandoned as Amy and Miyumi entered the office to join them for the now ritual end-of-day drinks session.

# – TEN –

The helicopter contracted to ferry supplies and guests to Ogg circled low over Oban so that its pilot-owner, Robbie, could point out the warehouse Amy had rented as a supply depot. Over the past two months he had flown almost daily trips to the island, transporting tradesmen and building materials.

James was seated in the front between Robbie and Miyumi, necessitating him leaning into the girl and absorbing the pleasurable aroma of her perfume to look out the side window. She wore brown Edwardian laced boots, black tights, a fawn-coloured corduroy skirt and matching jacket over a black woollen polo neck, and on her head, a perky brown beret. To James she looked a dream, and his fear grew that somehow the visit to Ogg would be a disaster and that his new-found happiness would become abruptly terminated.

'Firth of Lorn,' Robbie sang in his Scottish lilt and James leant across Miyumi again.

'Isle of Mull,' Robbie continued. 'Basically part of the mainland.' A few minutes later they passed the Island of Coll and were over open water. Below lay the uninviting grey sea of the Hebrides, its white-frothed waves rolling and rushing in angry surges. The helicopter bucked and jolted in the high winds. Please let it be all right, James prayed silently.

'I'll show you Barra first as it's the last inhabited island,' Robbie said, and he passed James a map of the Hebrides chain. James spread it on his knees and Miyumi huddled closer as together they studied it.

Twenty minutes later they reached Barra. As if in answer to James' prayer the wind now died away, and from the air the island with its central peak, rolling hills, white beaches and the picturesque village of Castlebray looked invitingly tropical. James' spirits rose.

Now the helicopter swung south and Robbie reeled off the names of the surprisingly pleasing-looking unoccupied islands, with their hills and bays and beaches: Sandray, Pabblay, Mingulay. In the early spring sunshine they bore no resemblance to the bleak imagery of Ogg which had absorbed James over the past year.

'I can't believe these islands are unoccupied,' Geoff said. 'They look terrific.'

'They were once,' Robbie responded. 'Over two thousand years ago. Occasionally I bring archaeologists out to them. You can still find pagan carvings and megaliths and those sorts of relics lying about. I don't know about Ogg though. No one's ever wanted me to take them there. It's coming up next. Ogg's not hilly like these islands. Sometimes it can be a wee bit tricky dropping the helicopter when the wind is up but we're lucky today.'

Suddenly, ahead lay Ogg, which had by now acquired almost mystical proportions in everyone's minds. 'I'll give you a quick tour,' Robbie said.

Despite the wind having faded and the sea becoming almost placid and transformed to an inviting blue, approached from the north Ogg had an ominous, fortress-like character as the sea built to a swell and exploded spectacularly against the cliff-face. They followed the coastline and came to a thick forest where nestling in the lee of the trees, impressively grand in its isolation, lay Ogg Castle, James' birthplace and future home. The castle was a hive of activity with the framework of its sprawling extension, stacks of building material and numerous lilliputian workmen, some of whom waved as they swept across.

The helicopter now turned east and flew over the tussocky Upper Ogg plain, scattering sheep in its path. They reached the dividing escarpment and below it, sheltered under the cliff-face, saw the tiled roof of the almost completed killer-sheep lodge with its large central building and two appendix arms of guestrooms extending outwards at 45 degrees. The land between this triangle was lime green from the air.

'Lawn's coming along nicely,' Robbie said. 'They only sowed it three weeks ago. It will be ready for its first cut any day now.'

Behind the lodge a quarter-mile-long tiled path led to the escarpment cliff-face. Newly planted trees were dotted ten deep along the path's sides and at its end lay a long concrete trench facing the thickly tree-planted land between it and the cliff-face. Freshly sown grassy spaces, on which the sheep were to emerge, were positioned at thirty-foot intervals facing the trench between the trees. A tiled roof on poles sheltered the trench, providing protection from the elements for the Japanese marksmen.

As with the castle, numerous workmen were visible and a large tent city lay to the rear of the complex. A small bulldozer was busy flattening a dirt road linking the lodge with the village and harbour.

They reached the harbour, now empty of boats. 'All out fishing,' Robbie remarked and they passed over the row of cottages. A solitary figure emerged from the cottage adjacent to the kirk and shook his fist at the helicopter. Misinterpreting the hostile gesture, Miyumi waved back. At the end of the road, facing down its length to the kirk could be seen, conspicuous and absurdly disproportionate to the row of crofters' cottages, the newly created Oggonian fifth-century warrior king Mugan statue, which James had last seen under construction in the Romanian factory three months earlier.

'I'll drop the helicopter behind the kirk,' Robbie said. 'You can have a look at the village, after which we'll whip over to the lodge and then on to the castle,' and he began the descent.

On the ground they waited until the rotor blade slowed then Robbie climbed out, strolled round the front and unlocked the passenger door. Gingerly they stepped down and, bent double, ran across to the rear of the kirk. 'I'll wait here for you,' Robbie shouted above the hum of the slowing engine.

Geoff led the way round the side of the old stone building and they found themselves in an ancient weed-strewn graveyard. 'Christ, look at this,' Geoff shouted triumphantly as he studied a moss-covered headstone. '1882.'

'Here's an even older one,' Amy cried. 'Listen,' and she recited 'Margaret Collay – born 6 February 1786, died 12 November 1851.'

'This is fantastic,' Geoff enthused. 'We'll polish them all up and tidy the graveyard. Another photographic feature for the Japanese wives. We'll bang in a few extra ones Romania can knock up going back hundreds more years. We could make them really interesting; you know ...' he thought for a while, '... people living to 110, or hanged for being highwaymen; that sort of thing. Brasch will come up with some good ideas; it's his sort of territory.'

'I rather think a prerequisite for being a highwayman is having

249

some highways,' James said stiffly. He was keen to end the discussion out of concern for Miyumi's reaction. But Geoff's exuberance was not so easily checked.

'You know what I mean though,' he continued excitedly. 'It will add to the interest if they've been exiled here. This place ...' he waved his arms expansively, 'Christ, it's got tremendous potential. We could turn it into a major attraction once Brasch is on the job.'

'Isn't it more in the American tourist line?' Amy questioned doubtfully. 'I'm not sure the Japanese will be that interested.' She turned to Miyumi. 'What do you think, Miyumi? Will Japanese tourists find old headstones interesting?'

'Perhaps just a little,' Miyumi answered carefully.

'I thought the Japanese were into all this ancestor-worshipping racket,' Geoff exclaimed, puzzled by her hesitant response.

'These are not their ancestors.'

'Yeah, well, let's take a look inside,' Geoff muttered and he led the way round to the front of the kirk and then started as he almost bumped into a strange, block-headed figure standing hard against the kirk stone wall, his face inches from its surface. He was emitting a weird humming noise.

'Oops, sorry,' Geoff mumbled.

'Good morning,' James said politely, but the strange creature ignored them and continued gazing intently at the wall and humming loudly. Months later they were to learn this was Thomas the simpleton whose presence had been forewarned in the original consultants' report when Ogg had first been inspected for Alceides. Somewhat rattled, they approached the entrance and Geoff pushed open the ancient wooden doors. Inside lay six rows of dark-timbered pews, while at the front an elevated altar displayed a large leather-bound open Bible, but despite its age the church was unimpressive in its simplicity.

'Bloody Christ, we're certainly going to have to dress this up,' Geoff muttered as he looked about disdainfully. 'Not even any stained glass. I'll get the Polish lads to measure up the windows and we'll design a few interesting panels back in London. Brasch will enjoy ...'

'Aiee,' came a loud cry from behind them. Startled, the party turned to confront the disturbing spectacle of the Reverend McDonald framed in the doorway. He was clad in a McDonald tartan kilt and wore a drab grey knitted pullover, across which spread his shiny white tangle of beard.

'And what do ye think ye be doing?' he bawled then, as his eyes settled on Miyumi and Amy, 'in the holy kirk with heathens. Begone, begone,' and he stepped forward, waving his arms menacingly.

'Now just you look here, my good man,' Geoff spluttered pompously but he was cut short. 'And who might you be?' the Reverend McDonald demanded, pushing his face close to Geoff.

'Never you mind who I am,' Geoff responded angrily. 'This is who counts,' and he pointed to James. 'This is James Campbell, the Laird of Ogg, and this church,' and he gestured about the interior, 'is his property, and the land beneath it, and all the cottages.'

The Reverend McDonald studied James, his eyes narrowing. 'Campbell you say; so you've come back to disturb the peace with ye nefarious Campbell practices. Is it you be responsible for all these foreigners and tomfoolery constructions upsetting the good people?'

James stepped forward. 'I'm sorry if there have been any misunderstandings, Reverend. I am the Laird of Ogg and I have come home.'

'I'll have ye know the villagers are decent people,' the Reverend McDonald bellowed angrily. 'There's been no Campbell on Ogg for nigh thirty years, and now we are visited by pestilence.'

'Now just one moment,' Geoff said sharply. 'I think you'd better mind your Ps and Qs. If there's going to be any unpleasantness let me remind you we can throw you off this island. The church doesn't have a lease or any legal right to be here.'

'Simmer down, Geoff,' James said quietly. He turned to the cleric. 'Reverend, we won't be disturbing life on the island other than in good ways. We're going to provide indoor plumbing, running water and electricity, all free to all the cottages and that includes yours. And for those who want it we can provide employment in the resort we're building. There'll be some tourists coming once a week to admire the kirk, otherwise you won't know they're here.'

Geoff's commercial instincts came to the fore and he joined in James' peace-making overtures, adopting a more conciliatory tone. 'There'll be lots of nice new money to go in the plate every Sunday, Reverend. And we'll bring you a handsome varnished wooden box with a slot at the top for donations. When the tourists come they'll pop money in it, mark my words. We'll do you a printed notice to go with it.'

These observations had a thawing effect on the Reverend McDonald as he weighed the possibilities, but abruptly his face darkened again.

'And it be you responsible for that pagan apparition frightening the good people?' he demanded, pointing a long, bony arm through the open doors to the statue at the end of the road.'

'Ah,' said Geoff, 'Mugan. No, Reverend; you've got it wrong. Important early Christian figure.'

'Who?' the cleric demanded.

Geoff looked at James who looked at the Reverend McDonald then quickly looked away again. Geoff came to the rescue. 'Actually, I haven't got the details here right now,' he said hurriedly. 'But we'll let you know. Still, you will have noticed the heathen head the Christian's holding.'

Sensing the earlier-won ground slipping away in the impasse which now settled over the confrontation James had an inspiration. 'The tourists won't bother you, Reverend. As I said, they'll quietly visit the village once a week, make a donation to the kirk and leave. But you'll be pleased to know our first lot are a party of McDonalds from America. They'll be here in a month.'

'McDonalds you say,' the Reverend McDonald said, rolling the name around as if tasting a particularly appealing sweet. 'Aye man, and why be McDonalds coming to a Campbell den?'

'There'll be no Campbells coming here, Reverend,' James battled on. 'But when the McDonalds arrive perhaps you'd honour us with your presence at dinner. I'm sure they'd be delighted to meet you.'

'They're rich American McDonalds,' Geoff added, slipping into the path James had carved. 'They could be substantial donors to the kirk. They know what's right and wrong. And now, if you'll excuse us we must be going,' and he gestured to the others.

Leaving the Reverend McDonald muttering in the doorway alongside the derelict humming figure still pressed up against the wall, they left and walked down the cobbled road past the cottages, none of which showed any sign of life. A gentle breeze ruffled the harbour, otherwise the village and its surroundings were deathly still. They stopped before the Mugan statue and gazed up at it.

'Lucky we didn't bother with a plaque,' Geoff said. 'The brochure will be sufficient to explain it to the tourists. But if there's any sabotage we'll bum-rush that old bastard off the island double-quick.'

'What is this please?' Miyumi asked.

There was an awkward silence before once more Geoff stepped into the breech. 'Like I said, important historic figure, Miyumi. James will explain it all to you in due course but we'll have brochures in Japanese so the tourists understand. I imagine they'd like to be photographed in front of it, don't you think?' he asked somewhat hesitatingly. The party looked at the girl and waited nervously for her response.

Miyumi studied the statue expressionlessly then stepped closer. Reaching upwards she rested her hand briefly on the severed head dangling from Mugan's left hand.

'Yes,' she said after some consideration. 'They will like this very much.' Geoff exchanged a triumphant look with James. They had called it right. Ogg would be a success.

# – ELEVEN –

Scarcely a day passed during James' first year on Ogg when he was not reminded of Geoff's praise of Professor Parkinson. Often each morning the tasks confronting him seemed overwhelming yet, miraculously, by day's end they were usually all achieved. James could but marvel at the truth of the Parkinson maxim, 'Time expands to accommodate the work available'. He had adopted the nightly practice of sitting with Miyumi over pre-dinner drinks, sometimes at the lodge but mostly at Ogg Castle, enjoying with quiet satisfaction the scene of excited Japanese men recounting their golfing and killer-sheep triumphs to one another and their ever-patient wives.

By the end of the first year Ogg's permanent population had risen to over eighty and the resort, although it was not yet operating at full capacity, usually numbered as many guests. Most of the staff were Ukrainian. The secrecy requirement had led to an all-morning talk-fest during the planning period in London and the debate as to their desirable nationality had only been resolved by taking the problem to Brasch.

Once more James had been fascinated by Brach's succinct analysis, as concurrent with his consumption of a dozen chocolate eclairs, he peeled off the necessary criteria.

'One,' he said biting an eclair in half. 'Non-English-speaking.'

'Two,' as he popped the other half in his mouth. 'Non-Japanese speaking.'

'Three,' and he reached for another eclair. 'High-education-standard country.'

'That's not the case with Kanju and the Latin American girls,' James interrupted.

'True,' Brasch replied, munching happily. 'Different considerations.

We needed coloured girls and there were no non-English-speaking, high-education countries with coloured people. Didn't matter in Kanju as for the clever stuff; monitoring the golf scores in particular, Juma wanted to train his own people.'

'Fair enough,' James conceded and Brasch continued his recital.

'Now where was I? Yes. Four, an extreme poverty and high unemployment country so as to value job and endure isolation uncomplainingly.' And so he continued, methodically polishing off the chocolate eclairs while listing other necessary criteria including familiarity with extreme cold, European so as to pass off satisfactorily as Scottish and not look silly in kilts, no special dietary, religious or other peculiarities which could cause difficulties. Eventually he concluded, 'It all points to the former Soviet Union. The central European states from Estonia down to Serbia are out. Too close to the west so have acquired some civilisation sensitivities and might smell a rat. Innocent gullibility is an absolute prerequisite. Russians are a possibility but may have too high expectations unless we comb some of the central regions. Problem is, in the more remote parts they all look too brutishly degenerate to even pass as Scots. Go a hundred miles east of Moscow and you're into Brezhnev facial types. The Japs are a refined race and won't pay good money to look at that sort of thing.'

His huge paw reached for the last eclair and he studied it sadly, then in two bites it was gone. 'Ukrainians,' he announced conclusively. 'Fit the bill perfectly.' He contemplated this conclusion for a moment, then added, 'Only problem I see is they're a good-looking race. Might lack credibility to pass as Scots.'

'Hang on a minute! I'm bloody Scots,' James protested.

'Exactly! You know what I mean then,' Brasch retorted mischievously. 'Seriously though,' he added, 'you can't deny that Scots can sometimes be a bit grim and pinched looking. Ukrainians have wide open, regular-featured faces. It could be a plausibility issue.' Just as James began further objections he was interrupted by Geoff. 'The Ogg clients are coming straight from Japan then returning immediately. It's not as if they're touring Scotland first. We had the same concern with the Latinas in Kanju until we realised almost the only Africans the Kanju guests encounter on their trip, thank God, are our Latin American girls. Same goes with Ogg. The only Scots they'll meet will be Ukrainians. As a Scot you should be pleased,

255

James. It will certainly leave a better impression of Scotland than would otherwise be the case. Anyway,' he said conclusively, overriding James' protestations, 'we're only interested in what pleases the clients, so Ukrainians it is.'

A week later Geoff and James had flown to Kiev and placed a half-page newspaper advertisement, translated into Russian by the newspaper's advertising staff, for highly paid, one-year terms of employment abroad.

The hotel had provided a translator and they had witnessed a near riot when more than three thousand hopeful job-seekers had clamoured outside for appointments. They had first engaged Oleg, a 40-year-old nuclear physicist who spoke excellent English, as the overseeing manager for the Ukrainian staff on Ogg. Thereafter he had effectively taken over the interviewing and over four long days the exercise had been completed.

The chosen 60 comprised 25 young men and 35 young women selected for their prettiness, all but four of whom had university degrees.

Twelve of the men were to work as golf-course electronic greens manipulators, four as greenkeepers and groundsmen, and another four as fairway ball-stealers on the six fairways where dips in the level, achieved by the bulldozer, another Brasch idea, made this possible despite the current absence of tree cover. Specialist staff employed included an electrician, a plumber, a carpenter and a motor mechanic. The girls, some of whom had doctorates, were all to be housekeepers, golf-score manipulators, waitresses and laundry and kitchen workers.

A bus duly transported them to Riga where a decrepit Latvian ferry had been engaged to take them to Ogg. The ship headed west and sailed in large circles between Norway and Iceland for twelve days to give credibility to the Ukrainians' understanding that they were going to northern Newfoundland, this being a Brasch suggestion in the interests of security. In due course it berthed in Ogg harbour, the largest vessel ever to call there.

As Brasch had predicted, with one exception the Ukrainians were first-rate. Only the electronic golf-course manipulation proved a problem, provoking frequent rages from the laird, Guy Sanderson. The necessary pin-point scoring precision implicit in golf seemed lost on them, and their sloppiness with this task was the sole source of dissatisfaction in their engagement. In every other respect they were co-operative and willing. All happily wore kilts and eagerly competed to be Highland dancers, aided by the incentive of more money.

The Highland dancing troupe was a Brasch idea to which James, mindful of the success of Kanju's traditional African dance performances and the need for supplementary entertainments for the Japanese wives, readily concurred. But a problem arose with training them.

Walter McNabb, a crusty old head greenkeeper from Aberdeen, had been employed to take charge of the golf course, his secrecy assured by his massive salary, and his value enhanced by his ability to double as the resort piper. McNabb had proffered the services of his elderly spinster sister who had devoted her life to teaching Scottish dancing. She had been duly helicoptered to Ogg and by the end of a week's tutorage the troupe had mastered, albeit clumsily, some basic Scottish dances.

But watching them perform James felt dissatisfied and he faxed Brasch outlining his concerns. The Japanese ladies always applauded politely but to James they lacked the chutzpah of the Kanju traditional dances, while as an entertainment they put a damper on the Japanese men's celebratory mood in the lounges each evening.

Brasch's response had been reprimanding. The object of the exercise, he wrote, is solely entertainment. The clients were in no position to question the performances' authenticity, nor would it occur to them to do so. The important points, if the guests were to be satisfied, were that the dancers must be young and attractive, their performances erotic, and as with Kanju, so long as the dances were represented as authentic traditional Oggonian culture, anything went. Most important, their kilts must be shortened and looser, they should wear nothing under them, the girls must have buttonless shirts open to the waist and not wear bras and, Brasch advised, he had ordered a set of dildoes to be dispatched for the male dancers from Romania. He further advised that Geoff had engaged a Soho strip-club choreographer who would arrive in a fortnight to put the troupe through its paces.

Other than in the dancers' shortened kilts the Oggonian traditional dances, Brasch wrote, should be identical to the provenly successful Kanju traditional dances if the desired level of client satisfaction was to be achieved. An important prerequisite, he added, was the pre-performance explanation of the dance's cultural significance so the clients could happily wallow in eroticism without embarrassment or guilt.

On receiving this advice James fretted for a week about Miyumi's reaction. He resolved the difficulty one evening by first plying her with wine then, once she was happily relaxed, entertaining her with an account of the Kanju dances and the guests' positive reaction.

'But why did I not see those on the videos?' Miyumi asked, a question James had anticipated and turned to his advantage.

'There are so many ancillary entertainments adding to the Kanju experience which we must introduce on Ogg, and as the videotape only lasts two hours, I suppose Brasch confined it to the main things,' he explained. Thereafter as new features were devised and Miyumi witnessed the favourable audience responses, she became an enthusiastic accomplice in their creation.

One unexpected difficulty arose with McNabb, who protested at the corruption of Scottish culture. James instructed Guy to take a firm line with him and the Scot's ingrained deference to Sanderson, to whose great pleasure McNabb always addressed as 'My Lord,' saw him begrudgingly continue to play the bagpipes during the Ukrainians' erotic cavorting.

A mini-crisis arose one night not long after these weekly Scottish cultural performances began when as the girls cartwheeled about, their kilts falling over their heads exposing all and their breasts occasionally bouncing free from their open shirt fronts, James observed one of the guests filming the performance with a video camera. He recalled Juma's warning announcement to the Kanju guests about the sacredness of the Kanju traditional dances and the required prohibition on filming and photography and thereafter Toshio, the Japanese head chef, delivered a similar pronouncement before each performance. He read and eventually memorised a tediously lengthy account that James had drafted and Miyumi had translated, explaining the sacredness of the traditional Oggonian Scottish dances they were about to witness and the necessary ban on recording. The guests reluctantly but, being Japanese, obediently complied with the ban. James had deliberately made Toshio's recitation lengthy and dull so as to reinforce the cultural character of the performance.

Looking back over the year James concluded that despite the daily problems – usually supply issues which were always quickly attended to following a fax to Amy – by and large things had gone remarkably well.

The laird, Guy Sanderson, had worked out very well and on learning the true nature of the Oggonian exercise had entered into the spirit of it with enthusiasm. As Mr Upton, despite his cynicism about actors, had predicted, he had proved to be an intelligent and first-rate manager and he provided James with an appreciated male companionship. A non-smoker, he readily accepted an unlit pipe as part of the laird imagery, jabbing with it theatrically to emphasise his points.

In his first week on Ogg, James had motorcycled down to the harbour and introduced himself to the two owners of the fishing boats, Alex and Andrew. Both had greeted him cordially and James had invited them back to the castle for dinner which resulted in the older man, Andrew, abandoning fishing and donning a kilt for the sheep-master job, which he had subsequently handled with great enthusiasm.

The killer-sheep exercise had been trouble-free from the outset, thanks to Andrew's competence. Each morning he led the dozen Japanese hunters, clad in military fatigues and holding their rifles ready for any unexpected rogue killer-sheep attack, running in line in crouching position to the safety of the covered trench. Each hunter carried a small backpack supplied by the lodge which contained a supply of blank bullets, a thermos flask of coffee and a mid-morning snack. At midday lunch was brought across under armed guard, at four o'clock whisky was ritually served, and at five, the shooters returned with their armed escort back to the lodge. Later they would gather in the lounge for some serious pre-dinner Oggonian whisky consumption, usually paid for by the day's successful shooter.

One nuisance of the killer-sheep exercise was the constant barrage of client questions about their history and habits. James eventually resolved this by writing an explanatory pamphlet which was translated into Japanese by Miyumi and then printed in Japan with appropriate ferocious illustrations.

In his first tentative effort James allowed himself only limited licence although by the time for reprinting three months later, such was his creative pleasure in the exercise and his confidence that

259

anything in print would be accepted unquestioningly by the Japanese, this time he really went to town.

'More than 160 deaths through killer-sheep attacks have been recorded over the last two centuries on Ogg, the last in 1988 when an Oggonian horseman was brought down by a pack-hunting flock of sheep and both he and his horse were devoured. Such is their ferocity they have been known to leap from the Upper Ogg cliff-face on to crofters 60 feet below, and there have been sightings of entire flocks plunging over the cliffs into the turbulent seas and attacking and destroying passing whales.'

The pamphlet was enhanced with illustrations of flocks of sheep viciously ripping apart a frantically leaping whale as they clung to its side, of sheep dragging down a panic-stricken deer and swallowing men head-first, only their lower torso and legs visible, hanging from the sheep's mouth. All of this heightened the shooters' sense of adventure, although Miyumi reported that many of the wives fretted for their husbands' safety during the day and were visibly relieved each evening at their safe return. The brochures were avidly read and when nothing was challenged James became even more emboldened; on wet days, contentedly engaged in increasingly outrageous Oggonian history and culture pamphlets.

Alex no longer made the often precarious trips to Castlebay as the resort purchased his catches at premium prices, and he often called up to the castle in the evenings for some companionship over a few drinks.

It became plain to James that the two fishermen had comprised the upper strata of pre-Alceides Oggonian society. Aside from the Reverend McDonald's small stipend they alone earnt cash and their contacts with the outside world, albeit confined to Barra thirty miles to the north, elevated them to figures of respect.

The excellent relationship with Alex and Andrew proved a boon in dealing with the crofters. For the first time the villagers earnt money through providing fresh vegetables and eggs to the castle but they could not be persuaded to increase production, preferring to remain indoors, joyously engrossed in their newly discovered television game shows and soap operas.

Enraptured at their abrupt change of fortune they readily complied with James' request, conveyed through Alex, to remain out of sight during the Japanese ladies' kirk, village and Mugan statue visits. Their shambling and demented demeanour was inconsistent with the imagery of the Ogg warrior race that James promoted in his historic brochures which the kilted young Ukrainians upheld so well with mock battles as a preamble to their erotic dance performances.

Only the Reverend McDonald and Thomas the simpleton remained outside the two fishermen's unspoken authority, the former through belligerence and the latter, stupidity.

Frequently the laird would return enraged after escorting village tours which had led to confrontations with the Reverend. The cleric particularly objected to the glass box fixed to the wall inside the kirk in which was displayed Mugan's ancient gold sword with which, as James had outlined in his Mugan pamphlet, the warrior saviour had beheaded over six hundred enemies during his lifetime. The sword's immense appeal to the Japanese was offset by the cleric's objection to it and it only remained in the kirk after a threat by James, in a rare loss of temper, to expel McDonald from the island. On that occasion the parson had retreated muttering to his cottage.

The Reverend had resisted the Polish contractors' attempts to electrify his cottage and, according to Alex and Andrew, now devoted his Sunday sermons to the evils of television, interspersed with insults directed at the Japanese heathens besmirching the island. But his message was lost on the crofters, the soaps' and game shows' powerful pull easily surpassing their sinful character, which reduction of influence only served to intensify the cleric's hatred of the newcomers all the more.

From Alex, James learnt that the Reverend McDonald came from a long line of proselytising missionaries and that his father had actually been killed by a crocodile in Uganda. According to Alex this incident preyed obsessively on the parson's mind and was a frequent sermon topic, sermon villains, currently the Japanese 'heathens', always being accorded the ultimate McDonald epithet of 'crocodiles'.

The problem of Thomas the simpleton was more one of embarrassment. James learnt that Thomas had devoted the past twelve years to standing all day, drooling and humming with his face to the kirk's wall, in the same spot adjacent to the front door. No one knew why, and prior to the newcomers' arrival, no one cared.

Alex's appeal, on James' bequest, to Thomas' mother fell on deaf ears, for not even the allure of television could separate him from the attractions of the wall.

'Bloody embarrassing,' Guy repeatedly complained to James. 'Upsets the ladies. We've got to do something about it.'

Eventually James came up with an idea. It was explained to the Japanese ladies that Ogg had a unique justice system, unchanged for the past 1,700 years. All crimes were divided into two punishment categories. The more extreme were subject to beheading, the instrument for which the ladies were about to see in the kirk. Everything else was subject to a sentence of standing staring at close range at the kirk wall and depending on the nature of the offence, the sentences ranged from a day up to a month. If they were lucky, the laird explained, they may well see an offender being so punished. Unfortunately, this device did not work for while inspecting the beheading sword plainly appealed, on observing Thomas, according to Miyumi, the Japanese ladies felt discomforted and became upset.

Just as they were beginning to despair the Thomas problem was resolved by Andrew who suggested paying Thomas' mother £1 a week to have him watch the sheep on Upper Ogg, a proposal she quickly accepted. Thereafter, each morning Thomas rose at dawn and stumbled across to a small shelter built for him on the clifftop, well away from the castle and golf course. There he resided, slobbering and humming as he watched the sheep grazing before returning to the village at sunset.

The various entertainments and background photography innovations which had been devised back in the London planning stages all added to the increasingly rich Oggonian tourist experience.

The shop attached to the castle which was managed by two Japanese girls, was from the outset a tremendous money-spinner. It sold kilts, tartan plus-fours, golf equipment, Oggonian woollen pull-overs imported from New Zealand and relabelled, Romanian-made Oggonian antiquities, Oggonian honey suitably re-labelled and shipped in from the mainland (for appearances' sake James had placed clusters of bee-less beehives about the island) and Oggonian whisky, both malt and blended, which had been bought cheaply in large quantities from a Bulgarian manufacturer and again suitably re-labelled.

James took particular pride in the ancient whisky-still constructed by the Polish contractor, visits to which were a regular part of the laird's conducted cultural tours. The still consisted of a stone room which had been aged two centuries over three days by the Romanian specialists. They had first hammered the building with axes and tilted it slightly askew by shunting it with the bulldozer, then they had applied acids. They had concluded their craft by lighting fires alongside both the outer and inner walls. A load of 300-year-old timber, trucked across Europe from the Romanian factory and brought over from the mainland by Alex, was used to build the wooden floor, ledges and barrels, and a shiny copper vat purchased from a Dundee jam manufacturer was installed. A thatcher was flown in from the Orkney Islands to construct the roof, and the ancient whisky-still was almost complete. But not entirely.

The finishing touches were achieved by Amy's purchase from a used-machinery dealer of a small 80-year-old letterpress printing machine. Partly hidden behind the ancient timber planking, with just a few of its highly polished levers and wheels and a brass manufacturer's plate exposed, once set in motion it delivered a satisfying clanking and rumbling. Open sacks of sawdust, the top six inches covered with barley, leant against an interior wall.

Once a week a paraffin oil lamp and a pile of peat were burnt inside overnight and this combined with the occasional spraying about the interior of a bottle of Bulgarian whisky, rendered a pleasantly smoky, whiskyish aroma. The still was James' pride and joy, so much so that he occasionally accompanied the laird when he escorted the Japanese wives on Oggonian relics tours. But listening to Sanderson outline its 300-year-old history and explain the printing machinery's whisky-making process dismayed James, when he observed that this was always received by the Japanese ladies with only polite detachment. Their sole interest lay in photographing one another, both inside and out, and once this was done, the historic and manufacturing explanations James had concocted fell on plainly disinterested ears.

Following this disappointment, and conscious of the Kanju maxim of keeping the wives happy while their husbands were sportingly preoccupied, James had Miyumi analyse the wives' behaviour. After accompanying Sanderson on eight Oggonian antiquities tours and recording the time spent at each relic by the Japanese wives, mainly photographing each other, a clear pattern emerged.

The ladies' principal activity, averaging 108 minutes daily, was tea-drinking and gossiping. This was followed by 23 minutes gazing at the flower gardens McNabb had created which rose to 44 minutes when park benches were installed. Next came the shop at 57 minutes.

Admiring the lawn's centrepiece fountain scored 14 minutes which rose to 21 when goldfish were added. The antiquities tour was particularly disappointing, the Mugan statue receiving only 7 minutes, the kirk 9 and the whisky-still 12. The remainder of the ladies' day was occupied with meals and in the evenings, listening to their husbands boasting about their killer-sheep and golf triumphs.

James discussed these figures with Miyumi and a plan of action was devised to create more time-filling diversions.

First the flower gardens were extended, which when completed lifted flower gazing to 63 minutes. An old freighter destined for scrapping was acquired, and with Robbie hovering overhead to lift him off, Alex steered it at top speed one full tide up onto the rocks, where it became firmly wedged. This wreck proved a great success with the ladies, more so when James' subsequent explanatory brochure was produced. Accompanied with gruesome illustrations it outlined how the freighter had been passing half a mile offshore only to be attacked by a 50-strong flock of sheep who, having leapt off the cliff into the foaming sea, had swum out to the ship, somehow scrambled aboard and killed and eaten the crew.

James constantly marvelled that no one ever questioned the killer-sheep stories, which inspired him into even more outlandish pamphlet-writing. These accounts compounded the Japanese huntsmen's sense of bravery and triumph when their turn arose to pot one, although, Miyumi reported, the wives anguished even more about the dangers their husbands faced. To provide comfort to the terrified ladies the laird carried a gun when he escorted them on their Oggonian tours, to deal with any possible rogue killer-sheep, although it was emphasised that apart from the copse facing the trench, sheep never ventured on to Lower Ogg. It was explained that an unseen and in fact non-existent security fence and trench among the newly planted trees prevented their access to the golf course on Upper Ogg.

Apart from killer-sheep anecdotes, after six months James realised that the only interest the wives had in Oggonian history and culture was in large tangible items to be photographed standing before. A megalith was planned but then discarded for its lack of interesting features, and instead a large boulder in the centre of Lower Ogg was carved into an Easter Island head by the Romanians, flown over for the task. James wrote a brochure explaining its historic significance as a fifth-century deification object and evidence of Oggonian sea-faring history.

'It is now widely accepted by historians,' he wrote, 'that Oggonians were the greatest seafarers in history and undoubtedly preceded Columbus in discovering America. The famous Easter Island heads were carved by Oggonian colonisers, evidence of this lying in the last remaining identical statue on Ogg which, scientific testing reveals, predates those on the Pacific island. Oggonian relics found in the Andes, backed up by DNA testing, prove the Incas were direct descendants of Oggonian colonisers. The great Oggonian Imperial era saw Oggonian culture spread across the Pacific. The similarities between Tahitian drum dances and Hawaiian hula dancing and the Oggonian traditional dances still performed to this day are apparent to all.'

The tennis court discussed back in London was built but rarely used, the Japanese wives being content simply to be photographed standing holding racquets alongside Miyumi.

While during the past winter bad weather had never deterred the golfers and killer-sheep huntsmen, James was initially concerned about entertaining the wives on inclement days. But observing them it seemed, and indeed Miyumi confirmed, that they were content to sit for hours before the fire, gossiping and drinking tea, this activity broken only by lunch, morning and afternoon tea and purchasing excursions to the shop. Despite that, James threw himself into the task of completing the castle furnishings.

Amy's purchasing trips to northern township auction houses rendered up plenty of battered old oak tables, sideboards and cracked leather chairs, stuffed salmon and gamebirds, old well-oiled cricket bats and tarnished silver trophies, stags' heads, milkmaid and Scottish highlander bronzes and Victorian porcelain bowls, and James eagerly awaited each new shipment. Once these were placed around the corridors, Ogg castle gradually took on the sought-after rumpled Scottish castle atmosphere. The finishing touch, however, arose during one of James' Oggonian history pamphlet-writing sessions and he faxed Brasch with his instructions.

As a result, four hundred Victorian-era lithographs, drawn to James' design and displaying episodes in Ogg's rich history, were completed in Romania. Most were in sequences of four and their age was easily achieved, so James learnt, by dotting them, once drawn on the computer, with dabs of brown paint to acquire the necessary foxing, then soaking them in milk and allowing them to dry in the Romanian sun. Once framed and hung about the castle corridors and in the bedrooms, studying them became a major attraction for the Japanese ladies on wet days.

The most popular were those showing the killer-sheep in action. In sets of four these displayed in one sequence: first, a kilted horseman desperately fleeing from a pursuing flock of ravenous sheep, fear evident in both horse and rider's eyes, and in the second, the flock leaping at the horse, some gripping its flanks, while the rider, twisting in the saddle, slashed at them with his sword. The third showed the horse lying kicking on its side while sheep tore at its throat and in the background the rider endeavouring to flee on foot. The final sketch in the set portrayed the flock devouring the horse, its bare, flesh-torn ribs exposed, while the rider, his legs protruding from a sheep's mouth, was being swallowed head-first.

Another set displayed the Great Oggonian Massacre of 1832, illustrating over a sequence of four sketches the attack on the village by a flock of two hundred sheep, the villagers cowering on the cottage roofs, mothers clutching terrified children to their breasts while the men vainly attempted to stave off leaping sheep with pitch-forks, the sheep charging the wooden cottages, and then some cottages collapsing and the villagers tumbling down and being borne off in the sheep's fangs. The final lithograph in that sequence showed the rebuilding of the cottages with stone. This set inspired James to write a brochure describing the episode as a turning point in Oggonian history when wood was replaced with stone as a building material and pointing out that the tilt in the whisky-still, achieved six months earlier with the bulldozer, had arisen from a frenzied mass charge by 60 sheep in 1884.

Killer-sheep attacking whales, climbing the sides of passing ships as the sailors desperately tried to fend them off, and leaping from the cliffs on to seals frolicking in the surf eventually exhausted their potential as a lithograph subject and James turned his mind to other episodes in Oggonian history. These he had painted as huge canvases in Romania, and once framed and displayed about the castle they added immensely to the overall ambience. Mugan leading his Oggonian warriors into battle against Vikings provided many bloodthirsty topics, and James noted the appeal of one in particular, a

266

massive oil painting showing Mugan standing on a rock, roaring victoriously as he waved his sword overhead while surrounding him over four hundred blood-dripping Viking heads were displayed on the ends of pikes. Other paintings portrayed Mugan wrestling with a huge bear, lifting a Viking longboat by its bow as its 40 crew tumbled backwards into the sea, carrying a boulder four times his bodysize and finally, as an ancient seer, sitting on his throne lecturing to his 27 offspring who were gathered at his feet.

More recent historic oil painting scenes showed kilt-clad Oggonian battalions led by pipers, massacring the French at Waterloo, Cossacks in the Crimean War, wild-eyed fuzzie wuzzies in the Sudan, Zulus in South Africa, and Germans in the trenches of Flanders. Turks, Egyptians, Red Indians, Solomon Island savages, New Zealand Maoris, Afghans; the list of battle victims portrayed all testified to the Oggonian warrior tradition, although James took care to avoid any Oriental vanquished enemies. Less popular topics were those displaying Oggonian craftsmen and artists down through the ages. But, by and large, once the lithographs and oil paintings were manufactured and displayed, the interior of Ogg Castle was complete.

The acquisition of a stag and four hinds enhanced the exterior atmosphere as most mornings they could be seen from the dining room window, nibbling the choice grass at the edge of the forest.

By the end of the first year all of these efforts had considerably heightened the Japanese wives' Oggonian experience. The biggest success, however, came from the building of stables, the employment of three more kilt-clad Ukrainians as stable-hands, and the introduction of gentle horse-trekking which the ladies took to with gusto, such was its novelty to them.

It had taken twelve months of trial and error but the new attractions seemingly created a full and exciting experience for the wives, more so once routines were established to ensure each intake covered every Oggonian offering. Now, Miyumi reported, they all left at the end of their visits bubbling with appreciation and undertaking to return.

For the first time in his life James felt purposeful and fulfilled. Most of all, thanks to his relationship with Miyumi, he was immensely happy.

Only the Reverend McDonald remained a problem. Had James remembered the donation box proposition hastily broached in the initial confrontation with the minister the cleric may possibly have accepted the new order uncomplainingly. But with the constant pressures of establishing Ogg this undertaking slipped James' memory and Guy's periodic run-ins with the churchman during village tours entrenched an abrasive relationship. James began to plan the Reverend McDonald's ejection from Ogg but as the danger of the cleric recounting the island's activities overwhelmed his nuisance value, it was not until two further years had passed that a solution finally presented itself.

# – TWELVE –

With the onset of summer and increasing sunny days a date was finally set for a long-planned fishing trip with Alex. Early on the agreed morning Miyumi and James motorcycled across the island to the harbour with a luncheon hamper. They chugged out into the placid open sea, eventually anchoring a mile offshore where fishing with hand-lines they hauled in over forty cod keeping Alex busy on the filleting table. Late that day they returned happy and slightly sun-burnt to find Geoff had arrived with the helicopter bringing in a new batch of guests. It was three months since James had last seen him, and over pre-dinner drinks Geoff explained his presence.

'I needed a break so I thought I'd pop up and wave the flag. Christ I've been busy. Brasch has come up with a sensational new scheme. Our New York office sounded out the market and we've had a terrific response. We're trialling it next week in India. Naturally I'm going and I'd like you to come along for the ride.'

'Tell me about it,' James said eagerly.

'It's vintage Brasch lateral thinking. Apparently he was pondering about the regular outpouring of Holocaust books and television documentaries and it puzzled him, the continuing interest that is. So on a hunch he checked it out and, sure enough, he found that despite all the extensive reviews of every new Holocaust book, very few people actually bought the damn things, which is what he suspected. But, even though it's six years since he left the building, he recalled that bookshops always carry a huge section devoted to the Nazis and in particular to Hitler, mostly pictorials.'

'He's right actually,' James reflected. 'They do.'

'Precisely. But it's not the done thing to review such books, not that they're really reviewable, being just clones of one another. The

269

important point is people keep buying them, and despite all the carrying on about the Holocaust, it's actually Hitler in the pre-war years which fascinates them. Judging by the poor book sales, they're suffering from Holocaust industry fatigue. Brasch came up with an explanation. It's supposition of course, but if the reaction from our clients is any guide, I think he's got it. Put his finger right on the button in fact.'

'But what is it?' James demanded curiously.

'You recall when I first explained how the Presidential and Royal Tour business came about?'

James thought briefly. 'Ah yes. Your father's friendship with the financier Goldsmith.'

'Yes, yes,' Geoff said hurriedly, 'but do you remember why? Goldsmith wanted mass public adulation and cheering crowds; all the flannel we deliver with our Presidentials and Royals. Well, Brasch made the connection between that craving and the continuing public fascination with Hitler. He claims the one thing which still holds everyone awestruck after seven decades is the bloody Nuremberg Rally. You know, Hitler up on a pedestal raving and giving the Nazi salute and 100,000 stupid robotic stormtroopers sieg heiling back and all the swastika banners everywhere. Let's face it though, it was fantastic theatre and probably the turning point which reinforced the Nazi hold over Germany.'

'I don't see the angle,' James said, puzzled.

'All of that's just preamble. The really, really big attraction is Hitler ranting. God knows, we've all heard the recordings. You can't deny it's gripping stuff; beginning with a whisper then building up to all that rage and passion. And it's not just bloody Hitler. Look at the Castro clown. He's apparently marshalled as many as 200,000 and bawled at the poor buggers for six and seven hours at a time. It's characteristic of every dictator, bellowing at the masses with lengthy tirades from a balcony. Ceausescu used to do it, so did Peron and Mussolini and the Gaddafi goose in Libya. But there's no doubt Hitler was the all-time champion. Sure, Castro could go on the longest with all that undergraduate socialist stuff when he wasn't boring everyone to tears about the sugar harvest. Castro was never more than an infantile clown and not really what I'm on about. You can't argue that as an orator Hitler was bloody exciting. Only a Martian might not be moved – but then I suppose on the other hand what would a

Martian make of ballroom dancing or a million other things people do? Brasch partly attributes Hitler's platform success to language. He claims German lends itself to menacing tirades, with all those harsh guttural consonants. Much tougher for Castro and Mussolini and Peron to intimidate with Spanish and Italian. Too many vowels. They're lovers' languages, not warriors' or tyrants'. Brasch says Hitler wrote in *Mein Kampf* that all epoch-making revolutionary events have been produced by the spoken, not the written, word.'

'Absolute crap,' James snapped.

'Be that as it may,' Geoff continued blithely, 'Hitler clearly believed it and arguably he proved it, at least in terms of creating the Third Reich.'

'Then he argued against his own book, literally and figuratively. Everyone knows *Mein Kampf* sold millions of copies and launched the Nazis.'

'Funnily enough, I actually said that to Brasch,' Geoff retorted excitedly. 'He claims *Mein Kampf* only created the initial interest but it was the oratory which really made the difference and transformed interest to involvement and he insists it was the Nuremberg Rally spectacle which finally got the buggers. Plus, he says, those who argue the pen is mightier than the sword invariably are those who wield the pen and are simply pushing their own barrel and it was Hitler's oratory which actually won the day.'

'Oh come on, Geoff. You make it sound like admiration. People are only still fascinated because of the huge number of deaths Hitler caused.'

'But that's the point,' Geoff cried. 'That's what we all assume. Brasch claims it's nonsense, attributable to the persistent Jewish demonisation of Hitler. Understandable from their point of view of course, keeping up the pressure that is. But as Brasch says, if the on-going fascination with Hitler is because of that, there would be an even bigger demand for Stalin books because he was responsible for four times as many deaths. And Mao caused more deaths than Hitler as well and there's no interest in him either. Brasch says that when it comes to genocide you can't go past the Spanish conquistadors and 70 million South American Indians wiped out and what interest is there in that? And what about Genghis Khan? His tally of killings has been estimated at as many as 60 million. Who's interested in him? Bloody nobody! You remember I told you how we have ten top history professors on the payroll as fattie-finders. On a hunch Brasch wrote to them all and discovered that over 60 per cent of current history doctorate thesis writers choose some aspect of Hitler as their subject. The profs are in despair, but it proves Brasch's point about the ongoing obsession with bloody Hitler.'

'It's you who's missing the point,' James protested. 'Hitler set out to kill entire races, or at least with the Jews and Gypsies he did. It's the sheer horror of that which grips people. With Stalin and Mao it was misadventure rather than intent.'

Geoff shrugged. 'I said exactly the same thing to Brasch. He argued that if that was the source of fascination there would be a Pol Pot book industry and there's not. And Pol Pot was yesterday, not way before most people were born, like Hitler. Pol Pot's killings were just as deliberate and certainly more significant in a scale sense, yet let's face it, who gives a damn? I tell you, it's a style thing. Stalin, Pol Pot, Mao, Castro; all that crowd were bloody boring. They lacked theatre. God knows, they even made a virtue out of austerity and drabness. Look at their clothing; that says it all. Brasch claims the most overlooked factor in explaining communism's failure was its relentless dreariness. People react positively to style and panache, as we prove with our Royal Tours, and there's no question Hitler delivered that. Look at his plans for Berlin; the grandiose intentions to build a golden metropolis. He gave the buggers something to be passionate about, and understood and applied the bread and circuses strategy. Stalin, Mao and the rest only ever offered bread and even then they failed at that. But here's the point. Where Brasch sees a brand new market is like I said; he claims the turning point for Hitler, the single event which consolidated his power and made him seem invincible, was the Nuremberg bloody Rally. People love mass hysteria. He's right you know. Look at Cup Finals. Why attend when you can see it better on television and without the inconvenience and cost? It's the mass hysteria; it's exciting, bloody exciting in fact to be there and be part of it. Well, our clients want that same excitement but being who they are they want to be the focal point of it and not just in the audience – and we can deliver it to them.'

'Oh yes, so what's proposed?' James asked cautiously, once again mentally bracing himself for a fresh Alceides outrage.

'Don't you see? It's obvious. Next week in India we're packing fifty thousand locals into a stadium. It's all organised. We're giving them a dollar each in rupees, payable on exit when it's all over. We're filling the front rows with five hundred of the buggers in black uniforms and jackboots. Half of them will hold up a pole with a large placard showing a photo of the client's head. We've got lots of black and red banners with menacing fascist-type lightning symbols, and the only accessories we need are a podium and a microphone for the client to orate from. We've organised a flashing light behind the podium which the speaker can't see and doesn't know about, and when it goes on they all have to cheer. And we've trained two hundred supervisors who for three dollars each in rupees per rally move about threatening to throw out anyone slacking on the cheering front, not that it should be a problem. A dollar's meaningful money where we're trialling it next week. The client can really let off steam before a huge, cheering audience. Basically it satisfies the same mass adulation craving the Royal and Presidential Tours deliver. I tell you, James, it's a wonderful concept.'

'And the clients are into that?' James asked, not hiding his astonishment.

'In it! We've been knocked over in the rush. We made a marketing video basically showing the Nuremberg Rally but guaranteeing a minimum fifty thousand assembly and we signed up fifteen for a $250,000 fee, plus disbursements, inside a fortnight. They're all existing Presidential and Royal clients. Honestly, James, I'm really excited about it.'

'It's bloody absurd,' James spluttered. 'And anyway, won't it mess up the Royal Tour business?'

'No way. The thing about the Nuremberg Rally industry is it's a very male thing and doesn't involve the wives. Women are innately one-on-one naggers; not ranters to the masses. Anyway, you saw the Queen in Madagascar, specially with the executions. Believe me, the wives won't give those up lightly and will harass their husbands to keep buying Royals and Presidentials. I'm not worried about that. Matter of fact, it will be helpful if it takes some pressure off the Head of State Tour business. Bookings-wise we've a full house for the next eighteen months and can't keep up with demand unless we can open up suitable new territories and find another Hodgie or Rama which, I might add, in both cases ain't easy. The good thing is that the client frustration is producing healthy growth in the sale of extras as they make the most of their tours. Over the last six months hangings are up 63 per cent although decapitations have dropped a bit. Bit of a worry there but Brasch is working on it. But execution revenue increments overall are significantly higher because we've been offering group hangings at a 40 per cent discount per victim for a minimum of five at a time and they've sold very well. Flogging sales are rising and village virgin deflowerings are steady. So are statue sales, although they're placing real pressure on Romania now we've used up our Lenin stocks. We've got a man from our Indian office in North Korea right now actually. He's negotiating to buy a dozen Kim Jong Il statues which we can replace with our clients' heads. It will relieve the pressure on our sculpting staff. I'd send one to you here, with a change of head of course, but they're unsuitable for Ogg.'

'Oh! Why's that?' James asked, as always eager for fresh background photography objects for the Japanese wives.

'They're all scholarly poses. A figure just standing with a book under his arm is quite unappealing to the Japanese ladies; saints and scholars that is. Not their sort of thing at all. They're more into the warrior and decapitation themes. Right Miyumi?'

'Perhaps,' Miyumi replied flatly, displaying no emotion.

'But there's no reason why Ogg couldn't have a great scholar in its history,' James insisted, reluctant to pass up the opportunity of a reheaded Kim statue and another brochure exercise.

'No, no, no,' Geoff said brusquely. 'Look; our New York office sent one of their staff down to Venezuela last week and he bought the cast of a Simon Bolivar statue on a rampant rearing horse. It's on its way to Romania now and we're expecting good orders for that, with the client's head on of course. More action-packed and heroic than the boring Lenin or Kim poses.

'We'll send one of the Simon Bolivars up here with a change of head to whatever's appropriate. Much easier to fit into Oggonian history and certainly more appealing to the Japanese ladies.'

'Fabulous,' James exclaimed, delighted at the prospect of composing another Oggonian history brochure. He thought for a while. 'We could stick it out on the cliff-face with the sea crashing against the rocks. It could be described as the site of …' he paused and thought for a moment, then added excitedly, 'it could commemorate the great battle of Ogg when Oggonians drove off the Spanish Armada forcing them to head south and tackle the English from the sea, thereby debilitating the …'

'OK, OK,' Geoff interrupted impatiently. 'I'll have Romania dispatch you one with a sixteenth-century Oggonian warrior head. But coming back to the Nuremberg Rally industry; no the Head of State Tour industry won't be affected, not so long as the bloody wives are involved, and with the few chaps who go alone there's still virgin deflowerings and floggings and executions and statues, none of which the Nuremberg Rally industry will be offering. Mind you, I suppose we should consider hangings with the Nurembergs. They'd certainly help create the right tone; maybe floggings too on reflection, but we'll play it by ear at this juncture until we see how the rallies pan out. I'm telling you, James; this one's going to be big. It's the same market but a quite different service and as I said, we've got a huge unfulfilled capacity now we're having to ration Head of State Tours. Best of all, it's so easy to organise and it's all over inside a day.'

'I still find it extraordinary,' James commented thoughtfully. 'After all, if it's simply adulation then the Royals and Presidentials deliver that in bucketfuls even if the clients do have to wait for a crack at them.'

'You're missing the point,' Geoff snapped impatiently. 'There's a different dimension to it altogether. As Brasch said, given the right opportunity and circumstances everyone has a bit of Hitler in them. Well, we're providing that opportunity and the right setting for them to really let off steam. Monarchs and presidents can't behave like that. Also, our super-rich clientele hate waiting. They're used to having anything they want on demand and it reflects badly on Alceides when we can't deliver. Where the Nurembergs are particularly important is as an ultimate replacement for the Royals. As I've always said, the Head of State Visits have a limited life with the growth of tourism everywhere.'

James pondered Geoff's comments. 'What about the ranting? I mean what will they say?'

'We offered to write them maximum one-hour deliveries but so far they've all turned us down. They're insisting on doing their own. Brasch is quite disappointed as he was looking forward to drafting them. Who knows what will happen and what problems may arise but make no mistake, on the basis of initial reaction it looks a winner. I'd like you to come along. You can be a background high-ranking military man again on the stage. We need a few be-ribboned military personnel for this one but otherwise no specialist extras are needed, at least not in the official party.'

James looked at Miyumi, who lowered her head. 'How long will I be away?' he asked.

'I'm leaving London early next Tuesday so you need to be down the night before. We'll be in Delhi by evening and will helicopter up to the territory the next morning with the client. There'll be a motorcade into the stadium, the client starts raving about eleven so we'll be back in Delhi that afternoon and can zip back to London. So what's that?' Geoff stopped and mentally added the days. 'Basically from leaving to returning, four days; only two actually in terms of being away altogether.'

James paused and Geoff, sussing the situation added, 'I'd suggest you bring Miyumi, but it's not as if you'll see India in a tourist sense. It's virtually non-stop travel other than half a day in Rampathal. That's the town we're doing it in.'

When James still said nothing and Miyumi continued to sit, her hands in her lap and eyes downcast, Geoff proffered a fresh suggestion.

'Look. I'm participating in another Royal in Mauritania next month. Come along for that as the Admiral and bring Miyumi. She can be a lady-in-waiting and there'll be another medal in it for you. I'll be the Field Marshal as usual. Monster's not coming as they provide their own executions there; real ones in fact. But we can shoot over to Kenya afterwards and spend a few days with Monster and have a few laughs. That gives you plenty of time to organise management in your absence. What do you say?'

Noting the alarm on James' face Geoff quickly qualified his suggestion. 'Another thing,' he said hastily. 'We can see Kanju's new traditional dance. You realise,' he added, emphasising each word, 'there's an entirely fresh batch of Latinas there now and a new traditional dance performance.'

James relaxed. 'That sounds terrific. I'd love to come to India and Miyumi and I will certainly be starters for Africa but perhaps not to Mauritania. We can wait a month or so for another Royal and anyway, with the golfer numbers starting to build up here I'll need to stick around to iron out any wrinkles.'

'Excellent. Naturally we'll be videoing the inaugural Nuremberg for the client, but also for Brasch to evaluate. He studies every Royal and Presidential to monitor for improvements, but this being a new venture, we need all the on-the-spot input possible. There are bound to be unexpected problems and with the passing of time we'll doubtless add numerous embellishments until we have it right. Amy's coming along for that purpose and we're picking Hodgie up in Athens on the way as I'll value his assessment. He'll be first-rate as Goering. He's already made the uniform. I'm hoping he'll get a taste for a senior military role and abandon this absurd passion for being a bishop.'

'Oh yes,' James said cautiously. 'And who did you have in mind for me?'

'Brasch thought you'd be an excellent Martin Bormann. I'm going as Goebbels. The uniforms and jackboots are in the London office ready for fitting next week.'

James looked troubled. 'Can't I be Rommel?' he asked after a thoughtful pause.

'Certainly not. Quite the wrong image altogether. Far too soft. There has to be an air of menace about proceedings.'

'So who's first? Who's the client?' James enquired.

'We're kicking off with Max Mulder, the Alabama breweries baron. He's a bit of a redneck and he's been one of our best Royal Tour clients. Always a big buyer of executions and floggings, and there are nine statues of him in various African and Indian towns. Hodgie gets along with him particularly well which is another reason I want him there for the inaugural. If anything goes wrong he'll be useful to pour oil on troubled water.'

'No one will understand what Mulder's saying,' James ventured.

'Precisely. Don't you see; that's the best bit. Even though the clients don't know that, if they really unleash there'll be no repercussions. The important thing is that the rally cheers on cue so the light-master has a vital role and must listen carefully to the rant. That's me on this trip actually,' Geoff added. ' I'll be holding a remote which will connect with the cheering light.'

James mulled over the proposal. Eventually he spoke. 'One thing I'll concede. It certainly involves a lot less organising than the Head of State Tours.'

'Oh but it's much better than that,' Geoff said excitedly. 'Once we've ascertained the depth of the market, and if it's as big as we think it is, we can turn an entire city into a full-time Nuremberg Rally centre. It will become its principal industry. We're kicking off in Rampathal as it fits the bill perfectly. It's one of our Indian Head of State Tour locations. It's miles from anywhere, no one goes there, it's dirt poor; just subsistence farming with an annual income per capita of 23 dollars. There's 60,000 people in the city and surrounding district and best of all, believe it or not, there's a cricket stadium which will be perfect for the rants. If we can get the rallies up to one a week we'll damn near triple the locals' annual income at a dollar each per outburst.'

'They might all stop farming and starve,' James suggested drily.

'Don't be silly. They've got to eat. We're only taking three or four hours a week out of their normal routine. The thing is, by maintaining one place as a permanent Nuremberg Rally centre we can open an office there, build nice bungalows for our staff and really develop it by training an officer corps and having lots of goose-stepping practice and sieg heiling sessions and all the rest of the Nazi carry-on. It's potentially a wonderful new industry; precisely the sort of thing India should be encouraging rather than all that Gandhi spinning wheels and austerity rubbish.'

'That was half a century ago,' James objected.

'True,' Geoff conceded. 'But look what they replaced it with. Protected industries, monopolies, bureaucratic empire-building, all with the predictable disastrous outcome. There's no doubt Indians were immensely better off when we ran the show. Well, here we are returning to straighten them out; in a small way of course, I don't want to overstate it. Nevertheless, we're showing them the future and spreading enlightenment, just as we did two hundred years ago. India's future lies in developing a sophisticated service sector, not with primitive food growing. If all goes well and the Nurembergs demonstrate the potential we think they have then we'll ship out a permanent staff of four actors for the key roles – you know, Goering, Himmler and the rest of that crowd. Anyway, we'll have a better idea about its potential after next week. So what's for dinner? I'm bloody hungry,' Geoff added, rubbing his stomach.

# – THIRTEEN –

After picking up Hodge in Athens and refuelling, the jet headed east towards Turkey from where it would fly over Iran, Afghanistan, Pakistan and on to New Delhi.

James was delighted to see the Australian again. The memories from his Madagascan royal tour often recurred and he had frequently asked Geoff about Hodge's activities. As it transpired the Bishop was in a buoyant mood. He had just completed a Royal Tour in Benin where a new innovation, hand-lopping of thieves, had been introduced.

'Beautiful spectacle,' he enthused. 'Clients were bloody delighted. We did four at $10,000 each. They provide a very nice build-up for the decapitation as a culmination event.'

'How did it work?' James enquired cautiously.

'Same as the beheadings. We had a stock of latex hands and stumps lying in goat's blood out of sight. The condemned collapsed below the parapet after the amputation and slipped on a blood-covered stump like a glove. Then Juma reached down, waved the imitation amputated hand and jerked the victim up so everyone could see the bleeding stump. Bloody Queen loved it. A damned good tour apart from the dwarf problem.' He looked across to Geoff. 'You'll have to ship me in another set of the bastards. I lost the latest lot in Benin.'

'Jesus, Hodgie, what this time?' Geoff enquired anxiously.

'I told you about the lion.'

'Yes, yes. The tame one you bought from the Nigerian circus for the procession. Why, what about it?'

'Well, it was tame up to a bloody point. Perfectly OK with normal people – the band, the crowd noise – none of that bothered it. Marched along nicely in the procession on the leash with its minder just in

279

front of the royal carriage and went down a treat with the locals. But things turned to lard during the execution. Bugger me, all eyes were on the beheading and when we turned round, the bloody lion had eaten both dwarfs, or at least, their bottom halves. Didn't fancy their heads and I don't blame it either. I gave them, the heads that is, the last bloody rites. First time I've had a crack at that. Quite enjoyed it actually although not as much as confessions. It's all on the video because the bloody fool video-operator thought it was part of the ceremony. I'm worried he's missed the execution which will piss off the client if he has.'

'Christ almighty, Hodgie, did Their Majesties see it?'

'Too bloody right they did. The client was Remedios, the Washington tobacco trial lawyer, and they don't come more brutish than that bastard. Couldn't give a stuff about anything but money so naturally that came up. Remedios complained he hadn't bloody ordered any dwarf-eating so I said we were tossing it in free and after that he was OK. Matter of fact that night the Queen asked for a repeat performance on their next tour. I quoted $50,000 per dwarf on account of them only being half size. Now the lion's got a taste for them we could be on to something here if you can maintain supply from India.'

'You can forget about that,' Geoff snapped. 'We'll have a look at the video back in London. If the video-operator missed the execution Brasch can splice one in from a previous tour. In the meantime we've six hours to India. It's a good opportunity to get into the mood,' and he produced four large pictorial books from a bag: *A History of the Nazis*, *The Rise of German Fascism*, *Hitler* and *The Third Reich*.

James thumbed through one. He had seen it all before: the goose-stepping, saluting, mass adulation, medals and menacing insignia, the parading and posturing. 'Here's a thought,' he said pensively after ten minutes had passed in silent study. 'I think I've discovered an interesting difference between Hitler and other dictators, and specially the communists.' He drew their attention to a double-page black and white photograph showing Hitler taking the salute before a mass march-past of goose-stepping soldiers. 'Look at this. There are no tanks, no armoured cars, no weaponry of any type. The men don't even carry rifles or have pistol holsters.'

Geoff studied the photograph then flicked through his book to similar scenes. 'My God, you're right. Remember the annual May Day parade photos in the communist era. Our newspapers ran them regularly every year. Potato-faced lumps muffled up in greatcoats on a podium, and below a parade with endless streams of missiles and tanks and armoured cars. You're absolutely correct; Hitler was different. It's as if he's emphasising the power of the people as opposed to the anonymous State epitomised by its weaponry.'

'Something like that,' James agreed. 'Of course it could be chance, after all there were no missiles in his day.'

'No, that's not it,' Geoff said thoughtfully. 'The communists paraded heaps of tanks and other military vehicles and they all existed in the thirties. You've definitely discovered something, James, and I don't think it's chance. It's bloody clever, quite subtle in fact. Emphasising people rather than weaponry threw the spotlight on Hitler as the key person; the only stand-out one in fact; everyone else is a mass of bodies.' He flicked over some more pages. 'Look at this,' he said, excitedly pointing to a large black and white photograph. 'Whenever it's march-pasts and orations Hitler's always alone on the podium. The group shots with Goebbels and Himmler and the rest of them are never the big ceremonial performances. There are lessons here from this in terms of client satisfaction. Alceides' clients want the focus on them, just like Hitler. General Rama has been talking about knocking up some bogus aluminium missiles and tanks for the Nuremberg stadium entries if it all goes well. I think we'll scrap that approach.'

'You're bloody right, mate,' Hodge said. 'Remember Hitler flogged the master race theme. That's putting the focus fair and bloody square on to people. Probably why they gave the Jews such a pounding. Maybe Hitler saw them as their only other rivals with their chosen people bullshit.'

'Here's another dimension to it,' Geoff enthused. 'All the dreary ones – Stalin and Mao and Kim in Korea and the like – all ran personality cults with statues and pictures of themselves everywhere. Hitler never did any of that despite supposedly having the genius propagandist in Goebbels. All Goebbels' efforts were about fascism and the Fatherland and so on, never about Hitler, and yet in a sense through understatement Hitler achieved a god-like status. It's amazing no one's researched any of this.'

'So you don't have to be obese to come up with ideas,' James teased.

Geoff laughed. 'Brasch will certainly be jealous when I tell him about this.'

'How's Brasch going?' Hodge enquired.

'He's been moving up over the past month,' Geoff said. 'Hit 465 pounds last Thursday. We'll pull him back to around 420 over the next month. Pity really; he's at his most productive in the high four hundreds.'

'Actually, that brings to mind something I've been meaning to raise,' James said. 'Are the new trainees performing?'

'They certainly are. We've only got one malingerer, still around the 340-pound mark no matter how much we stuff him with fattening food. But the other two have passed 400 and are beginning to produce results.'

'Anything interesting?' James enquired.

'One of them, Walters in our investment division, last Friday reached 410 pounds and has produced two exciting new concepts. He's discovered an arbitrage situation between certain currencies and particular commodities. Where an exporting country is dependent for a minimum of 25 per cent of its receipts on a particular commodity and a corresponding importing country spends a minimum 25 per cent of its import expenditure on that same commodity, Walters has discovered a time lag of about a week before the currency of the loser adjusts in cases where the commodity price moves sharply, whereas the exporting country's currency reacts immediately. He's studied the empirical evidence of eight commodities and 42 countries and he's absolutely right.'

'That's rather confusing,' James said. 'I don't understand. Give me an example.'

'I can give you lots of examples, such as diamonds with South Africa and Belgium, or oil with Nigeria and Japan, or cocoa with Ghana and Switzerland. What Walters found is that if, say, the commodity price rises sharply, the positive effect is immediate on the producing nation's currency but there's about a week's time lag before there's a corresponding negative reaction on the purchasing nation's currency. If the commodity price falls then the opposite happens. Either way we arbitrage the lag nation.'

James thought for a while. 'So you're saying people react immediately to good news but delay on bad news.'

'Precisely. That's what Walters' evidence suggests. Everyone treats good things as reasonable and permanent and bad things as unfair and likely to correct themselves, which of course they don't, at least not immediately. We gave it a small trial run last week when there was a big drop in platinum futures. We sold short the rand and picked up over seventy thousand dollars with no outlay. That was just a dabble as we're still not satisfied about downside risk factors, although Walters claims he has that covered. If he's right we're laughing. He's currently researching some other ideas that are similar in principle. Once he passed 400 pounds he became incredibly productive.'

'What's his other idea?' James asked.

'It's along the same lines,' Geoff said. 'Amy helped him with the research as Walters' fingers are now so fat he has difficulty handling paper. He's studied the past five years' currency movement forecasts by economists; you know, the tripe the newspapers run every January predicting economic factors like the fate of the pound in the coming year and quoting a bunch of well-known economists. What he's found is that when it comes to currency value prophecies, without exception they're always 100 per cent wrong. If they pick the pound to rise against the dollar, invariably by year end the opposite has happened.'

'Is there always a consensus view though?' James queried.

'The interesting thing is that the economists always agree on the trend and differ only in degrees of margin in the movement,' Geoff replied. 'Walters has been checking out other currencies and so far he's completed research with the yen and the Australian dollar and found exactly the same thing; that is, that the forecasters are without exception always diametrically 100 per cent wrong.'

'So where's the angle?' James asked.

'Next January we're going in big. We'll wait for the inevitable prophecies in the British and Australian and Japanese newspapers, then we'll margin-bet against the economists' predictions. On the empirical evidence it looks fail-safe. Hodgie's in next year's punt and sticking in half a million quid of his own money.'

'Christ, the way I'm going,' Hodge said, patting his bulging midriff, 'I'll be transferring to the London office soon to join Brasch and the other fatties. I'm getting too bloody old for all this gallivanting about.'

'They're too obese for sex,' Geoff hinted.

'Yeah, well there's that,' the Australian conceded. 'Maybe I'd better stick to the bloody Church for a while yet.'

'Did you employ any more tubbies?' James asked.

'Yes. I interviewed eight and we took on two which brings the stable up to six. They're ensconced on the seventh floor right now but they're still virtually anorexic. Only in the 300-pound range. Could be another eighteen months of solid eating before they ripen to a fruitful stage.'

'So if the malingerer doesn't perform, what happens to him?'

'Well obviously he'd have to go. The problem, of course, would be getting him out. Once they're over 350 pounds they can't fit in the lift, let alone walk down the stairs. We'd have to starve him. But it's too early yet to form a judgement. Anyway, it's unreasonable to expect all of them will be winners. Walters is certainly looking good and so's Ralston, in fact arguably better. He's concentrating on the Head of State Tour division and originated hand-lopping when he was only at the 350-pound mark. Now he's into the 400s he's spitting ideas out.'

'A promising lad,' Hodge said. 'He was right on the button with the hand-lopping.'

'Anything interesting with the other ideas?' James enquired.

'Actually, there's one that's got me starting to fizz. Problem is, I don't think there's much money in it, but our New York office did a sampling with some of our clientele and six promptly expressed interest.'

Amy put down *The Third Reich*. 'It's a wonderful idea. Let James decide. The money doesn't matter; it would be such fun.'

'Well there's that,' Geoff conceded. 'Difficulty is, if it went flat it could discourage the clients. Apart from some minutiae we've always had happy and satisfied customers. This one only appeals to the super-rich billionaire category and we don't want to jeopardise any of them. They're not exactly thick on the ground.'

'Oh, Geoff. Don't be such a spoilsport,' Amy protested. 'What can go wrong?'

'But what is it?' James demanded expectantly.

'Begging.'

'Begging?'

'Yes, begging. Ralston's thinking is that a billionaire would be captivated by a diametrically opposite experience, so long, of course, as it's only for a few hours. The idea is to fly the client to a begging location – India, that sort of place – outfit him in a dhoti, dirty him up a bit and let him lie on the pavement with a begging bowl for a few hours.'

Once again James found himself staring at Geoff with disbelief. 'It's ludicrous,' he spluttered. 'Anyway, why do they need you? They can do it themselves, but, for Christ's sake, I mean why would they want to?'

'That's easy to understand. It's standard human nature in its perversity; the absolute opposite experience of the client's everyday life. One day he's in his luxury Manhattan high-rise office wheeling and dealing in hundreds of millions; two days later he's sprawled in a Calcutta gutter begging for rupees, then bang, he's back in the high-rise. It's like a private joke. It appeals to their sense of humour.'

'It's absurd. Anyway, why involve Alceides?' James pressed.

'Absolutely essential. Basically security, which is why we have to fly them to India rather than give them a run in a London subway. Bloody important; after all, the client would look a real goose if anyone recognised him. The deal is the client strolls out of his hotel and into our van. We dress him in filthy-looking rags, smudge up his face with dirty smears and drive him to the location. Our chaps linger nearby to protect him should anything happen. God knows what, but who can tell? It could be rival beggars or a policeman or whatever so our chaps are important to provide protection should anything go astray and then, of course, to get him back in the van, cleaned up and returned to the hotel. We've quoted a $50,000 fee to handle the whole exercise so it's not exactly a big money producer, which is another reason why I have some reservations.'

'And they've bitten?' James said, not hiding his astonishment.

'That's the worry,' Geoff replied. 'Take Goldsmith. You remember I told you he was the first ever Presidential. Since we started he's averaged two Royals or Presidentials a year but last year he only did one, notwithstanding the new executions attractions. I'm worried they're getting bored by it, specially when Goldsmith snapped up the begging proposition so enthusiastically.'

'So why the hesitation?'

'Apart from the meagre fee, what if they don't actually enjoy it? That's what bothers me. One flat experience and they could begin to lose interest in all our services.'

James pondered the problem. After some thought he said, 'The way I see it the client satisfaction will rest on the take. These people are passionate about success in anything they do, even begging. So long as they're successful beggars it's my pick they'll be regulars.'

'Precisely,' Geoff said. 'That's the worry. What if they're duds and no one gives them anything?'

'But don't you see,' James said excitedly. 'It's so easy. You just pay Indians to drop rupee notes in their bowl at regular intervals. The clients will be rapt. If they become repeat customers you keep a record of each trip's take and ensure they do better every time they return, just like the golfers at Kanju and Ogg.'

'You're bloody right,' Hodge said. 'I know the bastards. I can hear them now, boasting about how bloody good they are at it.'

Geoff grinned. 'James, my boy. That's twice in one day. Any more of this and we'll get rid of Brasch and the others. Well done.'

'Well, it's pretty damned obvious,' James said modestly.

'Oh yes. It always is after someone else has thought of it first.'

Geoff became pensive. 'I wonder how you'd go if we fattened you up; not overdoing it or anything,' he added hastily as James started. 'But say around the 300-pound mark. It does seem to make a difference and given your ideas at your current weight, you could be a real star with a bit more padding.'

'Thanks for the offer but I'll stick to Ogg.'

'Pity. Anyway, you've certainly solved the begging concern.'

'Goodie. So we can do it,' Amy exclaimed, clapping her hands.

'There you go,' Geoff said to her. 'You've been on two Royals and a Presidential and you've watched most of the videos of the others. You're bored by them now, admit it.'

Amy considered the suggestion. 'Yes, I am. I do admit it. It's not like if you've seen one you've seen them all, but they still are a bit repetitious. I worry that the clients will become bored too.'

'You're worrying unnecessarily,' James suggested. 'You're looking at it from your perspective rather than the client's. You're watching a Head of State Tour, either in the flesh or on video, every couple of weeks. The client is only involved every nine months or a year. Also, your role is as a bystander; the client's is centre stage. Anyway, there are the new schemes, the Nuremberg Rallies and begging, to work through to provide variety; not that I think I'm wrong.'

Hodge, who had been uncharacteristically silent, now spoke up. 'I'll tell you what it's about,' he said. 'I'm not surprised bloody Goldsmith's a starter. I've organised two of his Royals and one Presidential. He's got a sense of bloody humour. Only a few of our clients have and they see the Head of State Tours as a wonderful joke. The rest take them bloody seriously, mark my words. But by

Christ I'll tell you this, most of the clients and none of their wives will be in the begging lark.'

'Oh, why's that?' Geoff asked, alarmed.

'Because most of them really believe they're kings and queens and presidents when they're on the job. They buy our service to elevate their current standing, not just to experience something different. But I can see you attracting the humorists like Goldsmith or Wilbur bloody Wellbeing, the pretzel king. His Royals are always a hoot. He won't buy executions or floggings but he's big on statues and dishing out medals and not averse to a round of deflowering. He'll lap up the begging deal.'

'It's the money that's my biggest concern,' Geoff said gloomily. 'We average nearly a million dollars in fees from every Head of State Tour with the statues and deflowerings and executions included. We can't hit them for more than $50,000 for a begging tour.'

'Yes, but they're so easy compared with a Royal. You can make up for it by volume,' James countered. 'Anyway, you said last week at Ogg, there's no falling off in demand.'

Geoff brightened. 'That's true. I guess we just have to be careful when we're introducing these new attractions not to saturate the market.'

'Tell you what,' James suggested. 'As there's not much money in it, why not throw the beggings in free with the Royals to enhance them? On the night off during the tour the king could slip out into the town suitably disguised and do a spot of begging for an hour or so. In the context of what he's there for it would be specially attractive. Don't charge for it, instead offer it as a fresh innovation to keep them stimulated. If John's right and only some take it up then so be it. That's the way I'd handle the saturation threat.'

'That's fantastic thinking, James. There's no doubt we're wasting you at Ogg.'

'None of the Queens will allow them to do it,' Amy said. 'I was a lady-in-waiting on a Royal in India once. You remember, Geoff; you were the hangman on that trip.'

'Ah yes, Nicolais, the shipping tycoon. Regular customers. Only do Royals though.'

'Well all I can say is if that old dragon Mrs Nicolais is typical then the Queens will never allow their husbands to beg,' Amy continued.

'She really believed she was a Queen. It was most unpleasant being her lady-in-waiting; all that bossiness.'

'She's bloody typical, believe me,' Hodge grumbled.

'The Queens need not know,' James suggested. 'The King can slip away for an hour, ostensibly to discuss planning or the Queen's tour complaints.'

'I think that's it,' Geoff said pensively. 'I'll tell New York to offer it on the next Royal and we'll see how it goes,' and he picked up his Nazi book and continued reading.

# – FOURTEEN –

James climbed out of the Delhi hotel pool alongside the Alceides party breakfasting on the terrace and was introduced to the client, Max Mulder, a short, slightly built American with large protruding ears. Geoff outlined the day's procedures.

'We'll leave for the airport at 9.30 and don our uniforms in the helicopter. Then on arrival, it's into the jeeps and straight to the stadium. It's not a Head of State tour so, Max excepted, nobody does anything other than look threatening. Max stays aloof throughout. He travels alone in the first jeep, standing with his right arm extended in salute.

'You met General Rama, Max, on your Royal in India last year. He'll follow you into the stadium. Hodgie and I will be in the next jeep, then Amy and James. We remain seated throughout, looking grimly straight ahead, as the focus must be entirely on Max. There'll be nine other jeeps behind, each carrying two stormtroopers. It's all a lot simpler than a Royal but the effect should be excellent if everyone sticks to the plan.'

'What role's Amy playing?' James enquired.

'She'll be in uniform to avoid standing out,' Geoff explained. 'But she's not involved in the proceedings. She'll be on stage taking notes for future reference. You've got your notebook?' he asked Amy. 'Record every observation and remember, so as to distinguish Max from everyone else, it's dark glasses on throughout for everyone. Should add a nice menacing touch. We'll do a lap of the stadium through the assembly then pull up in front of the stage. The leader, the Führer, call him what you will,' he said, looking at Max, 'mounts the stage and is followed by the senior officers. That's General Rama, James, Hodgie and me. The stormtroopers then come up from each side of the stage and line up at the rear. They've all been primed by Rama. Remember again; this is not a Presidential or Royal. Only the leader acknowledges the crowd. It's permanent grim demeanours bordering on repressed anger for everyone else.'

'So what happens when we're on stage?' James asked. 'Are you sort of the MC?'

'Certainly not. As I said, the focus is entirely on the leader. Max goes straight to the microphone and lets them have it. He starts with a prolonged salute and will receive the appropriate response. You have your notes?' Geoff asked Mulder.

'Ah do,' Mulder drawled. 'Ahm looking forward very much to this rahly. Thars a few things I sure wanna get off mah chest.'

'Great,' Geoff enthused. 'That's what we're here for. Remember, Max, you can say what you wish without fear.'

'That's what ah intend to do,' the American replied emphatically and then, to emphasise the point, he added, 'The only reason ahm here is your Noo York people assuring me ah can say what needs to be said and ah intend to say it.'

'You go for it, Max,' Geoff encouraged him. 'I can promise a very receptive audience.'

Two hours later the party departed in a military helicopter and headed east towards Nepal.

'Rama borrows it from the army for $1,000 a pop to one of his old mates,' Geoff explained. 'Having a former General has proven a boon with our Head of State Tours here in India.'

Everyone climbed into their uniforms. All but Mulder's were black with silver lightning insignia on the two high collars. Mulder was conspicuous in his crisp white, heavily braided uniform with gold insignia and white jackboots.

'You look tremendous, Max,' Geoff enthused. 'There's just one thing, if you don't mind a suggestion.' He turned to Amy. 'Have you got an eyebrow pencil?'

Amy rummaged in her bag and brought out her make-up kit.

'Let's see how this looks,' Geoff said as he carefully painted a toothbrush moustache on Mulder's upper lip. When he was finished Amy handed the American a small mirror from her make-up bag.

Mulder studied his reflection and his eyes lit up. 'Why! Ah do believe that provards a farn touch,' he enthused, and for the rest of the journey he sat quietly studying his notes.

Forty minutes after leaving Delhi they reached Rampathal. It looked vile and appeared to comprise a sprawling mess of rusting tin-roofed slums divided by a putrid green, slow-moving river, its banks dotted with sari-clad figures laying out washing. There were no public buildings other than some garishly coloured Hindu temples and no structure higher than two levels.

'Look at it,' Geoff enthused. 'It's hard to believe we might turn this dump into a shiny new metropolis. I feel like Father Christmas flying in with gifts.'

As they flew low over a crowded central square, Geoff drew their attention to numerous statues dotted around its edge. 'All past Royal and Presidential clients,' he observed cheerfully.

On the outskirts lay the stadium which, as they drew closer, proved to be simply a cricket ground bordered by tiered seating and surrounded by a ten-foot-high brick wall. At one end lay an elevated platform with a backdrop of thirty-foot-high black banners bearing large silver lightning insignia. Centre-piece, an even bigger banner with a huge portrait of Mulder, angled to hide his ears, was clearly visible. The spectacle delighted the American.

The cricket ground was filled with the 50,000-strong hired army standing in formation companies of two hundred each. Many waved as the helicopter passed over before descending in a field at the rear of the stadium.

The party disembarked and were saluted with the fascist gesture by the eighteen waiting black-uniformed, jackbooted stormtroopers. Mulder, with the experience of past Head of State Tours, solemnly reciprocated. General Rama was introduced, everyone boarded their jeeps and a few minutes later the convoy entered the stadium.

A wall of noise hit the motorcade when it emerged on to the cricket ground as the assembly, eager to earn their rupees, greeted them tumultuously. As the convoy passed down the lanes between the company formations, many broke rank to wave and cheer.

The soldiers wore brown military tunics and caps bearing the lightning insignia, although the variety of trousers diminished the effect of an orderly army. Every third man held aloft a ten-foot-high bamboo pole displaying a placard portrait of an earless Mulder, while others brandished poles carrying black banners with the silver lightning insignia.

Beethoven's Fifth boomed from the loudspeakers, competing with the cheering. James, staring blankly ahead, could see Mulder in the front jeep standing erect, his right arm extended in the fascist salute. His rigidity contrasted with the undisciplined rabble swirling about his jeep and emphasised his stature as the central figure of the proceedings.

Eventually they arrived at the foot of the platform. In careful formation with Mulder leading the way, they climbed the steps. General Rama, Hodge, Geoff and James sat on the four chairs at the rear of the stage, gazing sternly out at the wildly cheering stadium. The stormtroopers formed into a line, nine on each side of the seated foursome, and struck a menacing posture, legs apart and arms folded across their chest; surveying the scene through their dark glasses.

Centre-piece was a podium encased in a black cloth with the silver insignia on its front. Mulder strode briskly to it and, extending his right arm, stood for a full minute, his eyes gleaming fanatically, as he basked in the sustained acclamation from 50,000 throats and the reciprocal salute from the black-uniformed, jackbooted stormtroopers in the front rows.

Finally he lowered his arm, and extending his uplifted palms, he brought the cheering to a close. Simultaneously Beethoven's Fifth faded and died over the loudspeakers.

Geoff reached into his tunic and pulled out the remote for the applause lights which Rama had given him. 'Here we go,' he muttered to James. 'Let's hope this damn thing functions. Anything working in India is usually a miracle.'

But here they did not go, as for half a minute Mulder stared accusingly at the masses paraded before him. 'The fucker's lost his nerve,' Hodge muttered.

But not so. With a penetrating opening salvo which resonated around the stadium, causing a discernible tremor of fright, Mulder screamed, 'Whart's wrargnn with the warld?'

An eerie silence fell as Mulder glared menacingly at the packed stadium then, 'Ahm gonna tell you-all,' he shrieked, followed by another theatrical pause.

But abruptly the mood changed as he now reverted to a confiding tone, delivered initially in a near hush but rising in volume as it continued. In short, sharp sentences Mulder launched into the autobiographical recitation Americans find compulsive whenever they encounter strangers. Ominously this began at the beginning. 'When ah was a little boy, no harher than a grassharper's leap ...' but to James' relief it soon became clear that this was merely a device to deliver a series of homilies, 'larnt on mah daddy's knee.'

The theme of these childhood teachings was disclosed as pleasantries about respect for one's fellow men and James sensed Geoff's frustration as he fidgeted with the remote, lacking appropriate opportunities to unleash the cheering. Was it going to be an embarrassing disaster? Fortunately this conversational approach was suddenly abandoned when, following another long pause, Mulder leapt half a century and returning to his opening Hitlerish scream, demanded, 'Whart have ah larnt?' – pause – 'after fifty years on this warnderful Gard-given earth' – pause – 'Ah've larnt ...'

What Mulder had 'larnt' was the extreme shortcomings of 'nigras' and the price their existence extracted from everyone else's happiness.

Soon Geoff was busy with the remote and as Mulder warmed to his task, his delivery becoming ever more passionate and the cheering more frequent and prolonged.

'Ah say' – pause – 'send them back to Arfricar,' – thunderous applause.

'Ah say' – pause – 'they belargn in the jungle,' – more stupendous cheering.

Not content with these solutions to the 'nigra prarblem' and encouraged by the reception, Mulder now reverted to more drastic remedies.

'Ah say ... string 'em up harr,' this followed by prolonged cheering, initiated by Geoff.

'Ah say ... frar 'em in the charh,' bringing a tumultuous acclamation which ran for a full minute.

James sneaked a look at his watch. Mulder had been ranting for 23 minutes. How long, he wondered, could his voice last and the audience enthusiasm be sustained?

But Mulder was not yet done. Apparently the problems of the world were not confined to 'nigras'. Barely pausing for breath, Mulder, who from behind resembled an agitated Mickey Mouse, launched into a fresh tirade. Treacherous Japs, slit-eyed Chinks, grasping Jewboys and the Pope were all frustrating human happiness through their existence and Mulder reeled them off, with outlines of their sins, always concluding with the common solution of their immediate elimination.

There was one final problem to be dealt with – Indians. Now bulb-eyed Mulder really unleashed, reaching new heights of passion which startled James in its ferocity.

'Filthy, stinking …' 'larhest of the larr …' 'varmin of humanity …' 'scum of the arth …' After each shrieking vehement observation Geoff allowed the cheering to run longer than before until finally Mulder reached a crescendo, his screams now rising to a hysterical level as he demanded an immediate nuclear bombing blitz across India.

Sated, he held both arms aloft then moved to the front of the podium. Eyes glazed but fervent, he stood for a full minute, his right arm extended in the fascist salute.

Sensing their obligations were concluded, the assembly rose to the occasion and surpassed their previous efforts with deafening acclamation, the waving banners and Mulder portraits adding to the grandeur of the spectacle.

James gazed astounded at the frenzied scene but was jolted from his reverie by a dig in the ribs from Geoff. 'Come on, it's over,' he hissed, and with the cheering lights turned off, the noise quietened and faded.

As Mulder came back round the podium the seated men rose.

'That went bloody well,' Hodge muttered. 'Enjoyed it enormously. But Max missed a few points …' but he was interrupted in these musings by Geoff urging, 'Come on, you two.' They followed Mulder and General Rama down the steps and were soon driving in the same formation back through the assembly. As before, Mulder in the front jeep stood, his right arm extended in salute, as they passed through the frenzied audience, out of the stadium and back to the helicopter.

They boarded and Mulder fell back in his seat, emotionally drained. He called for a whisky which Amy poured before handing around a tray of sandwiches and savouries.

'Bloody good speech, Max,' Hodge said as he also took a whisky. 'Agreed with every word.'

'Why thankey Bishop,' Mulder replied graciously. 'Ah must say ah enjoyed it very much. You-all did a farn jarb.'

James looked out of his window and saw Geoff in heated discussion with General Rama. Shortly after Geoff boarded carrying two videos, and they were off.

'A moving rendition, Max,' Geoff said as he settled into his seat. 'You made some interesting points.'

'Wa'll sarn, ah been studying these prarblems a very larng tarm.

There's a lotta mah issues ah sure would like to elucidate. There's things the warld needs to know about the last four Democrat Presidents that would curl your socks up, boy.'

'Perhaps you'd consider a repeat performance?' Geoff suggested eagerly.

'You can book me in, sarn.'

'No more Head of State Visits then, Mr Mulder?' Amy quizzed.

'Missy, if it was over to me ah'd say ah've had mah fill of Royal Tars now you're provarding this farn new service. But ahm afraid there's mah little lady-warf to contend with. Ah don't think Mrs Mulder would allow me to starp our annual visits.'

'Quite right; you must look after Mrs Mulder,' Geoff said, visibly relieved.

'Perhaps Mrs Mulder could go alone,' James suggested. 'She could be the monarch, just like the Queen of England.'

'My God, James. That's a fantastic idea,' Geoff exclaimed. 'Why haven't we thought of it before?'

Mulder shared Geoff's enthusiasm. 'Sarn, ah do believe that's one cracker of a prarpasition,' and for the rest of the journey they excitedly explored the possibilities.

At New Delhi the officials stamped everyone's passports, the party shook hands with Mulder who boarded his Alceides jet for America, and they took off in the other jet to London from where Hodge would take a commercial flight to Johannesburg. It was 2.30 p.m. From the time they had left the hotel, travelled to the airport, helicoptered to Rampathal, conducted the inaugural Nuremberg and returned to Delhi, a mere seven hours had elapsed. They would arrive home around midday and James could be back at Ogg by the evening.

'We've a problem with Rama,' Geoff remarked as they settled down with pre-dinner drinks. 'Oddly enough he took exception to Mulder's speech. I said to him, what does it matter? The audience had no idea what he was saying but that only made it worse. Rama seemed particularly upset about the cheering when Max was making his Indian observations. I can't understand it. He's always seemed such a reasonable chap.'

'Tell him to get stuffed,' Hodge bellowed, his face reddening with outrage. 'He can bloody well change places with me if he doesn't like it. Organising that rally was a piece of piss compared with State Visits. Bloody uppity darkies; they're all the bloody same with their imagined racial slights. I get sick and bloody tired of them carrying on with this racism garbage.'

'Yes, well, be that as it may,' Geoff said. 'I reminded the General that Mulder paid $250,000 and, like you, Hodgie, he's on 10 per cent commission. Strangely enough it didn't make much difference. People can be peculiar. What on earth did he expect, a recitation of the Lord's Prayer?'

'They're bloody hopeless,' Hodge snorted. 'Even the ones we try and bloody educate. Personally I thought it was a bloody well-argued rendition, even if Max missed a few points. Bloody Rama shoulda been taking notes to learn a thing or two instead of this Goddamned snivelling.'

'I'm sure he'll simmer down,' Geoff responded. 'It was only the Indian stuff he objected to. Up until then he told me he agreed with Mulder. Anyway, overall for a first-up I thought it went extremely well. Certainly the client's happy and that's the main thing. Doubtless we'll add embellishments along the way. What were your impressions?' he asked Amy.

'It was definitely a success,' Amy said. 'But no embellishments. It's the absolute opposite of a Royal so the trick is to keep it simple. There were two forces at play; first, the massed assembly and their cheering and second, the focus on Mulder. The contrast was brilliant. It was exactly like James pointed out coming over about Hitler's performances.'

'So no criticisms?' Geoff concluded contentedly.

'Not a lot,' Amy replied. 'Apart from the stormtroopers the soldiers were awfully scruffy and they must be trained to hold their formation during the motorcade in and out of the stadium. It would make such a difference. They were really only an audience rather than an army and that diminished the effect.'

'That will come with practice,' Geoff said calmly. 'Remember this was just a trial, but now it's a goer I'll fax Rama to set up a permanent Rampathal base and begin regular training sessions. Now we know it works we can afford to invest in uniforms. We knocked up the tunics and hats for $2 each in Bangladesh but in the light of events we'll complete the full kit. I'm so excited. It's a wonderful new industry; everything we hoped for,' he concluded dreamily. 'And fantastic for Rampathal. It's the dawning of a new golden age for the town. It gives one a warm feeling ...'

'That's not all,' Amy interrupted Geoff's musings. 'The uniforms were wrong. Mulder should have been in black; you, James and John in khaki, and the stormtroopers in brown.'

'Max stood out like dog's-balls,' Hodge protested. 'Whatta ya on about?'

'Yes he did,' Amy conceded. 'But in quite the wrong way. White is the colour of purification. You know that with your Bishop's garments. Indians in particular are sensitive to its symbolism. Wearing white diminished Mulder's menace.'

'Maybe you're right,' Hodge conceded. 'I'll hang on to mine in case I ever have to step in as a General on a State Visit – not that I bloody intend to,' he added hurriedly, noting Geoff prick up his ears.

'Also, the music's wrong,' Amy persisted. 'You just need massed drumbeats. Adds to the menace and simplicity. You could play it over the speakers.'

'Amy's correct,' James contributed. 'Keep it simple, sharpen up the troops, and if I can add two suggestions: have a dozen stormtroopers wearing dark glasses on motorbikes leading the motorcade, and heighten the podium by at least six feet. It could have steps behind it. It would really compound the dictator raving from a podium effect, and throw even more concentration on the client as the key figure.'

'All excellent ideas,' Geoff enthused. 'We used two cameramen to cover all angles. We'll watch the videos tomorrow with Brasch before we do the client's copy. Brasch will have his own thoughts for sure,' and he called to Miriam for champagne to celebrate the new industry.

Later that night over Iran, James noticed Amy and Geoff had dozed off so he tentatively broached a subject he had been itching to raise with Hodge. 'Have you seen Nicole lately?' he enquired lightly.

'Who?'

'Nicole. You know, the lady-in-waiting I was on the Royal with.'

'Oh, her. The tart you were having it off with. Yeah. She came with us last month on a Royal down in the south.'

After a pause and affecting nonchalance despite his voice rising an octave, James asked, 'Lady-in-waiting or village virgin?'

'Nah. Lady-in-bloody-waiting again. It was for Lester Lumpington, the junk bond king. His bloody wife always comes so the poor bastard isn't allowed deflowerings. A good tour though. Our first group hanging. We had five swinging together, yielding a tidy $250,000.

Bloody impressive spectacle. Had to train eight new execution staff to back up our permanent mob. It was all hands on bloody deck, I can tell you.'

Relieved, James changed the subject. 'How are the troops going? Have you managed to sharpen up their marching? I remember you weren't very happy about them when I was there.'

'Too bloody right I have. Sorted those bastards out once and for all. Turned out the Battalion Commander was a devout Catholic fanatic. Once I learnt that I threatened to excommunicate the bastard if he didn't straighten the army out. Haven't had a problem since.'

James stared. 'But you can't do that,' he spluttered. 'Only the Pope can excommunicate people.'

'Fuck the Pope. When it comes to ecclesiastic matters on the State Visits I'll call the shots,' and with that Hodge rose to wake up Miriam for more whisky.

When he returned James asked, 'Have you been back to Fianarosa?'

'Going there next month with Alfred Duval, the Chicago chicken tsar. He'll be President of Tanovia. Another first with this one. We're building an archway in the main drag; the Duval Commemorative Arch, with the Tanovian coat of arms at the top. Never done an arch before. Should look bloody good. It's under construction now.'

'His wife going?' James enquired edgily.

'Yeah. Bloody strange woman. Some sort of religious nutter. Won't do executions but we've sold them a dozen floggings. She's big on those and we're picking up another fifty grand for the Davina Duval Memorial Hall. We slipped the mayor a grand to rename the town hall after her.'

'Oh well, more medals for the Indian hotelier I assume,' James remarked pleasantly. 'He'll be pleased.'

'That'll be the fucking day,' Hodge retorted sharply. 'I've knocked that right on the bloody head and sorted the little bastard out once and for all. In return for taking over the hotel plus all meals, liquor and the town hall banquet I've made him honorary bloody consul for Hamastan. We've given him a consulate brass plaque with the Hamastanian coat of arms on it for the hotel doorway and a framed certificate of appointment. He damned near pissed himself with excitement so I've probably stuffed up again and been too generous. If his grotty hotel was better I might take a different view. Could even make him an Earl if he caught me in the right mood. Same goes with the Turk. He's feeding the troops again in return for sitting at the head table at the banquet and an autographed photograph of the Tanovian President in full regalia. That's probably a fairer exchange.'

James was conscious of his own Hamastanian medal in its silk-lined box in his study and empathised with the Indian. 'Well, I suppose it's not a bad swap, becoming consul that is,' he said. 'After all, there'll be future tours and more medal opportunities with those.'

'Have you gone bloody mad?' Hodge barked incredulously. 'We're not dishing out consulates for a single bloody tour. It's for a lifetime servicing of hotel rooms, food and drinks. We'll keep the little shit up to scratch by making the consular appointment annually renewable.'

'Good Lord, that seems a bit tough,' James exclaimed. 'Surely the lustre will fade once he realises he's never going to actually do any consular activities.'

'I'm not a bloody fool, son,' Hodge grumbled. 'Goddamn it, I've never seen anyone so happy. It's the bloody Indian's crowning achievement. He'd rather die than lose it. Did you ever see the little bugger's framed certificates?'

James remembered them vividly and he nodded.

'Well, pride of place among them now in a stupid baroque gold frame is his consular certificate of appointment. Romania knocked it up and did a damn fine job. Hamastanian coat of arms, flourishing signature of the king, the bloody Indian's name printed in scroll script, a red seal in the bottom corner; the whole goddamn shooting box. The little bastard stands gazing at it for hours every day I'm told. He's got velvet curtains on each side of it which he pulls across every night and then each morning has the pleasure of a new unveiling. He's put in a row of plastic seats so viewers can sit and admire his rubbish on the wall. As he's one of the few employers in town the seats are filled all day with bastards hoping to get jobs, and that causes his existing staff to put in an hour or so admiring each day after work to keep in good. The Indian's ecstatic with all this fawning. Don't tell me it's not a fair exchange.'

'Oh, well then; I suppose if he's happy,' James conceded reluctantly, but Hodge was not done.

'Also we printed him consular letterheads with the Hamastanian coat of arms. Anything he writes on official business comes to us in Tana to supposedly go into the Hamastanian diplomatic pouch. That way we can deal with it. We allow a few weeks to lapse then send a reply back from the Hamastanian Foreign Office which we knocked up some flashy letterheads for. The little bastard's flat out dealing with official correspondence. It's become a bit of a hobby writing the stuff for Radama our office accountant; you remember him, the joker we hanged in Ambarosita.'

'But what sort of official business?' James enquired, puzzled.

'Lots of bloody things. For a start there was Hamastan's National Day so the little wanker hosted a celebration party in the hotel. Sent out smart invitations we printed with the Hamastanian coat of arms nicely embossed in gold. I went down for the first one. The bloody Indian was cock-a-hoop standing in a receiving line with his fat wife and daughters greeting the guests and wearing his medal, delivering a speech, calling for a toast to the King, flying the Hamastanian flag outside; the usual shit. God knows I suffered enough of that embassy crap when I was in the judging racket in Malawi. It all went off bloody well. The mayor was there wearing his medal and gave a speech in reply. Don't you worry about the Indian having nothing to do. Actually it's proven a hell of a good idea as next year we're doing a Hamastanian Prime Ministerial Tour down there and we've been able to lumber the Indian with all the planning work.'

'Prime Ministerial Tour; that's a new one isn't it?' James queried.

'Yeah. It's another Brasch concept. He's pushing developing special relationships between specific territories and our different nations so after the Tanovian tour next month they'll all be Hamastanian in Madagascar from then on. Got a lot of merit too as it saves costs and makes planning easier. We're dishing out more consulates across Africa on the same basis. So next year it's a Prime Ministerial Tour, then that'll be followed by a Crown Prince Visit, and maybe then it'll be time for a return Monarchial; all Hamastanian. The funny thing, so Radama tells me, is that we're starting to get genuine correspondence like trade enquiries. It's certainly brightened up the bloody Indian's life.'

'What is it you don't like about him?' James asked abruptly.

Hodge looked puzzled. 'Whatta ya mean, don't like?'

'Well, you seem to have a somewhat aggressive attitude towards him. I was just wondering why?'

'Horseshit,' Hodge exclaimed angrily. 'I've got nothing against the little bastard. As far as Indians go that is.' Noting James' sceptical look he continued, 'Listen mate, don't lecture me about a fair bloody go; I'm a trained judge remember. I'm used to dealing with the darkie mind and I've learnt to keep my bloody guard up when these buggers try to pull the bloody wool over my eyes, like copping one of our medals for instance. Cock-ups like that can wreck the show.'

James stared hard at Hodge and fleetingly wondered if he was pulling his leg. Curious, he pressed on. 'If you don't mind me mentioning it, John, what puzzles me is why the Indian doesn't suspect anything. After all, you turn up as a manager in civvies to organise things and then you return as a bishop. Surely he must find that odd?'

'Turn up in civvies! Have you completely lost your head? I'm never out of my bloody vestments when I'm on the road. Christ, man, I'd be lost without them. Get no bloody respect at all.'

'But … but …' James spluttered, 'I mean what about the bad language and that? I mean surely …'

'What fucking bad language?' Hodge protested. 'I'm a bloody holy man. I can do what I bloody well like. Jesus Christ, compared with the antics of Indian holy men, I'm a veritable angel.'

James decided to drop that line of enquiry. 'What I don't understand,' he puzzled, 'is surely given all that involvement the Indian would look up in an atlas to see where Hamastan is and maybe even want to go there?'

'Don't be bloody ridiculous. There wouldn't be an atlas within a hundred miles of the joint. Anyway, we gave him a map of Hamastan for his wall which Romania knocked up. Mountains and rivers and towns and cities with just a hint in their names, suggesting Hamastan's somewhere near Slovakia. The Indian's got it framed in the lobby. You're right about him wanting to go there though. The little prick raised it when I was last down. I cited the 1786 Hamastanian Constitution which requires all diplomatic appointments to be non-nationals who have never been to Hamastan. Told him because the consulateships were so prestigious it was a decree innovated to avoid corruption in the appointments. Told him he'd be welcome to visit but it would automatically cancel his consular appointment so that was the end of that.

'He seemed relieved actually so I suspect the little bugger was just going through the motions to show enthusiasm as he's probably an illegal resident in Madagascar. Wouldn't want to show up at an airport with an Indian passport and a 20-year-old, expired thirty-day visitor's visa. They'd bum-rush him out real quick, specially if they found out about the hotel and realised they could get their hands on that. Anyway, like I said, he's never been happier. When the Prime Minister tours next year he'll present him with a gold and blue sash to wear on official occasions and who knows, if he catches me in the right mood and performs up to scratch, like I said, I might cop him a bloody earldom. It'll be his crowning achievement.'

'So no medals this time,' James ventured. 'I thought the clients liked presenting them.'

'Too bloody right they do but discretion's called for. We're dishing out three in Fiana with the Prime Ministerial visit next year. I'm copping one this time which I might add is bloody overdue, the mayor's wife gets one and also the local police chief. A bit remiss there; he should've been top of the list on the first tour. It's important to have the coppers on side. Anyway, why the interest? Keen to be an Admiral again. You're welcome to come.'

'No, no,' James said hurriedly. 'I'm far too busy at Ogg.' He reached up and turned off the light and not long after he fell asleep.

# – FIFTEEN –

Two months after returning from the inaugural Nuremberg Rally James received a fax from Geoff:

You will recall I mentioned the Simon Bolivar on a rearing horse statue cast we purchased from Venezuela. It arrived three weeks ago at Constanta, the Black Sea port twenty miles from our factory where all our raw materials are routed, and apparently looks fantastic. The factory has cast the first four with our various clients' heads on them and three are on the high seas to Africa and India. They should stimulate a resurgence after the dreary old Lenins. I suspect the conquering hero look is precisely the image the clients have of themselves and we should have thought of this before.

I didn't forget you, in fact, yours with a wild-looking warrior's head, was the first off the line. It's currently being transported overland in four pieces which will need to be welded together and will arrive in the Oban warehouse late on Thursday. Alex can sail over to pick the crates up and we'll fly up a welder and a concrete contractor to build a plinth to sit it on. They will arrive on the helicopter on Friday the 4th and as the statue is hollow and not very heavy, the helicopter will lift the crates off Alex's boat and take them to the site.

In the interim, if you haven't done so then start writing the brochure explaining it. I recall you suggested a Spanish Armada theme. It will be another background photography object for the Japanese ladies. We don't need an explanatory plaque as your brochure will cover the story and it will avoid any unpleasantness from the Reverend McDonald.

PS Hodgie has lost another dwarf. Accidentally speared through the heart during a welcoming tribal dance on a Royal to Upper Volta last week. Went down well with the Queen apparently so Hodgie slugged them $20,000 as a disbursement and they paid up like lambs. The Indian office is combing the subcontinent for fresh stock although the way Hodgie is using them up it won't surprise me if we exhaust the entire supply. We may have to look to South America at this rate of consumption.

After breakfast James took a mug of coffee to his study and as the rain beat against the window he contentedly began writing:

Ogg has played a significant role in British history. There is compelling evidence that the sixteenth-century Spanish military command planned to invade England from the north by first conquering Scotland.

Because of its secure harbour and anticipated easy conquest, Ogg was chosen to become the initial Spanish foothold in Britain. But the Spaniards seriously miscalculated in underestimating the notorious ferocity of Oggonian warriors, led by the famous sixteenth-century Oggonian chieftain Cona. Just as the Vikings had discovered eight centuries earlier, defeating the Oggonians in hand-to-hand combat proved beyond any conventional army's capability.

As the first three Spanish Armada galleons sailed into Ogg's harbour they were met by a hail of flaming arrows which set them alight and caused the rest of the fleet to quickly retreat. The forces from the burning ships clambered ashore where they were brutally decapitated by the waiting Oggonian warriors. This was the traditional Oggonian battle strategy due to its discouraging effect on enemy forces, as is epitomised by the centuries-old statue of Mugan holding a freshly decapitated head.

The remaining ships, their forces now hugely demoralised, turned tail and headed south where they were defeated by Sir Francis Drake. However, military historians generally credit the victory to the great Oggonian chieftain, Cona, in destroying the Spanish spirit and will to fight. It is in no small measure due to

Ogg's legendary warrior tradition that Britain is not today a Catholic colonial outpost of Spain.

The statue of Cona commemorating the victorious Battle of Ogg stands at the cliff-face at the end of the lodge garden, and is one of Ogg's most treasured icons. It is in a safe killer-sheep-free zone so visitors may inspect it without concern.

James read what he had drafted and chuckled as he contemplated the villagers as descendants of a ferocious warrior race. At this point Miyumi came into the study brushing raindrops from her face.

'What are you writing, my darling?' she said putting her arms round James from behind and hugging him.

'A new brochure for you to translate. Run and get me another coffee while I finish it,' and inspired by Miyumi he continued his tract.

It is unclear how the tradition arose but it is widely believed in Oggonian folklore that by sitting quietly for an hour at the base of the statue, women acquire a powerful sexual allure. Many scientists have studied the statue's aphrodisiac effect and confirmed its existence, but they are unable to explain this mystery of science.

To this day young Oggonian brides traditionally place a miniature of the Cona statue in their bedroom. These are available for purchase in the resort shop and are reputed to have universal applicability in respect of their aphrodisiac properties.

From time to time after storms, relics from the three destroyed Spanish galleons are flushed from the harbour floor. These are periodically on sale at a fraction of their market value in the resort shop. All sales of Spanish relics are subject to the purchaser assuring the shop manager that he or she is a genuine collector, respectful of the relics' historic significance, and are not mere speculators intending to on-sell at profit.

James again read what he had written. Yes, he thought, that's not bad. Romania can knock up a line of Cona aphrodisiac statue miniatures. The Japanese wives will lap them up. He would fax Brasch for ideas on Spanish armada relics for Romania to produce, and he began composing a covering letter to Brasch to send with his brochure text.

A few hours later a fax came back from Brasch:

Good work on the Spanish Armada concept. The warrior factor will appeal to the Japanese men and the aphrodisiac angle will certainly capture the women with the Cona miniatures.

We've instructed Romania to produce a first run of fifty miniatures to trial although I'm confident they will sell well. Suggest you start them at £50 and if they go as anticipated then lift the price.

Re Spanish Armada relics, I'm inclined towards a line of Spanish coins of the period. Romania's geared to coin production and can age them with an acid bath. There's something about coinage which always appeals and if they're ancient, then all the better. I've sent details to Romania of our version of Spanish coins of the period, and we will have a hundred each of two different ones for you in about a month. I suggest you kick them off at £30 each.

As for other relics, I'm disinclined towards historic marine objects, astrolabes and the like, as they don't really mean much to the punters. Spanish helmets and swords should sell well but we'll try a line of Spanish plate of the period first and see how you go before we explore other items. You may not know it but after the defeat of the Armada a number of commemorative coins were struck in England and we could easily reproduce those, but as Alceides policy is never to counterfeit actual coins, I've had to create our own version for the Spanish ones. Mr Upton has always been a stickler on this point with the Head of State Tours. He says no one can touch us on the currency issue so long as we're giving away our own coinage.

Re your brochure text. My only suggestion is to add a piece about the statue being commissioned by Queen Elizabeth I as an expression of gratitude to the Oggonian warriors. It's another interesting angle and after a few months' battering from the elements the statue should look the part although I presume the factory has done some appropriate ageing. I've instructed Romania to send a photo of it to the Tokyo office for the brochure cover design.

James pulled out his copy of the original text and worked in the Queen Elizabeth twist. It was now ready for Miyumi to translate and fax through to Tokyo.

He felt a surge of satisfaction at his creation, and then a slight reticence as the thought suddenly struck him of the Reverend McDonald's likely reaction when the monument appeared. Still, in the final analysis they held the trump card and if McDonald became too troublesome they could always eject him from the island.

# – SIXTEEN –

Fax Memo to James, Ogg
From Brasch, London

James: Your excellent sales results with the Cona aphrodisiac miniatures and Spanish Armada relics suggest the Ogg market has an unfulfilled capacity for tourist items of an antiquity persuasion.

Write a brochure outlining the golden age of Oggonian culture. Throw heavy emphasis on the paintings and skilled craftsmen of the era. Place it about the late fourteenth century and Romania can produce antiquities consistent with that period in Europe.

On the painting side, emphasise Ogg's fame in the Renaissance period for its miniature oil paintings. Vera's icons and Kanju primitifs don't keep her busy enough so she can turn her hand to some fifteenth-century miniatures on canvas. We can present them in old timber frames made from our 400-year-old timber.

We'll avoid religious themes which could deter the Japanese. I'll dispatch a series of prints of non-religious Renaissance paintings to Vera so she understands what's required – maidens in their boudoirs, mounted knights against a background of rose-covered walls, possibly some banquet scenes – it depends how the sales go, but as presumably only the Japanese ladies will purchase, delicate feminine themes will be the order of the day. We'll pitch it to Botticelli, Dürer and that crowd's style, which should connect with the Japanese ladies.

In respect of crafts, I think ornate metallic cups, bracelets, rings, bowls and the like should go well so long as they bear some resemblance to traditional Japanese style for such objects. I'll research that and come up with some designs for Romania.

Given the Japanese taste for netsukes, we could create some similar small carved wooden objects. We'll have Romania do a run of small Ogg Renaissance carved figures, so give that a good trot when you describe the Oggonian golden age of creativity. I'd do it myself but I know you enjoy developing the island's history.

Ageing the metallic stuff 500 years will require new technology as the soccer matches won't work for heavier metal objects. I'll tell them to bang them all together with small rocks in a concrete mixer and churn away until the appropriate appearance has been achieved, which hopefully will do the trick. We will need to look at the canvas as well but ageing that should be less trouble.

James read the fax twice, contemplating with increasing excitement the possibilities. The shop would need to be expanded; a pity, as the garden along its walls was now well established. Still, the plants were tough creatures and easily transplanted; mainly hydrangeas, geraniums and pelargoniums. The Japanese preferred well-lit, spacious shops without clutter, and satisfying their appetite for antiquities was the first requirement.

He rose and drew forth a volume from the growing library of reference books regularly dispatched from the London office. *A Pictorial Guide to the Renaissance* looked just the thing and he plucked it from the shelf and settled back on the couch, pen and notebook at hand, for a pleasant afternoon's research.

# – SEVENTEEN –

'My assessment is you're about six months away from everything running smoothly with a full house of 150 golf couples plus the killer-sheep brigade,' Geoff said contentedly as he sank into an armchair beside the fire and took a sip of his whisky. He was at Ogg on his monthly visit and had just completed a round of golf with James, unaided by the electronic putting.

'I still want to take it slowly,' James cautioned. 'Our biggest problem is the golf scoring. Using non-English-speaking Ukrainians has been fine from the secrecy point of view but God knows, they certainly think differently.'

'No work ethic you mean?' Geoff quizzed.

'That's what I first thought but now I don't think it's laziness. They've been first rate on every count except the all-important golf score rigging. They just can't seem to get it right. I suspect it's an attitude thing about doing something precisely and quickly. They're not used to that and it's critical with monitoring the golf scores. We sent two home last week which sharpened the others up so hopefully they'll come right. On the other hand the Japanese kitchen staff are outstanding. It would be great to switch entirely to them but bang, there goes security. Anyway, we can't put them in kilts and pass them off as Scots. The Ukrainians have been excellent on that front, specially the traditional dancing.'

'I'm sure you'll sort it out,' Geoff said encouragingly. 'Monster had the same problem at the beginning and fixed it.' He paused, frowning. 'It's five years ago now so I can't quite recall what he did but it was some sort of punishment with a bit of an angle to it. But it certainly worked. I was talking to him on the phone last week and he mentioned he's coming to London for a university reunion next month. He suggested he might come up afterwards to have a look at your operation so you could ask him then.'

'That would be terrific,' James enthused. 'Tell him I'd love to see him.'

'Remember our original profit projections,' Geoff said. 'They're out the window now. Dad was right about the golf course. Our latest assessment shows Ogg will be netting about £15 million annually when it's fully operational. You're going to be very rich, old man.'

'Yes. I've more or less got used to that prospect,' James replied blithely. 'Everything else going well?' he asked, changing the subject.

'Yep. Kanju runs smoothly. We're building an adjacent golf course resort, so Monster will have his hands full bringing that into operation.'

'What about Hodgie? How are the Royal Tours going?' James asked.

Geoff frowned. 'I'm a little worried about him actually. He's been a bit odd lately. Sort of detached and lost his fire. Something's up. I spoke to him last week and asked if everything's OK and he said yes, but there's definitely a mood shift. Can't put my finger on it. If he packs up I rather think we'd call it a day now with African Head of State Tours. Finding another Hodgie would be a tall order, and with Kanju and Ogg and the Nurembergs and Indian Royals going so well, I ask myself, why bother?'

'It's a hell of a lot of work from what I saw,' James said. 'Maybe he's just burnt out or bored by it.'

'No, it's definitely not that. Sure there's lots of detail but it's all well-programmed now and his staff handle most of the donkey work. Anyway, he enjoys State Visits and is hardly in it for the money any more. Apart from the problem of the increasing tourist numbers, the tours are going OK and the demand's certainly there; it's just Hodgie. He's sort of different. Amazingly polite and mild natured. I'm not used to him like that and it makes me uneasy. He promoted himself to Archbishop two months ago so at first I thought it was that and he was taking his ecclesiastic duties more responsibly. But now I'm not so sure. It's definitely something outside the job. My pick's a health scare but I can't draw him on it. Anyway, work-wise it looks like he's struck a deal with the Benin government for regular monthly official State Visits so the operation could become fairly routine if he can snare a few more co-operative governments. Perhaps I'm worrying unnecessarily. We'll see.'

'Have you tried the begging exercise yet?' James enquired, as always fascinated by Alceides operations.

'We certainly have, three times now in fact. The first two went to plan and now they want us to organise a contest. You know how damned competitive those billionaire types are. The first two both came from New York and knew each other. Apparently they were boasting about how good they each were at it, one thing led to another and the next bloody thing they've placed a million-dollar bet on who can out-beg the other and we have to organise it. Could be a problem as essentially we have to choose a winner. If we make it a draw they're bound to be suspicious.'

'Good Lord! With a million dollars at stake that's a hell of a dilemma.'

'I know,' Geoff said gloomily. 'At the moment they're still arguing over rules; you know, no white sticks or artificial aids like imitation stumps for arms, how much physical contact is acceptable, such as clutching at punters' sleeves and so on. It's a damn nuisance. We can hardly refuse on the grounds of being too busy as the one thing they've agreed on is that the begging time will be one hour so they know we could easily squeeze it in. I really don't know what to do about it. Brasch is thinking up fresh things for them to quarrel over setting rules about but sooner or later they're going to reach agreement.'

'Still, otherwise the begging went well?' James enquired.

'We gave it a crack again last month with Brandon Branstoke, the Memphis breakfast bran baron during a Royal in Guinea. Hodgie said that went OK too. He made sure plenty of punters dropped cash in Branstoke's begging bowl. Reported the client was happy but, as I said, he's in a funny mood. I couldn't draw him out much now he's become so subdued. It's all rather suspicious.'

James rose and threw another log on the fire. 'And the Nurembergs. They're going well too?' he enquired.

Geoff brightened. 'That's why if anything happened to Hodgie's operation I wouldn't really mind. The Nurembergs are going sensationally. Far better than we ever anticipated. You wouldn't know Rampathal now, or the stadium. We're banging through a rant every week. Thanks to our regular Tuesday training sessions the troops are right up to top Nazi goose-stepping and sieg heiling standard. We've added a lot more features such as mass hangings which provide the right tone. Being India we're discounting executions to $40,000 a head so the clients are buying them in bulk. The clients love it and we're booked up nine months ahead. If it holds up we'll open a second venue to deal with demand. The only problem is it's put huge pressure on Romania providing banners with so many different clients' heads on them. We may have to set up a factory in India or Bangladesh.'

'So who's running the Nurembergs?' James asked as he topped up their whisky glasses.

'Actually, that's worked out very well. General Rama's back on Head of State Tours as we have permanent on-the-ground Nuremberg staff. We've built new headquarters. I'm quite proud of it; a very smart four-storey air-conditioned apartment building on the square. We bought up one side and built a nice plaza with a fountain in the middle and air-conditioned shops. They're the first glass-fronts the town has seen. We shipped out three of the actors you helped interview and they play the roles of Himmler, Goebbels and Goering permanently. They're in heaven. Never had so much money and they enjoy bullying the troops at Tuesday practice. They're never out of their uniforms and strut around Rampathal where they're treated with great respect which, being actors, is a new experience so you'll appreciate why they're so ecstatic. You remember that poor old sod who burst into tears when we interviewed the actors for Ogg? He's out there as Himmler. A lifetime of being bullied has certainly brought the Nazi out in him. Now the boot's on the other foot, by all accounts he's running a reign of terror, to very good effect on the goose-step training front I might add. A very happy chap, make no mistake. Indians' inclination to behave as a rabble has been a problem but we're up to about a hundred who've mastered goose-stepping in unison. Once they crack it we pay them an extra 50 cents per Nuremberg and that inducement seems to be working. We've even established a special corps as an SS division. They get $5 a rally and have crew cuts dyed blond. All these embellishments, specially the mass hangings, certainly get the clients going and we've been able to increase the fee by $100,000. They all seem to have plenty of bees in their bonnets they want to get off their chests.'

James laughed. 'I can't imagine Indians goose-stepping. Somehow they don't have the right image for bombastic behaviour.'

'Be that as it may,' Geoff responded, 'when you think about it, training Indians to goose-step has considerable virtue. It teaches them to act in concert which their current inability to do is a major national shortcoming. Look at their emphasis on personal cleanliness, side by side with a total disregard for everyone else in chucking rubbish about everywhere. Plus it teaches them discipline, which absence is another national characteristic, and it also induces some bloody enthusiasm instead of their usual lethargy. We really are doing God's work with the Nurembergs. We're aiming at a thousand goose-steppers by the end of the year. Once we've managed that we'll introduce grand march-pasts with the client taking the salute. Should be a magnificent spectacle, specially as we've shifted all the statues from the town square out to the stadium where now they form a Grand Avenue. Also we've built a replica Brandenburg Gate at the stadium entrance. Believe me, it's all very Albert Speer and the clients certainly love it. Rampathal's booming now. We've tripled the town's income and put in a sewage system and water supply. We gave the local police chief a jeep and a new air-conditioned police station in our building and he's on a $5,000 annual retainer, which is triple his salary, so now we've complete control of the district and any problems are quickly resolved. Most important, he gives the bum-rush to any freeloading hippy no-hoper, which India abounds in, so security's not an issue. I tell you, James, everyone is very happy. The whole exercise makes me enormously proud when I see how much good we're doing. Honestly, I feel like Mother Teresa at times.'

'I see,' James said obliquely. After a pause, he added, 'Frankly, I'm staggered at the level of demand. After all, lashing out about some obsession and getting it off your chest is all very well but doing it to an audience who don't understand a word you're saying seems totally pointless.'

'Well I can tell you this, the demand's certainly there. Once they have a taste of it, to a man they're rebooking for another go within a week. We've stopped marketing it as we have 32 regulars all wanting to sound off every couple of months.'

'But no one understands what they're saying,' James persisted.

'We've been monitoring that. With the army cheering and sieg

314

heiling, once the clients warm up they simply don't realise it. Bear in mind they don't know about the cheering lights so they think the responses are genuine. Also, they fly into Delhi the night before the rally and all the hotel staff speak impeccable English. As I said, the clients are all convinced the audience is totally with them. That's where the has-been actors have proven a real plus. With the first few Nurembergs General Rama was controlling the lights monitor and getting it all wrong. The ranter would pause for breathe and Rama would unleash a round of sieg heiling. Brasch picked it up watching the videos. Now one of the actors controls the lights and with their sensitivity to the theatrical, they let rip the cheering or sieg heiling at the appropriate moments.'

'What about the speeches?' James asked, shaking his head in wonderment. 'Still all racist stuff?'

"Fraid so, or most of them anyway. The usual targets; blacks, Jews, Latinos. Brasch watches all the videos and every now and again calls me up to have a look at some of them. My God, some go over the top, specially when they put on the Hitler moustache.'

'Like what?' James enquired, his interest fully aroused.

'Last week Brasch called me to watch Hunter Huntington, the Texas tyre tycoon. Bloody unbelievable. He delivered an hour-long screaming rant about his ex-wife. Christ it was chilling, especially the last twenty minutes when he outlined the various ways he'd like to see her die. A lot of Edward the Second stuff with red-hot pokers up the bum, that sort of thing. There's no doubt the cheering eggs the speaker on. Mind you, that's been a problem. We've had to set up a full-time medical clinic with a throat expert to deal with hoarseness so now, an hour before each rally, every soldier is tested to make sure he's up to scratch, otherwise he's sent home without pay. It's a big exercise monitoring 50,000 but we've got it fairly smooth so our officer corps checks the lot inside an hour before each rant. That's why we're considering a second location. Two hours a week of cheering and sieg heiling seems about the limit the throat can take, otherwise we'd increase productivity in Rampathal. We run two lights now; a red one for sieg heiling and green for cheering. The only negative is we've lost Rampathal as a Head of State Tour location. The locals won't cheer gratuitously now we're paying them to do so. It's a terrible indictment on human nature when you think about it, specially the lack of respect, given that the visitors are Heads of State. I tell you, James, there are times I become quite despairing about human nature.'

'Yes,' James replied wryly. 'I wouldn't worry too much. I suspect humanity will struggle through despite those lapses. But tell me about the rants, or at least the other ones, you know, not just carrying on about blacks.'

'I'd say 65 per cent deliver racist speeches. But ex-wives, business partners and Democrat Party politicians are recurring topics. Hillary Clinton's had a fair old thrashing from some of them. We don't like them doing political speeches as they don't buy any executions. When the subject's race we can usually rely on picking up another two hundred grand with a decent group hanging. Fortunately, only about 10 per cent do Democrat politicians. Actually, some are quite educational. For example I didn't know Jimmy Carter was a convicted rapist, did you? Swain Spolkington, the Kentucky carrot king, did an entire Nuremberg on it.'

'Very interesting,' James said quietly. 'Tell me more.'

'Well, you can never be quite sure what they'll say. Take Henry Longhurst, the zinc mining tsar. He's normally quite a dignified aristocratic type. Always treats his Royal Tours very seriously. He launched into a terrible tirade about Bulgarians. We found out afterwards he'd blown $50 million in some investment scam there after the communist collapse. And Max Mulder, who you will recall was our pioneer Nuremberg, came back for a second crack and took the reintroduction of slavery as his theme. Quite well argued actually. I think he could be on to something there. Backed it up with mass floggings and two hangings. Mind you, I was a bit worried about Rama given his peculiar attitude to Max the first time so I flew Hodgie up from Madagascar to keep an eye on things. In the event there was no problem and apparently Rama agreed with Mulder this time. Funny really, Rama going off like that the first time when Max touched on Indians.'

'You don't suppose that's possibly because Rama is an Indian?' James hinted.

'Oh come now. We're in the service business. It's not for us to question the clients' opinions. And talking of the service business, that's why I'm so proud of what we've accomplished with the Nuremberg Rally industry. It's nice to do something with an altruistic touch. In just one year we've advanced Rampathal's economy by what would normally take two hundred years. We've switched it from a redundant hand-to-mouth agrarian structure to a modern service economy by the application of western know-how. I feel damned proud about it and I don't mind saying so.'

'Oh lay off, Geoff,' James muttered. 'You're proud of shifting an entire community from honest productive endeavour to masquerading as Nazi stormtroopers, just to satisfy the fantasies and prejudices of nutters with too much money.'

'Come, come, James,' Geoff scolded. 'You lack imagination, a regrettable shortcoming in an age of constant change. You're like a condom on the penis of progress. As always when you've encountered an Alceides operation, you've leapt to judgement without any depth in your analysis. If you'd had any say the pharaohs would never have built the pyramids. It's the outcome that matters. Apparently most of our stormtroopers have stopped growing rice now they're into a wage economy. Surely that's a good thing?'

'And that's advancement, is it?' James mocked.

'Too damned right it is,' Geoff countered. 'If you did your homework you'd know India produces more rice than it consumes. And why? Because it rots in warehouses as the Indians who need it can't afford it. In cutting production we've restored some balance to that situation. And how? By satisfying the fantasies you ridicule. What does it matter? Allowing the clients to vent their prejudices, as you put it, alters nothing. No one understands what they're saying and regardless of our service they're going to hold those views anyway.'

'Perhaps you're right,' James conceded. 'I suppose it represents a transfer tax on prejudices, from the rich to the poor.'

'And a progressive shift from brawn to brain activities,' Geoff added. 'That's the real achievement.'

'Yes. Well perhaps we'll have to disagree there. I don't quite categorise bawling sieg heil as an intellectual vocation.'

'The main thing is client satisfaction and that's evident from the rebookings,' Geoff said, impatient with James' moralising. 'It's all very satisfactory and the clients' enthusiasm is perfectly understandable. They're all used to being speakers at black-tie dinners to a select fifty, and having to utter platitudes for fear of offending someone. With our Nurembergs, being able to unleash without fear of consequences is a wonderful pleasure. Best of all is doing it in front of a massive cheering audience. If you think about it very few people in history have done that; you could list them almost on one hand – Hitler, Castro, Billy Graham, Peron, um ...' Geoff paused as he searched his mind for names.

'Yes, but the clients are talking, or should I say shrieking, nonsense,' James muttered.

'Get real, James,' Geoff said, annoyed. 'So were Hitler and Billy Graham and the rest of them; talked absolute tripe, the lot of them. Everyone knows that. You can't rave common sense to 50,000 people. It would sound ridiculous. Simply wouldn't work. It has to be nonsense to justify shrieking and an appropriately hysterical audience response.'

The two fell silent while James pondered this proposition, puzzled by the dilemma Geoff's claim raised in his mind. There was a peculiar logic to his argument. Talking sense while shrieking hysterically seemed fundamentally at odds. Talking quietly, sense or not, to a huge audience also seemed a strangely perverse concept. Did it follow, he wondered, that people talked the most sense on a one-to-one basis, and their rationality decreased as the size of their audience grew? He was interrupted in these musings by Geoff breaking the silence.

'Look, I'm taking a trip out to Rampathal soon; important to keep abreast of things. You might like to come along. Bring Miyumi. We could be tourists – visit the Taj and that sort of rubbish.'

'I don't know about that,' James said pensively. 'We'd love to but with so much happening here, it's probably wiser to wait a bit although we could certainly do with a break. I'll think about it. Tell me,' he said, changing the subject, 'how are Brasch and the other brains-trust fatties going?'

A worried look crossed Geoff's face. 'Bit of a problem there. Amy's been hammering their Cambodian lady minders but for some reason they've all gone out of control. Brasch is nearly 500 pounds and the rest are well over 400 and we can't seem to get them down. None of them can stand up now and it's creating all sorts of difficulties.'

'So the ideas are drying up,' James queried.

'Yes and no. At first when their weight soared they were even more productive. They'd all slide into their wheelchairs each morning and somehow manage to shower and shave but that's virtually all they were capable of doing. The thing is we don't want to lose them, and our tame medico insists we will if we don't get them each down at least 100 pounds. So last week we began a more severe regime on the food front and told them it's for their own good. Now they're all sulking and productivity has faltered. I certainly don't want that as there are some really promising new concepts in the pipeline.'

'What's Brasch come up with?' James enquired hopefully.

'It's not Brasch. He's been in a bloody bad mood for three months now and been totally unproductive ever since I put an end to the Second Comings.'

'Second Comings!'

'Haven't I told you about that?' Geoff sighed resignedly. 'Brasch came up with it after we ended the Dalai Lama and Papal Visits four years ago. But what he refuses to face is it's still the same old problem with religion and that's boredom.'

'But what is it?' James cried.

'His idea is to go into some small backward village, say about five hundred souls; there's heaps of suitable places in Latin America and Africa – and stage a Second Coming.'

'But how? What's he got in mind?'

'First we have about fifty extras in priests' and nuns' outfits descend on the village and announce they've come from all over the world. They've all been told by angels or visions or whatever, that the Second Coming is going to occur in the village the next day and they get the locals lathered up into a fervour, praying and what have you. Has to be a Catholic place of course to make sure they're gullible enough to buy into the deal. Then we drop the client off on the town's outskirts, dressed in a shimmering white robe and a false beard. He bowls into town with a shepherd's crook and a swag of disciples in tow and our extras fall about fawning, whereupon the problem starts. What does the bastard do next?'

'What does Brasch suggest?' James asked faintly.

'Oh, he came up with a few ideas; nothing very original though. Some multiplying of loaves and walking on water and soul-saving illusions but it's bloody well not good enough. It still gets back to religion's fundamental problem and that's tedium. It's all very well the client playing God, and obviously they'd love to be in it, but once they've belted out a few miracles and blessings then the novelty fades.

Anyway, Brasch has wasted enough time on it so I knocked it on the head once and for all and he's been in a bloody mood ever since, just like he was over the San Francisco McDonalds that time.'

'So what about the new chaps? Have they come up with anything?'

'Not worth going into yet. They're mostly financial engineering things and still at their conceptual stages.'

'Nothing touristy or targeting the super-rich?' James pressed.

'Just one. I'm not sure about it. One of the new intake came up with it. I've thrown it at Brasch as my idea to see if he can add to it.'

'Tell me, tell me,' James said eagerly as he topped up Geoff's glass.

'Actually, it was you wanting the old freighter for Ogg which spawned the idea. Like the State Visits and executions and the Nurembergs, it's the same old power thing that's the angle.'

'Well come on. Spit it out.'

'Basically we buy an old bomber plane from the Russians which we can get for about $200,000, then we buy up old freighters; the world's awash with them and we can get 'em for peanuts. We take them out to sea and let the clients bomb and sink them. Our New York office made some enquiries and the market's definitely there, but flying the planes is the problem. As I see it the clients would never spare the time to learn to fly and somehow the whole thing falls apart if they're simply passengers with a pilot. Pity really. New York reported it definitely touched a chord when they outlined it to the clientele. We'd provide a video of the entire performance starting with the client at the controls, the background aircraft noise and then up ahead, the ship in the distance. Filming the bombing and subsequent explosion and sinking may require a cameraman on a helicopter nearby but it would certainly provide a splendid spectacle. Still, I don't see how we can overcome the difficulties.'

James pondered the proposition. 'Scrub the Russian bomber. Buy an old prop plane with dual controls. The pilot can take it off and land it but once in the air a child could handle it. Flying a plane is dead easy, so much so you could actually show them on the job if they don't already know how.'

'That's not the main difficulty,' Geoff said gloomily. 'The problem is accuracy. Bombs are incredibly expensive and we're told by Air Force personnel we checked with that even when you're flying old crates it's still damned hard to land one on a target. Four misses, the profit's gone and worst, the client's unhappy. You know how important client happiness is to Alceides.'

James poked at the burning logs then looked up. 'The answer's easy,' he said. 'Let them drop imitation bombs which will cost virtually nothing to make. You could even make them out of plywood. Matter of fact you need not actually have any at all. Just have a lever the client pulls which he thinks releases bombs. Mine the ship and as the plane passes over and the client pulls the lever, it can connect to a remote which sets off the explosions. The client will think he scored a first-run hit.'

'My God, James,' Geoff exclaimed excitedly. 'That's bloody brilliant. Goddamn it, I've said it before. We don't need the tubbies. You should be at head office.'

'Actually,' James said coolly, 'I think it's childish.'

'Who cares about that if the clients like it? We'll cop a hundred grand profit on each bombing run and anyway, think of the valuable economic role we'll be playing destroying all those redundant freighters. Geoff swirled his whisky and became thoughtful. 'You know,' he said after a pensive pause, 'I wouldn't mind entering it for one of those industry awards.'

'Rubbish,' James retorted. 'You're forgetting a key point your father emphasised when I first came on board, about the importance of monopolies. Let people know and the next thing you'll have competitors undercutting you. Stick to receiving your own medals on Royal Tours.'

'I'm a fool,' Geoff exclaimed, slapping his brow. 'You're quite right.'

'On reflection,' James said, 'you could make a tremendous spectacle of the ship going up, or I suppose I should say going down. You could dowse it with petrol so it burns ferociously once the first explosion occurs. I assume that's the sort of thing the clients require to satisfy some sort of deficiency in their lives.'

'Do I detect a slight tone of disapproval?' Geoff teased.

James shifted uneasily. He took a sip of his whisky then, speaking slowly and thoughtfully, he said, 'I'm not suggesting we're taking advantage of people, and I know you will talk about client satisfaction and all of that but everything's so damn bogus.' He hesitated, then continued, 'You will say look at the money we're making, but in a funny sort of way I feel like we're losers from it all.'

'What on earth are you on about?'

'It's just that if you accept the principle of no free lunches – you know what I mean – then it does seem to me we're trading our self-respect in providing Alceides services. OK, so the clients are happy with their delusions, but surely if Brasch and the others are clever enough to think up all these things then why not instead think up useful and productive activities? It's as if the starting premise must always be spurious. I'm probably not making myself very clear,' he blustered.

Geoff stared at him wide-eyed. 'Oh don't come the boy scout with me,' he sneered. 'If the client's happy what else counts? Does a restaurant make value judgements for obese patrons ordering fattening dishes; does the dress shop deter customers choosing unsuitable garments? I challenge you to name a single commercial activity or transaction where one couldn't hypothesise a parallel situation. The customer is king, it's the marketplace in action and if the customer's happy then why have qualms about it? It's all perfectly harmless.'

'It's not the clients I'm talking about,' James replied quietly. 'It's me, and also Miyumi for that matter. We don't dispute the customers are happy. It's our happiness we're considering. Surely you'd feel better if you were actually doing something meaningful and constructive.'

'As far as I'm concerned that's precisely what I'm doing,' Geoff said icily. 'We're in the entertainment business making the clients happy and that in itself is meaningful, plus we're having a few laughs and best of all, we're making heaps of money. And if you want to be altruistic then there's the economic benefits we're bringing to our Third World locations. What's come over you suddenly with all this hand-wringing preciousness? You make our activities sound like some sort of Faustian bargain.'

'Up to a point, yes, I think they are,' James said quietly.

'Bloody rubbish and, as always, a huge exaggeration,' Geoff retorted angrily. 'Why is it necessary to constantly remind you that our services are voluntary exchanges between two willing parties? Nothing else counts and nothing could be fairer.'

'But don't you see,' James persisted, 'I agree with all of that. I'm not making the criticism from the clients' viewpoint; I'm making it from mine. It's irrelevant whether it's fair or whether the clients are happy. It's how we, or in this case Miyumi and I, feel about it.'

'You've been working too hard. You're losing your sense of humour.'

'You're probably right,' James said dolefully. 'Sorry to be a bit glum. It's like I said though. So much clever thinking and energy; all for illusions. I just think if we applied the same effort to something truly useful and constructive, we'd feel a hell of a lot better about ourselves.'

'Get real,' Geoff said incredulously. 'You've studied economics and should know better. Confine everyone to useful and constructive activity, as you put it, and 95 per cent of people would be unemployed. It's a measure of progress when a society employs most of its people in nonsense activities. You want useful and constructive endeavour. Well I'll tell you where to find it. Pick the poorest countries in the world and you'll find absolutely everyone's engaged in productive activity, usually growing rice and mending their thatched roofs in a hand-to-mouth primitive existence. Alceides is in the vanguard of civilisation. We are the future; a shining beacon of light showing the way ahead. Look at Rampathal. Before we arrived every bastard was growing crops from dawn to dusk and was dirt poor. Now they've been elevated to Nazi stormtroopers, which inexplicably you seem to object to, yet compared with the past they're prosperous and can afford the luxury of importing their food from neighbouring regions, plus they're enjoying heaps of leisure time and money. Goddammit, James, you're preaching Gandhi-ism and look what that delivered.'

'It must be some puritan streak in me,' James teased, conscious yet again of the accuracy of Geoff's outburst.

'It's worse than that, mate. Listen, if there was a market for constructive stuff as you put it, we'd be in it. Economic history shows there's a direct relationship between reward and the absence of basic worthiness in what one does. The more useful something is, the less it's rewarded; the more unnecessary, the higher the returns. We don't make the rules; we're simply responding to the realities of the world.'

The two remained silent, gazing at the fire. Eventually James spoke. 'You're right about one thing. Miyumi and I certainly need a break. We've been working too hard and we're too isolated. As you can see it's leading to an unhealthy introspection,' he joked.

'Never a truer word, old man. With Hodgie going all peculiar, being worryingly nice and polite and the fatties' health problems, the last thing I need is you turning wishy-washy on me. Tell you what.

Why not make a definite plan when Juma's here to come on a decent trip. Bring Miyumi. We'll nip over to Kenya to drop Juma off and stay a few days to have a look at the new golf course. Then we'll all join Hodgie on a Royal as I want to see what's up with him. It'll give you a chance to earn another medal. Then we'll rip up to India, take part in a Nuremberg and do a spot of touristing.'

'You've got me on the medal,' James laughed and for the time being at least, the crisis of conscience was over. But as it transpired, only temporarily.

# – EIGHTEEN –

Unseasonal drizzle was sweeping across the island in squalls when Geoff departed the following morning on the helicopter which had brought in a new party of Japanese.

James looked out through the rain-pounded dining room windows at a Japanese foursome, undeterred by the weather and about to tee off. Three wore newly purchased tartan plus-fours beneath transparent plastic waterproof gear. The current intake's group clown, as always a short stocky man, was ludicrously clad in a kilt and waving his driver threateningly at the heavens while his huddled companions dutifully tittered. James comforted himself with the thought that in four hours they would be back indoors, showered and triumphant, enjoying an afternoon's boastful fireside golf recollections and heavy consumption of Oggonian whisky. He looked around the dining room at the wives chatting contentedly over pots of tea and for a moment envied their placidity in settling for a day beside the fire in the main lounge.

The weather would induce duffed shots, necessitating rapid recalculations by the Ukrainians in the golf control room. Reluctantly James rose and headed for the basement to supervise the score adjustments, annoyed this was still necessary after the months of training. The Ukrainians' inability to make quick calculations was irksome but James brightened when he remembered Juma would be arriving next month. Monster had managed to train the Kanju tribespeople despite encountering similar difficulties, and James resolved to enlist his assistance in dealing with the problem.

While fumbling with the keys at the control room door James suddenly remembered the pile of London newspapers Geoff had brought up for him. To hell with it, he thought, Sanderson can handle the Ukrainians, and he returned upstairs and instructed a waitress to bring him a pot of coffee.

The fire in his study was welcomingly ablaze when he arrived. James picked up the telephone and instructed the operator to find the laird and send him to his study. A few minutes later Sanderson, dressed in a kilt, an unlit pipe in his mouth, entered the room.

'I'm sorry, Guy, but I've a busy schedule today,' James said. 'I want you to supervise the Ukrainians. Take a tough line and pay particular attention to anyone constantly miscalculating and we'll dump him. I'm fed up with their cock-ups so it's over to you to straighten things out. Another thing; if the rain keeps up put two of the waitresses in the shop to help out this afternoon. You know what the ladies are like when it's wet. They'll go into a buying frenzy after lunch.'

'Shit, James; I've got an Oggonian relics tour this morning,' the laird protested.

'Postpone it until the rain clears. I doubt the ladies will mind as it'll be hopeless for photography and that's all they ever want. They looked happy enough just staying indoors gossiping. The golf score adjustments are much more important. Look here; you're supposed to be an actor. Why not give the Ukrainians a bit of the Stalin treatment? Maybe they'll respond to that.'

'Bloody Ukrainians,' Sanderson muttered as he turned to leave. 'I'll give them a damn sight more than Stalin.' He paused at the door. 'You know what would be a good idea. We should build a gulag-type concentration camp out on the cliff-face. We could sentence them to a couple of days out there every time they messed up. Bread and water, leaking cold barracks, someone in a guard's uniform bawling at them, which is a job I'd happily do myself, the rottweilers pacing the barbed-wire boundary snarling at them, the threat of the torture chamber; I suspect they'd react positively to all of that – after all, historically that sort of thing's part of their culture, isn't it? What do you think?'

'I think you're a silly bugger,' James laughed. At that moment the crack from a bevy of gunshots was heard. Good Lord, James thought. The easterly gale must be truly ferocious to carry the killer-sheep gunshot reverberations so loudly across the island. Normally they could only be heard on still days, and then only faintly. It would be hell out there on the golf course today. The snug comfort of his study put him in a benevolent mood. 'Tell you what,' he said. 'In view of the weather knock another two strokes off everyone's scheduled scores. It'll be their lifetime highlight and the awful weather will magnify their sense of achievement and keep them eager for the remaining days if the rain sets in.'

'What about a Tiger Woods?' Sanderson suggested. 'We haven't done one of those for some time now.'

James thought for a second. 'OK,' he said. 'But remember. Be careful and pick one of the top golfers,' and Sanderson left the room in a happier mood.

A Tiger Woods was a James innovation which he had passed on to Juma via the London office. It required discretion for plausibility but the aftermath was always massive champagne sales with the chosen one joyfully picking up the bill. Periodically a good golfer would be programmed to birdie seventeen consecutive holes and conclude with a hole-in-one on the final par three to finish with a mind-blowing 53 round. Mishaps would be countered with an eagle on the next hole. The weather seemed to be worsening and a Tiger Woods would certainly encourage the others for the morrow. There would be much gaiety tonight and James reminded himself to change into a kilt for dinner, which invariably heightened the guests' appreciation of their environment and also to notify McNabb to be ready with his bagpipes to pipe the lucky golfer into the dining room. That always went down a treat.

James inserted a Mozart sonatas CD in the player, poured himself a coffee and sank blissfully into an armchair before the fire. He picked up a three-day-old *Times* from the pile of newspapers and settled in for a contented morning's reading. Fifteen minutes later, towards the end of the newspaper, he started. Gazing out at him was a studio portrait of Jane, affecting the ethereal but intense look she always adopted when in the public gaze. Alongside, another photograph displayed a plump, double-chinned male wearing a bow tie and a supercilious grin. James read the text:

The engagement is announced of Miss Jane Felicity Harrington-Smith, the only daughter of Dr Hugh Harrington-Smith, Professor of Art History at Sussex University and Mrs Amelia Harrington-Smith the well known potter, to Mr Claude Egbert Ebbington, eldest son of the Reverend Xavier Ebbington and Mrs Daphne Ebbington of Bath. Miss Harrington-Smith is a prominent Arts Council official and Mr Ebbington is recognised as a leading British contemporary art expert.

'Bloody hell,' James muttered. He felt a twinge of guilt at his abrupt departure from Jane's life and his failure to communicate since arriving at Ogg three years earlier, a sentiment that was quickly submerged beneath one of relief. Jane's engagement put a firm closure on that part of his past. He wondered how Lucinda had taken the news, as she read *The Times* and again he felt guilty for he had not contacted her since his father's funeral. Perhaps a trip to Edinburgh with Miyumi might be a good idea although then again, he pondered, it might not. Lucinda was the ultimate conservative and he was unsure how she would respond to the Japanese girl. On the other hand Angus' reaction would be predictable. Miyumi's prettiness would ensure she passed with flying colours in his brother-in-law's assessment.

James reread the text. Egbert. Where had he heard that before? Then he remembered; it was Brasch's dreaded source of shame. James laughed out loud. Somehow it was fitting, and he mentally pictured Jane bossing Ebbington about. He looked the type who would relish such treatment – arguably it would be a marriage made in heaven. James contemplated whether he should write Jane a congratulatory letter. Probably better to let sleeping dogs lie, he concluded. At that point the door opened and Miyumi entered. James quickly folded the newspaper and greeted her cheerfully but Miyumi did not reply. She sat on the edge of the other armchair facing him, her eyes brimming with tears.

'What's up, sweetheart?' James asked lightly, endeavouring to hide his alarm. Miyumi was not given to emotional displays, indeed he had often marvelled at her undemonstrative reaction to the periodic crises which had arisen in Ogg's management.

Miyumi lowered her head then looked up again. 'I think I'm pregnant,' she whispered, barely audible and again she hung her head and dabbed at her eyes with a handkerchief.

James' mind swirled, overcome with a mixture of emotions. Somehow Miyumi's bombshell seemed appropriate following the revelation of Jane's engagement. It was like pieces of a jigsaw, the one announcement seemingly logically following the other. He rose and put his arms round the girl. 'Well now, if that's the case why are you crying?' he heard himself saying as if somehow detached from his body and an observer of the scene.

Miyumi raised her tear-streaked face and looked at him searchingly.

'Most people are pretty happy to make that announcement,' he added manfully and Miyumi rose and with a half-gasp, half-laugh she hugged him tightly.

Half an hour later, like Jane, James found himself engaged to be married.

# – NINETEEN –

The visit by Ogg Castle's first scheduled guests, the five San Francisco McDonald couples, began to acquire legendary proportions due to its frequent postponements. The first arose of necessity during the Ogg planning period but over the next three years by the McDonalds themselves, who made numerous rebookings then abrupt postponements.

James did not want them now the original baronial castle hosting concept had been abandoned and on receiving advice of yet another booking date he faxed Geoff instructing their trip be cancelled. It would put unnecessary pressure on Guy, he explained. He's up to his neck with his management responsibilities but at least with the Japanese he doesn't have to concern himself with lairdish authenticity. As it was they couldn't accommodate the Japanese golfer and killer-sheep hunter demand so why waste beds and put a strain on everyone?

He immediately received a fax back from Geoff.

'I'm fully sympathetic with your arguments,' Geoff wrote. 'The problem is Brasch. You'll remember the original Ogg Castle concept was his idea and he hugely resented us abandoning it after Dad raised his objections. To appease him we agreed the already booked San Francisco McDonalds trip would proceed as a one-off. Brasch is still smarting about abandoning his concept and for three years he's made a childish fuss about letting them visit, just to prove his point. Nuisance though I know it is, please run with it just to shut him up. After all, it's only four days.'

So James had dispatched a fax agreeing to the San Francisco McDonalds' visit in a week's time. He was about to call Sanderson to explain the situation, when relations with the Reverend McDonald reached boiling point and abruptly the laird burst into the study holding a handkerchief to his bloody nose. It seemed that following an angry altercation in the kirk half an hour earlier, when the laird had been explaining the Mugan sword's macabre history to a party of twenty Japanese ladies, the Reverend McDonald had punched Guy on the nose then snatched the sword from its display cabinet and threatened the ladies. They had fled shrieking from the kirk and returned distressed to the castle. James was not surprised, as he had warned Sanderson to ensure he wore the McDonald tartan when conducting village tours, especially considering the name Sanderson belonged to the McDonald clan. But his appeals had fallen on deaf ears. Sanderson objected to the dark green and red pattern and had persisted with the brighter Cameron tartan which, he asserted, suited his colouring better.

'After he hit me I whacked him with my sporran,' he boasted. 'That's when he grabbed the sword. The bloody man's dangerous, James. I'm not going back.'

'Right! That's it,' James said angrily. 'This time he's gone too bloody far. He's on his bike out of here.'

But how? The risk of the Reverend McDonald returning to the mainland and drawing attention to Ogg, even if he was not fully cognisant of its realities, was too dangerous to chance. After Guy left James paced the study searching for a solution. The cleric must go; that was clear and go he would, but how to destroy his credibility so that anything he said would be instantly dismissed as a nutter's ravings. James mentally reviewed all he had learnt about the clergyman from Alex and then, remembering Alex's remarks about the Reverend McDonald's crocodile obsession, an idea began to form.

By the end of the day he had hatched a plan which, with Juma's co-operation and a little luck, might do the trick. James picked up the telephone and instructed the operator to find the laird and Miyumi and send them to his study. To Guy's delight and Miyumi's reservations he outlined his scheme.

An exuberant laird left to instruct the Ukrainians' supervisor what would be required from the Scottish dance troupe as their part in the plot. Somewhat hesitantly Miyumi agreed to her role of explaining to the killer-sheep lodge guests, whom the exercise would involve as unwitting bit players, the special entertainment they would be fortunate to witness, since they were present on the first full moon night at the height of summer. As she was to explain, it would be an ancient Oggonian ceremonial rite dating back 1,500 years, but never before witnessed by outsiders, a qualification James felt would guarantee their enthusiastic attendance.

A critical part in the proposed exercise depended on the Reverend McDonald's Bishop's response. Enlisting Sanderson, who applied all his thespian skills as the 'laird's private secretary', James eventually reached him on the telephone.

'Tragic state of affairs, Your Grace,' he explained. 'Things are now reaching a dangerous point and we simply can't cope any more. There's been a rapid deterioration over the past year and I'm afraid the Reverend McDonald is now in urgent need of closely supervised care. He's become obsessed with sexual perversion. There are only five elderly parishioners in the village but he goes on and on about it, accusing them all the time. Also, he insists they are Japanese which is a real mystery. And then there are crocodiles. He claims he is being stalked by one and that the devil is living in the swamp and comes out at night.'

The Bishop listened carefully. 'Yes,' he said thoughtfully when James had finished. 'When my secretary explained why you were calling I obtained the Reverend McDonald's file. I'm afraid we'd rather forgotten about him. You must appreciate that this sort of development with our elderly clergy is not uncommon. It can be a stressful task serving the Lord and sadly some of our soldiers of Christ fall by the wayside under the strain of battle.'

'I quite understand, Your Grace,' James said.

'Mind you,' the Bishop hastily interrupted. 'You must not think this is a normal case. Sexual perversion and devil obsessions, yes, quite standard occurrences, but I don't believe we've had crocodiles before and the Japanese accusation is perplexing. I should think it unlikely the Reverend McDonald has seen any Japanese people. Very strange, very strange.'

'I'm sure you're right, Your Grace,' James agreed.

The Bishop thanked him for his assistance, and was even more grateful when he learnt James would henceforth conduct the Sunday sermons so would not require a replacement. He gratefully accepted James' offer to have the Reverend McDonald delivered in a straitjacket by helicopter on the Bishop's west country manor lawn in two days' time.

'Crocodile arriving with Juma tomorrow as requested,' Geoff faxed in response to James' demand, adding, 'What the hell are you up to? It's a valuable animal so make sure you operate it properly. Monster knows how.'

The prospect of hosting Juma delighted James, after all it was three years since he had last seen him and there was much advice he sought applicable to Ogg. Additionally, there was the Reverend McDonald insanity exercise which, he was confident, once privy to the background, Monster would embrace wholeheartedly as a participant. By the morning of Juma's arrival, James was in a high state of excitement.

The days were now sunny and long and James waited expectantly outside on the lawn for the sounds of the helicopter. Just as the echo from a burst of gunshot reached him from the killer-sheep marksmen two miles away as the day's first killer-sheep was electronically propelled into a clearing, the helicopter swung over the trees and descended. A few minutes later James was shaking Juma's hand. Juma's bags and the crocodile crate were unloaded and they went inside to meet Miyumi and the laird. Afterwards they toured the island, James showing off the golf course, the whisky-still and the Easter Island head, then they examined the Cona statue before returning to the castle for lunch. Only the village and the killer-sheep operation had been omitted from the tour, for as part of James' plan it was important neither the Reverend McDonald nor the dozen killer-sheep hunters and their wives saw Juma. 'I'll show you those on Thursday,' James promised. 'After lunch I'll explain everything.'

During lunch Guy raised the Ukrainian problem with the golf scores.

'We had the same pwoblem,' Juma said. 'I'm surpwised Geoffwey didn't tell you how we fixed it. Must have slipped his mind.'

'But what is it?' James and Guy demanded.

'Torture. Worked splendidly.'

'I told you,' the laird said triumphantly, 'precisely what I've recommended.'

James looked at Miyumi, concerned about her reaction, but before he could defer the explanation to a later, private session, Juma elaborated. He had encountered exactly the same difficulty and fretted over it, and the solution had arisen when he recalled his earnest phase during his student years in London.

Inside a room at Kanju a large screen television with a single chair

333

facing it was placed. Persistent golf-scoring delinquents were strapped to the chair facing the screen, their wrists tied to the chair's arms to prevent them putting their hands over their ears to block out the sound. A wire was attached to the offender's chest, leading outside to a controller monitoring the punishment through a window in the door. If the offender closed his eyes or averted them from the screen he was given a sharp electric shock.

'But what did you show on the screen?' the laird demanded.

'Canadian Arts Council subsidised feature films,' Juma replied. 'I wemembered them from my student days. We gave them six hours' non-stop viewing. Sheer torture.'

There was a disbelieving silence, broken eventually by James. 'And that did the trick?' he queried doubtfully.

Juma laughed. 'Have you ever seen a Canadian Arts Council film?' he asked. 'Believe me, James. Six hours of those and you'd never sin again. Basically they're about gwim middle-aged women weeping and talking about themselves. I wowwied about overdoing it and dwiving our culpwits insane but six hours seemed just wight. The golf scores were OK after that. It worked, James. Twy it and you will see,' and he promised to send the videos which were no longer needed, such was the terror induced by the prospect of their compulsory viewing.

Later James outlined the Reverend McDonald problem and his scheme for fixing it once and for all. Initially Juma baulked, but after repeated assurances as to his safety, he agreed to participate.

The operation began the next morning while the killer-sheep hunters and their wives were breakfasting. Miyumi read aloud in Japanese the text James had composed.

'Today is the longest day of the year,' she recited. 'This evening an ancient Oggonian ceremonial rite will occur, as it has on this day ever since the sixth century. As a result of my personal appeal to the Oggonian High Chieftain, you are privileged to become the first non-Oggonians ever to witness it.'

A buzz of excitement ran round the room.

'Tonight is the full moon,' Miyumi continued blushing. 'At 8 p.m. Oggonian warriors and maidens from across the island will gather at the statue of Mugan to perform an ancient purification dance seeking the gods' blessings for the year ahead. To symbolise their purity they will of course be naked.'

This detail engendered an even more excited response from the men.

'Got 'em,' James thought happily as he stood in the doorway observing, and accurately guessing which part of the translation Miyumi had reached.

'Only younger Oggonians participate in this ancient rite,' Miyumi continued. 'Consequently you will be the sole observers as tradition requires older Oggonians to retire early, this being deemed to be a night for youth.

'Following the ritual dance the warriors and maidens retreat to the swamp adjacent to the statue. There they engage in the ancient ceremony of calling for the swamp monster to come forth. Rarely does this occur, indeed the monster's existence is dismissed by some anthropologists as a mere fable although there are older Oggonians who claim to have seen it. The monster is said to be mud-coloured and appear in giant human form, and it is believed to have the power of transforming itself into the Loch Ness monster, as the few claimed sightings in the last hundred years all coincide with no sightings that same year of the Loch Ness monster.'

Miyumi paused and glanced nervously at James, whereupon the room erupted into excited conversations. These quickly faded when she held up her hand indicating there was more.

'Oggonian folklore claims the monster is always accompanied by dangerous animals which are its guardians. It is believed that anyone who sights the monster is blessed with amazing good fortune for the remainder of their lives. Because of the threat from nocturnal killer-sheep as well as the possibility of the monster and the accompanying dangerous beast appearing, unlikely though this is, the men should carry their rifles fully loaded. We will leave the lodge at 7.45 tonight and drive to the village for the purification dance, then afterwards we will proceed to the swamp for the monster-calling ceremony.'

Leaving Miyumi with the excited guests, James climbed onto his motorbike and rode down to the harbour for the final briefing with Alex. Then he returned to Ogg Castle and collected the laird and Juma, and with the case containing the crocodile they drove to the swamp.

Juma broke open the case, spread the crocodile parts on the ground and carefully assembled it. Then they placed jumper leads on its battery from the Land-Rover and recharged it.

'It's got a five hundwed yard wange. Top speed of 20 km,' Juma explained, and they took turns running the crocodile through its paces with the remote. James soon had it mastered, and he steered it adeptly into the cover of some reeds then they returned to the castle with the packing case.

Alex was waiting for them. 'The Reverend McDonald, he took the bait,' he mumbled nervously. 'Worked himself into a great anger. He'll be there.'

'I hope you warned him not to intrude at the statue?' James cautioned.

'I did that indeed. I said about the disgusting dancing at the statue. And I told him afterwards they would all be going to the swamp for purposes of copulation but if he interrupted they would run away and there would be no sinning,' Alex said sheepishly.

'Excellent. And you've made sure the villagers will remain indoors?'

'Yes. I told them like you said that if even one came out you would take away all their televisions. They are afeared of that,' Alex said adamantly.

'Right. Now don't forget. Make sure you're hidden on the other side of the swamp by eight o'clock and I want to hear some really awesome howling from you and Andrew.'

At 7.30 Land-Rovers transported Juma, James and twelve blanket-clad Ukrainian Scottish dancers across to Lower Ogg then drove to the lodge for the Japanese guests. All the dancers were on £50 bonuses and were naked except for their McDonald tartan kilts and the dildoes the six men had donned. It was a warm midsummer's night and the full moon ensured excellent visibility.

At 7.55 p.m. they heard the Land-Rovers carrying Miyumi and the guests drive up to the statue of Mugan, 100 yards away.

'OK everyone, let's go,' James instructed, and the dancers dropped their blankets and ran in a line across the peat surface to the statue. Standing in a row about 20 yards away, Miyumi and the dozen Japanese couples waited, the men in their military camouflage outfits, each holding a loaded rifle.

Behind them, crouched under the wall of the end cottage and peering over its top, waited the scandalised Reverend McDonald. His outrage intensified when he observed the bare-breasted dancers' McDonald tartan kilts, and when they reached Mugan and began a high-kicking cavorting round the statue it was all he could do to

336

contain himself. But contain himself he did, conscious that worse debauchery was to come.

But it was all too much when the dancers suddenly dropped their kilts and now naked, pranced up and down on them. The clergyman rose, shaking as he gripped the wall and shrieked, 'Defilement, defilement.' But his voice was lost, for the dancers, now warming to their task, were loudly singing Ukrainian nursery rhymes, which had been explained by Miyumi as ancient Oggonian purification chants.

For two minutes, while the Reverend McDonald raged and the Japanese couples gazed awestruck, the dancers continued with the ancient Oggonian ritual. Then, as instructed, they bent, gathered up their kilts and trotted gaily back towards the swamp.

'Come,' Miyumi instructed the Japanese. 'Now is the swamp monster calling ceremony,' and she led the way as the exhilarated guests dutifully followed, the men with their guns primed for any stray killer-sheep. Behind them, muttering, stumbled the Reverend McDonald.

At the swamp edge, waving their kilts rhythmically over their heads, the twelve naked Ukrainians stood in a line chanting loudly in unison a poem known by every Ukrainian child.

'Heathens, defilers, speakers in tongues, besmirchers …' – the epithets tumbled from the Reverend McDonald hidden beside a bush as he awaited the promised crescendo of atrocities.

Miyumi's group stood to one side behind the Ukrainians. 'You must not be disappointed if the monster doesn't come,' Miyumi explained to the two ladies nearest her. 'It is 25 years since its last appearance but it is always worth attending for it means great good fortune to any who do see it.'

The ladies nodded dutifully, but barely had Miyumi finished speaking when an eerie howling from the swamp reeds penetrated the night, drowning the chanting as Andrew and Alex sprang into action.

Then, a mere dozen yards from the dancers, alongside a reed bed where he had been hiding, Juma erupted from the water, roaring and beating his chest, clad only in tight black underpants.

As instructed the Ukrainians instantly ceased chanting and fell to all fours facing Juma, their foreheads on the ground in obeisance, while for half a minute Juma splashed before them, pounding his chest and bellowing loudly.

Almost delirious, a lifetime's unswerving faith in the existence of evil now confirmed, the Reverend McDonald edged towards Juma as if drawn by some invisible force, muttering, 'The devil, Satan, demons …' but another burst of howling from Andrew and Alex brought him to a halt behind the terrified Japanese couples, their eyes fixed on the swamp monster.

Juma, his eyes blazing, turned to the Japanese and, pounding his chest, he splashed noisily out of the swamp towards them.

All twelve killer-sheep marksmen simultaneously lifted their rifles, aimed and fired their blanks. Juma staggered backwards, theatrically gripping his chest, then slowly regained his composure and roaring loudly, his arms flailing, he resumed his clumsy movement towards the Japanese.

The wives and seven of the men turned and fled to the Land-Rovers but five brave marksmen again raised their rifles and fired the second barrel. Again Juma gripped his chest, faltered and swayed before straightening and resuming his chest-thumping advance and the five Japanese froze, rooted to the spot.

Then, just as another burst of howling from Andrew and Alex rang across the swamp, Juma abruptly turned and, facing the water, shouted, 'Cwocodile, cwocodile,' as with jaws snapping the huge crocodile exploded from the water and ambled towards the Japanese. This was too much. Dropping their rifles they turned and ran shrieking to the Land-Rovers.

The crocodile now swerved towards the Reverend McDonald. Every imagined horror, perniciousness, atrocity and terror in a life mentally obsessed with such concerns, had in fifteen minutes been tangibly encapsulated before him. Now he faced the worst of all of his fears as the crocodile, its vicious jaws snapping, advanced on him.

Briefly through his delirious confusion he contemplated prayer but survival instincts quickly superseded faith and he turned and fled back to his cottage, gibbering incoherently.

Silence fell. Juma sat down on the grassy bank as James emerged from the reeds.

'I must say that was gweat fun,' Juma said happily.

'It was fantastic,' James added, joining him on the bank after he had steered the crocodile back into the reeds. 'You were first rate, Monster. Everyone did very well. Tomorrow comes the tricky part though when the helicopter arrives for bloody McDonald with a straitjacket and handcuffs.'

Andrew and Alex now plodded up. 'Well done, chaps,' James congratulated them. 'Excellent howling. Added just the right touch.'

'I fwightened the life out of the Japanese,' Juma boasted.

'You certainly bloody well did. You were fabulous when they shot you,' James replied. 'Excellent recoiling. You had me concerned for a moment there had been a cock-up and they had real bullets.'

'Not as much as me,' Juma said. 'That was the only bit I was wowwied about.'

Now the laird loomed up. 'Tremendous show everyone,' he said. 'I can't think when I've enjoyed myself so much.'

'You saw it all?' James queried.

'From go to whoa. Everyone was terrific. Bloody McDonald's fleeing was the highlight. Pity the croc couldn't have given him a nip on the backside though. I'd have loved that. But come on. Here come the Land-Rovers so we'd better get the dancers back. They're getting cold,' and the party rose to rejoin the jeeps and return for celebratory drinks at Ogg Castle.

# – TWENTY –

Hungover following the prolonged festivities of the previous night, James lay in bed recuperating in the warm morning sunshine flooding into his bedroom. His spirits rose when he heard the helicopter arriving, conscious it would be returning to the mainland in a few hours' time with the Reverend McDonald aboard and out of his life once and for all.

He lay mulling over the probable tussle, notwithstanding the Reverend McDonald's seventy years, involved in fitting the cleric into a straitjacket and handcuffing his legs and hands. Guy had eagerly volunteered to supervise the operation but he would need to enlist some of the stronger Ukrainian lads and James weighed up who could be spared. With the lovely weather the golf course would be packed so it would be all hands on deck in the scoring manipulation room and with the fairway golfball shifters. It would have to be the greenkeeping staff, he concluded.

Suddenly he remembered the five San Francisco McDonald couples were due in that morning on the helicopter. Reluctantly he rose, showered and shaved, donned his McDonald kilt and went downstairs to greet them. In the dining room he found Juma in intense conversation with the laird. Guy looked up, ashen-faced, as he arrived.

'We've got a bloody crisis,' he announced.

'It's a lovely day so cancel the crisis,' James replied gaily, pulling up a chair and feeling that no problem could supersede the joy of the Reverend McDonald's imminent departure.

'The San Francisco McDonalds have arrived,' the laird said gravely.

'So! We're expecting them. So what?'

'They're not bloody couples,' the laird spluttered then he quickly added, 'Or at least not in the usual sense. They're all bloody fairies.'

340

'Fairies?'

'Ponces, wind-jammers, pillow biters, bloody homosexuals,' the laird protested.

'Really! Are you sure?'

'Of course I'm bloody sure. I've spent my life in the theatre for Christ's sake.'

James stared at Guy, puzzled. 'I don't see the problem. Why does it matter?'

'Listen, James; they're not the pencil-moustached, gymnasium body beautiful, leather cap variety. They're as camp a lot as I've ever seen; all fluttering eyelashes and squeaks and mincing about and ...'

'So what!' James interrupted. 'They're only here for four days. Probably add a bit of colour to the place and be a damn sight less demanding on you than normal couples. In the circumstances you can lay it on thick with the laird stuff. I imagine the more theatrical you are the better they'll like it. On reflection I think it's probably a bonus.' He thought for a moment and then added, 'Actually, they sound like fun. I'm quite looking forward to meeting them.'

The laird cast a quick sideways glance at Juma.

Juma laughed. 'Oh go on, Guy. Tell James what's weally bothewing you.'

Somewhat hesitantly Guy muttered, 'They're black.'

'Black! What do you mean black?'

'You know; Afro-Americans or whatever the current fashionable term is.'

'Good God! Are you sure?'

'Of course I'm bloody sure. I'm not colour-blind. Furthermore, they're all wearing McDonald tartan kilts and I'm fairly certain they've got nothing on underneath from the glimpses I saw when they were climbing out of the helicopter. And now they've all gone off down to the village. I couldn't stop them. You know what bloody Americans are like. All that damned enthusiasm and wanting to see everything straight away. They insisted on walking and all flounced off on foot half an hour ago. It's the last thing we need this morning when we go to pick up bloody McDonald.'

'You're worrying unnecessarily,' James said. 'We're not due to grab him until after midday. The Church authorities are expecting him between one and two this afternoon. The San Francisco McDonalds will be long gone from the village by then.'

'Well I hope you're right,' the laird said sternly. 'But it will take them an hour to get down there and they are Americans, remember. They'll study everything at great length. With that lot the graveyard's good for half an hour alone. None of the Japanese are interested but these buggers will be different. I'm worried they'll upset bloody McDonald and something will go wrong. We want that bastard out of here today.'

'Absolute nonsense,' James said dismissively. 'You're making a mountain out of a molehill.' He turned the conversation to planning the Reverend McDonald's capture.

As events transpired, the laird was right to be concerned. The Reverend McDonald had spent the night hiding terrorised in a closet. At dawn, hunger had cautiously brought him out. Thereafter he had sat on his cottage roof, which he had reached by dragging outside a chair and his kitchen table and up-ending it, and there he had spent the morning muttering and scanning the horizon for crocodiles.

His mental state following the events of the previous night had now moved irrevocably from its normal borderline mild derangement to advanced lunacy. Had a dinosaur appeared, no question of hallucination would have arisen in the Reverend's crazed mind. He was ready for and indeed expected any contingency, no matter how preposterous.

In the event it was neither crocodiles nor dinosaurs but an even greater horror in the form of the San Francisco McDonalds who suddenly loomed up on the scene. The spectacle of ten frolicking, hand-holding, black men clad in his beloved McDonald tartan and entering his kirk induced a maniacally homicidal rage. Temporarily forgetting the crocodile threat, and foaming and muttering deliriously, he clambered down the upturned table and stumbled across the road to the kirk.

Meanwhile, in the kirk a false sense of security induced by not having seen a soul since leaving Ogg Castle, aided by an ungodly disposition and combined with the cavalier irresponsibility common to all when abroad, induced an irreverent mood in the San Francisco McDonalds.

Thus, when the Reverend McDonald flung open the doors and beheld the sacrilegious desecration of his beloved kirk he was suddenly transformed, the fears of the previous dozen hours being replaced by the frenzied super-strength of the redeemer. Smashing the display box to the floor the Reverend seized the sword and launched himself at the terrified McDonalds. With one wild slash which drew blood he dekilted the nearest McDonald and then another, whereupon the remaining eight, fearful of a similar dangerous defrocking, quickly released their kilts to the floor.

The unaccustomed spectacle of ten whimpering black men, naked from the waist down, temporarily paralysed the Reverend, and seizing the opportunity of the lull in hostilities the San Francisco McDonalds fled shrieking down the side of the pews and into the empty village.

A few seconds later, sword in hand, the Reverend McDonald burst out after them. Somehow through the deranged fug of his mind a brief flash of clarity shone and he raced across to Alex's cottage, seized the fisherman's bicycle and set out in unsteady pursuit. Had the San Francisco McDonalds headed for the Lower Ogg plain, especially given their forty years' age advantage, they would undoubtedly have escaped their pursuer. But being unfamiliar with the terrain they instead raced fear-stricken down the road towards the killer-sheep lodge with the Reverend McDonald in wobbly, sword-in-hand, baying pursuit.

It had been an unsettled morning at the lodge, the events of the previous evening having traumatised the guests. The terrifying swamp monster's bulletproof immunity and the unexpected presence of crocodiles in Scotland, when combined with the ever-present threat from the killer-sheep, had induced tearful pleadings from the wives to their husbands to remain safely indoors. In truth, and despite their outwardly expressed bravado, the Japanese men were very receptive to this proposition. Such was the scene confronting Miyumi when she drove up in a Land-Rover in mid-morning to find a confused Alex and the Ukrainian horse-trek guides waiting outside while debate raged in the dining room.

Calling for silence, she assured the guests of their safety. The swamp monster could not survive more than two minutes out of the water, she improvised, a skill that came readily to her after the past three years' practice. As for the crocodile, it never left the swamp monster's presence. Miyumi then delivered the *coup de grâce*, reminding the guests that having sighted a swamp monster, their lives were now destined to be blessed with permanent good fortune. Eventually all but two ladies were hesitatingly persuaded and Miyumi took Alex aside and instructed him that, as it was the group's last day, every shooter should be allowed to pot another sheep, while the sole hunter yet to be allocated one, should be given three kills. Nervously the men set out under armed guard for the killer-sheep trench while ten of the ladies climbed into Land-Rovers to be taken by the waiting Ukrainian stable-hands, confused by the delay and uncomprehending of the problem, for their scheduled horse-trek.

Only Mrs Kobayashi and Mrs Nomura remained unconvinced and stayed behind. After everyone had departed the two ladies sat in silent companionship in the sun-drenched lounge for ten minutes, increasingly imbued with a sense of disunity for their rebellion. As their feelings of guilt at such un-Japanese individualism mounted, and as the first comforting burst of gunfire from the killer-sheep trenches penetrated the silence, Mrs Kobayashi could contain herself no longer. 'Perhaps we could go into the garden and look at the flowers,' she suggested, and the two ladies rose and strolled across the lawn to a garden seat.

In truth Mrs Kobayashi was grateful to be alone with Mrs Nomura for she was in desperate need of a confidant. The week on Ogg had hitherto presented no opportunity for such feminine exchanges, with its organised events filling the days and the menfolk's raucous socialising each night.

She had pinned much hope on the Ogg trip, praying that Mr Kobayashi, once free of his twelve-hour work days and late returns every evening, which had been the pattern of the past two years, would notice her existence again. There had been other excursions abroad when she had accompanied him on business trips, but they had been even worse than at home for he was preoccupied with his meetings and she had scarcely seen him. She worried constantly that Mr Kobayashi's pride in his status as the Kobe ball-bearing king had replaced her in his affections. Disappointingly, however, the Ogg holiday had not seen the resumption of their former intimacies, for it had befallen Mr Kobayashi to be the last of the hunters allocated a successful killer-sheep shot. As each unsuccessful day's shooting at Ogg had passed he had adopted a brave face and manfully joined in his successful colleagues' celebrations, drinking ever more Oggonian whisky before collapsing despondent and intoxicated in bed each night. And now, with only one day remaining, he was imbued with a sense of failure and inadequacy.

Gently Mrs Kobayashi broached her anxieties with Mrs Nomura, and was greatly relieved after fifteen minutes of cautious exchange to discover her friend was also fraught with similar concerns. Each revealed that she had purchased a miniature Cona aphrodisiac statue, regrettably without results, although Mrs Kobayashi remained hopeful, having acquired hers only the previous day.

'Shall we visit the Cona statue?' Mrs Nomura suggested. The two ladies had both read with excitement James' brochure on the statue's sexual allure powers but they had hitherto not had the opportunity to spend the required hour at its foot. Now bound by their shared suffering they rose and, arm in arm, wandered across the lawn. For an hour, as instructed in the brochure, they sat in silent meditation at the statue's base and then, arms linked, they strolled back towards the lodge.

'Perhaps we are now too old and have lost our beauty,' Mrs Kobayashi ventured. But before Mrs Nomura could respond the two ladies halted horror-struck as seventy yards away at the end of the lawn, ten naked, slavering black men galloped into view and bore down upon them. It was every Japanese woman's worst nightmare. The two ladies had not anticipated such an immediate response to their statue pilgrimage, and certainly not in such volume and from such quarters.

It was then that Mrs Kobayashi remembered the swamp monster sighting assurance of good fortune. Could it be … but she dared not think the unthinkable and instead, her voice quavering, she said, 'It is best not to resist, my dear.' Taking care to first loosen their clothing, the two ladies lay down on the grass, exhilarated with expectation, closed their eyes and awaited their defilement. As the pounding feet neared, the ladies clenched their eyes even tighter and then suddenly the debauchers were on them, only to thunder past and disappear along the path to the killer-sheep trench.

Mrs Kobayashi sat up slowly, overwhelmed with a sense of rejection. 'It is safe now,' she declared sadly. 'We have lost our beauty.'

'Perhaps it is the good fortune we were promised which saved us,' Mrs Nomura suggested unconvincingly as the two ladies rose and disconsolately began retying their clothing. At that moment the wild-eyed apparition of the indecorously bare-legged Reverend McDonald, his kilt caught around his waist, pedalled into view.

A flicker of optimism crossed both ladies' minds but was quickly discarded. If the black rapists did not want them then surely it would

345

be too much to expect ... and they felt only the smallest disappointment as the Reverend McDonald, babbling incoherently, cycled past.

In the event their unhappiness was to end later that day when their menfolk returned, Mr Kobayashi borne aloft by his fellow hunters, having established an Oggonian one-day record of three kills, while Mr Nomura was almost as joyful from chalking up his second for the week. The promised good luck from the swamp monster sighting and the aphrodisiac properties of the Cona statue were plainly not mere fable, for coincidentally, and perhaps compounded by the effect of the Cona miniatures hidden under their beds, both jubilant husbands were sufficiently moved by their triumph to commence the evening's celebrations with a predinner ravishing of their spouses. Later that night the promised good fortune seemed limitless when, although by then in his cups, Mr Kobayashi briefly forgot his beloved ball-bearings and delivered a repeat performance in the early hours of the morning after he had finally staggered to bed. Mrs Kobayashi and Mrs Nomura were both very happy.

But all of those developments were preceded by dramatic midday events at the killer-sheep trenches.

Disturbed by the pounding footsteps of the approaching San Francisco McDonalds, the Japanese killer-sheep hunters had turned and, to their horror, recognised charging at them ten slightly smaller but ominously naked swamp monsters, notwithstanding Miyumi's reassurances. In their panic at the prospect of the possible depravity intended, they forgot the swamp monster's bulletproof powers and all lifted their rifles and blasted away at the oncoming McDonalds.

Hysterical from this fresh assault and nearing exhaustion, the McDonalds leapt over the trenches, providing the Japanese hunters a kaleidoscope of genitalia, and charged on into the killer-sheep forest. But not before the last of them was spotted by the Reverend McDonald who had emerged, jabbering deliriously and waving the sword, pedalling frantically down the path towards them.

Once more the terrified Japanese raised their rifles and unleashed a bevy of blanks at the demonic cleric who, flinging his cycle aside and swinging his sword wildly at the ducking hunters, jumped across the trench and followed the McDonalds into the killer-sheep clearings.

All of this was a source of astonishment to Alex, ensconced 200 yards away in his tree-hidden control hut watching on the television

346

screen. Unaware of the San Francisco McDonalds' existence and alert to his responsibility for the Japanese huntsmen's welfare, he rushed to the trench to find them frantically reloading their rifles to deal with any further assault. Inside twelve hours, and despite repeated assurances as to their safety, they had been charged by a chest-thumping swamp monster, pursued by a jaw-snapping crocodile, attacked by ten naked Negroes with doubtless unthinkable intentions, and then slashed at with a gold sword by a bullet-proof, bearded, bicycling, kilt-clad crazed clergyman. This was not the placid and civilised Scotland that had been portrayed to them in Tokyo. Now they trusted nobody and they braced themselves for fresh degradations.

'Follow me, men,' Alex commanded, but only four hunters left the safety of the trench and set out in a crouching run, guns poised, behind Alex in pursuit of the Reverend McDonald.

By now the San Francisco McDonalds were exhausted. On encountering the cliff-face they could run no more. They collapsed defeated in a gibbering heap and awaited the fate that as hated homosexuals and black men had always threatened in their minds.

The Reverend McDonald, eyes blazing and mouth foaming, arrived and stopped before them, relishing his moment of triumph before, sword poised, he advanced to finish them off.

It was at this moment, disturbed by the shouting and gunfire, that Thomas the simpleton rose from his shelter on the cliff-edge above and stumbled drooling towards a group of 60 sheep which had become disengaged from the main flock. Not without justification one promptly panicked and galloped over the cliff-top and the others, as is the wont of sheep, quickly followed. The four Japanese hunters following Alex emerged from the trees just in time to witness the sky darkened by a flock of ferocious air-borne killer-sheep apparently leaping from the clifftop in attack.

Once more they raised their rifles and blazed away, before turning and fleeing back to the security of the trench.

But the Reverend McDonald was less fortunate. Alone in the line of exposure, he was knocked askew by a falling sheep and fell groaning to the ground, his left leg broken.

Alex raced back to his hut to telephone Ogg Castle and ten minutes later the laird and James arrived in a Land-Rover. They recovered the sword, fitted the straitjacket on to the delirious cleric, handcuffed his wrists together and bore him back to the helicopter. Ten minutes later he was airborne and off Ogg for the first time in forty years. If not executed precisely as planned, his removal had nevertheless been accomplished and the laird opened a bottle of champagne to celebrate.

The San Francisco McDonalds were in a less festive mood. Once safely back in Ogg Castle, and following their desperate pleadings, they were scheduled to depart in three hours' time – four days earlier than planned and paid for – as soon as the helicopter returned from delivering the Reverend McDonald.

Later that day James again telephoned the Bishop.

'You've been wonderfully kind,' the Bishop said. 'We really can't thank you enough. I'm afraid this is as severe a case as we've encountered. But how on earth did he break his leg?'

'It was lucky we were down in the village,' James explained. 'We were called there by one of the crofters. He was on the roof of the kirk and apparently leapt off claiming a crocodile was attacking him.'

'Quite extraordinary,' his Grace muttered. 'Sexual perversion obsessions we can deal with. Perfectly normal with our older clergymen, although there are times I do envy my Roman brothers-in-arms. With their innately weaker characters my Catholic colleagues' clergy tend not to resist their unfortunate impulses so they do not incur the consequences of frustration. A lot less trouble I can assure you.'

'I once knew a Catholic bishop in Madagascar,' James ventured impulsively and immediately regretted it.

'Licentious I imagine,' his Grace proffered lightly.

James thought quickly. 'A practical man I would say, Your Grace.'

'Yes,' the Bishop said thoughtfully. 'I think I understand. But look here. You mentioned the sexual obsessions and as I have said that's all perfectly normal. But the crocodiles and Japanese; I must say they're new. Our people are certainly perplexed by those. Never had them before. No mention of lingerie?' he quizzed.

'No,' James replied. 'I can't say I recall that.'

'Yes, I see. Well that's a bit worrying. They usually go in for that; an odd fish indeed.' He paused for a few seconds and then added, 'The Dean tells me the Reverend McDonald has also been going on about Negroes. Given his history of being confined on Ogg, just as with the Japanese, I can't imagine he's ever seen one. I don't suppose you can throw any light on that?'

''Fraid not, Your Grace,' James replied. 'But you're quite right about the Negro carry-on and it's remiss of me not to mention it. It's just there have been so many things, you know, the Japanese and crocodiles and the depravities' unpleasantness. You must understand we're not used to this sort of thing on Ogg. Life is very quiet here.'

Suddenly the Bishop tittered. 'One thing he got wrong though,' he said.

'Flying sheep. He started on that as soon as he arrived. I could live with pigs. At least it would make some sense.'

James laughed dutifully. 'Yes; I had heard he'd mentioned that as well.'

There was a moment's silence, and then the Bishop said, 'When we last spoke, Mr Campbell, you kindly offered to take the church services at Ogg.'

'Yes,' James replied, detecting from the Bishop's tone that this was about to lead somewhere awkward.

'If you don't mind me asking, you do sound rather young.'

James relaxed. 'I'm 31, Your Grace.'

There was another ominous silence and then, 'That's a very good age, Mr Campbell. Have you considered a career in the Church?'

'Well, I'm afraid, that is, I'm extremely busy.' James thought quickly. 'Actually, I'm writing a book. It's why I'm on Ogg. Peace and quiet you see. I've still got three years of research and then of course …'

'That's perfectly all right,' the Bishop interrupted sadly. He sighed, 'It's the war you see. It ruined everything. I sometimes question whether we truly won. Everyone has had such high expectations since then. Wanting everything all the time. We've been unable to attract top-drawer candidates for the clergy ever since and well, I'm afraid with the Reverend McDonald you see the consequences.'

'A rotten apple in the barrel surely, Your Grace,' James generously suggested. 'I'm quite sure it will not have any detrimental effect on the Ogg parishioners' devotions. You can be assured I'll be keeping them up to scratch.'

'I'm delighted to hear it, Mr Campbell. Once again, I must thank you for all you've done. Perhaps it's my age but I have a strong sense of foreboding about the contemporary world. Your Christian spirit has rather renewed my optimism about the human condition.'

'I'm pleased to hear it, Your Grace,' James responded. 'But really it's nothing. One must do one's duty.'

349

'Quite so, quite so, it's just a pity so many others no longer feel the same way.'

Later in a curiously mixed mood of celebration and remorse, James joined Juma and the laird and became very drunk.

# – TWENTY-ONE –

For the first time since the inaugural Nuremberg two years earlier, James entered the Alceides building. He rode the lift to the third-floor office, emerging to find Geoff engrossed in a report.

'Good to see you, mate,' Geoff greeted him warmly. 'Look at this,' he grimaced, waving a sheet of paper. 'Another bloody cock-up. Why don't you pop up and visit Brasch? He knows you're coming and would love to talk about Ogg. It will give me time to sort this mess out, not that it's bloody sort-outable as far as I can see. We can shoot out and have lunch somewhere afterwards.'

'What's the problem?' James enquired.

'You wouldn't believe it. A real mess with Taiwan.'

'Taiwan! What on earth is Alceides up to there?'

'Well, it was actually a damn good idea in principle,' Geoff said grudgingly. 'One of the new tubbie trainees came up with it. Fellow called Bustin; well-named actually, he's bustin' out all over with ideas. Wrote his doctoral thesis on the history of papal entertainment. Said as bugger all was known about it he was able to speculate to hell and go off on all sorts of tangents. Unsurprisingly, he received a first-class honours pass. Once Dad heard that he knew Bustin would be a winner for Alceides. Bustin was spot on with this clever concept he devised the first time he saw a video of the Kanju operation. Still, if every cloud has a silver lining,' Geoff brightened, 'I suppose that fact alone is encouraging for the future. After all, he was only 315 pounds at the time which is a good 100 pounds short of the usual inspirational flow beginning. He's well over 400 pounds now so I'm anticipating great things from him. Anyway, the balls-up wasn't his fault.'

'But what is it; what's happened?' James urged, as always mentally bracing himself for a new Alceides lunacy.

Geoff frowned and hit his head with his hand. 'I broke the golden rule about owning things. Bought a bloody golf-club factory in Taiwan. You can imagine my father's reaction.'

'You bought a golf-club factory?' James repeated, astonished. 'Since when has Alceides gone in for conventional activities? If that's Bustin's idea I'm damned if I see what's so clever about it.'

'No, no; you don't understand. The idea was to make our own brand of Kanju golf club. It was a first rate concept too. We started selling them at $6,000 four months ago and so far we've knocked off over eighty sets a week and made over six million dollars. They only cost $130 in Taiwan so it's been a huge winner, at least up until this fiasco,' and again Geoff waved the paper he'd been reading.

'You're kidding me; $6,000 a set. That's huge money,' James exclaimed. 'Who buys them at that price and why? And if they only cost $130 to manufacture then surely they must be rubbish.'

'Well, you're certainly wrong on that assumption,' Geoff replied smugly. 'The very best quality brands only cost in that order to actually make. It's the same with all "me too" manufactured goods, whether it's pet food, tennis racquets, toothpaste, petrol, designer jeans; or anything else you care to name. Ninety per cent of the end-consumer's payment is absorbed in marketing costs. The biggest advertiser wins. Where we're creaming it is possessing a ready private market so we incur none of those promotional expenses.'

'Ready market! What do you mean?'

'Sorry,' Geoff apologised. 'I'm confusing you. We sell them to the Kanju guests. Nowhere else.'

'You certainly are confusing me. For the life of me I can't see why the Kanju clientele would buy new clubs. Apart from the fact that with their wealth they've probably already got the best brands available, if they're all shooting phenomenal rounds then the last thing they'd contemplate is to change their clubs.'

Geoff laughed. 'Let me explain. The idea Bustin came up with was quite revolutionary. Basically the scheme was to reverse the standard modus operandi at Kanju. As you know, most of Kanju's guests are repeat customers. Some are on their fourth and fifth trips now and they take for granted knocking up sensational scores from day one. You remember I told you when we were out in Kenya that the one flaw, the only one I might add, in the golfing exercise is that the joy from the sensational scores is diluted by the fact that every

352

other bugger's turning them in as well. Bustin recognised the opportunity that presented straight away and came up with this terrific angle. I was going to get on to you about it for Ogg.'

'But what is it?' James demanded, his curiosity now fully aroused.

'We gave it a trial run four months back. Juma wasn't too happy about it. Argued why risk a winning formula? As I pointed out to him,' Geoff continued, adopting a slightly schoolmasterly tone, 'I like to think of our operations as fluid and Alceides as having a radical progressive outlook, you know, always striving to do things better, not passively accepting the status quo, constantly elevating …'

'Yes, yes, I know all that,' James interrupted Geoff's familiar refrain impatiently. 'But what was the scheme?'

'We waited for a new guest intake to arrive and on the first day we turned off the electronic greens and confined the ball-shifting lads to just stealing their balls. Out the golfers went, naturally all expecting to shoot phenomenal rounds as per normal. Needless to say the first day was a massive disaster in terms of their expectations and when they'd finished their rounds they all trooped back in crestfallen and predictably moaned to the golf shop pro when they came in for new balls to replace the ones we'd nicked. He's not really a professional of course – we hardly need that at Kanju – he's really just a shop assistant but we call him the club pro for image reasons.

'As instructed the pro listened to them complaining then suggested they change their clubs and try our brand. Loaned them our new Kanju sets to have a trial run with the next day. Most accepted and we restored the electronic putting and fairway lads on the job, but just for them of course. The punters who were still using their own clubs had another bad day. Needless to say after a second disastrous round they saw the light and were quickly into the Kanju clubs, specially after they'd listened to all the others raving about them that night. The cost didn't matter as it's nothing to them. In fact nearly all of them give us their old clubs rather than lug two sets back home so we've picked up another one and a half million dollars there so far, flogging them to our golfball buyer in Nairobi. They're all name brand sets so it was a great deal for him. He shipped them down to South Africa where the money is. The only initial drawback was a 20 per cent fall in champagne sales as naturally no one was buying on the first day but we ended up making a turn on that as well by lifting the champagne prices 20 per cent to compensate. Now we gross the same money but provide a fifth less product. Clever isn't it?' Geoff grinned.

'As always I'd call it devious rather than clever,' James responded coolly. 'But you haven't told me the problem.'

'This,' Geoff said waving the paper again. 'It's an email from Monster. A new dispatch of a thousand sets of Kanju clubs arrived yesterday from Taiwan and they're all bloody left-handed. Now we've got no stock for the next four weekly golfer intakes before a fresh supply arrives.'

'Hardly the end of the earth, surely. You'll catch them on their next trip, no doubt. But how did this left-hand botch arise?'

'Look at this,' Geoff said angrily, searching among the mess of paper on his desk and handed a sheet to James. It was a memo to the Taiwan factory from Geoff and read, 'Require run of left-handed clubs. Please advise. Note Kanju needs 1000 new sets by May.'

'It is a bit ambiguous,' James suggested.

'Rubbish. Plainly there are two messages there. Once everyone at Kanju started buying our sets we realised we were missing out with about a tenth of the market who were left-handers. I didn't know if our factory was geared up for those, thus the "please advise" bit. The other was just a reminder about normal supply deadlines for the new intakes.' Geoff became pensive. 'You know, James, in some respects this mishap is a windfall in reminding me how blessed we are with our operations. This sort of stuff-up by all accounts is an everyday event in conventional commerce and explains all the stress and duress incurred by the modern executive. Compared with orthodox business, life's normally a cock-up-free cruise in here. The blunder was mine for not sticking to the tried and true Alceides formula and instead buying the factory.'

'But I don't see how that makes any difference,' James said perplexed. 'You'd still have a thousand left-handed clubs. Your memo wasn't as clear as it should have been.'

'That's not the point,' Geoff said dismissively. 'Of course we'll unload the left-handed sets over about eighteen months. I'm not worried about that. The point is this blow-up made me realise the one flaw in the Bustin brainwave and that is it's a oncer. By the end of a year we'll have fitted everyone into our clubs. Of course we can run the factory for another year supplying Ogg brand sets for your customers, but after that I'm stuck with a bloody useless Taiwanese golf-club factory. If I'd practised my father's doctrine the collapse of demand would be the factory's problem, not ours. Manufacturers are used to all that upsy-down fate. We're bloody well not.'

'You could sell it as a going concern or market the clubs elsewhere,' James suggested.

'Don't be ridiculous. If the order book is zilch the factory's going-concern value is likewise and we're certainly not getting into that competitive rat-race on the open market. You're forgetting the secret of our success. Dad explained to you three years ago about creating monopolies to avoid all of that.'

'I hate to tell you this and be a party to the outrage but there is a fairly obvious solution,' James ventured.

'Tell me, tell me,' Geoff cried. 'You're so good at problem-solving, right up there in the Brasch league.'

'Then why haven't you thrown it at Brasch?'

'Can't do that. He doesn't know about the scheme and obviously I don't want him suspecting there are other tubby brain-trusters on board. Anyway, he's sulking at the moment because of the diet and he's being totally unco-operative. So come on; what's the answer?'

'Well, first you might have to downscale the factory and just gear it to Kanju and Ogg consumption which will mean acquiring a warehouse to stock up in the off-year.'

'Off-year! What do you mean?'

'It's simple,' James said. 'But I shouldn't really be telling you this. However,' and he sighed resignedly, 'all you do is allow the punters to use their new clubs for a couple of years. In the interim you manufacture and stack up a supply with a different brand name and then you repeat the exercise; you know, turn off the electronic greens and all that again, then sell them the new brand. I suppose the only redeeming feature is that $6,000, outrageous though it is, is as you say neither here nor there to the clientele.'

'James, that's absolutely brilliant,' Geoff cried. Then noting James' reservation, he added, 'You shouldn't moralise about these matters. You said it yourself, the money's nothing to the clients; it's just small change and, anyway, don't forget most of the Kanju intakes turn a pretty big profit on their annual visits from our self-fulfilling sharemarket tips. So call the new clubs a tip to us for the tip to them; and talking of that, remember the Japanese and Americans are tipping races. If nothing else their generosity when they leave reflects the

355

happiness we bring them. We pay our Latin girls well, but my God, they really clean up on the tipping front. Every week the departing customers spray $100 bills around like confetti, they're so happy and rejuvenated.'

'Good Lord! Surely the girls aren't having it off with those old buggers?' James responded, plainly shocked.

'No, no. That's precisely my point. If they were then one could understand the tips. As I said, the clients' generosity simply reflects their overwhelming happiness, which let me emphasise,' Geoff said slowly, 'is solely due to us.'

There was a lull as both men fell into a contemplative mood. Eventually James said, 'I know you have a rationalisation for everything and frankly I admit it's always hard to quarrel with it. It's just, where do you draw the line? There has to be one and something intuitively tells me you step way over the mark with all of these money-making stunts.'

'I don't see why there need be a line,' Geoff said, a puzzled look crossing his face.

'OK. If there's no standard, no line, then why waste time with golf clubs? Do it easier. Sell the poor buggers magic pills which knock eight strokes off their best round and then work the course to deliver it. Simple placebos will be sufficient.'

'That's absolutely brilliant,' Geoff said, wide-eyed.

'I was bloody well joking,' James shouted.

'I don't care. It is bloody brilliant. Christ, imagine what we could charge for hole-in-one pills.'

'Oh for God's sake,' James groaned. 'You really are ...' but he was interrupted by loud guffawing and thumping and then a methodical, indecipherable chanting from overhead.

'It's bloody Brasch,' Geoff muttered. 'He must be watching the video of last week's Nuremberg. This building's hopeless with its paper-thin floors. I know exactly what he's up to all the time.'

'I'll go and say hello to him and see you later for lunch,' James said, and he rose and left Geoff mulling over the hole-in-one pills proposition.

# – TWENTY-TWO –

James knocked tentatively on Brasch's door then cautiously opened it and stepped inside, only to recoil from the deafening noise. The room reverberated with a machine-like rhythmic chanting: 'Sieg heil, sieg heil, sieg heil.'

In the middle, kaftan-clan, blubbery and wheelchair-bound lay Brasch, his attention fixed on a large screen suspended across the bookshelves. A jackbooted, black-uniformed figure, standing erect on a banner-shrouded podium and wearing a toothbrush moustache, his right arm pointing skywards, could be seen giving the fascist salute. Behind him eight corpses dangled from scaffolds. A seemingly endless stream of sieg heiling, blond crew cut, brown-uniformed Indians, their right arms extended and their heads turned rigidly towards the platform, goose-stepped past the podium. Geoff was right; the has-been actors dispatched to India had certainly smartened up the troops.

For a few seconds James stood transfixed by the spectacle until suddenly he started as he recognised the mock Führer. It was the New York financier, Andrew Clifford, the Hamastanian monarch on his Madagascan tour three years earlier.

It was then Brasch noted James' presence and he clicked off the video with his remote. 'James, how nice to see you,' he wheezed in a thin, reedy voice, so different from the booming resonance of their previous meetings. 'Geoff mentioned you were coming to London.'

James was shocked by Brasch's dissolute appearance. He seemed immensely more elephantine; his face sprawled and slopped like a massive blancmange down and across his kaftan, while his hair hung in lank shoulder-length strands.

'How are you?' James mumbled.

'Not good, James, not good,' Brasch whimpered, plainly struggling to speak. 'As you can see, they're starving me,' he gasped.

At that moment Hoon emerged pushing a tea trolley. She placed it alongside Brasch and, head subserviently down, scurried from the room.

The trolley contained a huge mug of coffee and a plate with four chocolate cream eclairs. Brasch looked at them wistfully, a tragic expression crossing his massive countenance, and for a brief, alarming moment James feared he was about to weep.

'You won't want any of these I assume,' Brasch mumbled and he picked up the plate with both hands and hugged it to his chest.

'No, no,' James said hurriedly. Visibly relieved Brasch carefully plucked an eclair from the plate and in two bites it was gone. The remaining three were disposed of in quick succession.

'They're starving me, James,' Brasch bleated again when the last one was gone and, crestfallen, he studied the empty plate.

'I'm sure that's not true,' James consoled him. 'I know they're concerned about you possibly getting overweight.'

'It's bad for a chap not to eat, James,' Brasch gasped.

James changed the subject. 'I say, I caught a glimpse of the Nuremberg on the screen. Wasn't that the fellow I did the Royal with in Madagascar?'

'The very same, the very same,' Brasch wheezed.

'Can't imagine him ranting,' James said. 'He hardly said boo during the entire three days in Madagascar. How was his Nuremberg?'

Brasch began to laugh, gasping and squeaking, his body shuddering in ripples of convulsions which cascaded down his kaftan. 'He's no orator,' he cackled. 'Read a half-hour address from notes … hee, hee … on … on … hee, hee … fiscal …' Brasch could go no further and erupted into a terrible coughing fit, his massive frame shuddering as tears streamed down his face. Eventually he settled. 'Fiscal policy,' he croaked and again he collapsed, shaking with laughter. 'I'll show you,' he wheezed, as he reached for the remote and wound back the tape for thirty seconds.

James studied the screen. Clifford was at the podium, head down, reading laboriously in a leaden monotone from his notes. 'Responsible fiscal policy must pay cognisance to the wider framework context of monetary price settings,' he droned.

Suddenly the green light behind him flashed and Clifford started, seemingly perplexed as the stadium erupted in a pandemonium of cheering. Pavlovian-like he shot his right arm skyward and stood erect, eyes blazing fervently for the minute the acclamation lasted. The light went off, the cheering died away and Clifford returned to his recitation.

'Conversely, monetary policy, albeit independently instigated, must necessarily reflect the underlying democratic elements implicit ...' Clifford plodded on stodgily in this vein for another two minutes until, pausing for breath, he allowed the light-master a further opportunity. This time the red light flashed and as the stadium exploded in an ear-splitting series of thunderous 'sieg heils', Clifford, blinking furiously, looked up puzzled and then again jerked his right arm skywards, his eyes lit with passion as he wallowed in the tributes.

Brasch clicked off the remote.

'Not exactly a scintillating performance,' James commented. 'I can't imagine why Clifford wanted a Nuremberg.'

'Rampathal reported he was thrilled with it all,' Brasch spluttered. 'With his wealth no one's ever told him he's a prosaic bore. The cheering merely confirmed his own heroic view of himself.'

'He can't be that dumb,' James asserted.

'Can't he?' Brasch quavered. 'Are you sure? Hepplethorne sent me a note which suggests otherwise.'

'Hepplethorne! Who's he?' James asked.

'Hepplethorne's Goering,' Brasch wheezed. 'Former Royal Theatre actor. In his post-performance report he said Clifford asked his opinion about distributing a free pamphlet ...' Brasch again broke into quivering, out-of-control mirth ... 'distributing a free pamphlet ... hee, hee, hee ... across India ... hee, hee, hee, promoting his fiscal policy thoughts ... in view of the audience enthusiasm ...' At that Brasch shook and rumbled and rocked with uncontrollable laughter. Eventually he composed himself. 'Strangest Nuremberg we've ever done,' he said joltingly, his huge body shuddering with the effort to speak. 'Can't afford any more like it ... upset the troops. Cheering and sieg heiling standards bound to decline. They don't understand what the clients are saying but the normal screaming deliveries wind them up to respond appropriately. But enough of that. Tell me about Ogg.'

James recounted all that had evolved, periodically prodded by Brasch for elaboration. But after half an hour, noting Brasch's increasing difficulty in speaking and his obvious fatigue, he made an excuse and departed, not mentioning the subject of his lunch appointment with Geoff.

Back downstairs he did not pull his punches. 'I'll wager Brasch will be dead soon,' he snapped, 'I told you it would come to this. It's tantamount to murder.'

'Suicide,' Geoff replied detachedly, folding his papers into neat piles. 'If Brasch dies it will be misadventure.' He rose, opened a cupboard door and reached for his jacket. 'How many chocolate eclairs?' he asked coolly and on being told, 'Well, there you are. Up until a month ago it was twelve every morning tea, another dozen with lunch and the same again at afternoon tea. Then he knocked off a further batch before bed. Now he's on one-third rations. He's not dying; he's just despondent because of the diet. We're doing a complete purge and taking him all the way back to 400 pounds. He'll be right as rain once he gets there.'

'Well I'm not so certain,' James said angrily. 'He's in such poor shape he can barely speak. What about the other fatties? Are they in the same boat?'

'I told you at Ogg,' Geoff said coldly. 'They all went on an eating binge. Once they passed 450 pounds they became totally preoccupied with non-stop gorging. We're doing our best. Do you think we're happy about it?'

'You mean new ideas productivity is down?' James quizzed suspiciously.

'New ideas productivity is non-bloody-existent,' Geoff snapped.

'I've been thinking about the fatties and what you told me three years ago,' James said. 'You know, about only choosing history students.'

'So?'

'Well, I'd have thought you could make the same case for using classics students.'

Geoff looked at him sharply. 'You know damn well my father wouldn't do that to classics students,' he said curtly. There was a silence, then he added, 'Look, I might be the manager but I don't make all the rules. Some things are out of my hands.'

'An admission of guilt, surely?' James said coldly but Geoff said nothing and they left the office.

They walked to the restaurant without speaking. After they had placed their orders James broke the silence. 'You realise Ogg's running smoothly now. All the wrinkles are ironed out and Sanderson has management well in his grasp.'

'Why are you telling me this?'

'I think you know but I'll say it anyway. Ogg doesn't need me any more.'

'Then take more holidays. Get a flat in London and spend two weeks here with me and two weeks there, or whatever arrangement suits.'

'No.'

'What do you mean no?'

'Look, Geoff, you can't seriously expect me to spend the rest of my life on Ogg. I'm 31. I want to do something.'

'You are doing something and you're making a fortune as well,' Geoff said flatly.

'What's the point of me at Ogg, specially if my heart's not in it? Sanderson does the job very well and furthermore he loves it. He can't believe his luck. I'm totally redundant. The same goes for Miyumi now that Hiroshi effectively runs the killer-sheep lodge. Miyumi's just twiddling her thumbs. Even the Ukrainians have finally mastered the golf-scoring after we punished them with the Canadian Arts Council films.'

'Miyumi should be up at the castle then, looking after the golfers' wives.'

'That's exactly where she has been for the last six months. But we've got five Japanese staff there and any one of them could handle her job very well. The last year completed everything. The golf-course is in tip-top shape, specially after we barged in all the sand for the bunkers. Alex is routinely bringing in oil for the generators on the towing barge, the daily plane service has cut supply costs and is landing comfortably on the par five sixth hole now we've extended it; everything's running totally smoothly and frankly, it's a bore now.'

'The deal was a partnership with an owner-operator,' Geoff said sharply.

'That was to develop Ogg. Now it's established and going well, there's absolutely no need for me to remain. Aside from that Miyumi's seven months pregnant and can't possibly stay there any more and I intend to be with her.'

361

'Really,' Geoff exclaimed. He looked searchingly at James. 'Well, I suppose congratulations are in order.'

'Thank you.'

'Tell you what,' Geoff said, brightening. 'Why don't you come and work with me in London as an ideas man? God knows you've been right up to Brasch standards at times.'

'I don't think you understand,' James said quietly. 'I want out. I'm not comfortable about it all, particularly the tubbies, and I don't want to debate it. I want you to buy me out.'

'Buy you out! It's out of the question. You know Dad's theory about landowner partners.'

'It's a theory, Geoff, that's all. You've got my £50-million secrecy agreement contract.'

'I'm not sure that's good enough. There's too much at stake. With your pejorative attitude to Alceides activities you're a hell of a risk.'

James leant back in his chair and looked Geoff firmly in the eye. 'You may not believe this,' he said, measuring his words carefully. 'I actually don't have a negative view of Alceides. Oh, don't misunderstand me,' he added when Geoff gave a mocking laugh. 'I thought the icons in Romania were a bit naughty but then I ended up doing the same thing at Ogg and I actually don't feel bad about it. As you always said when I questioned things, all that counted was the customer's happiness and I've seen the pleasure Oggonian antiquities bring their purchasers. And how can I quarrel with the golf exercises? The customer's joy is beyond argument. The State Tours are harmless, although I can't see why Hodge won't pay for purchases and services instead of dishing out medals to those poor buggers.'

'The answer to that is simple,' Geoff retorted, plainly annoyed. 'Offer them the choice and they'll take the medals every time. That's evident by the fact that they do so when they don't have to, like the Indian hotelier you saw in Madagascar. He could charge the earth and we'd have to pay. Instead he opts for the medal.'

'The poor little bastard,' James muttered.

'What do you mean by that?' Geoff asked sharply. 'Christ Almighty; Hodgie had him appointed an Earl last month when they did their first Hamastanian Ducal Visit. By all accounts he's insufferably happy.'

'Look, I don't want to quarrel with you,' James said appeasingly. 'I've told you and I mean it. Apart from Brasch and the other fatties, which I think is a disgrace, I'm perfectly comfortable about Alceides' activities. Well, the floggings are dreadful but fortunately I've never witnessed those. It's simply that I'm redundant now on Ogg so I want to move on. Managing a resort for the rest of my life isn't my bag.'

'Is it the Nurembergs?'

James sighed. 'The worst I could say about those is they're bad taste but if that was a crime half the population would be behind bars. I've been thinking a lot about the Nurembergs since you were up at Ogg and we had that discussion about the impossibility of talking sense to a mass audience.'

'So the Nurembergs do bother you then. Admit it,' Geoff demanded.

'Not in the least. What I realised was that Hitler and Castro and Franco and Billy Graham and all the other podium ranters all have one thing in common which we overlooked. And then it occurred to me that exactly the same characteristic applied to Alceides' super-rich clientele.'

'Oh yes,' Geoff said suspiciously. 'So what's that?'

'They're all buffoons.'

'Buffoons! How can they be buffoons to get where they did?'

'They probably can't. But let's face it. Enough's known about the dictators once they made it to make it fairly clear they certainly all became buffoons. And frankly, what I've seen and you've told me about your super-rich clientele, they all seem to be buffoons to me and I'm sure they couldn't have started that way. My theory is, it's a variation on the absolute power corrupting thing. Absolute power evolves into buffoonery. I've tried and I can't think of any other explanation.'

'I don't see why that should bother you.'

'It doesn't. As I said, I'll admit to one concern only and that is the fatties. I don't think it's necessary and I don't think it's a parallel to, say, exploiting the super-rich's craving for adulation. That's harmlessly filling a gap in their lives. With the fatties you're encouraging and exploiting a very serious character weakness. Frankly, I believe if anything kills Alceides it will be that situation. I have an ominous feeling about them.'

Geoff laughed. 'Sounds like superstition to me,' he mocked.

'On your head be it,' James said with a shrug.

'So what is it you want then?'

'I told you. I want you to buy me out.'

'And what will you do?'

'I'm not entirely sure. If we can agree on a price Miyumi and I may go to Vancouver.'

'Vancouver! Why Vancouver for Christ's sake?'

'I was dragged along there once in my old job when I was in the New York office. They thought my English accent would help their solicitation to underwrite a city debt issue. I fell in love with the place. So too with Miyumi. She won the Canadian Open there six years ago and stayed on for a week afterwards. Also, it's only a short hop to Japan which is another plus for her visiting her family from time to time. Anyway, we thought if we can negotiate a buy-out of Ogg we'd shift there and give it a go.'

'But what will you do in Vancouver?'

'I honestly don't know. At this stage it's only an idea. We might take an apartment for a month and fossick about to see how we feel about it. But it's not cast in stone.'

The two sat without speaking for a minute. Eventually Geoff said, 'So what do you think your freehold and quarter share in the business is worth?'

'If it makes you comfortable I'll retain the freehold with Alceides as lessee. But I'm equally happy to sell it to you for a million quid, reflecting its rental income. The business is now in full swing. My assessment is it will clear six million pounds this year and nine next year. I think twenty million for the freehold and my quarter interest is a pretty good buy for you. Ogg really is flowing smoothly now but I'll stay in touch and you have my word; if ever there's a management crisis I'll return and run the show until it's smooth sailing again. You can contract me to that if you wish.'

Geoff stood up suddenly. 'I'm going back to the office,' he said abruptly. 'My father's flying in tonight so I'll discuss it with him. Come in tomorrow morning.' Leaving James to settle the bill, and without a goodbye, he left the restaurant.

# – TWENTY-THREE –

Geoff was staring abstractly out of his window when James arrived the next morning. 'I've talked to my father. We prefer the status quo,' he said bluntly, without any greeting. 'I want you to reconsider shifting to London and working here as an ideas man while keeping your quarter interest in Ogg.'

James and Miyumi had spent the previous evening discussing the options and had allowed the possibility of such a response. The London proposition was not without merit. It would certainly be stimulating and great fun thinking up new ideas to cater to the super-rich's craving for adulation. Additionally, the three days they had already been there had reinforced James' view that city life hugely outweighed the rural option. While their time on Ogg had been satisfying during the establishment stages, the prospect of returning now seemed abhorrent.

Encouraged by James' hesitation Geoff added, 'Naturally we would entertain an equity participation in any new ventures you instigate.' Suddenly his normal confidence evaporated and he looked unsure and almost frightened. He adopted a pleading tone. 'Don't go, James. It would be terrific to have you working here.'

James sat down heavily in an armchair. 'I've told you the truth about Ogg. Miyumi and I are no longer necessary. You've got enough on your plate now with Ogg and the Nurembergs and Kanju and Hodgie's tours. You don't need me and you don't need new schemes.'

'We've lost Hodgie,' Geoff said abruptly. 'We're closing Africa down.'

'Good God; what's happened?'

'I told you at Ogg he's been behaving strangely lately. Now he's tossed it in. He called yesterday.'

'But why, what's happened?'

'It's ludicrous,' Geoff muttered, shaking his head. 'He's in love.'

'In love? You're pulling my leg.'

'I wish I was. You're not going to believe this. He's in love with a bloody Ugandan nun. She's half African and half Indian. I warned him to leave them alone and now look what's happened. Some people just can't be helped, although you'd expect better of Hodgie. Still, as the Bible says, as you sow etcetera, so he'll just have to bear the consequences. She's made him give up the tour business and go straight after the dopey bugger told her what it was all about. I've a suspicion she could be a bit prudish.'

'That's extraordinary,' James spluttered. 'Do you know what he's going to do?'

'He's become all righteous and conventional. It's a terrible thing to see happen to a man, specially at his age.' Geoff shook his head sadly. 'He's bought a bloody luxury game resort in Namibia. Had us liquidate his investments and wire all the funds to his Hong Kong account yesterday. That's why I don't want you to go. It feels as if Alceides is collapsing about my head; all the old team disappearing suddenly.'

'Oh, lay off it, Geoff. You always said the Royal Tours had a limited life with the growth in tourism everywhere. They couldn't have lasted much longer anyway. There was bound to be an exposure sooner or later, leaving one of the clients looking a damn fool.'

'Look, I agree with that. It's actually already happened. I told you in Madagascar, we only gave it a few years. At first I thought it must have been that incident in Benin which made Hodgie go strange but now the awful truth's out.'

'What incident in Benin?'

'Haven't I told you about that?' Geoff said, surprised. 'Mind you, it must be three months since we last saw one another. The Benin crisis has certainly preoccupied us here.'

'But what happened?' James demanded.

'Bloody Taylor Tedford the Chicago pork-belly prince was doing a Presidential. Fortunately he was on his own as he's big on village virgin deflowerings. Halfway through the second day during his statue unveiling he spotted a familiar face staring flabbergasted at him from the crowd. It was one of the partners in the law firm he uses back home. Thank God Tedford promptly told Hodgie who immediately had some of our army personnel arrest the lawyer. We're still holding him prisoner under guard in a house in central Benin. Apparently he's involved in some sort of church group which dishes out aid to West Africa and he was over there regarding that.'

'Jesus Christ, Geoff. What are you going to do?'

'Well at this juncture, we're not quite sure. We sent a note to a Benin newspaper demanding a million-dollar ransom on behalf of the Benin Revolutionary Front and that gave us a few weeks' leeway while the authorities wasted time enquiring about the Front. But the bloody American State Department's putting heat on the Benin government. Our thinking is to hold him in captivity another six months then drug him, fly him to India and drop him off while he's still unconscious, stark naked in some town. By the time all that's sorted out and he finally gets home, if he starts on about Tedford everyone will assume he's delirious and won't take him seriously. Running about naked in India should destroy any credibility, specially when he insists he was in West Africa. That's the great thing about using our Alceides jets to transport the clients. We simply leave the US and head for the Bahamas, and of course we've got the authorities on side in all our tour location countries so no passports are needed. If it really comes to the crunch Tedford can show his passport as evidence he was in the Bahamas at the time. We've shifted his statue to another town so that'll be another nail in the lawyer's credibility coffin if he starts babbling on about Tedford and tries to have someone check out the statue. Still, the whole affair reinforces the difficulty of finding tourist-free locations when Chicago lawyers start touring in bloody Benin.'

'That's outrageous.'

'Couldn't agree more,' Geoff said, misunderstanding James' remark. 'We certainly must protect the clients. Furthermore we can expect more of these sorts of incidents. We've tossed it around and can see no answer. For example, there's not much point disguising the Heads of State; you know, wigs and that sort of thing, as it takes away all the fun when they watch the videos and they're unrecognisable. Anyway, it's not losing the Royal Tours as such which is bothering me; it's losing the super-rich market if we can't cater for them. That's why I want you on board to help with new ideas. We can't just rely on the Nurembergs as only about a third of our billionaire clientele are into those. The fatties have ground to a halt.

Personally, I believe they're on strike because of the dieting regime. Bloody Ralston's even taken up writing poetry; that's how vicious they've become. It's sheer bloody malice I tell you.'

James thought quickly. 'I'll tell you what I'll do. Shift the fatties out to a private hospital in the country and offer them employment when they get down to 200 pounds. I don't know how you will get them out of the building. You'll probably have to hire a crane and take out the windows and maybe even part of the walls. But if you do that, then I'll join you here.'

'No,' Geoff said flatly. 'It's out of the question.'

'Why not?'

'I raised your concerns with my father. He's adamant and won't budge on it. He considers the fatties concept his greatest achievement. The fatties stay. Even if we did what you said, what if they then turned out no good? We can't sack them with them knowing what they know. Anyway, as you said yesterday, on my head they be.'

'But why assume they'll be no good?' James pressed. 'They know the score. I think you could be pleasantly surprised. Turn them into more normal human beings and they'll certainly have more energy.'

'I suggested that to my father,' Geoff said wearily. 'He won't hear of it. He claims people who boil down from obesity inevitably become obsessed with their weight and never stop and we'll end up with a building full of skeletal horrors. It'll be gymnasiums and a total preoccupation with losing even more weight. Plus they'll be able to leave the building and for the first time in their lives be normal human beings wanting to do normal things. Imagine the trouble that'll create with girlfriends and wanting to travel and play golf and go to shows and all the other rubbish normal people do. They'll be useless once they go under 250 pounds.'

'Then I definitely want out,' James said flatly.

Geoff stared at him coldly then turned and picked up a document and a cheque from his desktop. 'Sign Ogg over to us here; it's a quite straightforward and simple contract and here's a bearer cheque for £15 million.'

'It's worth more than that, Geoff. You know that. Let's go to lunch and talk about it.'

'Take it or leave it,' Geoff said curtly.

'I'd like to talk to your father about this,' James said coolly.

'You're wasting your time. I suggested he come in for this meeting and he refused. To be frank, he considers your attitude one of betrayal and ingratitude. He's upstairs in bed reading Thucydides and I can tell you he only ever does that when he's upset.'

'I'm sorry he feels that way,' James said firmly. 'Personally I think the past three years have been mutually beneficial. Because of me you have Ogg and I'm certainly grateful for all I've experienced. But Brasch and the other tubbies are not something I want to be part of. Apart from its immorality I have a strong sense they will be the death-knell for Alceides, otherwise, to be honest, I wouldn't be averse to joining you here.'

'That's childish,' Geoff snorted. 'You make far too much of a song and dance about them. You have absolutely no respect for free will.'

'So be it,' James said and he read the sale note. As Geoff said it was straightforward. He signed, took the cheque and without speaking left the room. For the last time he left the building. Outside he encountered Amy emerging from a taxi laden with the bunches of flowers she placed each week throughout the building. He held the door open for her as she clambered out, then took the flowers while she paid the driver.

'They're very upset, James,' she said sadly. 'Hodge leaving has rattled them and with the fatties on strike and now you going, it's all too much. Maybe you'll change your mind after a break.'

'Maybe,' James said conciliatorily, and he kissed her cheek then headed for Piccadilly.

By the time he reached Hatchards where it had all begun three years earlier, his anger at being shortchanged had dissipated. What the hell; he had almost £4 million in his account from his Ogg rental and quarter-share earnings to date and with the £15 million and Miyumi's fortune they were rich. James crossed Piccadilly and headed for his St James bank to deposit the cheque. The teller started when James presented it and two minutes later he found himself in the manager's office being served coffee.

'Naturally, Mr Campbell, we're here to assist,' the manager oozed, clasping his hands before him. 'We have a wide range of interest-bearing products you might care to consider. Now if you ...' but he was interrupted in his sales pitch by the shrieking of a siren from outside. As it faded another quickly replaced it and then eight more in quick succession. 'I really question whether that appalling racket is necessary,' he spluttered angrily. 'You'd think the city was falling down.'

Little did he realise how near the mark that comment was.

Four minutes after James left the Alceides building, Brasch, desperately reaching for a chocolate eclair which had slipped from his fingers to the floor, rolled his massive bulk too far across the wheelchair, fell and crashed through the hugely overburdened two-hundred-year-old timber floor, crushing Geoff below him and killing both of them instantly.

Slowly the remaining timbers subsided, bringing down Brasch's thousands of books, and with the building's delicate balance destroyed, the entire structure imploded.

The eight fatties above crashed through simultaneously, all the way to the ground floor. The walls slowly crumbled and within minutes flames from the kitchens where the Cambodian ladies had been cooking the fatties' reduced lunches tore through the rubble. The Alceides building was no more.

# – TWENTY-FOUR –

'IRA OUTRAGE' the headline screamed above a front-page photograph showing the burning rubble which had been the Alceides building, surrounded by frantic firemen and policemen. For the tenth time James, lying in bed, read the accompanying newspaper story, his mind reeling with shock.

He briefly considered not telling Miyumi, concerned how she would cope with the news. She had left the hotel only ten minutes earlier for a walk, having first brought in the newspaper hanging from the doorknob. Miyumi had really only known Geoff, although she had met Amy when she first arrived in London three years ago. There had also been the single lunch with Mr Upton, which hardly counted, and James had only recently mustered the courage to tell her about the fatties and the Cambodian widows. Her distaste at their plight had influenced his decision to leave Alceides. But she was now seven months pregnant and James worried about the effect the shock might have on her. If he told her he knew she would become intense and solemn but her eyes would brim with tears in off-guard moments, cracking the stoic reserve she would outwardly adopt.

James studied the photograph again. No doubt about it. It was definitely the Alceides building. The address, plus the recognisable façades of the adjacent buildings, put it beyond question. Then he remembered the sirens he had heard yesterday and he shuddered at the realisation of his near miss. He mentally ran through who was in the building when he left. Poor Amy had just returned, Geoff was certainly a goner, as was Mr Upton in bed reading Thucydides at the time. Brasch, the other fatties and the Cambodian widows were surely all history. 'Some badly burnt bodies have been recovered,' the report said, but no number was given.

But why on earth would the IRA target Alceides, he wondered? Could it be chance or misadventure? He quickly dismissed that possibility. Given Alceides security there would be much more accessible targets and he puzzled as to how the IRA could have gained entry.

Mr Upton had always been a mysterious figure and while nothing about Alceides would surprise him, the thought of Mr Upton as an undercover anti-IRA agent didn't ring true. After all, he chose to live in Spain and rarely came to England so he was unlikely to be a fanatical Anglophile engaging in clandestine-type activities.

The inside story was entirely journalistic speculation. Plainly neither the newspaper nor the authorities had any idea who had occupied the building, the report indicated that neighbours had been unhelpful, and a statement from a police spokesman soliciting information from the public made it clear they were in the dark.

Suddenly alarmed, James remembered his cheque then he relaxed. It would be processed. He felt slightly ashamed for thinking about it. Lucky for Hodge, though, he thought. Tracing his funds would have proved impossible and he had uplifted them in the nick of time. But what of Monster's investment capital? Could that be accessed?

He considered Kanju and the other operations. What would happen to them? James lay back in bed calculating the number of people affected in Africa, India, London, Ogg and Romania. Then there were the Tokyo and New York offices and the pilots, and Mr Upton's Peruvian mistress in Ibiza, and just recently he had learnt of Taiwan so who knows what else might exist that he was unaware of. The realisation dawned on him that he alone was possibly in a position to salvage the situation and that everyone's fate rested with him.

He leapt out of bed, showered and left the hotel. The Alceides building, or what remained of it, was only a ten-minute stroll and he felt drawn to it as if taking a last look at a deceased family member. In the event his efforts were in vain as he was halted by heavily manned police barricades a block from the site. 'Only residents and office occupants allowed any further, sir,' a policeman insisted.

James returned to the hotel, bought the other morning newspapers and wandered into the breakfast room. All the newspapers front-paged the story but apart from expressing varying degrees of outrage at the IRA, none knew more than the others which was effectively nothing.

After breakfast he returned to his suite and telephoned Sanderson.

'Go to my study,' he instructed him. 'There's a business card in my second left-hand drawer with the name Juma Kensorati on it. Call me back with the phone number.'

Half an hour later he was explaining to Juma what had occurred and was relieved to learn that the Kanju investment funds were held in their own name under Juma's control. 'The helicopter fwom Naiwobi is due in half an hour,' Juma said. 'I'll take it back and be in London tomowwow.'

James was on the telephone booking a room in the hotel for Juma when Miyumi returned slightly flushed and in a happy mood, carrying a bunch of flowers for the room.

James showed her the newspapers. As he had expected she became very still, but as he had also anticipated, very soon her eyes were damp.

'No point moping in here,' he said briskly. 'We'll need to stay in London longer than planned. What's done can't be undone so we must get on with things. You were going to buy your pregnancy clothes today. Hanging about here is pointless,' and Miyumi somewhat reluctantly agreed, and half an hour later left to go shopping.

There was much to decide. He weighed up whether he should contact the police but quickly dismissed the notion. It would save a great deal of police time if he enlightened them but would similarly open up a dangerous hornet's nest of endless questioning, and the inevitable full-scale revelation would be disastrous for Alceides' ventures.

The existing operations, James concluded, should be saved. Fundamentally, Geoff's constant rationalising about them was right. Largely they produced happiness while simultaneously creating a great deal of employment. It was then he recalled Geoff's explanation three years earlier about compartmentalising and his course of action became clearer. He did not want to return to Ogg, nor was there any need for him to do so. Monster could take the whole show over and his people could receive the benefits. He might have to shift to London and set up office to pull all the strings; then again it could be possible to run the entire operation from Kenya. James realised he was probably going to have to stay in London for a time to help Monster take control and re-establish new headquarters. The thought also crossed his mind that it would be a simple matter for him to step in and take over. He would certainly become immensely rich. Only he knew of the compartmentalising, and he recalled his visit with Geoff to the administration offices. Could he find them again, he wondered. Pending Juma's arrival, he decided to use the day on that task. The take-over exercise would be a dead duck if the accounting administration had shifted since his visit there three years earlier.

James left the hotel and engaged a taxi, explaining to the driver that he wanted to tour every street in Hackney. Half an hour later they were cruising the grim suburb when suddenly, before them lay the corner cake shop. Telling the driver to wait, James leapt out of the cab and walked back along the street.

There it was, the Encyclopaedia Sales sign exactly as on his previous visit. James paused and gathered his thoughts. What was the manager's name and for that matter what was his? He had been Lord something or other. He'd have to bluff it.

He opened the door, entered the gloomy hall, pushed the lift button and emerged on the first floor. Nothing had changed. No one greeted him. He stood vacantly for a while then approached the nearest fat harridan.

'Is the manager in?' he enquired.

'Albert's in the loo,' she said flatly, not lifting her head.

Albert – that was the name, and James fixed it in his memory and made a mental note to record the street address.

Suddenly Albert emerged from the rear. On spotting James he scuttled forward nervously. 'Lord Bellvue,' he exclaimed. 'It's a pleasure to see you again.'

'Just in the neighbourhood,' James said authoritatively. 'We've had a few management changes so I'll be back in a day or so to introduce you to Mr Kensorati who's replacing Mr Upton now that he has shifted to our New York office.'

'Certainly, sir,' Albert replied, without any suggestion of surprise or questioning. After some small talk James left and returned to the taxi. He borrowed a pen and notepad from the driver, wrote down 'Lord Bellvue' and 'Albert' and then at the end of the street recorded the name 'New Shamrock Street' and they returned to the West End.

In the hotel foyer he purchased the afternoon newspapers and took them into the coffeeshop. The Alceides building story still dominated the front pages but had now taken a new turn. The IRA had indignantly denied responsibility in a manner that suggested such conduct was beyond the pale while the police had searched the land titles and ascertained the name of the ownership entity. With this information, aided by an Oxford University classics don, they were now working on a strong new line of enquiry. James folded the newspapers and went upstairs. Later that evening over dinner he outlined the options to Miyumi.

They could step into control and become enormously rich. Alternatively they could do so jointly with Juma, and after an initial establishment period adopt a more passive arms-length, profit-sharing role. Or they could help Juma set up a new management structure then walk away and continue with their existing plans. The first option was quickly rejected and eventually they decided to sleep on the question of continuing involvement pending discussions with Juma the next day.

The following morning, after Miyumi had left for her walk, James turned on the television news. The gnome-like figure of the bearded Foreign Secretary holding a Downing Street doorstep press conference filled the screen. Overnight, it transpired, the investigation had progressed and, as the Foreign Secretary pompously explained, while enquiries were still being completed, thanks to outstanding police detective work assisted by the classics scholar and a London University Balkans expert, there was now clear evidence suggesting the Alceides building was a Macedonian or possibly Montenegrin base and that its destruction was the work of the Serbian government.

'I want to make it very clear,' the Foreign Secretary thundered, 'neither this government nor the British public will tolerate Balkan ethnic strife being transferred to our shores. I have summoned the Serbian ambassador to my office later this morning and will be conveying to him in the strongest possible terms the seriousness with which my government views this matter.'

A dozen reporter voices all simultaneously shouted questions. Eventually one prevailed over the babble. 'Will the government be pursuing any reprisal actions?' he bawled.

The Foreign Secretary drew himself up to his full five feet six inches and puffed out his chest. 'A number of options remain open and at this juncture none have been discarded,' he said haughtily and then turned and retreated inside Number 10 to discuss the matter with the Prime Minister.

The camera panned to the television reporter. 'That was the Foreign Secretary outside Number 10 Downing Street announcing immediate military action against Serbia for its bombing destruction yesterday of a Mayfair building,' he said excitedly. 'Earlier today we spoke to Mr Cyril Smudge, the taxi-driver who was on the scene minutes before the bombing. Mr Smudge has been helping the police with their enquiries.'

A large oafish face now filled the screen.

'Can you tell us what you saw, Mr Smudge?' the interviewer pressed.

'I dropped off a young gel wif flowers at the building. She was deffnly foreign lookin', Greek like or one of them Mickey Mouse places; know wot oi mean. And this geezer come outta the building and bailed her up and she got upset like and went inside and the bloke shot off towards Piccadilly.'

'Could she have been Macedonian or Montenegrin in your expert opinion, Mr Smudge?'

'Deffnly. Both of them.'

'And the man you saw, Mr Smudge. Are you able to describe him?'

'Yeah. Deffnly a wog. I see 'em all in my profession so I know me nashanallies. Deffnly one of them dodgy Slav types; know wot oi mean?'

'Serbian perhaps, Mr Smudge?'

'Deffnly!'

'Assisted by Mr Smudge, the police have produced an identikit picture of the suspicious man and have requested that anyone who was in the vicinity of Dover Street or Piccadilly yesterday and recognises this portrait, should contact them immediately,' the announcer recited.

A line drawing of a male face now appeared on the screen. Not only was it flawed by the addition of the moustache Mr Smudge had 'deffnly' recollected, it otherwise bore no resemblance to James.

James sighed and turned off the television. Juma would be arriving at eleven and just as he rose to shower and go downstairs to breakfast Miyumi returned. She seemed in a happier mood.

'I've been thinking, James,' she said brightly. 'Let's go out tonight with Juma to help forget about everything.'

'Well of course we'll be having dinner with Monster,' James replied, puzzled.

'No, no. I don't mean just dinner. We can do that later. Let's go to a show.'

'A show!'

'Yes, you know, a stage show. Do you know what I'd like to see? *The Mousetrap*. I've heard it's very good.'

James looked sharply at Miyumi. Her expression was without guile as she waited expectantly for his reply. His mind raced. He felt intuitively that his response would mark a watershed in deciding his future. Eventually he spoke.

'That's a terrific idea, Miyumi. I'll telephone now and make a reservation.'